George E. Raum

A Tour Around the World

George E. Raum

A Tour Around the World

ISBN/EAN: 9783337193935

Printed in Europe, USA, Canada, Australia, Japan

Cover: Foto ©Andreas Hilbeck / pixelio.de

More available books at **www.hansebooks.com**

A TOUR

AROUND THE WORLD

BY

GEORGE E. RAUM

BEING A BRIEF SKETCH OF THE MOST INTERESTING SIGHTS
SEEN IN EUROPE, AFRICA, ASIA, AND AMERICA,
WHILE ON A TWO YEARS' RAMBLE

NEW YORK
WILLIAM S. GOTTSBERGER, PUBLISHER
11 MURRAY STREET
1895

A TOUR

AROUND THE WORLD.

CHAPTER I.

AFTER a ten days' voyage by steamer across the Atlantic from New York, we reached the Emerald Isle, landing at Queenstown, a city situated at the southern extremity of Ireland, in Cork Harbor, and admirably defended by two strong forts. It contains about 10,000 inhabitants, and has few attractions for tourists; but is a favorite resort for invalids on account of its mild climate. Here the Rev. Charles Wolfe, who wrote the famous poem, "The Burial of Sir John Moore," died of consumption in 1823.

After passing our baggage through the Cus- tom House, an hour's time was quite sufficient to note the few points of interest the place presented, and taking rail for Cork, we skirted the beautiful river Lee for twelve miles, passing several ancient castles and lovely modern country-seats.

At Cork we took carriage, and drove for six miles along the banks of the Lee to Blarney Castle, over a road considered the most charming in Ireland, passing the Castle of Carrigrohane and the Bridge of Inniscarra built by Cromwell in the 16th century.

Blarney Castle was the stronghold, and long the residence of the royal race of McCarthy, by whom it was built in the 15th century; all that now remains of it is a donjon tower, 125 feet in height, with walls 14 feet in thickness, which rendered it impregnable before the introduction of gunpowder. The chief attraction of this castle is the famous Blarney-stone, which is supposed to endow whoever kisses it with that gift of persuasive eloquence so characteristic of the Irish nature. This stone, which bears the inscription, "Cormach McCarthy, 1446," is placed near the top of the tower, and is both difficult and dangerous of access; but a substitute is shown the less venturesome below, which is said to possess the same virtue as the original. On the river side is shown the place where the defenders of the castle poured down hot lead upon Cromwell's attacking forces, and beneath are the donjon cells, three by five feet in dimension, and ventilated only by an inch hole. An underground passage, also hewn from the solid rock, connects the castle with a cave some three hundred yards beyond, while the grounds surrounding the castle are noticeable both for their beauty and their historic interest.

Returning to Cork by a different road, one has a lovely bird's-eye view of that city, picturesquely situated on the Lee. It was here that William Penn became a convert to Quakerism, and near by the place where Sir Walter Raleigh lived, planted the potato, and scented the air of Hibernia with the fragrant weed of our own Virginia.

Leaving Cork by rail for Bantry—distance 70 miles—we passed through primitive Ireland, seeing much ignorance and squalor, barefooted, ragged mendicants preferring their claims upon our time and charity at every turn, and miserable huts with straw chimneys and dirt floors—man and beast sharing alike such poor comfort as might be found within them.

Passing along the bogs one sees men and women busily engaged cutting turf—a species of black mud composed of decayed vegetable matter, which, after having been dried a month, is used by the natives for fuel.

Continuing by stage, a distance of eleven miles, we reached Glengariff, a charming resort surrounded by high peaks and lovely lakes. The climate here is delightfully mild; flowers blooming a month in advance of the season elsewhere,

while its surrounding views and historic scenes —
among which may be noted Cromwell's Bridge
and the Martello Tower — render it a locality well
worth visiting.

At Glengariff we took a wagonette and drove
to Killarney, a distance of 40 miles, passing
through the beautiful and extensive estate of
Lord Bantry, viewing at a distance "The Nob,"
" Eagle's Nest," and other features of the wild
mountain scenery.

Arriving at the Lakes of Killarney, so justly
celebrated for their exceeding beauty of scenery,
we contracted with the proprietor of the hotel to
send ponies, boats and carriages to different points
on the lakes.

At an early hour in the morning we drove,
attended by a guide, a distance of nine miles to
the Gap of Dunloe ; stopping en route at the Castle
and Cave of Dunloe, at the cottage of St. Patrick,
the tutelary saint of Ireland, near which, legend
avers, he exterminated the last of the Irish snakes ;
and at the home of Kate Kearney, where one of
her descendants dispenses " mountain dew " to
the thirsty wayfarer.

At the entrance to the Gap we mounted ponies,
and rode a distance of five miles, through a narrow
mountain defile, passing Macgillicuddy's Reeks,
and several small lakes ; into one of which the
author of the Colleen Bawn cast his heroine.

At the head of the upper lake we entered a

small row-boat, and proceeded to view the pic-
turesque scenery bordering its shores. We passed
Lord Brandon's cottage, "Eagle's Nest," and
McCarthy's Island; shot the rapids under the old
Weir bridge; crossed the "Meeting of the
Waters" and landed on Dinish Island.

From here we drove to the Torc Cascade, and
thence to the historic ruins of Muckross Abbey.
This is a grand, old, ivy-covered ruin, in the centre of which stands a yew tree 440 years old, and
surrounding it are the tombs of the McCarthy, the
Moore, and other names of ancient Ireland.

Ross Castle—three miles distant—is another
fine ruin which withstood the assaults of Cromwell in the 16th century; also to be noted are,
the castle of Lord Kinmare and the ruins of Innis-
fallen, so celebrated by Moore in song. Joined to
the harmonies of sight were those of sound,
throughout this delightful tour; mountain and
lake returning echoes from violin, bugle and
cannon.

From Killarney to Dublin—a distance of 112
miles—one passes through a country of no special
interest. This city, situated on the Liffey, has a
population of 340,000 inhabitants. Its principal
buildings are the "Castle"—the official residence
of the Lord Lieutenant; the Bank of Ireland—
formerly the House of Parliament; Trinity College; and the "Four Courts." The finest streets
are Sackville and James, on which are erected

monuments to William III., Nelson, Wellington, and O'Connell, and among other places of historic interest there also is pointed out the spot where Emmet was hung.

Phœnix Park—one of the most beautiful in the United Kingdom—contains the private residence of the Lord Lieutenant of Ireland, who may be seen driving, surrounded by a strong escort of cavalry. The blood of his predecessor, Lord Cavendish, and that of Secretary Burke, was still fresh upon the spot where they were assassinated, May 6th, 1882; the day previous to our arrival.

From Dublin we went by rail to Portrush, a small bathing place in the north of Ireland, and from there, by jaunting-car, six miles to the Giant's Causeway. This is a basaltic promontory from ten to five hundred feet high, and consists of prismatic columns fitting side by side with such uniformity, as to look like the work of art; the heating of the rock, and its sudden cooling, is supposed to be the cause of this remarkable formation.

The Castle of Dunluce, four miles from the Causeway, is the finest ruin in the north of Ireland. It is built on a rock and is connected with the mainland by a stone bridge only twenty inches in width.

Belfast, the second city in size in Ireland, contains but little to attract the transient visitor, and from here we took the steamer across the Irish sea, to Scotland.

CHAPTER II.

SAILING up the river Clyde, we passed large numbers of ships in course of construction, from the formidable man-of-war and fine merchant ship, to various small sized craft destined for lighter service.

Glasgow, the commercial capital of Scotland, is finely situated on the river Clyde at the head of navigation. It was here that James Watt, in 1763, first applied steam as a motive power. The city has a population of 512,000 inhabitants, and contains many handsome buildings and fine statues. St. George's Square, centrally located, contains the monuments of Sir Walter Scott, the Duke of Wellington, James Watt, Prince Albert, and Queen Victoria; and is surrounded by the Royal Bank, Mechanic's Institute, Royal Exchange, and Post Office. The city is noted for its abundant supply of fresh water brought from the romantic Loch Katrine—a distance of 40 miles.

The Great Western Cooking Depôt, established by one of her philanthropists, is a novel and an admirable institution, where a most excellent meal is served to the working people at three-pence (six cents) each.

The most important object to be seen in Glasgow is the cathedral, which ranks next to Westminster in the kingdom; particularly admired for the rich coloring of its stained-glass windows. It is situated in a picturesque spot, partly surrounded by an old churchyard or necropolis, which rises terraced in the background, and contains some beautiful monuments, the most conspicuous of which is that erected to the memory of John Knox, the great Reformer. The cathedral was built in the 12th century, is in the form of a Latin cross, and of the Gothic style.

The University, a fine building, costing millions of dollars, is located on high ground sloping to the river Kelvin, and commands a fine view of the city.

Ayr — 40 miles from Glasgow — has 18,000 inhabitants, and is situated on the Ayr river, which is crossed by the "twa brigs," immortalized by Burns.

On the site of the prison where Wallace was confined a structure now exists called the Wallace Tower, in front of which is a statue of that hero, and in the Tower are the clock and bells of the old donjon steeple.

Two miles from Ayr is the cottage, divided

into two rooms, where the poet Burns was born, January 25th, 1759, and the bed yet stands in the original niche where the poet first saw the light of day. Two miles from this is " Alloway's auld haunted kirk," which has been immortalized by Burns in his " Tam O'Shanter." In the adjoining churchyard are the graves of Tam O'Shanter, or Tam Laughlin, from the farm Shanter, and those of the poet's parents, on the headstone of which is inscribed the following beautiful epitaph, written by Burns, on his father :

" O ye, whose cheek the tear of pity stains,
    Draw near with pious rev'rence and attend !
Here lie the loving husband's dear remains,
    The tender father and the gen'rous friend.

The pitying heart that felt for human woe ;
    The dauntless heart that fear'd no human pride ;
The friend of man, to vice alone a foe ;
    For ev'n his failings lean'd to virtue's side."

The "auld kirk" is in ruins, but the interest of the locality is centred in the graveyard.

A short distance to the west is the well where Mungo's "mither hanged hersel," and near by is a fine monument to Burns, in the interior of which are relics belonging to him — original manuscript, wedding-ring, a lock of his Highland Mary's hair, and two bibles given her by the poet. In a cave on the grounds is a monument to Tam O'Shanter and Souter Johnnie, and a few steps further on

the "auld brig o'Doon," over which Tam took
his famous nocturnal ride.

From here we drove back to Ayr by another
road, passing the cottage where two of Burns's
nieces live — old ladies upward of eighty. We
then visited the tavern where Tam and Souter
Johnnie used to meet and carouse, sat in their
chairs, and drank from their cups.

Sixteen miles from Glasgow is Dumbarton
Castle. This fortress stands on a rocky height
six hundred feet above the river, commanding
extensive views in every direction, the ascent
being made by many steps cut in the solid rock.
The armory contains the sword of Wallace, which
is more than seven feet long, and over the inner
gate is a room where he was confined a prisoner;
the face of Wallace and that of Monteith, his
betrayer, being cut in the stone wall outside. To
this castle Mary Queen of Scots was brought
when a child. Charles I., and Cromwell successively occupied it, and Queen Victoria visited it
in 1847.

Two miles from here is Cardross Castle, where
Robert Bruce died in 1329.

Arriving at Balloch Pier, on Loch Lomond,
we sailed for two hours amid the many beautiful
islands which gem its surface, surrounded by
exquisite mountain views, passing Ben Lomond, a
high mountain peak, in the distance, and nearing
Rob Roy's cave and rock, where he suspended

his prisoners by a rope until they agreed upon what ransom they would pay.

At Inversnaid we landed and took stage through a mountainous country — the scene of Sir Walter Scott's Rob Roy — to Stronachlacher, passing on the roadside a stone cottage, once occupied by Helen MacGregor, Rob Roy's wife.

Here, by steamer "Rob Roy," we sailed through Loch Katrine, which teems with the poetry of Scott's " Lady of the Lake," passing the island where Rob Roy put the steward ashore and left him, after taking his money ; Ellen Douglas' Isle, the Silver Strand, Ben Venue, and the place where James and Roderick Dhu first met.

From the end of the lake we drove through the Trossachs—a wild, heather-grown gorge, and stopped at the hotel of the same name, for a brief rest. Continuing our drive we passed Ben Lodi, Loch Venachar, and Coilantogle's Ford, where the combat took place between Roderick Dhu and Fitz James, after Roderick had discharged his obligation of conducting him there safely.

From Callander we went by rail to Stirling, a place of great antiquity ; with a population of 13,000.

Stirling Castle, around which is centered so much of historic interest, is built upon a rocky elevation of 380 feet; the battlements of which command a magnificent view. Secure on account of its central location and inaccessible situation, it early became a place of great importance, and was for a long time the residence of the kings.

Inside the castle walls is the palace built by James V., and ornamented by statues of himself and his favorite courtiers. In the chapel adjoining, Mary was crowned Queen of Scots, and her son, afterwards James VI. of Scotland and I. of England, baptized.

It was the birthplace of James II., and of James V., and a favorite residence of James VI., who was crowned in the old church near by; John Knox preaching the coronation sermon.

One of the most interesting places in the castle is the Douglas room, in which William, Earl of Douglas, was assassinated by James II., after that monarch had promised him safe conduct. Here is shown the window from which the lifeless body was thrown; also the secret stairway leading from this room, by which the king sometimes left the castle in disguise. From the battlements, no less than eight battlefields are in sight; on one of which Bruce secured the independence of Scotland, by his victory at Bannockburn, in 1314; and on another where William Wallace achieved a great triumph over the English in 1287.

A drive of four miles from Stirling brought us to Cambuskenneth Abbey, where are interred the remains of James III. On the way we passed the Wallace Tower—an immense monument built at a height of 200 feet; Darnley's house; and Queen Mary's palace.

Edinburgh was first called Edwin's borough, from the fact that King Edward pitched his tent on the rock where the castle now stands. The city, which contains 230,000 inhabitants, is situated on both sides of a deep ravine, and, for its size, is one of the most imposing, interesting and magnificent cities in Europe, and has often been styled "the modern Athens." Princes and George streets are the fashionable thoroughfares, lined with elegant buildings and fine monuments; the most conspicuous of which is a monument to Sir Walter Scott, 200 feet high, with a statue of himself and dog under a stone canopy surrounded by fifty smaller statues representing characters in his novels.

Edinburgh Castle, whose origin is clouded in obscurity, is one of the fortresses which, by the articles of union between England and Scotland, must be kept fortified; and is teeming with romantic and historic interest. Sir William Kirkaldy defended it thirty-three days for Mary, Queen of Scots, against the combined armies of England and Scotland. The room is shown where that unfortunate queen became a mother; and the window where her son, when only eight days old, was lowered in a basket, to be conveyed to a place of greater safety.

In a room over one of the inner gates, the

Duke of Argyle slept, the night previous to his execution; and in the tower, strongly guarded, are the crown jewels of Scotland, consisting of crown, sceptre, sword, plate, and decorations set with precious stones. These were lost for over a hundred years, and but recently found by Sir Walter Scott, in an old chest in the castle.

Mons Meg, a gigantic cannon, twenty inches in diameter at the bore, used in 1514 at the siege of Norham Castle, is to be seen on the battlements.

The Museum contains many interesting relics, among which are the "Maiden" or guillotine, used in the time of the Covenanters; the stool which Jeanie Geddes threw at the Dean of St. Giles; thumb-screws, and other instruments of torture.

The National Gallery is filled with rare specimens of art, and on this spot formerly stood the house where Lord Darnley was blown up.

Holyrood Palace, built in 1501 by James IV., was the home of that lovely but unfortunate queen, Mary Stuart, in which she lived with Darnley for a time. Among the apartments shown, are Lord Darnley's rooms, hung with fine tapestry; and in his bed-chamber, the bed occupied by Charles I. From Darnley's apartments leading up to Queen Mary's rooms, is a private staircase by which the assassins of Rizzio ascended to murder that unfortunate secretary. Mary's supper room, an apartment so famous in Scottish history, was the scene of Rizzio's murder, which took place while he was at supper with the queen.

The objects of interest in the old quarter of Edinburgh are John Knox's church and tomb; Greyfriar's cemetery, where 18,000 martyrs are buried; the Heart of Mid-Lothian, a large stone heart, marking the spot where the prison once stood; and the Grass Market, formerly a place of execution, where the Dukes of Argyle, Montforth, and many others of more or less note were beheaded.

Roslin Chapel, built by the St. Clairs in the 11th century, and in which they were buried in armor, is particularly noted for its fine carvings and Gothic architecture. The Apprentice Pillar, for which the apprentice lost his life, having completed it while the master was in Rome in search of a design, is exceedingly beautiful. Roslin Castle, a short distance from the chapel, is situated on a cliff overhanging the river Esk, and among its subterranean dungeons is one which was occupied by Queen Mary for several weeks.

Walking along the river, a distance of two miles, through a romantic and lovely ravine, we reached Hawthornden, the home of the poet Drummond. Here is to be seen the sword of Robert Bruce, and the caves in which he and Wallace took refuge at different times. These caves are cut in the rock underneath the poet's

residence, and connect with Roslin Castle by a
passage under the river.

Melrose Abbey, the chief attraction of a small
village of the same name, on the river Tweed, is
an old, roofless, ivy-covered ruin.   It was founded
in 1136 by King David I., who lies interred here
with his queen.   Here also is buried the heart of
Robert Bruce, Michael Scott, the wizard, Alexander II., the royal family of Douglas, Brewster
the historian, and Tom Purdy, Sir Walter Scott's
forester.   The old clock, which time has robbed
of both figures and hands, still denotes the hour,
which is sounded by strokes of the old bell.   In
the centre of the Abbey stands a broken column,
which was the favorite seat of Sir Walter Scott
when he came to gather fresh inspiration from the
grand and varied beauty of the scene.

From Melrose, a drive of four miles brought
us to Dryburgh Abbey, the burial place of Sir
Walter Scott, and the most picturesque ruin in all
Scotland.   Adjoining the Abbey are the remains
of the cloister; and a hole in the wall of a cell
shows where refractory monks were punished by
having their hands wedged in with wood.

Leaving Dryburgh — the home of the dead —
we drove seven miles to Abbotsford, the late
residence of Sir Walter Scott, a most imposing
mansion, situated on the banks of the river
Tweed, in the midst of well-kept grounds.   The
study contains his leather arm-chair, pipes and

canes as he left them. The library has some twenty thousand volumes, and in it are the chairs presented him by George IV., and Pope Pius VII., the portfolio, pen-case, and cloak-clasps of Napoleon, taken at the battle of Waterloo, locks of Wellington's and Nelson's hair, Rob Roy's purse, Helen MacGregor's brooch, Tam O'Shanter's snuff-box, and Robert Burns's drinking-glass. The drawing-room is elegantly finished in carved wood, and contains many handsome paintings. The armory is a small room, with arms tastefully arranged on the walls, among which are the swords of the Earl of Montrose and of Colonel Scott, Napoleon's pistols, Rob Roy's shield and gun, the spurs of Prince Charlie, and the armor of James VI. ; besides these is a candlestick formerly belonging to Bruce, the crucifix carried by Queen Mary to execution, her money-box, and the keys of Loch Leven Castle. From the armory a door opens into the dining-room, where Sir Walter died, his couch commanding a view of the river Tweed from the window. The main hall, a beautiful apartment of carved wood, marble floor, and stained-glass windows, is hung with arms and armor of all descriptions ; and in it is seen a clock of Marie Antoinette, a cast of Bruce's skull, and that of one of a life-guard, who killed thirteen men with his fist at Waterloo, Napoleon's armor, the keys of the old tolbooth — the Heart of Mid-Lothian—and the clothes, shoes and hat last worn by

Scott. In the grounds, near the main entrance, is a bronze monument placed over the remains of the author's favorite dog, Meda.

Truly a baronial mansion, and one full of interest.

CHAPTER III.

LONDON.— ITS ENVIRONS.

LONDON, the metropolis of the United Kingdom of Great Britain, and the largest city in the world, is situated on the Thames river, 45 miles from its mouth, and has a population of nearly 4,000,000. The older portion of the city is on the north bank of the river, and embraces but a small part of the area of modern London; it is of great antiquity; but very little being known of it previous to the time of Nero, when it bore the dignity of a Roman colony.

Starting from the Bank of England, the treasury of Great Britain, and commercial and financial centre of the city, we drove past St. Paul's Cathedral, Temple Bar — where formerly stood one of the old gates of the city, the Courts of Justice, the old graveyard, near by — made mention of by Dickens in " Bleak House," where little Joe peered through the railing, at the grave of his only friend,

Temple Church, where Oliver Goldsmith is buried, and Somerset House. Continuing down the strand —one of the principal thoroughfares of the city, on which are located many of the theatres, we reached Charing Cross—a locality which takes its name from one of the five crosses which mark the resting-places of the funeral procession of a Queen of England.

Trafalgar Square, the finest in the city, is overlooked by the principal hotels, and contains a beautiful monument to Nelson, surrounded by fountains and colossal figures of recumbent lions, and other statues.

In a narrow street leading from the square, is still to be seen the " Old Curiosity Shop," presided over by an old Jew and his little daughter—completing the picture so touchingly described by Dickens.

Continuing through Pall Mall, where are situated the principal club-houses, we passed the Crimean monument in Waterloo Place, Marlborough House — the residence of the Prince and Princess of Wales, St. James' Palace and Park, Buckingham Palace — the Queen's city residence, and Wellington's statue, located at Hyde Park Corner—the fashionable quarter of London.

Hyde Park, the great pleasure drive of the city, contains 350 acres, and is laid out with fine carriage-roads and paths intersecting each other at every point; the portion called Rotten Row be-

ing devoted exclusively to equestrians. On the
southern limit of the park stands the Albert
Memorial, said to be the finest monument in the
world, and costing $500,000. The four large
marble groups at the outer corner represent Europe, Asia, Africa, and America; the upper corner marble groups, Agriculture, Manufacture,
Commerce, and Engineering; while the carved
figures which surround the base number 169, and
represent renowned painters, poets, sculptors and
statesmen. The monument is of brown stone,
180 feet high, and under the canopy which is
studded with 12,000 stones, is the sitting figure
of Prince Albert in gilt.

The Zoological Gardens of London contain the
largest collection of animals, birds and insects
known in the world; the larger animals being
particularly fine; the fashionable day to visit " the
Zoo" is on Sunday, when admittance is gained
only by card.

The Tower of London, supposed to have been
commenced by Julius Caesar, is situated at the
eastern extremity of the city, and covers 12 acres
of ground. On the river-side is the entrance,
called the Traitor's Gate, through which prisoners
of state were conveyed in boats after trial. Within
this famous structure are numerous buildings, including barracks, armories and towers, viz: the
Bloody Tower—where Richard III. murdered his
nephews; the Bowyer Tower—where the Duke

of Clarence was drowned in a butt of Malmsey
wine; the Brick Tower—in which Lady Jane
Grey was confined; the Beauchamp Tower—the
prison of Anne Boleyn, and numerous others of
equally historic association. In addition to the
original use of the Tower as a fortress, it was
the residence of the monarchs of England down to
the time of Elizabeth, and a prison for state criminals.

Numerous are the kings, queens, warriors and
statesmen, who have not only been imprisoned,
but murdered within its walls; among whom
were Catherine Howard, Sir Walter Raleigh,
Somerset, Sir Thomas Moore, William Wallace,
and King John of France. In the Tower inclosure is the Horse Armory, built in 1826—
an extensive gallery in which is a finely-arranged
collection of armor used from the 13th to the
18th century; including suits worn by the Prince
of Wales—son of James I., Henry VIII., Dudley,
Earl of Leicester, Charles I., and John of Gaunt.

Queen Elizabeth's armory is filled with old
arms artistically arranged on walls and ceilings,
representing floral and other designs; instruments
of torture are numerous, among them being the
block on which Lords Kilmarnoch and Balmerino
were executed in 1745. The Jewel House contains all the crown jewels of England—crowns,
scepters, swords, orbs and maces of gold studded
with precious stones; Queen Victoria's crown

containing the celebrated Koh-i-noor diamond,
and the heart-shaped ruby worn by the Black
Prince; while St. Peter's chapel is interesting as
the burial place of many royal victims. The war-
dens of the Tower still dress in the costumes of
the Beef-eaters of the time of Henry VIII.

Westminster Abbey was founded in the year
610, and within its venerable walls repose the
ashes of kings, queens, and distinguished men —
the first interment being that of King Harold.
Their respective places of rest are marked by
sumptuous monuments in marble and bronze.
Among them are the tombs of Edward the Confessor, Edward I., Edward III., Edward V., and
Edward VI. ; Richard II., Henry III., Henry V,
and Henry VII. ; James I., Charles II., William
III., and George II. ; Queens Mary, Elizabeth,
Mary of Scotland, and Anne ; also the remains of
the two princes murdered in the Tower. In the
Poets' Corner lie Milton, Dryden, Chaucer, Spen-
cer, Garrick, Dickens, and others noted in the
world of letters. In the opposite transept, allotted
to statesmen, are Pitt, Wilberforce, Palmerston,
Canning, and a host of other distinguished names.
Separating the transepts is the altar, where the
sovereigns of England have received the crown
from the hands of the Archbishop since the church
was built ; and in the rear of the altar stands the
old coronation chair of England's sovereigns,
beneath which is the famous stone on which the

Scottish kings were crowned, brought to England by Edward I., in 1297. In the nave of the church are slabs on the floor, memorials of Livingston, the African explorer, Peabody, the philanthropist, whose remains were afterwards removed to America, and Charles Robert Darwin, the great philosopher of this age.

The British Museum is a magnificent edifice in the Grecian style of architecture, and contains an immense and ancient collection of original manuscripts; Egyptian, Greek, and Roman antiquities, mausolea, the Winged Bulls from Sennacherib's palace at Nineveh, Assyrian relics, the Elgin statuary, and zoological and mineral collections.

In the Egyptian department, besides many of the oldest stone inscriptions known to exist, is the Rosetta stone, carved with hieroglyphic, enchorial, and Greek characters, dating 200 years B.C., and discovered by the French in 1799. This stone was found near Rosetta, in Egypt, and was instrumental in enabling scholars to decipher hieroglyphic characters, and through them to learn much of ancient history.

The Kensington Museum, located in a park of the same name, covers many acres of ground, and requires a day simply to walk through it, bestowing only a hurried glance at the most important objects. It has an extensive and valuable collection of antiquities, ceramics, bronzes, Japanese wares, silver and gold plate, ancient furniture and tapestry, mosaics, terra-cottas and sculpture. The galleries are extensive, and contain some fine paintings, among which are "Napoleon's Farewell to France," and the "Death of Amy Robsart." The East India Museum connected with this building, comprises a very rich and curious collection of Oriental arms, costumes, and carvings, presented to the Prince of Wales by the native princes of India, on the occasion of his travels through that country.

The Houses of Parliament — magnificent buildings, where the sittings of the great council of England are held, and where the laws of the realm are framed — are located on the Thames, and cover eight acres of ground. There are five hundred apartments in these buildings, and the Victoria Tower is 336 feet high. Nearly 500 statues are distributed about the building, and numerous beautiful paintings and frescoes adorn the walls and ceilings. In the House of Lords, rich in gildings and carvings, is the throne-chair, used by the Queen when she opens Parliament. The House of Commons is small and plainly finished. It has a free-and-easy appearance, the members having no particular seats assigned them — benches being used instead of chairs — and they loll about with their hats on during debate.

St. Paul's Cathedral, in the most central part

of the metropolis, is on the site where formerly
stood another cathedral 400 years previous to the
Norman conquest. From the pavement of the
crypt to the top of the cross surmounting it, it is
375 feet, and the minute hand of the clock in the
belfry is said to be ten feet in length. In the
body of the cathedral are fine monuments to
Nelson, Wellington, Collingwood, Picton and
other heroes, while in the crypt are the remains
of the architect, Sir Christopher Wren, and those
of Wellington and Nelson, in granite tombs,
surrounded by constantly burning torches. Here,
also, is the catafalque, formed of captured cannon,
which bore Wellington's remains to their last
resting-place.

The National Picture Gallery in Trafalgar
Square contains numerous gems of painting and
statuary; most of the pictures are old, and from
Biblical subjects, principally of the Italian, Spanish,
French and Flemish schools, and some of the best
works of Raphael, Correggio, Rubens and Murillo,
are to be found here.

The Royal Mews — or stables — at Buckingham Palace, contains one hundred horses; those
used on state occasions being magnificent animals
of a uniform cream color. The carriages are of
great variety: the state carriage, heavily gilded
and ornamented, and weighing several tons, being
the handsomest in the collection. The harness
belonging to this equipage glitters with burnished

brass, and weighs 500 pounds to the horse, often causing the animal to fall beneath its burden.

Madame Tussaud's Wax-works is one of the great sights of London, and is said to be the finest collection of the kind in the world; the models exhibited being the result of many years' patient and careful study. The suite of rooms in which the collection is displayed is gorgeously decorated and gilded; the walls hung with crimson cloth and costly oil paintings. The figures comprise 300 portrait models of celebrities of ancient and modern times, including the complete line of the kings and queens of England, and images of the Pope of Rome, Napoleon I., and the Czar Alexander II. of Russia, lie here in state. The costumes are the identical ones, or correct copies, of those worn by the originals of these effigies, and are valuable both from their intrinsic worth, and for their historic accuracy. Curious and life-like characters are those of an old man seated upon one of the benches in the midst of the spectators, moving his head while taking snuff, apparently absorbed in watching the moving crowd around him; and of a beautiful woman reclining in uneasy slumber, her breast heaving with evident agitation — the night previous to execution. The Chamber of Horrors contains the figures of notorious criminals, and the guillotine used in France during the Revolution.

The collection also includes a large number of

relics of Napoleon, among which are his camp-chair, table and carriage, taken at Waterloo; Voltaire's chair, and the key of the Bastile.

On June 3d, 1882, we witnessed a review of the military or " Trooping of the Colors," as it is called — in St. James' Park, in honor of Queen Victoria's 63d birthday. The celebration was attended by many distinguished guests, including the Prince and Princess of Wales and family, the Countess Burdett-Coutts and others.

Spurgeon — London's noted preacher — may be heard Sundays in the Tabernacle, which seats 5,000 people, and is always crowded by attentive listeners — chiefly of the middle and lower classes — apparently absorbed by his simple and earnest eloquence.

The Derby race at Epsom is celebrated once a year, when all classes make it a holiday. The steam-cars run from London to Epsom Downs, but to go by the road is to see London on wheels: from the four-in-hand private drag, elegantly mounted, down to the costermonger's cart drawn by the smallest donkey. Leaving the Grand Hotel on top of a four-in-hand coach, with a few friends, we started at 10 A. M. by the road, a distance of 16 miles, to Epsom, and soon joined a tide of humanity bound for the same place. On the ground were 400,000 people. The races, six in number, were exciting; but more interesting than they, were the great mass of humanity; the

numberless side-shows of every description, and
the wandering minstrels moving about the grounds
seizing every opportunity to earn a small pit-
tance, rendered the scene a perfect carnival.

Windsor Castle is situated on the river Thames,
20 miles from London.   It has been the favorite
seat of the sovereigns of Great Britain for the past
eight centuries, and, even before Windsor Castle
was founded by William the Conquerer, the Saxon
kings resided on the spot.   The rooms shown to
visitors are the Queen's audience and presence
chambers, the reception, throne, Van Dyke,
Rubens and Zaccarelli rooms, and the banqueting
hall, all of which are elegantly furnished and hung
with fine paintings and Gobelin tapestry.   St.
George's Chapel in the enclosure, is a splendid
specimen of Gothic architecture; in it the Prince
and Princess of Wales were married with great
pomp.   In the vault lie the remains of many of
England's sovereigns, including Henry VIII. and
his queen, Jane Seymour, George III. and his
queen, William IV. and his queen, Charles I., and
the Princess Charlotte.   It is in this chapel the in-
stallation of the Knights of the Garter takes place.

The Albert Chapel, a memorial to the Prince
Consort, was originally erected by Henry VII. as
a place of sepulture for himself.   Afterwards Cardinal Wolsey obtained a grant of it from Henry
VIII., and prepared it as a receptacle for his own
remains.   This chapel has been embellished with

unsparing magnificence by Queen Victoria, in
memory of Prince Albert, and the interior is said
to be the richest in the world. The entire vaulted
roof has been covered with mosaic figures, ornaments and inscriptions, with gold-enamel, in bas-
relief; the floor and walls are beautifully inlaid
with every variety of highly-polished marble and
agate, in exquisite designs, and the window is of
stained glass, with full-length figures of Henry
VIII. and Wolsey. In the centre of the building
is placed a cenotaph with a recumbent figure of
the Prince in armor, and on it is inscribed :

> " I have fought the good fight ;
> I have finished my course."

The Crystal Palace at Sydenham — an hour's
ride from London — is an interesting place to
spend a day, affording an opportunity for the
study of both nature and art. The gardens are
very fine; their beautiful walks, serpentine
streams, statues, fountains and lawns, rendering it
a delightful resort. A portion of the building is
appropriated to tropical trees and plants ; another
to courts of Egyptian, Greek, and Roman sculpture and architecture, which contain copies of the
masterpieces of the great sculptors of both ancient and modern times.

Kew Garden, the most complete botanical
gardens in the world, cover several hundred acres

of highly cultivated ground.   It has an extensive
palm house, and many conservatories.

From Kew we drove through Bushy Park,
noted for its avenue — a mile in length — of
chestnut-trees, planted by William of Orange,
and dined at the famous inn, the " Star and Garter," near the entrance to Hampton Court
grounds.

Hampton Court, the palace presented to
Henry the VIII. by Cardinal Wolsey, is situated
near the banks of the Thames, and surrounded by
extensive grounds.   In the vinery is a grape vine
112 years old, bearing annually 800 lbs of fruit.
Near the entrance is "the Maze," whose devious
and intricate windings afford much perplexity and
amusement to the unwary visitor.   The palace is
of red brick, with stone ornamentation, and was
the birthplace of Edward VI.   Here, the masques
and tournaments of Philip and Mary, and of
Elizabeth, took place; and also the celebration of
the marriage of the daughter of Cromwell to Lord
Falkinbury.   The interior of the palace has an
extensive collection of paintings and tapestry, the
latter representing incidents in the history of
Alexander the Great; and among the portraits
are the beauties of the Court of Charles II.   In
the bedroom of William III. is the state bed of
Queen Charlotte, hung in embroidered satin
draperies.

Embarking from here in one of the small boats

which daily ply the Thames, we skirted the banks
of Battersea Park, passed the Houses of Parliament and Cleopatra's Needle, steamed under
Westminster, Waterloo, Blackfriars and London
bridges, over the subway and tunnel which connect, under water, both banks of the river, passed
the Tower of London, and landed at·Greenwich,
noted for its fine observatory, from which point
the world's time is computed.

CHAPTER IV.

OXFORD: LEAMINGTON: WARWICK: KENILWORTH:
COVENTRY: STRATFORD-ON-AVON: CHESTER: LIV-
ERPOOL: LANCASTER: BOWNESS: ENGLISH LAKES:
PENRITH: CARLISLE: NEWCASTLE: YORK: SHEF-
FIELD: ROWSLEY: MANCHESTER: RHYL: CONWAY:
BETTWS-Y-COED: FFESTINIOG: BRIGHTON: PORTS-
MOUTH: COWES: NEWPORT: SOUTHAMPTON.

OXFORD, situated at the confluence of the Cher-
well, Thames, and Isis rivers, has a population of
40,000. It was once the favorite residence of
Canute, and of Henry I. and Henry II., during
which time the valiant son of the latter, Richard
Cœur de Lion, was born. The city was stormed
in 1067 by William the Conqueror; the part of
the castle which he erected still stands, and is now
used as a jail. Oxford is noted for its University,

which consists of 19 colleges, one of them having been founded by Alfred the Great. In front of Baliol College is a beautiful monument marking the place where Ridley, Latimer, and Cranmer were burnt at the stake. In the museum, among other interesting relics, is Guy Fawkes' lantern, used by him in the celebrated Gunpowder Plot.

Leamington, on the river Leam, is a beautiful city, with lovely parks and wide streets, lined with trees, and has a population of 23,000. It is noted for its medicinal baths, and is environed by six battlefields, viz., Eversham, where Prince Edward defeated Simon de Montfort; Tewksbury, where the Yorkists defeated the Lancastrians; Bosworth, where Henry VII. defeated Richard III., and ended the War of the Roses; Edgehill, which begun, and Naseby, which terminated, the conflict between Charles I., and the Parliament; and Worcester, where Charles II. made a last effort to reverse the fortunes of Cromwell.

Warwick Castle, two miles from Leamington, guarded by embattled walls and stupendous towers, covered without with ivy, and adorned within by frescoes and paintings, is situated on elevated ground, which slopes down to the Avon. It is at the present time, notwithstanding its antiquity, considered one of the most magnificent castles in the kingdom, its history dating back to the Conquest. The principal towers which guard its walls are Caesar's, Guy's, and the Clock, beneath which are donjons formerly used for prisoners. In the great hall of the castle are Cromwell's helmet, the horse-trappings used by Queen Elizabeth, and the sword and porridge-pot of the nine-foot giant, Guy, Earl of Warwick. It was here that Queen Elizabeth stopped over night on her way to visit Dudley, Earl of Leicester, at Kenilworth, and though several centuries have elapsed since then, the arrangement of the room she occupied remains the same to this day, under its present owner, Earl George Guy Greville. In the conservatory is the celebrated Warwick vase, found at the bottom of the lake at Hadrian's villa; it is a fine specimen of Grecian sculpture, cut from a single block of marble, and will hold 188 gallons.

In the town of Warwick is St. Mary's Church, where there are many fine monuments, that of Richard Beauchamp, Earl of Warwick, being one of the finest in England. Here, also, is buried Dudley, Earl of Leicester, one of the favorites of Elizabeth, the fickle queen, lying by the side of his third wife, who survived him. His first wife was Amy Robsart, whose sad fate needs no reminder; his second likewise died — of poison — at the hands of her cruel lord, and the third escaped the same fate through a mistake, Leicester himself taking the poisoned draught intended for her; these crimes being induced by his ambitious designs to obtain the hand of Elizabeth.

Leicester Hospital, which furnishes a life home for twelve veterans, was endowed by Dudley, and is an ancient and picturesque building.

Kenilworth Castle, three miles from Warwick, is one of the grandest ruins in England, its ivy-covered walls teeming with the romance of history, which the eloquent pen of Sir Walter Scott has transmitted to posterity. The castle was founded by Geoffrey de Clinton, and Henry III. gave it to Simon de Montfort; John of Gaunt and Henry IV. both occupied it, and Elizabeth presented it to her favorite, Leicester, who entertained her here with royal magnificence. Those portions of the ruins which are in the best state of preservation are, the banqueting hall, where feasts and revels were held with boundless extravagance, and the tower, in which the unfortunate Amy Robsart was confined previous to meeting her terrible fate. From Kenilworth we continued to Guy's Cliff, the romantic spot where dwelt the Saxon hero, Guy, Earl of Warwick, who retired here to a hermit's cave, after a series of marvellous achievements, and thence we drove to Stoneleigh Abbey, the residence of Lord Leigh, who has an area of 6,000 acres, with a well-stocked deer park and fine grounds.

Coventry, five miles from Kenilworth, is noted chiefly as the scene of the Lady Godiva's ride through the streets, clothed only in the mantle of modesty, prompted by the cruel taunt of her hus-

band, King Leofric, who consented, on these
terms, to yield to her a charter freeing the inhabitants from the unjust taxation to which they had
previously been subjected.   The effigy of Peeping
Tom, whose curiosity cost him his sight, is yet to
be seen on the sight of his cobbler-shop, the place
where he was discovered.

Stratford-on-Avon, the birthplace and burial-
place of Shakespeare, is eight miles east of Warwick.   The house in which this immortal genius
was born is quaint and humble, and remains the
same as when Shakespeare occupied it.   In one
room of the house are preserved relics of the
bard, his signet ring, sword, manuscripts, and
other documents bearing in the cross-mark of his
father and sister, evidence of their illiteracy.

Near the town is the old church in which
Shakespeare lies buried, his wife and daughter
lying on either side of him ; and in a niche in the
chancel is a bust of the bard, which is considered
the most authentic likeness extant.

The slab over his grave bears the inscription,
written by himself, which has guarded his remains
from the hand of desecration to this day :

> " Blest be he, who spares my bones,
>   And curs'd be he, who moves these stones."

One mile distant is the cottage where Anne
Hathaway lived; the house, with its furniture —
including the bench where Shakespeare made love

to her — remains unchanged; and is occupied by
an ancient dame, a descendant of the Hatha-
ways.

Chester, one of the oldest cities in England,
founded by the Romans, is on the river Dee, completely surrounded by a wall, two miles in circuit,
which is now used as a promenade. From the
Phœnix Tower, on the walls, Charles I. witnessed
the defeat of his army by Cromwell's forces. The
castle, erected in the time of William the Conquerer, is well preserved; and the Cathedral is a
venerable structure on the site of an ancient Saxon
monastery. The characteristic feature of the town
is its antique and singular looking houses, with
side-walks for pedestrians on the second story,
which are bordered by shops.

Liverpool, on the river Mersey, is noted for
the magnificence of its docks, which cover 200
acres in extent, and has 15 miles of quays.

Lancaster, on the Lune, has a fine castle; and
is noted for the part it took in the Wars of the
Roses. The town received its first charter from
King John, and now gives the title of Duke to the
Prince of Wales.

Bowness, on Lake Windermere, opposite Belle
Isle, is a charming spot; and from the overlooking heights are afforded the loveliest views of lake
and landscape. Windermere, the most beautiful of
all the English lakes, is eleven miles long and one
wide; small steamers ply its waters, threading its

islands, and affording glimpses of the lovely villas nestling among the hills on its banks.

Taking stage from Bowness we followed Lake Windermere, passing Wray Castle and Ambleside; then Rydal Waters, on which is the home and favorite seat of the poet Wordsworth; "Dove's Nest," where lived Mrs. Hemans; the cottage where Coleridge lived and died; and lastly the lakes Grasmere, Thirlmere and Derwentwater. Near the latter are Keswick and the beautiful falls of Lodore, described by the poet Southey, whose remains lie in the churchyard near by.

Penrith, environed by the seats of many of England's nobility, is noted for the ruins of its fine castle, which was once the residence of Richard III. From here, continuing our route, we stopped at Carlisle, in order to visit its ancient castle and cathedral; then passing through Newcastle, noted for its coals, whence the expression, "carrying coals to Newcastle;" and Durham, celebrated for its fine breed of cattle, we reached York.

This city, situated on the banks of the Ouse, whose history dates back 1000 years B. C., has a population of 55,000. It is partially inclosed by ancient walls, the top of which afford a delightful promenade and a fine view of the city and suburbs. It is claimed that Constantine the Great was born in York in 272 A. D., and that his father, Constantius, died here in 307 A. D.

This city has always held a conspicuous place

in all disturbances of the country, particularly in the Wars of the Roses.   Its objects of greatest interest are, the old castle built by William I., the Cathedral, the second largest in England — its length being 524 feet — and the ruins of an ancient picturesque abbey, situated on the banks of the river Ouse.

From Sheffield, a city of 285,000 inhabitants, chiefly noted for its manufacture of cutlery, we reached our next point of destination, Rowsley.

This place is the nucleus from which excursions are made to Matlock Baths, the vicinity of Byron's home; and to Haddon Hall, a glorious old ruin teeming with romance, which dates from the time of William the Conqueror.

From Rowsley a beautiful drive brought us to Chatsworth Hall, the magnificent residence of the Duke of Devonshire, considered the finest home of any private individual in the world.   The park comprises 2,000 acres, and the gardens and conservatories are marvels of taste and beauty.   The picture-gallery and hall of sculpture contain a number of masterpieces, and the walls and ceilings are rich in frescoes.   All that wealth and refined taste could procure are here combined to charm the sense.

Manchester, the great manufacturing centre of England, is celebrated for its immense cotton mills, and its iron and brass foundries.   From here we continued by rail through northern Wales to visit its seaside resorts and picturesque coast scenery; stopping at Rhyl and Llandudno, the most fashionable bathing-places; Conway, with its romantic old castle; and Bettws-y-Coed, two miles from which is the Fairy Glen and Cascades. At Ffestiniog we took a miniature railroad with a track only 23 inches wide—the narrowest in the world—which conveyed us for 20 miles through the immense slate quarries of that country; and brought us to Portmadoc, where we resumed the broad guage and continued our journey along the coast, via Shrewsbury, to the southern shores of England.

Brighton, 55 miles south of London, the fashionable watering place of England, has a population of 100,000. The favorite drive, five miles in extent, borders the beach, and affords a continuous view of fashionable equipages, and of the bathers beyond, sporting in the waves.

Portsmouth, a fortified city, is the great naval arsenal of the United Kingdom, and a principal seaport of the English Channel. Its extensive storehouses contain every article required for the use of the navy, and in the harbor is stationed Nelson's flag-ship, the old Victory, on which the hero breathed his last, during the Battle of Trafalgar.

Newport, the capital of the Isle of Wight, is in a valley surrounded by gardens, groves and orchards. Carisbrooke Castle, one mile from

Newport, is an old historic ruin, and one full of interest. Here Charles I. fled for safety, and was afterwards confined a prisoner by the Governor, who had guaranteed him protection. A window, from which the unfortunate king attempted his escape, is still shown, with the iron bars partly filed asunder; also the room in which his daughter, the Princess Elizabeth, was found dead, her face on an open Bible at the passage, " Come unto me all ye who are weary and heavy laden, and I will give ye rest."

Cowes, on the north coast of the same island, has many lovely drives and fine residences. Among the latter is Osborne, the summer palace of the Queen, surrounded by a large park, about two miles distant from the town.

Returning to Southampton, a seaport on the English Channel, we took steamer for Havre, and bade a lingering farewell to the shores of old England.

CHAPTER V.

HAVRE: ROUEN: PARIS, — ITS ENVIRONS.

CROSSING the English Channel, we landed at Havre, a strongly fortified seaport town on the northern coast of France, with a population of

93,000, and next to Marseilles in commercial importance. From this point Richmond embarked,
with troops furnished by Charles VIII., to meet
Richard on Bosworth field. Here Bernadin de
St. Pierre, author of Paul and Virginia, was born ;
and the rocks near by were his favorite haunts.

Rouen, on the banks of the Seine, is in the
midst of a highly-cultivated country and picturesque scenery. The cathedral, whose outer walls
are ornamented with many statues, has, among
its monuments, one beneath which rests the heart
of Richard Cœur de Lion.

A donjon is shown in the Market Place,
where Joan of Arc was confined after her capture
by the French ; and in the Place de la Pucelle is
a monument erected on the spot where the Maid
was burnt at the stake, in 1431.

Between Rouen and Paris the railroad follows
the winding course of the river Seine, affording
many varied and picturesque views.

Paris, the gayest and most beautiful city of
the world, is situated on level ground on both
banks of the Seine, and is a place of 2,225,000
inhabitants. It is the centre of fashion and
luxury; has many fine and interesting palaces
and cathedrals, beautiful parks, and wide, clean
streets and boulevards lined with rows of trees,
and ornamented with costly statuary and elaborate
fountains.

The Garden of the Tuileries is laid out in

avenues and flower beds, and adorned with statuary in marble and bronze, the finest of these being the Laocoon and the Rape of Sibyl.

The Place de la Concorde, the handsomest square in Paris, is embellished by two elaborate fountains and eight colossal statues, representing the principal cities of France, that of Strasburg being draped in mourning. The Obelisk of Luxor, which was presented to the French Government by Mahomet Pasha of Egypt, now stands in the centre of the square where formerly stood the guillotine, on which were executed Louis XVI., Marie Antoinette, Madame Elizabeth, Robespierre, and, in one year and six months, 2,800 people.

The Champs Elysées, a grand avenue a mile and a half in length, bordered by trees and walks, and diversified by booths and cafés, is the fashionable drive and promenade of Paris. At the end of this avenue is the Arc-de-Triomphe built by Napoleon I., in commemoration of the victories of the French army under the Republic and the Empire. It is one of the finest in the world, is 160 feet in height, and was erected at a cost of $2,000,000. The bas-reliefs upon its sides represent: "The departure of troops to the Frontier in 1792," "The Taking of Alexandria," "The Blessings of Peace," and "The Triumph of Napoleon."

The Colonne Vendôme, an imitation of Trajan's

column, towers 142 feet high, and is surmounted by a statue of Napoleon. The metal of which it is composed is the melting of 1,200 guns taken from the Russians and Austrians; and the reliefs in bronze represent scenes in the campaign of 1805.

The Colonne de Juillet, of bronze, 154 feet high, and surmounted by a figure representing the Genius of Liberty, stands where was once the Bastile, a state prison, destroyed by the Communists during the late Revolution, and was erected to the memory of those who fell in defence of public liberty in 1830.

The statue of Marshal Ney occupies the spot where he was shot, condemned to death for again joining Napoleon's standard after his return from exile, and the equestrian statue of Joan of Arc is conspicuously situated opposite the Louvre.

The Bois de Boulogne, said to be the finest park in the world, embraces 2,250 acres. The roads are beautifully graded, and bordered with trees. The paths diverge from the main avenues in most graceful curves, which, with the lakes, grottoes and cascades, unite in rendering it a perfect harmony of nature and art.

The Buttes Chaumont, a beautiful park in the suburbs of Paris, was the last work of Napoleon III., and is a miniature rocky wilderness, with lakes, cascades and stalactite grottoes. It occupies a high elevation overlooking Paris, and was the stronghold of the Communists in May 1871,

from which point they threw petroleum shells into
the city.

In Père-la-Chaise cemetery, named after La
Chaise, Jesuit confessor of Louis XIV., are the
tombs of myriads of distinguished dead. Here
lie buried Abelarde and Héloise, Marshal Ney,
"the bravest of the brave," Lafayette, Demidoff,
Racine, Lafontaine, Thiers, Rachel, Eugene
Scribe, Rossini, Chopin and Cherubini, and many
of the generals and savans of the time of Napoleon I.

The Pantheon, a magnificent building, modelled after the Pantheon at Rome, has a lofty
dome 270 feet high, and serves as a place of sepulture to many of the great men of France; such
names as Voltaire, Rousseau, Marshal Lannes,
Montebello, Mirabeau and Marat, which history
has rendered immortal for good or evil.

The Catacombs of Paris, which were once immense quarries of stone, undermining one-tenth
of the area of the city, were in 1786 converted
into a depository for the dead ; when the bones of
3,000,000 people were collected from all the
cemeteries, and brought hither on funeral cars,
followed by priests chanting the service for the
dead. The principal entrance is through the
Porte de l'Enfer, or gate of hell, and ninety steps
lead down to this gloomy subterranean city. On
either side of the narrow passage ways which
intersect this labyrinth, are massed bones and

skulls, arranged in various hideous designs; and here and there are placards, upon which are inscribed quotations appropriate to the sepulchral surroundings.

The Sewers of Paris are among the wonders of subterranean architecture, being only inferior to those of ancient Rome. The main sewer is travelled both by boat and tramway, which transport the visitor, a distance of several miles, from the Madeleine to the Châtelet Theatre.

The Palace of the Tuileries, now in ruins, was burnt by the Communists, May 23, 1871. It was built in 1564 by Catherine de Medici, on the site of an old tile factory, from which it derived its name. Here, in 1572, its wicked founder gave a fête, four days previous to the massacre of St. Bartholomew, in presence of both Catholics and Protestants, and had her son, Charles IX. represented by tableau driving the Huguenots into hell. This was the prelude to the massacre of 25,000 innocent people. Here, in August 1792, the Swiss Guard were killed, and in the Place du Carrousel Louis XIV. gave, in 1672, that splendid tournament which was attended by guests from all parts of the civilized world.

The Palace of the Louvre, which takes its name from Louvrie — a resort for wolves — is a magnificent gallery of art. It was commenced by Francis I. and added to by Napoleon I. and Napoleon III., and embraces several acres of ground.

It was from the southern window that Charles IX.
gave the signal for the massacre, and fired on the
victims of St. Bartholomew.   In the picture gallery are " The Ascension " by Murillo, and " The
Madonna and Child " by Raphael, besides other
celebrated paintings of the old masters.   The
sculpture gallery contains the famous Venus de
Milo; also statues of Minerva, Melpomene, Augustus Caesar and other celebrities of antiquity.
In the Egyptian department are relics brought
from Egypt by Champollion, the antiquarian, and
by Napoleon Bonaparte — sphinxes, reliefs and
statues rifled from the palaces and tombs of the
Theban kings.

The Palais Royal was erected by Cardinal
Richelieu in 1630; and presented by him to
Louis XIII.   In 1793 it was confiscated by the
Government, and at present its gardens — inclosed
by numerous jewelry shops dazzling with the
glitter of gems and gaslight — are open to the
public.

The Palace of the Luxembourg was built by
Marie de Medici, and was bequeathed by her to
the Duke of Orleans.   It is now used for the sittings of the Senate ; and what was formerly the
throne-room, elegantly frescoed and gilded, is now
the Council Hall for its members.

The Palace of Justice, which includes the
Courts of Law, has within its inclosure the Con-
ciergerie, used as a prison during the Reign of

Terror. Here most of the political prisoners of the Revolution of 1797 were confined, and the cells occupied by the unfortunate Louis XVI. and his family, also that of Robespierre remain unchanged.

Notre Dame, one of the old landmarks of Paris, was built in 1160 by Alexander III., Pope of Rome, who at that time had taken refuge in France. Before its magnificent altar have transpired many of the notable events of history; here Napoleon solemnized his marriage with Josephine, and here the First Consul assumed the crown of Empire.

In the treasury of the Cathedral are kept the plate and jewels of the church; the rich robes of the ecclesiastics, and the embroidered coronation mantle of Napoleon; a piece of the True Cross, and a fragment of the Crown of Thorns. At the top of one of the square towers hangs the famous Bourdon bell, which recalls to mind the poor hunchback of Victor Hugo's novel of Notre Dame. It weighs 32,000 pounds and requires the strength of eight men to ring it.

The Church of St. Roche, belonging to the wealthiest parish of Paris, was commenced about 1633; the corner-stone having been laid by Anne of Austria and Louis XIII. From the steps in front of this church Bonaparte levelled his cannon on the mob during the Directory.

The Madeleine, built in 1764, during the reign

of Louis XV., was a place of refuge, in 1871, of the Communists who were shot down without quarter within its walls, regardless of the shelter of its sanctuary.

The Sainte Chapelle, erected in 1245, during the reign of St. Louis, is a fine specimen of Gothic architecture; its stained glass windows illustrating scenes from the Old and New Testaments. In the wall is a small grated window, through which Louis XII., fearing a closer contact with his subjects, listened to the services of the church.

The Hôtel des Invalides, covering 31 acres, was built by Louis XIV. in 1670, for 5,000 pensioned soldiers. The gilded dome, which is 340 feet from the ground, can be seen for miles off; and beneath it is a circular crypt 20 feet deep, with polished granite walls, and adorned with marble reliefs. The mosaic pavement at the bottom, represents a wreath of laurel, from the centre of which rises the massive porphyry sarcophagus which contains the ashes of the great Napoleon. Twelve statues surround the monolith, and record his principal victories; not far off are Vauban and Turenne; while Jerome and Joseph Bonaparte, are near him — in death as in life. Over the door of the crypt are engraved the hero's last words: " I desire that my ashes may rest on the banks of the Seine, in the midst of the French people whom I have loved so well."

The Church of the " Invalides," which over-

shadows the tomb of Napoleon, is adorned with
battle-flags taken by him in Egypt. Every Sunday, at 12 o'clock, a military Mass is performed to
the beat of the drum, when the veterans, some of
whom are blind and crippled and bent with age,
march in to the sound of military music, escorted
by the Veteran Guard. While they perform their
devotions the organ renders the "Vox Humana"
—a wonderful imitation of a choir of human voices
heard from a great distance; and altogether the
service is very impressive and beautiful.

The Grand Opera House on the Place de
l'Opéra, is the finest building of the kind in the
world, having cost the nation nearly $20,000,000.
and was built in 1860. The carriage-way leading
to the Imperial box, the grand staircase, promenades and buffets, are excellent specimens of
architectural skill, while the entire interior is gilded
and frescoed with lavish extravagance.

The Gobelin Tapestry Works, founded in 1450
by Jean Gobelin, was for a long time a private
establishment, but in 1662 passed into the hands
of the Government. The carpets and hangings
made here are unrivalled for their fineness and
brilliancy of color, and are mostly copies of Le
Brun's paintings. At one time they were destined
chiefly for palaces, and as gifts to foreign poten-
tates, but can now be purchased at fabulous
prices.

The Hôtel de Cluny, built in the 15th century

by the abbots of Cluny, is at present a museum
containing a valuable collection of objects of art
and antiquities of the Middle Ages. Among
these may be seen specimens of Flemish tapestry,
Roman sculpture and carved altars.

The summer concerts on the Champs Élysées
are both novel and interesting. Stage performances are given in the open air, the audience being
permitted to smoke and drink during the entertainment.

The students' balls in the Latin quarter now
take the place of the Jardin Mabille, and are notorious for the license permitted its frequenters,
the style of dancing witnessed there, being more
free than elegant.

The Palace of Versailes, 16 miles from Paris,
was built by Louis XIV. about the year 1670.
Wishing to build a palace which would eclipse
any other in Europe, he employed the celebrated
architect Levan to design the building, Le Notre
to plan the grounds, and Le Brun to decorate the
apartments. Sixty miles of country were purchased for this purpose, hills were levelled and
valleys raised, and water brought from great distances to supply the numerous fountains. Over
$200,000,000 is said to have been expended, and
that, with the extravagance of the Court, im-
poverished France, and was the indirect cause
of the Revolution of 1789. Approaching the
palace on either side are colossal marble statues

of warriors and statesmen; and in the centre of
the court is the bronze equestrian figure of Louis
XIV. The grounds surrounding the palace are
magnificent; lakes, grottoes and statuary diversi-
fying the landscape. Fifty-six fountains of elaborate design complete the beauty of the scene; one
of them, Neptune, having seventy jets, which
throw water to the height of 75 feet, and which
costs $2,000 each time its waters play. In this
palace Louis XIV. died, Louis XV. was born,
and escaped being assassinated by Damiens, Marie
Antoinette was attacked by the mob, and from it
Louis XVI. addressed the infuriated populace.
After the fall of Napoleon I., it was occupied successively by Louis XVIII., Charles V., Louis
Philippe, Napoleon III., and Thiers. Here Queen
Victoria was entertained, in 1855, by Napoleon
III.; and here King William of Prussia was declared Emperor of Germany in 1871. The paintings, frescoes, and statuary of the palace are exceedingly fine; notably a marble statue repre-
senting the last moments of Napoleon I., and
paintings of his coronation before the altar of
Notre Dame, and of the presentation of standards
to his army by this great general. Within the
limits of Versailles are the Grand Trianon built by
Louis XIV. for Madame de Maintenon; the Petit
Trianon, built by Louis XV. for Madame du
Barry; and the Swiss cottage, in which the lovely
but heedless Marie Antoinette sought relief from

the irksome trammels of the etiquette of the
French Court. Among the state carriages and
sleighs are those of many successive sovereigns,
the most magnificent of these being the state
carriage, built for the coronation of Charles X. at
a cost of $200,000, last used by Napoleon III., and
considered the finest in the world.

The Palace of Fontainebleau is 40 miles from
Paris, and dates from the reign of Louis VII. in the
12th century. Here, the Great Condé died, and it
was here the son of Louis XV. fell a victim to
poison in 1765. Here, Queen Christina of Sweden caused her secretary, Monaldeschi, to be
assassinated ; and here Charles IV. of Spain was
kept in captivity ; as was also Pope Pius VII.,
retained by Napoleon Bonaparte in 1812, for a
space of eighteen months, for the purpose of in-
ducing him to resign his temporal power. Here
was pronounced the decree of divorce between
Napoleon and the unhappy Josephine ; and, here
also, where he signed his abdication, and took
leave of the remnant of his old guard, who had
followed him through all the vicissitudes of war
until the moment of his departure for Elba. This
was the subject of the celebrated painting : " Les
Adieux de Fontainebleau."

In one of the apartments of the palace is still
to be seen a table, upon which the deposed sovereign signed his abdication, and which bears a deep
gash from the pen-knife of the incensed hero. In

the midst of the grounds is a lovely lake, in the centre of which is an island containing a small pavilion, reached only by boat, where Napoleon was wont to retire with his generals to discuss military measures.

St. Cloud Palace, six miles from Paris, on the Seine, is now in ruins, having been ' shelled in 1870 by the French from Fort Valerian, in order to dislodge the Prussians who occupied it. It was built in 1658 by Louis XIV. and presented to the Duke of Orleans; and was afterwards purchased by Louis XVI., for Marie Antoinette. Here Henry III. was assassinated; and here again, Napoleon Bonaparte laid the foundation of his power; and later, in 1815, Blücher held his headquarters. It was here that Charles X. signed the fatal ordinance which cost him his throne; and here the capitulation of Paris was signed in 1871. The palace stands on an eminence overlooking Paris, and is surrounded by beautiful grounds, in which is a cascade noted for its size and beauty.

Malmaison, formerly a hospital, but afterwards selected by Josephine as a place of residence after her divorce from Napoleon, and elegantly fitted up by him, is situated ten miles from Paris. Here the Emperor was in the habit of visiting his divorced wife; seeking its retirement to plan some of his campaigns, and here he came to bid a last farewell to Josephine, ere he took his departure for Elba. In the adjoining church are fine monuments over the remains of Josephine and Hortense.

The Palace of St. Germain crowns the summit of a terraced elevation commanding a fine view of the valley of the Seine and the heights of Mount Valerian. It was here that Francis I. was married, and James II. of England passed the period of exile.

Sèvres, where is manufactured the most beautiful porcelain ware, was founded in 1737, and has been in the hands of the French Government for over 100 years. The process of manufacture is most interesting, and the show-rooms contain beautiful and valuable copies on porcelain of paintings from Raphael, Michael Angelo, and Titian.

St. Denis, six miles from Paris, is chiefly interesting on account of the Abbey church which has been the burial-place of the kings of France, from Dagobert, 580, to Louis XVIII. During the first revolution, by decree of the Convention the tombs were rifled of their contents, and the remains of kings and queens thrown into one common ditch. In the royal vault are the remains of Marie Antoinette, Louis XVI. and Louis XVIII., and among the magnificent monuments are those of Henry II. and Catherine de Medici, Louis XII. and Anne of Brittany, Francis II., Henry III. and the Duke de Berri.

In the crypt is kept the sarcophagus in which Charlemagne was interred at Aix-la-Chapelle.

CHAPTER VI.

BRUSSELS, the capital of Belgium, is on the river
Senne, and has 171,000 inhabitants. The fortifications of a century ago have all been removed,
and on their site are beautiful boulevards and
walks bordered with stately linden trees extending
for five miles around the city. The handsomest
square is that directly in front of the king's
palace, containing several fine fountains. Among
the statues seen are those of Geoffrey de Bouillon
and Leopold I., and also that of the Mannikin—a
fountain, remarkable for its peculiar and unique
design.

The Bois de Cambre and Forest of Soignies
are the fashionable drives, which extend for miles
in the suburbs of the city.

Among its finest buildings are the old and new
Houses of Parliament, the latter having cost
$10,000,000.

The Hôtel de Ville, erected in 1400, is one of
the largest and most remarkable edifices of the

Gothic style; its pyramidal tower rising 364 feet high. In one portion of the building are the Senate and Assembly rooms, adorned with portraits of late kings and members, while in another are the keys of the city; and here the drawing of the National Lottery takes place. The ball-room is elaborately carved and hung with some fine specimens of Gobelin tapestry; it was here the Duke of Wellington attended the ball given by the Countess of Richmond the night previous to the battle of Waterloo.

The old palace built in 1300, was formerly the residence of the Spanish and Austrian governors of the Netherlands, but is now a museum; and contains a large collection of paintings and curiosities.

The Wiertz Gallery of paintings is a most peculiar collection by this eccentric artist. In it are pictures representing Napoleon in hell; a woman who had been buried alive breaking from the cerements of the grave; a scene in the infernal regions; Quasimodo, the hunchback of Notre Dame; and Life and Death, represented in the forms of two young girls; all of which are of the same repulsive character.

Brussels was once famous for the manufacture of carpets, but they are now no longer made here. Lace is an important article of manufacture and export, those varieties generally preferred being Point, Point Appliqué, Duchesse, and Chantilly.

In the factories are the partly-underground work-rooms, in which women weave the dainty webs of lace in the damp and semi-obscurity, where more than half their lives are spent. Owing to the extreme delicacy of their work, only a ray of light is allowed to rest upon the one spot on which their gaze is riveted. We saw old women and young girls, their eyes dim to all objects save that to which their sight was trained.

The battle-field of Waterloo, twelve miles from Brussels, is of less extent than one would imagine from the importance of the contest, and from pre-conceived ideas, the line of battle covering an area of scarcely three miles. In "Les Misérables," Victor Hugo has given a magnificent description of this celebrated battle. On the field we noted many points of historic interest—the "Cross Roads,"—Wellington's headquarters—"La Belle Alliance,"—those of Napoleon—directly opposite each other, and only a mile apart; "La Haye Sainte," the headquarters of the Hanoverians; and "Hougomont," with its brick walls, burnt crucifix, and well once filled with human skeletons. We also saw the place where the Scotch Grays charged, the spot where the heroic Highland piper sat, with both legs shot off, cheering on his countrymen with the sound of their beloved bagpipes, the locality where Ney fought so desperately, and the sunken road of Ohain, into which the charging troops of France, inadvertently plunged, horse and man, to their destruction.

Vilvorde, 6½ miles from Brussels, is particularly noted as being the home of Tyndale, the translator of the Bible, who suffered martyrdom here in the cause of religion.

Antwerp, on the right bank of the Scheldt, is the chief port of Belgium, and has a population of 163,000. It is one of the most strongly fortified cities in Europe, and before the 15th century was almost without a rival among the commercial cities of the globe. The treaty of Westphalia, in 1648, almost ruined her commerce, but Bonaparte made it his naval arsenal, and since that time it has somewhat recovered its former prestige. Rubens, Vandyke, Jordaens, and other great masters, were natives of Antwerp, and the best of their productions are found here to-day.

The Cathedral, a magnificent specimen of ecclesiastical architecture, is of vast dimensions. In the tower, the steeple of which is 466 feet in height, are eighty-two chime-bells, which are noted for their sweetness and purity of tone. The interior of the cathedral corresponds in grandeur with the exterior, being elaborate in carvings of brass, marble and wood. Here is Rubens' masterpiece, the Descent from the Cross ; also his Resurrection, Elevation to the Cross, and Assumption of the Virgin.

The Church of St. Jacques is the handsomest

in the city, and contains the vaults of most of the leading families of Antwerp. Among these is the tomb of Rubens, who lies buried behind the high altar.

In St. Paul's Church is Rubens' painting of the Scourging of Christ. The grounds belonging to the church contain a representation of Mount Calvary. At the summit of this rocky elevation — 100 feet high — is an image of Christ on the Cross, at the base of which is a model of the Holy Sepulchre; and below this is represented the infernal regions filled with people in torment, while life-size figures of apostles, saints, and angels, are grouped, standing and hovering about the scene.

The Museum, which has a splendid collection of paintings, comprises the choicest specimens of the Flemish school. Here is Vandyke's masterpiece, the Crucifixion, Quentin Matsys' Descent from the Cross, Van Lerins' Lady Godiva, and Rubens' Crucifixion of Christ between the two Thieves. Near one of the churches is an iron canopy of marvellous design, the work of Quentin Matsys, the blacksmith artist of Antwerp. He fell in love with the daughter of a celebrated painter, but the obdurate father refused consent to his suit, resolved that his daughter should wed only with one of his own calling. Abandoning the anvil, Quentin Matsys assumed the brush, and eventually surpassing her father in his own art, won the daughter's hand.

Rotterdam, the second city in Holland in point of population and commerce, has 153,000 inhabitants, a magnificent harbor, superb docks, and many canals, these latter are as numerous as the streets, and upon them is done the principal traffic, communication being maintained by draw-bridges and ferry-boats. The houses are of red brick, tall and quaint, thoroughly Dutch in aspect, one general feature being an arrangement of two mirrors placed at an angle outside the windows, giving the inmates views of all that is passing in the streets.

Rotterdam was the birthplace of Erasmus, the celebrated Dutch scholar, and his statue in bronze adorns the market-place, while in the park stands the marble statue of Holland's favorite poet, Tollens.

Scheveningen, a fashionable watering place, is three miles from the Hague, environed by fine residences and a wooded country; it is much fre-quented by the Dutch for its fine beach and surf bathing. From here Charles II. embarked for England after the downfall of Richard Cromwell.

The Hague, originally the hunting-seat of the Counts of Holland, and so called from the hedge which surrounded their lodge, is indebted to Louis Napoleon for conferring upon it the privileges of a city, and at present ranks as the political capital of the kingdom. The streets are wide and lined with trees; the principal buildings being the King's

Palace, the Queen's Cottage, and the Museum, which contains Rembrandt's celebrated painting of an Anatomical Examination, and Paul Potter's Bull, the latter valued at $100,000.

Amsterdam, "the dike or dam Amstel," is built on piles, and intersected by canals which are spanned by 300 bridges dividing the city into ninety islands. Diamond cutting has here attained its great perfection, and gives employment to hundreds of men and women; the polishing is done with diamond dust on a wheel which revolves at the rate of 2,000 revolutions a minute, and the cutting is done by hand with a like stone; hence the origin of the expression "diamond cut diamond."

The palace is occupied by the king for only one month of the year. The ball-room, 125 feet in length, is finished in Italian marble, and is considered one of the finest in Europe. The Jews' quarter in Amsterdam is occupied by 60,000 of that race; and the characteristic type is marked on every face.

Zaandam, on an arm of the Zuyder Zee, six miles from Amsterdam, has a population of 13,000. Its inhabitants are primitive both in customs and dress; the streets are narrow, paved with brick, and without sidewalks; the houses are very small, quaint and painted green, as a rule, and the whole town is scrupulously clean: a horse or other beast of burden being rarely seen. Zaandam is noted

for its 400 windmills, and for its being the scene
of the self-exile of Peter the Great, who resorted
thither, disguised as a common workman, to learn
the art of ship-building; the cottage in which he
lived, containing his work-bench, bed and chairs.
is still extant; and a tablet over the mantel, placed
there by the Emperor Alexander, bears the inscription: "Nothing too small for a great man."

Bremen, built on both sides of the Weser, has
a population of 113,000. It was formerly an independent and free city, but was added to Prussia
in 1867, and is now garrisoned by troops of the
German Empire. Its harbor is good, and ship-
ping extensive; its snuff manufactories are the
largest in the world.

Hamburg, a free, imperial city of Germany, is
on the Elbe, 75 miles from its mouth; population, 290,000. It is one of the most important
commercial cities of the world, and its lines of
steamers run regularly to China, Japan, the West
Indies and America. It has some fine public
buildings and handsome streets, but nothing of
special interest to detain the traveller.

CHAPTER VII.

COPENHAGEN, the capital of Denmark, is on the east coast of the Island of Zeeland, and has 236,000 inhabitants. The city is enclosed by a line of fortifications — now used as a promenade — mounting 150 cannon; and the harbor is protected by the Castle of Frederickshavn, which is considered impregnable.

Rosenborg Palace was built in 1604; it ceased long ago to be a royal residence, and contains at present a collection, belonging to Danish kings, made at the death of Christian IV., in 1648. Several rooms are devoted to relics of each of the kings — comprising the furniture, arms, jewels and garments of the different eras, and the banqueting hall, hung in tapestry, contains the coronation chairs made of the ivory of the narwhal, considered in former days worth its weight in silver.

Thorwaldsen's Museum, built in 1848, for the exclusive purpose of containing the works of this famous sculptor, is of the Grecian sepulchrai style of architecture, surmounted by a bronze figure of Victory in a chariot, driving four fiery horses. The whole number of Thorwaldsen's works in this museum are 300 ; among them are Jason and the Golden Fleece, which first gave the sculptor his renown; an equestrian figure of Prince Joseph Poniatowski, Pope Pius VII., the Graces, Night and Morning, the Ages of Love, and the bust of Martin Luther ; this latter, his last work, was left unfinished. In the centre of the court lie the remains of Thorwaldsen, whose name and genius command the highest love and respect. The tomb is a simple, ivy-covered, granite slab, his greatest monument being his works, which surround him.

Christiansborg Palace contains the royal picture gallery, with fine paintings by Danish artists. Among them are Christian II. in Prison, and Samson at the Mill, by Block; A Fisherman's Home, and Rent-day, by Dalsgand. In the banqueting room is Thorwaldsen's famous frieze of Alexander's entrance into Babylon.

The Cathedral of Notre Dame is adorned exclusively with the works of Thorwaldsen, whose remains were followed here by the royal family, and all the high officials of the Government. These works comprise twelve colossal marble statues of the Apostles, a Figure of Christ, and, the gem of all, the kneeling figure of an Angel holding a shell, which forms the baptismal font.

Trinity Church, with its famous round tower, was erected by Christian IV. for an observatory. The tower is ascended within by means of a spiral inclined-plane, up which the Empress Catherine, in 1716, drove four horses, Peter the Great preceding her on horseback.

Elsinore, 40 miles north of Copenhagen, is situated on the Sound, only a mile distant from the Swedish coast. Here is the Castle of Kronborg, a fortress commanding the Sound, erected in 1574 for the purpose of collecting dues enforced on all vessels going to or coming from the Baltic. The place is interesting from its association with Shakespeare's tragedy of Hamlet, the battlements of the square tower of this castle being the scene where the ghost of Hamlet's father "was doomed for a certain term to walk the night." On a terrace to the north of the town, in a grove of trees, is a pile of stones shown as Hamlet's grave, and close by is Ophelia's brook.

Many of Shakespeare's dramas, modified and embellished by fiction, are founded on fact. Hamlet was really a native of Jutland, a section of Denmark, where his father was a famous pirate-chief, and associate governor with his brother of the northern portion of the country. Hamlet's father had married the daughter of the Danish king, and was subsequently murdered by his own brother, who married his widow, and succeeded to the government of the whole of Jutland. Hamlet, who was a pagan, deeming it his first duty to avenge his father, feigned madness in order to encompass his ends, and contriving to slay his uncle became Governor of Jutland, and was eventually killed in battle. The name Hamlet, pronounced by the Danes Amlet, signifies madman.

Jönköping, on the southern extremity of Lake Wetter, is an old Swedish town, which was set on fire in 1612 by Gustavus Adolphus, to prevent it from falling into the hands of the enemy. It was here that, in 1809, the treaty of peace between Sweden and Denmark was signed. This town is best known as the place of manufacture of the famous Swedish matches, made without sulphur or phosphorus, and since imitated in other countries.

Gottenburg, the first commercial, and second largest city in Sweden, has a population of 75,000. It is situated on the Gotha river, and has a fine harbor, but is by no means an attractive city. The military governor resides here, and in the building occupied by him Charles XI., of the Palatinate line, died in 1660.

The Gotha Canal is the general name given to the entire water highway between Gottenburg and Stockholm — each artificial connection having its individual name — which joins the waters of the North Sea to those of the Baltic. The total length of the entire route is 260 miles, while the artificial portions are 57 miles in length, and include 53 locks. The work on the canal was begun in the 16th century, and was in course of construction during the reigns of successive monarchs. Travelling through this route one sees most wonderful specimens of engineering, and while the steamer ascends, through numerous locks, apparently a succession of gigantic steps, one has an opportunity to explore the surrounding country, and to see some of the grandest scenery and finest waterfalls in Sweden.

The Falls of Trolhätta, at the outlet of Lake Wener, seven in number, 108 feet in height, and covering a distance of 480 feet, are sixty miles from Gottenburg. The view obtained of the Rapids, and of the whole series of falls, from a rocky eminence overhanging the river, is one of extreme beauty. The locks on the Trolhätta canal are 19 in number, the oldest of which was constructed in the reign of Charles XII. by the great engineer and celebrated founder of the religious sect, Swedenborg.

Christiania, the capital of Norway, with a population of 100,000, was founded by Christian IV. in 1624. The city is beautifully situated on a fiord, an inlet of the sea, gemmed with a number of small islands, and closed in by a range of hills thickly wooded with Norwegian pine. Although Nature has done so much to beautify it, the city is most commonplace and unattractive. The University museum contains a fair collection

of paintings, the finest of which is Tiedeman's
"Haugiauer," or, preaching in a cottage, much
admired in the Paris Exposition of 1855. Here,
also, is the Viking ship, found buried near the
coast, supposed to be a war vessel a thousand
years old, and containing the bones of human
beings and horses.

The Castle of Aggershuus, on an eminence
commanding the harbor, was built during the
14th century. It contains at present the regalia
and crown jewels; and is noted as having been
the place of confinement of the famous Hoiland,
the combined Robin Hood and Jack Sheppard of
Norway. This man was distinguished for his
generosity and kindness towards his associates,
and his devotion to the fair sex, while his robberies
were entirely confined to the rich; bolts and
bars were of no avail against his strength and
ingenuity.

The Parliament House, or Diet, and the City
Palace, are among the few prominent buildings of
the city.

Oscar's Hall, a summer residence of the King,
five miles out of town, is a showy building well
located on a neck of land, and commanding beautiful views of water and landscape.

Leaving Christiania by rail, we skirted a number of fiords, cascades and rapids, the mountain
views being among the finest in Norway; then
forty miles by boat on the Randsfiord, the most

beautiful of Norwegian lakes, and again by diligence to Mustad.

Mustad, on the summit of the mountain, consists of a few insignificant houses, and serves as a way station for travellers visiting the remote parts of Norway. The inn is primitive in its appearance and domestic arrangement. . Upon the register were only two names of English-speaking people inscribed within ten years; and on a table an old wooden-bound family Bible of mine host bore the date 1580.

After spending the night in this mountain retreat, we continued our journey to Lake Mjösen, which is over fifty miles long, and two thousand feet deep. Here we crossed over to Hamor, prettily situated on the lake, and a station on the line of railway to Trondhjem.

Trondhjem, on a fiord bearing the same name, at the terminus of the railroad, has 23,000 inhabitants, is the largest of the northern towns of Europe, and has the same latitude as that of southern Iceland. It was founded by Olaf Tryggvesson in 994, was formerly the capital of Norway, and here the kings of Norway and Sweden are still crowned. The city has suffered much from plague and conflagration. The streets are wide, well paved and clean, but the houses, built of stone or brick, are low and insignificant. The cathedral, where the kings are crowned, is of Norman architecture, and was erected in the 11th century. On its high altar is a reliquary which once contained the remains of St. Olaf, a former king, who destroyed the native temples, and established the Catholic religion with fire and sword. A well of water still to be seen in the church is said to have sprung from the spot where he was buried; and the fact of his remains being found in a perfect state of preservation was looked upon as a miracle, and they were placed in a silver reliquary studded with precious stones. His shrine became a favorite place of pilgrimage for the devout from all parts of Europe, until 1541, when the church was plundered by the Lutherans, and the remains carried off by the Danes.

The Castle of Munkholm, on an island opposite the city, was the place of imprisonment of Count Greffenfeld, the Grand Chancellor of Christian IV. of Denmark; and the stone floor of the cell is worn by his constant pacing to and fro during his twenty years' incarceration. The sad story of Count Greffenfeld gave Victor Hugo the foundation for his novel Hans d'Island.

At Hammerfest, the most northern city in the world, the midnight sun is visible in July, its reflected light extending some distance southward, so clearly that until midnight one can read without difficulty.

The people of Norway are of stunted growth, of pinched visage, and of a fair type, the result of the excessive rigor of the climate.

The peasant men wear knee-breeches, red shirts, sugar-loaf hats and fur-lined coats; while the costumes of the women are even more quaint and gaudy. Their habits are plain and unassuming, and their honesty and politeness proverbial. The houses in the country are roofed with earth, and entered from the second story; light — owing to the extreme cold—being admitted only through the door. The cariole, the summer mode of conveyance, is a peculiarly constructed vehicle; admitting but one person within its narrow limits, who must needs drive in an uncomfortably reclining position, while an attendant clings, as best he may, to the rear.

Stockholm, the capital of Sweden, with a population of 174,000, is built upon nine islands in Lake Malar and the Baltic sea, and, from its location in the midst of the waters, is styled the Venice of the North. Its name is derived from Stock(wood) and Holm(island). The city contains many squares and small parks in which are monuments in bronze of Charles XII. and Charles XIII., and an equestrian statue of Adolphus III. There is also a fine bronze group of two combatants, bound together by a leathern band about the waist, while the struggle between them with knives is thrilling and life-like, and symbolizes the national form of duel.

The Royal Palace, an immense building of granite and brick, commands a fine position on

the highest point of the centre island. The exterior is unprepossessing, but within its walls are
516 rooms and 32 kitchens. The apartments of
the king, queen and queen dowager are handsomely appointed, and filled with works of art;
the great gallery, the banqueting hall and the
throne room are spacious, and in the latter is the
silver throne, a present to Queen Christina from
Magnus Gabriel de la Gardie.

The Museum has a large collection of statuary,
antique arms and armor; relics and antiquities of
a succession of kings, and paintings both ancient
and modern. Among these are the Victor's Return, by Saloman; the Religious Fanatic, by
Tiedeman; After the Duel; and a portrait of King
Eric IV.

The Cathedral, where the sovereigns are first
crowned — for, in concession to the national pride
of the two kingdoms, now united under one ruler,
the ceremony of coronation is repeated in Trondhjem — contains an altar-piece finely carved in
ebony. Here are preserved the spurs and helmet
of St. Olaf of Norway, taken by Eric IV. from his
tomb in the Cathedral of Trondhjem.

The Riddarsholm church is now used as a
mausoleum for the royal family, and a receptacle
for trophies of the battlefields of the various
epochs of the history of Norway.

The Royal Library comprises 70,000 volumes,
and occupies an entire building. In it are auto-

graph letters of Richelieu, Voltaire, Alexander I. and Napoleon; a Bible dating 1521 with marginal notes by Martin Luther; and a curious volume called the Devil's Bible; this measures several feet in length, is bound in wood, and is written on the skins of 300 asses.

The Zoological Museum has the finest botanical, mineralogical and geological collection in the world; and was founded by Linnæus and other noted Swedish scientists. Among other interesting objects to be seen, is the largest specimen of an elephant's skeleton, and here also is a meteoric stone weighing 250 tons, which fell in the north of Sweden.

The Deer Park, with its lovely drives, villas, and cafés is a favorite afternoon resort. In its midst is the Palace of Rosendal, the former residence of Charles XIV.—better known as Bernadotte, one of Napoleon's renowned marshals.

Upsala, fifty miles from Stockholm, is one of the most attractive of the old-fashioned cities of Europe, and in its cathedral are buried Gustavus Vasa and Linnæus. Among the manuscripts in the library is a copy of the four Evangelists, written in letters of silver on parchment of the 5th century.

CHAPTER VIII.

ABO : HELSINGFORS : ST. PETERSBURG : PETERHOF : MOSCOW: SEBASTOPOL: WARSAW :

THE Russian Empire covers over one-half the area of the European continent, while its Asiatic possessions are three times the extent of those in Europe. The southern portion of Russia is for the most part a level plain, green in spring, parched in summer, and shrouded in snow in winter. The central section is, to a large extent, covered with timber, and is decidedly the most productive, while the northern part is beyond the limit of vegetation, and buried in snow and ice throughout the year. The natural wealth of Russia is enormous, especially in mineral productions, her mines embracing nearly every variety. Gold and silver mines are productive, and those of lapis lazuli, malachite, and jasper are the richest in the world.

The area of the Russian Empire embraces 8,352,940 square. miles, and contains 90,000,000 people, of which number

55,000,000 profess the Russo-Greek religion.
1,000,000 are Dissenters.
3,000,000 Roman Catholics.
2,500,000 Protestants.
2,000,000 Jews.
  250,000 Idolaters.
   50,000 Armenians.

The Empire is divided into 96 governments or territories, viz. :

50 in Russia, having	70,000,000	inhabitants.
12 in the Caucasus,	5,000,000	"
10 in Poland, "	6,000,000	"
8 in Finland, "	2,000,000	"
8 in Siberia, "	4,000,000	"
8 in Central Asia	3,000,000	"
——		
96	90,000,000	

The Russian navy comprises 275 vessels, and the army, on a peace footing, 800,000 men.

The religion of Russia exacts observance of its forms from the highest official to the lowest serf. The Emperor is the head of the Greek Church, which predominates, and all army and government officials are required to embrace this form of worship. Great wealth is concentrated in the Church, and images being forbidden pictures are substituted set in gold, and studded with precious stones of such great value that a guard is kept constantly on watch to protect them.

The lower classes are poor, ignorant and superstitious; and whether in church or on the street, are continually praying, making the sign of the cross, and prostrating themselves on the ground before one or other of the innumerable shrines to be found everywhere.

The drosky, the summer conveyance, is usually drawn by a single horse, but frequently one sees three driven abreast. The costume of the drivers is somewhat similar to a woman's garb — a full skirt, gathered in to the waist by a broad sash, and reaching to the ankle, allowing the heavy boots to be seen below it, and a tall, oddly-shaped hat completes this singular and not un-picturesque costume.

Abo, the former capital of Finland, is on an inlet three miles from the gulf, and has 23,000 inhabitants. This is the first point reached by steamer on crossing the Baltic from Stockholm. The cathedral, the first Christian temple in the Northern land, contains the novel and hideous spectacle of open coffins, displaying the embalmed corpses within.

Helsingfors, the present capital of Finland, with 34,000 inhabitants, has a strongly-fortified harbor, protected by the fortress of Sveaborg, called the Gibraltar of the North, which in 1855 was unsuccessfully attacked by the combined fleets of France and Great Britain. The Greek church, with a large gilt dome, surrounded by thirteen smaller ones, is conspicuous for some distance.

St. Petersburg, the Capital of Russia, at the mouth of the Neva, was founded by Peter the Great in 1703, and contains 668,000 inhabitants. It is built on several islands in the river marshes. Fifty thousand peasants were employed for years driving piles for a foundation, the Czar himself superintending the operations, and all conveyances approaching the city by land or sea were required to bring a certain number of stones. The river Neva, which flows throughout the city, is crossed by several bridges, some of which are built of boats. The streets are very wide and clean, and are paved with small stones; the houses are of brick, covered with plaster, and painted yellow, and the roofs red or green.

The finest monuments which adorn the city are those of an equestrian statue of Peter the Great; Catherine II. surrounded by her favorites; Nicholas I. on horseback, with bronze bas-reliefs at the base, and that erected to Alexander I—a highly-polished granite shaft, surmounted by the figure of an angel, the whole 150 feet in height. The shaft was cut from the quarries of Finland, and is

said to be the largest monolith in the world. Two
triumphal arches have been erected in commemoration of Russia's victorious arms — the Moscow
Gate, raised in honor of the army of 1826—1831,
is on the old road to Moscow ; and the Narva
Gate, opposite the palace, surmounted by an
image of Victory in a triumphal car drawn by six
horses, commemorates the return of the Russian
troops in 1815.

The cottage of Peter the Great, the first house
built in the city, was occupied by the Emperor
while superintending the building of St. Petersburg.   It is protected from destruction by an
outer casing, and contains three rooms, one of
which is now used as a shrine where devotees
come to pay their devotions.

In the Arsenal are large collections of arms and
standards captured from nearly every nation in
the world, comprising the earliest war implements
from guns made of rope, leather and wood, down
to the largest and most lately improved cannon.
Here are also displayed the uniforms and trappings of Peter the Great, Catherine II. and Alexander I.   The cannon foundry adjoining the
arsenal well repays a visit; for here are to be
seen hundreds of the largest cannons cast.

St. Isaac's Cathedral, whose foundation alone,
owing to the marshy nature of the soil, cost over
a million dollars, is of vast dimensions and of the
most costly material.   The centre dome, sur-

rounded by four smaller ones, overlaid with gold,
and ornamented with colossal bronze figures, is
supported by eighty pillars of polished porphyry
sixty feet in height, resting on pavement of marble and granite.   The interior is gorgeous beyond
conception; steps of porphyry, floors of variegated
marble, pillars of lapis lazuli, malachite and jasper,
walls and altars adorned with mosaics and paintings of saints, emperors and warriors, set in gold
and precious stones.   The priests dress in flowing
robes, wear their hair and beards long, and chant
the service loudly and with much ostentation;
while the worshippers prostrate themselves at full
length on the marble floor, or move about, kissing
repeatedly the pictures of their saints.

The Cathedral of St. Peter and St. Paul, situated inside the citadel, has by far the most gaudy
interior of any church in the city, being a mass of
gilt and glitter from floor to dome.   Here are interred Peter the Great, and all the succeeding
sovereigns of Russia down to the present time,
with the exception of Peter II., who was buried in
Moscow.   The tombs are uniformly of plain, white
marble, three feet in elevation, the surface of the
slab bearing only the Russian eagle in gold, and
an inscription on the end giving, according to the
custom of the country, the height and breadth of
the occupant at birth.   The tomb of the late
Alexander II. is guarded by day and night, and a
light kept continually burning above it.

The Cathedral of St. Petersburg, dedicated to Our Lady of Kazan, is on the Nevskoi Prospekt, and was built after the model of St. Peter's at Rome. In front of the cathedral are the statues of Prince de Smolenskoi and Barclay de Tolly, and within is the painting representing Our Lady of Kazan, set with jewels of fabulous value, and a number of flags and keys of walled cities captured in battle.

The Monastery of St. Alexander Nevskoi, built by Peter the Great for the remains of the Grand Duke Alexander, contains his tomb, which is of solid silver surmounted by angels. The bones of this saint, after their removal to their new place of sepulture returned again to the Volga, until Peter threatened the monks with punishment if they did not prevent the saint from continuing his midnight rambles. At this church may be heard the finest music in the city, chanted by 40 monks.

A shrine now marks the spot where the late Emperor Alexander was killed; and preparations are being made to erect a church on the same site in commemoration of that event.

The Winter Palace, though of great proportions, is of an unprepossessing exterior, being of brick with an outer coating of plaster painted yellow, and surrounded by neither trees nor gardens. It was formerly the winter residence of the Emperor and his court, accommodating 6,000 persons constituting his household. At present its finest apartments are closed, in accordance with a Russian custom commemorative of the decease of a former occupant. The crown jewels, kept here, are among the most magnificent in all Europe; one — the Orloff diamond, next to the largest in the world — weighing 194¾ carats; this gem was stolen from the eye-socket of an idol in the Temple of Seringham, India, was afterwards bought by Count Orloff, and presented by him to Catherine II.

The Hermitage connected with the Winter Palace was built in 1765 by Catherine II., for the purpose of retirement from the cares of affairs of state. Its halls and marble stairway are of vast proportions, supported by pillars of Finland granite. In the picture gallery are paintings of celebrated artists; the Last Days of Pompeii, by Brulow, and the Brazen Serpent, by Bruni, being fine specimens of Russian art. The gallery of Peter the Great contains that sovereign's working tools, and his iron cane weighing 10 pounds, besides other articles used by him, while throughout the galleries, in extravagant profusion are tables and mantels of malachite, jasper and lapis lazuli.

The Taurida Palace, now in disuse and going fast to decay, was the scene of the gorgeous entertainment given by Count Potemkin to his royal mistress Catherine II., a description of which exceeds in splendor the most extravagant conceptions in the Arabian Nights. The ball-room on this occasion was dazzling in the brilliancy of 20,000 lights, and in the midst of the magnificent chandeliers were stationed, in mid-air, the musicians who contributed melodious strains to this scene of enchantment.

The Palace of Peterhof, 12 miles from the city, has been occupied by successive sovereigns since the reign of Peter the Great, with the exception of the present emperor, Alexander III., who prefers to occupy a smaller palace near by. The grounds surrounding Peterhof are extensive and handsome, and rich in gilded statues and fountains ; of these the largest is one called Samson, which throws a jet 80 feet high, while environing this are smaller fountains, and cataracts extending a distance of 500 yards. The interior of the palace is filled with innumerable objects of virtù — tapestries, and tazzas of marble, porcelain, and malachite. One room contains 386 portraits, representing a peasant girl of each Russian province, an interesting and beautiful collection. At Montplaisir, a small palace in these demesnes, is the bed which was formerly occupied by Peter the Great, and in which he died; and in the Hermitage, also attached to the palace, is a curious mechanical arrangement, by means of which a dinner-table can be removed, through a trap, after each course, and returned with its appointments renewed.

Moscow, on the banks of the Moskva river, was founded in 1147, and contains 600,000 inhabitants. It was formerly the capital of the entire Russian empire, and is consequently more cosmopolitan than other cities of Russia. The streets are long, and, as a rule, wide, except in the older portions of the city, where they are narrow, and more available to pedestrians. The houses are fancifully ornamented, and painted in a variety of bright colors. The churches and public buildings are also of many hues, and with their numerous gold and silver domes and spires sparkling in the sunlight, offer a scene both quaint and dazzling. The men wear small caps, long coats and high top-boots, and the women are partial to gay colors. The horses, which are mostly black, and of Arabian and Russian breed, are models of equine beauty, and travel with the rapidity of the wind.

The Kremlin, or citadel, is in the heart of the city, and the wall in which it is inclosed measures two miles in circumference. It is entered by five gates, the most important of these being the Redeemer's Gate, over which hangs a picture of the Saviour, an object of great reverence to every Russian, from the Emperor to the lowest peasant, none of whom would presume to pass under it without removing his hat. Almost to this very gate the victorious Tartars advanced, time and again, but no further. The French tried to re-

move the picture, but every ladder with which
they attempted to scale the gate broke and fell
with the bold invaders. They next attempted to
demolish it with ball, but the cannon burst, and
they finally set fire to the walls, but the flames
miraculously recoiled before the sacred emblem.
The Kremlin is crowded with palaces, churches,
monasteries, arsenals and museums, in which the
Tartar style of architecture predominates. This
is the only part of Moscow which escaped the conflagration of 1812, when the Russians set fire to
their capital to prevent its falling into the hands
of Napoleon. At the St. Nicholas Gate, where
the French powder-train exploded, is now a
shrine where each Czar, before entering the city,
must first offer his devotions.

The Emperor's Palace in the Kremlin is built
on the site of an ancient Tartar palace, and has a
magnificent interior. The Red Staircase, which is
only used by the Emperor and Empress after
their coronation in the cathedral, but which Napoleon and his marshals ascended after the fall of
Moscow, leads to the banqueting room, where
the newly-crowned Emperor sits enthroned, wearing for the first time all the imperial insignia. In
St. Andrew's Hall, on a raised dais, stands the
magnificent throne of the present empire; and in
the hall of the Order of St. George the walls are
adorned with the names of the members in letters
of gold.

The Treasury occupies a wing of the palace,
and contains relics of great value; the large bell
once used to warn the citizens of impending danger,
weapons and trophies, gifts from foreign nations,
and cases of table service of gold and silver, once
the property of former czars.   Here, also, are the
chair on which Charles XII. was carried at the
battle of Poltawa, the baldachino, under which
the emperor and empress walk at their coronation,
the throne of Poland, brought from Warsaw in
1833, the ivory throne of Ivan III., who first took
the title of Caesar or Czar of Russia, the throne of
Alexis, brought from Persia, in 1610, studded with
countless diamonds, rubies, pearls and turquoises,
the double throne of John and Peter, with a recess
in its rear, in which their mother, concealed behind
a curtain, dictated to them their addresses to the
people, and those of the Empress Elizabeth, Paul
I. and Michael Romanoff, each sovereign of Russia having, according to custom, his own individual throne and crown.   The most valuable of these
latter is that of Catherine I., containing 2,536 diamonds, and an immense ruby bought at Pekin, by
order of Peter the Great; and those of John,
Alexis, Michael, and the King of Kazan.   Here,
also, are the coronation robes of Nicholas I., Paul,
Alexander I., and Alexander II.; of Anna and
Catherine II.   A glass case contains the Order of
the Garter, presented by Elizabeth to John the
Terrible, and the iron cane of the latter, with

which he killed his son. Among the many state carriages is one which once belonged to the Empress Elizabeth, arranged with every convenience for her habitation on the journey from St. Petersburg to Moscow.

The Cathedral of the Assumption, within the Kremlin, is one of the most interesting of the Christian churches of Russia. Here all the emperors are crowned, and a wooden throne is still extant dating 988 A. D., in which rulers of Russia, before the reign of Peter the Great, stood during divine service. Among the many relics displayed are a nail from the True Cross, a robe of the Saviour and a remnant of the dress of the Virgin; also an immense Bible presented to the cathedral by the mother of Peter the Great, which is encrusted with emeralds and rubies.

The Cathedral of the Archangel Michael, with its nine gilded domes, was built in 1332 to commemorate Russia's deliverance from a terrible famine, and is noted as being the last resting-place of all the sovereigns previous to Peter the Great. In the vaults below are the remains of the rulers of the Rurick and Romanoff dynasties, and among others are the tombs of John the Terrible and his son, whom he killed by a blow from his iron staff. A drop of the blood of John the Baptist, seen through glass, is an object of great veneration at one of the shrines.

The Cathedral of the Annunciation, where the

Czars formerly received the sacraments of baptism and marriage, is most peculiarly frescoed, and the floor is paved with blocks of agate — a gift from the Shah of Persia.

The House of the Holy Synod is celebrated as being the place where the myrrh or holy oil with which the children of Russia are baptized, is made and preserved. This oil — of which some four gallons are made every three years — is said to be sanctified by the addition of a few drops of the same oil with which Mary Magdalene anointed the feet of the Saviour: it is made from the choicest olives mixed with some sixty-seven different ingredients; the vessels in which this oil is prepared being of solid gold and silver. In the ceremony of baptism the priest uses a small camel's-hair brush with which, after dipping it in the oil, he makes the sign of the cross over the child's eyes, ears, mouth, hands and feet, that it may see, hear, speak and do no evil. The Synod also contains the church treasure, and the wardrobe of the patriarchs, some of which robes are elaborately embroidered in large pearls, and weighing as much as sixty pounds each.

The Ivan Veliki Tower — the lower part of which is a chapel dedicated to St. John of the Ladder — is 325 feet high, and contains over 40 magnificent bells. The Czar Rolokol — or king of bells — stands on a granite pedestal at the base of the tower. It was cast in 1730, during the reign

of the Empress Anna; is 21 feet high, 67 feet in
circumference, weighs 400,000 pounds, and is estimated to be worth $200,000.   During a fire which
once consumed the tower, this bell fell from its
position, breaking a small section from its side,
and buried itself in the ground, where it remained
under the accumulation of soil for 100 years.

The arsenal contains a sufficient number of
weapons to arm 150,000 men.   Along the outer
walls are ranged 875 cannons captured from other
nations; 375 pieces being those abandoned by
Napoleon in his disastrous retreat of 1812.

Just outside the walls of the Kremlin stands
the Church of St. Basil, differing in style and
architecture from any other church in Moscow.   It
has no less than twenty domes and towers, each
differing from the other in form and dimension,
and all gilded and painted in every possible variety
of color and design.   It was erected by order of
John the Terrible, who was so pleased with the
result that he caused the eyes of the architect to
be put out, that he might not duplicate it.   In the
basement are preserved the iron chains, belts and
crosses worn by St. Basil for penance.

The Temple of the Saviour is a modern structure erected to commemorate the defeat of the
French, and is probably the finest church in all
Russia.   It is of immense proportions, surmounted
by five gilded domes, the ceilings and walls of the
interior are exquisitely frescoed, the pillars are of

jasper, and the floor of highly-polished Labrador porphyry and marble ; the total cost of this edifice having been 19,000,000 roubles, or $14,000,000.

The Public Museum has a library of 16,000 volumes, and a fair collection of paintings. Several rooms are devoted to life-size wax-figures, representing the different races of the Russian empire, illustrating their dress, occupations and form of worship.

The Foundling Asylum, founded by Catherine II., is a Government institution, so extensive that it will readily accommodate over a thousand waifs under its roof. Here all infants are received without question, and admirably cared for up to a certain age, when they are provided with homes in the country.

Sparrow Hill, reached by a favorite drive of eight miles from the city, commands a splendid view of Moscow. It was from this point Napoleon Bonaparte viewed the goal of his famous campaign, and the road over which he marched is still called the Road of the Grand Army.

In Moscow, May 22nd, 1883, or May 10th of Greco-Russian calendar, we witnessed the coronation ceremonies of the Czar, Alexander III., and his Czarina Maria. The city donned her gayest holiday attire for this occasion ; buildings, both public and private, were hung with flags, festoons of gay-colored bunting and flowers ; arches covered with garlands of evergreens, and

decorated with paintings and monograms of
the imperial consorts spanned the streets at
frequent intervals. On the day previous to the
ceremonies, the Emperor and Empress, accompanied by the royal family, and escorted by 75,000
troops from St. Petersburg, arrived in Moscow, remaining in a palace outside the city, preparatory
to entering it in the pomp and magnificence of
the occasion.

At 9 A. M. on the morning of the grand
entrée, the streets on the line of procession were
required to be vacated by all save those taking
part in the ceremonies, and occupants of houses
compelled to submit their names to the police
department.

Owing to the wide-spread sense of insecurity
inspired by the actions of the nihilists, to whose
animosity the Emperor's father had but recently
fallen victim, and whose mysteriously-conveyed
threats filled his successor's heart with dread, the
utmost precautions against a similar catastrophe
were taken.

A hundred thousand troops lined either side
of the streets along the line of procession, and
behind them stood a secret organization, in plain
citizen's dress, sworn to protect with their lives
the person of the Emperor. Sentinels were stationed on every house-top, in every cellar, and at
the front and rear doors of every house. Officers,
mounted on handsomely - caparisoned horses,

patrolled the streets to ensure further security against the possibility of surprise. At precisely 1 P. M. cannons were fired, and bells were rung throughout the city, to announce that the royal procession had started, when both soldier and citizen removed his hat, and reverently crossed himself. The order of procession was as follows:

Chief of police and gens d'armes mounted.
Body-guard　　　　.　　　　.　　　"
Imperial horse-guards .　　.　　　"
Asiatic deputies .　　　.　　　"
Circassian deputies　　　　　"
Russian nobles　　　　.　　.　"
Palace officials　　.　　.　　"
The Emperor's hunters　　.　　.　"
Assistant masters of ceremonies .　　"
Grand master of ceremonies.　　.　"
Imperial grooms and Nubian attendants on foot.
High palace-officials in state carriages.
Court marshals　　　"　　"　　"
Imperial counsel　　　"　　"　　"
Russian nobles　　　"　　"　　"
Kings and princes in golden state carriages.
Imperial guard mounted.
Czar Alexander III., mounted on a white horse, and dressed in the full uniform of a general.
The Crown Prince and the Princes, his brothers, on black horses.
The Grand Dukes, on bay horses.

Ministers of State and War; mounted.

Foreign princes and suites, in state carriages.

The Empress Maria and young Princess, in a golden chariot, drawn by eight white horses, caparisoned with gilded harness and nodding ostrich plumes, attended by grooms and postilions in rich liveries.

Relatives of the Empress, in golden state carriages, drawn by six black horses each.

Relatives of the Emperor, in golden state carriages, drawn by six black horses each.

Other members of the Imperial Family, in gold and silver state carriages.

Empress' suite in carriages.

Imperial troops mounted.

Imperial dragoons.

Russian infantry.

At each of the old city gates salutes were fired, denoting the progress of the procession; and as the Emperor appeared in sight, loud and continuous acclamations arose from the multitude, resounding along the entire route of procession. As the Emperor passed the various churches and other religious institutions, priests appeared, bearing crucifixes, to bless him on his way. Arriving at the St. Nicholas gate the Emperor and Empress, in accordance with an old Russian custom, descended to offer a prayer and receive the blessing of the priest at the shrine of the Iberian Mother of God, before entering the Kremlin through the Redeemer's gate. Here a salute of 101 cannon was fired, and as the procession filed through every man, from the Emperor to the humblest of his train, reverently uncovered. Proceeding to the cathedral, prayer and thanksgiving were offered, and from here they finally entered the palace of the Kremlin.

Next day occurred the consecration of the imperial standard. During the three days following, while the Emperor fasted — taking only brown bread and tea — heralds, accompanied by squadrons of cuirassiers, chevaliers and life-guards, regimental bands, and several masters of coronation ceremonies in showy and picturesque attire, proclaimed the approaching coronations at the chief barriers and gates, and public places of the city; and after the herald's blast of trumpets, the multitude uncovered, and listened to the following proclamation read aloud by the Secretary of the Senate:

"Our most august, most high, and most mighty sovereign, Emperor Alexander Alexandrovitch, having ascended the hereditary throne of the Empire of all the Russias and of the Kingdom of Poland, and of the Grand Duchy of Finland, which are inseparable from it, has been pleased to ordain, in imitation of his predecessors and glorious ancestors, that the sacred solemnity of the coronation and consecration of his Imperial

Majesty, which his Majesty wills that his august
Consort, the Empress Maria Feodorovna shall
share, do, with the aid of the Almighty, take
place on the 15th (27th) of May, 1883. By the
present proclamation, therefore, this solemn act is
announced to all the faithful subjects of his Majesty, to the end that on this auspicious day they
may send up to the King of Kings their most fer-
vent prayers, and implore the Almighty One to
extend the favor of His blessing to the reign of
his Majesty; to the maintenance of peace and
tranquillity to the very great glory of His Holy
Name, and to the unchanging weal of the empire."

May 15th (27th) the coronation of the Czar
took place in the Cathedral of the Assumption,
which was filled to overflowing with the royal
family, foreign ministers and distinguished guests.
Out of the fourteen social grades of Russia, only
the two highest were admitted within the limits
of the cathedral. At 1 o'clock the Emperor and
Empress left the palace, and entering the cathedral ascended their thrones, Alexander occupying the ivory throne of Alexis Feodorovitch;
and Maria the silver and jewel-studded one of
Alexis Michaelovitch. After divine services and
prayers offered up by the metropolitans of Moscow, Kief, and Novgorod, high-priests of the
Greek Church, and the Emperor had professed the
orthodox Catholic faith, they invested him with
the coronation robe of ermine, saying: "Cover

and protect thy people, as this robe covers and
protects thee;" to which the Emperor made
answer, " I will." Then taking the crown from
the priests' hands, he placed it upon his own
head, and assumed the sceptre and orb. The
Empress then knelt before the Emperor, who first
touched her forehead with his diadem, and then
placed a smaller crown upon her head, after which
they both received the Holy Sacrament. The ceremony concluded, the imperial pair, wearing their
crowns and coronation robes, and preceded by the
priests, walked from the church to the palace
under a magnificent baldachino, or canopy of silk
and gold, surmounted by ostrich feathers of white,
black and yellow. This was borne by thirty-two
generals of the highest rank, guarded on either
side by noblemen, and followed by the royal
household. At the palace the Emperor and Empress received deputations from all parts of their
dominions, all of whom, agreeably to custom,
brought and presented, with many costly gifts,
offerings of salt and brown bread; a curious gift
being a bottle of fermented mare's milk, presented
by one of the Kirghiz from the Steppes. At night
the entire city was illuminated by a dazzling
glitter of 10,000,000 colored lights in every conceivable form and device, palaces, churches, towers, walls and gates outlined with innumerable
lights — a dazzling scene of indescribable magnificence.

The two weeks following were devoted to receptions and balls, while national fêtes and amusements of all kinds were provided on a large scale for the lower classes.

Sebastopol, on the Crimean Peninsula, has to-day a population of only 11,000, but its inhabitants numbered 25,000 previous to the Crimean war. It is surrounded, on every side, by strong fortifications, now abandoned according to treaty, but doing efficient service during the war of 1853-55, when Russia defended herself against the combined arms of England, France, Turkey, and Italy. Sebastopol presents a picturesque appearance, both on account of its situation and the numerous ruins resulting from the war, whole streets showing traces of the heavy cannon-ading, not a house being left habitable after the bombardment of eighteen months. On one side of the town is Malakoff, an eminence taken and re-taken repeatedly by the French and Russians, where so many thousands perished; beyond it is the Redan; two miles away Inkerman, on the road to Moscow; and ten miles to the east, Bala-klava, a small village, mostly inhabited by Tartars. In every direction, for several miles, are to be seen breastworks and fortifications, while the cemeteries contain the bodies of some 500,000 of those killed in battle.

Warsaw, the former capital of Poland, situated on the Vistula, has 337,000 inhabitants, of which number 40,000 are Jews. Having ceased to be a place of royal residence in 1831, its palaces are now converted into public offices and barracks. Of its churches, 90 are Roman Catholic, the remaining 10 being divided among the Protestant, Greek, Mohammedan and Jewish persuasions. The citadel is strongly fortified, and in its underground cells are kept political prisoners and nihilists, 25,000 soldiers being constantly on watch to prevent insurrections, and protect the Russian frontier. Among the statues which adorn the streets of the city is one of the astronomer Copernicus, who was a native of Warsaw, one of Sigismund III., in the palace square, and an obelisk to five Polish generals, who fell fighting for Russia against their own country. The park surrounding the old Saxon palace is a beautiful promenade, and a favorite resort of the beaus and belles of Warsaw. The Jews' quarter has some points of local interest; each shop bears its sign in four different languages; the men wear long coats, and a curl hanging over each ear, and the women wigs of false red hair over their own natural locks.

The Palace of Lazienski was the residence of King Poniatowski; it is situated on an island, in the midst of a lovely lake, and surrounded by beautiful grounds. A curious and interesting feature belonging to the palace is an open-air theatre, built of stone, and ornamented with statues, the audience being seated in an amphitheatre of stone

7

benches graded down to the water's edge; and
on a small island opposite, separated by a narrow
strip of water, and accessible only by boat, is the
stage where the performance takes place, while
gayly-lighted barks passing to and fro add ani-
mation to this already novel scene.

CHAPTER IX.

BERLIN : DRESDEN.

BERLIN, the capital of the German Empire, as
well as of Prussia, has a population of 1,123,000,
and is situated on the river Spree, which is crossed
by fifty bridges. It is one of the handsomest
cities in Europe, and is the great centre of intellectual and artistic development of Northern Germany. It is the home of many of the best German artists and scientists, and a place of various
and extensive manufactures.

Unter den Linden, so called from its double
rows of lime trees, is a beautiful avenue over a
mile in length, ornamented with statues, and lined
with palaces and other handsome buildings. Here
are continually to be seen the military, accompanied by fine bands, handsome equipages, and
crowds of pedestrians.

The finest monuments of the city are, the equestrian statue of Frederick the Great, in bronze, surrounded by his leading generals, and statesmen, 31 in number; the work of the famous German sculptor, Rauch; also those of Frederick William III. the great Elector, father of Frederick I.; Blucher, Bulow, Goethe, Schiller, and other prominent men. The Brandenburg Gate, erected in 1789, surmounted by Victory in a chariot, is a magnificent triumphal arch, facing the palace at the other extremity of the Unter den Linden. This gate leads into the Thier-garten, a lovely park beautifully arranged for promenading and driving; in it are several small inclosures for open air concerts, and in the centre of the park stands a column to Victory, surmounted by an angel, commemorative of the wars of 1864-66-71.

The Royal Palace, built by Frederick I., is spacious, and used on state occasions only; at its entrance are the bronze horses presented by Nicholas of Russia, and in the court the statue of St. George and the Dragon. The palace contains 600 apartments, magnificent in gilding and mirrors. In the throne-room is an elaborately-carved silver balcony, intended for an orchestra, and opposite the throne are golden shields, arranged on the walls as reflectors of the lights. The White Hall, used for state balls, contains the statues of the twelve electors of Brandenburg, and the banqueting hall, 70 yards long, is also the

picture gallery. In it are paintings of Frederick
the Great and his generals, Bonaparte crossing the
Alps, and the Coronation of William as King of
Prussia, at Königsberg, in 1861, and as Emperor
of Germany at Versailles in 1871. The chapel
seats 1500 people, and is walled and paved with
variegated marbles.

The Emperor's home-palace, while being elegantly furnished, and filled with works of art, has
every appearance of genuine comfort.

The Château Montbijou, formerly a palace, is
devoted at present to a collection of historical
relics. Frederick the Great is here represented in
wax, seated in his coronation chair, with his flute,
and surrounded by his favorite dogs and war
horse. In the room of Frederick William III. are
some specimens of embroidery done by the beautiful Queen Louise, mother of the present emperor ;
also are preserved Napoleon's hat, and all his
decorations, taken by Blücher at the battle of
Waterloo; and two cannon-balls welded together
as they met in mid-air at the siege of Magde-
burg.

The Royal Library contains Luther's Bible,
from which he made his translation; also the
translations of the psalms in his own handwriting,
Guttenberg's Bible, the first book printed with
movable type, in 1450; the prayer-book which
Charles I. carried with him to the scaffold, and
two hemispheres of metal, by means of which Otto

Guericke discovered the principles of the air-pump.

In the Cathedral are the coffins of Frederick William and Frederick I. and their queens, and here the Mendelsohn choir chant every Sunday; while adjoining the church is the Campo Santo, or royal burying-ground.

In the Royal stables are two hundred horses of choice breeds, chiefly black in color; but the state carriages, although of more substantial make, do not compare in elegance with those of France or England.

The Panopticon is a collection of wax-figures representing the monarchs and prominent men of Germany and other nations. A life-like group is that representing the Council of Arbitration held at Geneva, September 14th, 1872, and presided over by Bismarck.

In the National gallery is a fine collection from the best modern artists of Germany; among the 340 paintings on exhibition, are Jeremiah lamenting before Jerusalem, by Belderman; Jeptha's Daughter, by Richter; the March of Death, by Spangenburg; the Pursuit of Fortune, by Kenneberg, and some strong battle-scenes by various other noted painters. Of the groups of statuary we particularly noticed Faith, Hope and Charity, by Kiss; Hagar and Ishmaël, by Wittig; and Prometheus Bound, by Müller.

The Museum of Berlin, taken as a whole, is

scarcely inferior to any in Europe.   In front of the
building is an immense vase of polished granite,
66 feet in circumference, the largest in the world.
At one side of the entrance is a celebrated group
in bronze by Kiss, of an Amazon slaying a tiger,
and on the other, one by Wolf, of spearing a lion.
In the Egyptian apartment is a temple supported
by pillars, and enclosing statues of deities and
kings: also the tomb of a high-priest, brought
from Thebes, spices and other ingredients for em-
balming, and brass hooks used for drawing the
brain through the nose.   In the picture gallery is
a painting of the Temptation of St. Anthony, by
Teniers: the artist represents the saint in his own
person, his wife, with a small portion of tail visible
beneath the folds of her dress portrays the Temp-
tress, while the mother-in-law appears in the very
decided form of a devil.

Potsdam, 20 miles from Berlin, has no less
than five palaces, the summer residence of royalty.
The palace of Sans Souci, built by Frederick the
Great, is a low, unpretending building externally,
but replete with historic interest.   In the room in
which Frederick breathed his last is the clock
which stopped the moment of his death, its hands
yet pointing to the hour and minute.   Adjoining
the apartments of his royal friend and host, is
the bedroom of Voltaire, left undisturbed since his
occupation.   In the midst of the handsome
grounds stands the historic windmill which Fred-

erick desired to purchase on account of the ground
it occupied, but the miller refusing to sell, the king
brought suit and lost; whereupon he built the
miller a fine mill as a monument to Prussian
justice.

Charlottenhof, a villa in the same grounds,
built by Frederick William III., contains the
apartments occupied by Alexander von Hum-
boldt, and is built in imitation of a Pompeian
dwelling, with baths, fountains, statues and bronzes
taken from the ruins of Pompeii.

The New Palace, now occupied by the Crown
Prince, was erected by Frederick the Great at
enormous expense, after the Seven Years' war, in
order to show his enemies the extent of his re-
sources. The ball-room is built to imitate the
interior of a grotto, the walls and ceilings being
formed from shells and minerals of every variety,
interspersed at intervals by cascades and sta-
lactites.

Babelsburg, the summer residence of the
present Emperor, is a castle beautifully located
on an eminence overlooking the surrounding
country.

In the town of Potsdam is the Garnison
Church, its walls covered with flags taken from
the Austrians and French, where lie the remains
of Frederick the Great and those of his father,
Frederick William I.

Charlottenburg, a suburb of Berlin, contains

the palace built by the queen of Frederick I., environed by beautiful grounds with avenues of orange and pine-trees. To the rear of the palace is a mausoleum of granite, in which are the tombs of Frederick William III. and the beautiful queen Louise, father and mother of the present Emperor; also the heart of Frederick William IV. The recumbent figures repose on a marble sarcophagus, both masterpieces by Rauch; and on either side are marble candelabra representing, respectively, the three Muses and the three Fates. Anniversary services are held here twice a year; the subdued light shining on the marble figures through blue glass, giving a weird effect to the scene.

In Berlin we witnessed a grand review of the German army, some 40,000 men, by the Emperor William, who, though 86 years old, rode on horseback and looked every inch a soldier, while the troops, in their gay uniforms, commanded by officers the names of many of whom are historic, moved with wonderful precision and exactitude.

At the Royal Opera House the same evening, Satanella was especially rendered for his Majesty, who, with the royal family, occupied four boxes; and on each side were his ministers, generals and high officials, numbering about three hundred persons. Of the five hundred performers, two hundred were an unrivalled ballet of beautiful girls, the leading dancer, Fraulein Del Era, being considered the equal of the famous Taglioni. The scenery was superb and original; hell represented teeming with devils and imps, while heaven was a garden of blooming flowers, with statuary, fountains and music the danseuses embodying devils and flowers.

Dresden, the capital of the kingdom of Saxony, is on the Elbe, and has a population of 221,000. Its rich collections of works of art, its many men of learning and talent, its splendid opera, its educational advantages, added to its healthy and bracing climate, have made it a favorite residence of Americans abroad. The river divides the city into the new and the old town; in the former is an equestrian statue of Augustus II., while in the latter are the finest private residences, public buildings and squares, and the monuments to Carl Weber and Frederick Augustus; also a statue to Victory, commemorative of the war of 1871. Of its various manufactures, those of porcelain and musical instruments are the most extensive and celebrated.

In the Schloss, or Royal Palace, are the Green Vaults, a series of eight rooms, with a rare and valuable collection of precious stones, and carvings in ivory and crystal. One room contains the gala dress of the Elector of Saxony, consisting of coat and vest buttons, epaulets, sword-hilt, scabbard and buckles, all made of diamonds of the purest water, and weighing from 40 to 50 carats

each, while in another is the coronation robe of
Frederick Augustus II., when crowned King of
Poland. Among a number of immense pearls is
one as large as a hen's egg, which forms the
body of a statuette of a certain court-dwarf of
Spain. A great curiosity is a miniature court of
the Great Mogul, the throne being of gold and
silver, surrounded by 138 enamelled figures, set
with precious stones. The green diamond is
among the magnificent stones here exhibited,
which are worn by each queen at her coronation,
upon the delivery of which she is required to give
a receipt, and to return them to the vaults the following day. To give an idea of the immense
value of the collection, the contents of this room
alone is said to be valued at $15,000,000. The
great wealth here lying idle is accounted for by
the fact of the Saxon princes,—formerly the richest monarchs in Europe, having owned the Freiburg silver mines, and invested much of their
great wealth in precious stones.

The Japanese Palace, so called from its Japanese decorations, was built by Augustus the
Strong, as a summer residence; at present it is
devoted to a collection of statuary, and a library
rich in manuscripts, among them the conjuring
book of Dr. Faustus.

The Military and Historical Museum surpasses
all others in the variety, richness and quality of
its arms and trappings for both man and horse.

Among the relics are the cuirass, weighing 100 lbs., and the helmet 20 lbs., worn by Augustus, surnamed the Strong; also the horse-shoe which he broke in twain with the bare strength of his hand. Here, also, are the boots and saddle of Napoleon used at the battle of Dresden, and his slippers, worn at his coronation; an elegantly embroidered tent, taken from a Turkish general at the siege of Vienna, and the pistols worn by Charles XII. the day of his death. The suits of armor seen here are the finest ever made, some weighing as much as 200 lbs. and causing certain death to the wearer, if thrown from his horse. The China collection numbers 60,000 pieces, dating from the earliest manufacture in China, thousands of years ago, to the present improved styles of Germany.

The Picture Gallery of Dresden, so celebrated for its fine paintings by old masters, was respected by even those great despoilers of art, Napoleon I. and Frederick II., when taking the city. Its finest paintings are: the Madonna di San Sisto, by Raphael, purchased by Augustus III. from the Duke of Modena for $40,000; the Madonna and Burgomaster's child, Holbein's masterpiece; Correggio's Virgin and Infant Christ; also his Recumbent Magdalene; St. Cecelia, by Carlo Dolce; the Flight into Egypt, by Claude; Liotard's Chocolate Girl; Battoni's Penitent Magdalene; the Disputation between Martin Luther and

Dr. Eck; and Behind the Scenes; the two latter paintings by modern artists.

The Catholic cathedral is a large edifice ornamented with statues. It has a fine organ, and on Sundays the orchestra from the Grand Opera House discourses sacred music. Over the altar is the Royal box, connected with the palace by a bridge crossing the street, and ladies and gentlemen are compelled to separate, and sit on opposite sides of the church.

Meissen, 15 miles from Dresden, is celebrated for its porcelain manufacture of Dresden china. This was the first place in Europe where it was made, in 1705, Batticher, an alchymist, accidentally discovering the art, in his search for the Philosopher's Stone. Meissen is the terminus of the mammoth tunnel, 24 miles long, which drains the Frieburg silver mines; and here, also, is an old Gothic castle, formerly occupied by the Saxon kings.

From Dresden to Prague the railroad follows the river Elbe, and passes some old German and Austrian forts and castles, in the midst of fine mountain scenery, from which this section of country derives its name of the Switzerland of Saxony.

CHAPTER X.

PRAGUE: LINZ: THE DANUBE: VIENNA: SEMMERING-
PASS: ISCHL: GMÜNDEN: SALZBURG: KOENIGSSEE:
INNSBRUCK: BRIXLEGG:

PRAGUE, the capital of Bohemia, on the Mol-
dau river, has a population of 250,000, and is next
to Vienna in importance in the Austrian Empire.
It is located in a basin, surrounded by high rocky
cliffs, and is particularly noted for its manufacture
of Bohemian glass-ware, and for the fine garnets
it produces.   On the heights of Laurenziberg the
fire worshippers of old celebrated their peculiar
rites, and where the acropolis now stands, was
formerly the palace of Queen Lybussa, the
founder of Prague, a notorious wanton, who cast
her lovers into the river below, after becoming
weary of them.

The streets of Prague are for the most part
narrow and crooked, and the numerous arches and
gates spanning them add to their general antique
appearance, while the principal avenues are well
paved, and lighted by immense burners. Among
the statues ornamenting the streets are, the equestrian figure of Francis I., surrounded by sixty
characters in bronze, representing the different

provinces of Austria, and that of Von Radetz standing on his shield, borne by ten soldiers. A stone-bridge crossing the river has thirty-two life-size statues on either side of it, the centre one being a bronze figure of St. John Nepomuk, who was thrown from the bridge from this spot and drowned, by order of King Wencislaus, for refusing to betray the secrets of the queen, confided to him in the confessional. The five stars encircling his head are representative of those reflected in the water over the spot where the body lay until its recovery three days later.

It was in Prague that John Huss, born at Huss in Bohemia, first became imbued with the doctrines of Wickliff, and declared the worship of the Virgin and saints idolatory. In the museum still exists his autograph letter, challenging all who would to dispute with him on the articles of his belief. Being summoned to Constance, to render an account of his doctrine, and under assurance of safe-conduct from the Emperor Sigismund, he fell into the snare; for hardly had he arrived than he was thrown into prison, and suffered martyrdom at the stake, with heroic courage. Thus commenced the famous Hussite war led by John Zizka, who defeated the emperor; and it is said, at his death, gave orders to have a drum made from his skin, in order to inspire his enemies with superstitious alarm.

The Palace, or Hradschin, now occupied by

the Crown Prince of Austria, was formerly the
residence of the Bohemian kings, and contains
1,000 rooms.   Its chief point of interest is the
council chamber, where the imperial commission-
ers, sent hither with the most intolerant edicts
against the Bohemian protestants, were remorselessly thrown from the window, two crosses beneath still marking the spot where they fell. This
was in 1618, and the inauguration of the Thirty
Years' War, which secured the liberty of Germany,
and closed with the treaty of Westphalia, in 1648.

The Cathedral of St. Vitus, in the palace
inclosure, contains many fine monuments, besides
being a complete museum of relics.   Before its
high altar, the emperors of Austria are crowned
King of Bohemia.   In this church are the marble
tombs of Rudolph III. and other kings; a gorgeous shrine of silver, surrounded by angels, the
whole weighing 4,000 lbs. incloses a crystal coffin,
in which are the remains of St. John Nepomuk;
and in a side chapel, whose walls are of agate and
amethyst, is the tomb of Saint Wenzel, who was
murdered by his brother in the 10th century.
The Loretto Chapel is built in imitation of the
wandering house of Nazareth, and is considered
the most sacred shrine in Prague.   It contains
two rooms, counterparts of those occupied by
Joseph and Mary.   In the front room is a shelf,
on which Joseph kept his tools, and here, also, are
shown the leg-bone of Mary Magdalene, and the

skull of one of the wise virgins. The church treasury contains bones of Abraham, Isaac and Jacob, the pocket handkerchief of the Virgin, the tongue of St. John, a piece of wood and two nails from the True Cross, two thorns from the Crown of Christ, a fragment of the rope with which He was bound, the sponge with which He was given to drink, one of the palm-branches over which He rode ; also a candelabrum from Solomons' Temple, the bridal dress of Maria Theresa, worked by her own hands into a Mass robe, and divers church insignia of gold and precious stones.

The Thein Church, the oldest in Prague, still contains the pulpit from which John Huss, the celebrated reformer, preached, and the tomb of the great astronomer Tycho Brahe. It was here that the heads and hands of the Protestant leaders were buried, after having been taken down from the Gate Tower, where they had been hung to appease the anger of Ferdinand after the battle of Whitehill.

In the old Jewish synagogue, which dates back 1,300 years, are the ancient parchments of the laws which were found when the building was unearthed. The burying-ground adjoining is a curious sight, crowded with graves on top of graves, the tombstones lying one against another, some engraved with a bunch of grapes, the emblem of the tribes of Israel, and dating back to the 12th century.

The Wallenstein Palace, built by the hero and generalissimo of the Thirty-Years' war, is an immense structure, to make room for which 136 houses were torn down. The grounds within the palace walls are tastefully arranged, and in one room is preserved the war-horse of Count Wallenstein, shot under him in battle. It is said that he lived in a style of magnificence superior to that of the Emperor, being attended by sixty pages of noble birth, barons and knights. When he went abroad, over a hundred carriages were in his train, besides fifty of the finest saddle-horses, and he could travel for three hundred miles in a straight line, without quitting his estates. His income was $5,000,000 annually, but all was confiscated at his death by the Emperor, who, it is supposed, instigated his murder by poison.

The Rathhaus and the Square in which it stands are interesting, from their association with many remarkable historical events. During the Hussite troubles the mob entered the council chamber, and threw the German councillors out of the windows, upon the upraised spears of those below, repeating the same act of barbarity sixty years later, and in the square, John of Luxemburg, commonly known as the blind king of Bohemia, was wounded in a tournament

Linz, on the Danube, has a population of 30,000, and is the principal town of Upper Austria. In the Market-place stands the Trinity

Column, erected in 1713 by Charles VI., and in the Church of the Capuchins is the tomb of Montecuculi, a celebrated general of the Thirty Years' war. From the Tower of Freiberg, which was built by the Archduke Maximilian, and is surrounded by 32 forts, is obtained one of the finest views in Austria, the Danube winding its devious course through a varied landscape.

Taking steamer from this point to Vienna, a distance of 110 miles, one passes through the most beautiful and picturesque scenery of the Danube, which is bordered on either side with high mountain peaks, crowned by castles, monasteries, and ruins, and is to Austria what the Rhine is to Germany.

Vienna, the capital of the Austrian Empire, situated on the banks of the Danube, has a population of over 1,000,000 inhabitants, and is fifteen miles in circumference. The old town is in the heart of the city, and what was formerly its fortifications, is now the Ringstrasse — a broad and elegant boulevard three miles in circuit, bordered with trees and handsome buildings. Vienna has two large parks, besides many squares and gardens beautified with fine statues and lovely walks. More wealth is here represented than in any other European city of its size. Its people are light-hearted, gay and fond of music, and are partial to out-of-door amusements. The cafés and concert gardens are brilliantly illuminated at night, and

thronged with a pleasure-seeking crowd, all combining to render this city the second Paris of the
world.

In the Palace grounds, which are open to the
public, are the superb equestrian statue of Archduke Charles, representing him bearing a flag at
the battle of Wagram, and that of Prince Eugene
of Savoy. In the same grounds is a small temple built for the express purpose of containing
Canova's fine group of Theseus killing the Centaur,
which was cut from an immense block of marble.
The sculptor received the order for this piece of
statuary from Napoleon, who destined it for the
triumphal arch at Milan. A portion of the park
is appropriated as a concert garden, where every
evening the military band, and Strauss', led by
that excellent composer himself, discourse delightful strains of music.

The Imperial Palace, besides having many
large state apartments, contains the Grand Salon,
where the Thursday before Easter of each year the
Emperor and Empress wash the feet of twelve old
people brought in indiscriminately from the street,
in token of humility. In the bed-room of Maria
Theresa is the furniture which was once used by
her; and an adjoining apartment is hung with
40 landscape pictures made of Florentine mosaic
of great value and beauty.

The Imperial Library contains 1,000,000 volumes, and is said to be the largest in Europe; in

it are the psalm-book of Charlemagne; the MSS.
of Tasso's Jerusalem Delivered, and Dante's Divina
Commedia; and a military map of the Roman
empire of the 4th century.

In the imperial stables are several hundred
horses, white ones being used exclusively on state
occasions; and among the 100 carriages and sleds
are the coronation carriages of Maria Theresa and
Napoleon I.

Many rare and beautiful jewels of fabulous
value, are kept in the imperial jewel house, among
which are gems belonging to the imperial family;
the crowns of the Emperor and Empress of Austria, sceptres, orbs, Orders of the Golden Fleece,
and other national decorations.   Here is an emerald weighing 2,980 carats, and the Florentine
diamond, 133⅛ carats, lost by Charles the Bold
at the battle of Granson.   Among the historical
curiosities are the Turkish seal of the Sultan Mustapha II., the sword of Charlemagne, the horo-
scope of Count Waldstein; the carving-knife used
by Philip of Burgundy at the inauguration of the
Order of the Golden Fleece; a silver chain of one
of the Doges of Venice, the silver cradle of
Napoleon II., and the coronation mantle and
crown of Napoleon I. when crowned king of
Italy.   Among the sacred relics are the book of
the holy Gospel found on the knees of the Emperor
Charlemagne, when his tomb was opened by Otho
II. at Aix-la-Chapelle; the lance of St. Maurice,

with a nail from the Holy Cross set in the point
of the blade; a piece of the True Cross six inches
in length, and surpassed in size only by that preserved in Rome; a portion of the table-cloth used
at the Last Supper; a remnant of the apron worn
by Jesus when He washed the feet of His disciples;
a bone of the arm of St. Anne,—mother of the
Virgin; three links of the iron chains with which
the apostles, Peter, Paul and John were fettered;
a piece of the garment of St. John the Evangelist;
a tooth of St. John the Baptist, and blood of the
holy martyr, Stephen.

The Imperial Arsenal, a fine structure, is handsomely frescoed with scenes from the celebrated
battles of Austria, painted by her best artists, and
has 200,000 stands of arms and armor of every
period.   Of the historic souvenirs are the elk-skin
coat in which Gustavus Adolphus was shot at the
battle of Lutzen; the uniform of Prince Eugene
and the armors of Maurice of Saxony, and of
Alexander Farnese, Duke of Parma.   In the Hall
of Glory are fifty-six beautifully-carved marble
statues of Austria's monarchs and bravest warriors; also a colossal group representing Austria
shielding her provinces.   The court-yard contains
the monster chain, composed of 8,000 links, which
was thrown across the Danube in 1529.

The Cathedral of St. Stephen, in the heart of
the city, is an elegant Gothic building of imposing
dimensions standing on the site of an old cemetery

which Joseph II., for sanitary reasons, caused to be obliterated, and the human remains destroyed with quicklime. Near the top of the spire of this church, which is 450 feet high, is the watch-tower whence alarms are given in case of fire. Its bell weighs 358 cwt., and was made from 180 cannon taken from the Turks. The interior of the cathedral is rich in sculpture and stained glass, and in it are the tombs of Prince Eugene and of the Emperor Frederick I.

The Votive church, a modern and elaborate structure, was founded by the Archduke Maximilian—afterwards emperor of Mexico—to commemorate an unsuccessful attempt made upon the life of his brother, the present emperor, Francis Joseph I.

The Church of the Augustines, where the emperors of Austria are crowned, is embellished by the monument of the Archduchess Christine, a masterpiece by Canova. It is a pyramid of marble representing the entrance to a vault, with figures of Virtue, Benevolence and Humility in the act of ascending the steps. Here also is buried Dr. Van Swieton, physician to Maria Theresa, and one of the earliest authorities on vaccination. In the Loretto chapel are silver urns containing the hearts of the imperial family, their entrails being deposited in another church, and their bodies in a third.

The Church of the Capuchins is the royal

burial vault, in which may be seen the coffins of
Maria Theresa, Francis of Lorraine, Joseph II.,
Francis I., Marie Louise,—wife of Napoleon I.,
their son, Napoleon II., Maximilian, Emperor of
Mexico, and many other scions of royalty.

The Upper Belvidere Palace was built by the
Austrian General-in-Chief, Eugene of Savoy, in
1724, and was appropriated by Joseph II. for the
picture gallery of the imperial court. Besides the
portraits of Maria Theresa and Joseph II., are
Titian's Ecce Homo; Van Dyke's Crucifixion,
and portraits of the aged parents of Rembrandt
and of Denner, painted by these two artists.
Among the modern paintings are the Last Appeal, by Defregger; Hecuba weeping for her
children, by Russ; and the Queen of Naples
with her children on the way to prison, by
Engerth.

The Lower Belvidere contains the Ambras
collection, brought from the Tyrol by the Archduke Ferdinand: of these are suits of armor of
Maximilian, Ferdinand, and of his giant attendant,
eight feet in height; besides fine specimens of
carved ivory, and some portraits of the nobility of
Europe.

In the city Arsenal is the head of the Grand
Vizier Mustapha, a Turkish general commanding
at the siege of Vienna, in 1683, who was strangled
by order of the sultan for having failed to take
the city, and here also are his saddle and baton.

Mohammed's Green Standard is among the many
Turkish trophies here displayed; it is three by
four feet in dimension, of green stuff striped
with yellow, inscribed with mottoes from the
Koran, and the names of the first four followers
of the Prophet; Abu Bekr; Omar; Osman; and
Ali; this is carried in holy wars and raised only
on occasions of dire distress; and all who fall
fighting beneath this banner are assured of
Heaven.

The Cabinet of Antiquities has a large and
valuable collection of cameos; one of them, the
largest in the world being 26 inches in circumference, carved in representation of the Apotheosis
of Augustus, and considered the perfection of
art.

In the National Exhibition of Paintings—which
takes places annually were: the Dying Wish, by
Valentiny; the Virgin Consolatrice, by Bouguerau;
the Death of Wallenstein, by Piloig; the Pest at
Tournay, by Gallait; Leda and the Swan, by
Michael Angelo; and Io and Jupiter, by Correggio.

Schönbrunn, five miles from Vienna, is the
summer palace of the Emperor. It was built by
Maria Theresa, and is in the midst of beautiful
grounds in which are high hedges, Pompeian
ruins, and the Gloretta Temple. It was here the
assassination of Napoleon I. was attempted by the
German student Stapps, and the place possesses a

melancholy historic interest from its having been
the scene of the death of the young Duke of
Reichstadt — Napoleon II, in 1832, in the same
bed occupied by his imperial father in 1809. The
council-room of Maria Theresa; the tapestry
apartments, and Napoleon's bedroom are points of
much interest.

From Vienna we went by rail over the Sem-
mering Pass, which is 3,256 feet high, the lowest
in the Alpine range, passing mountain rocks towering over 10,000 feet, fertile valleys and beautiful lakes and cascades, forming the grandest
scenery of the Austrian Alps. There are many
exquisitely beautiful spots on this route which deserve more than a passing notice : Aussee, at the
junction of three rivers which form Lake Traun
is overlooked by Mount Loser, a peak 5,000 feet
high, and is celebrated for its whey cure.

Hallstadt, on the romantic lake of the same
name, is situated at the base of a mountain 7,000
feet high, which rises abruptly from the water,
leaving no place for a road ; communication being
maintained by steps, the houses resembling swal-
lows' nests clinging to the side of the rock.

Ischl, a small town on a river of the same
name, is a fashionable Austrian watering-place.
It is picturesquely located in a basin environed on
all sides by high mountain peaks, and is the site of
the Emperor's favorite summer palace. The extensive salt-works belonging to the government

are located at this place; the salt and mud baths, for which it is noted, attract large numbers of invalids.

Gmünden, a village of 2,000 inhabitants, is also a fashionable summer resort and one of the loveliest spots in Europe. It nestles on the banks of Lake Traun, which is nine miles long and one wide, hemmed in on all sides by mountain peaks, some of which rise almost perpendicularly to a height of six thousand feet. The shores of this lake are dotted with pretty villages and the villas of nobility; avenues of trees border the banks, and fanciful little boats whose oars keep time to the rhythm of the musical strains borne from the shore, float placidly on its glassy surface.

Salzburg, the capital of the Austrian province of the same name, is on the river Salza, and has a population of 20,000. The Castle of Hohen-salzburg, which crowns the heights overlooking the city, was the former residence of the sover-eign archbishop. In the Rack Tower is the cham-ber of torture, where many protestant victims were first hung to the roof with 150 lb. weights tied to their feet; and then allowed to drop into a terrible donjon below.

Salzburg was the birthplace of Mozart—1756 —and in the room where he first saw the light, are yet preserved his spinet and piano, and the MS. of his musical compositions written when only four years old.

In St. Peter's cemetery, which dates back to the 4th century, are vaults cut in the rock 200 feet from the level of the ground; and from a cave above, the hermit St. Maximus with his followers were thrown, in 477, when the town was destroyed by the German tribes. Here lies buried the great composer Haydn; and seven iron crosses indicate the number of wives of a certain man who murdered them in turn, by tickling their feet until death relieved them from their hilarious torture.

The Palace of Heilbrunn, four miles from the city is celebrated for its numerous fountains: the Neptune Grotto sending forth 5,000 jets; and a curious contrivance, worked by water-pressure, is a mechanical theatre, with 154 movable figures, representing a town in the full bustle of daily life.

From Salzburg, a beautiful drive leads to the Königssee, and we were well repaid by tarrying on the way to visit the government salt mine at Batrichgarden. Here after assuming appropriate costumes we entered the mine and penetrated through the salt tunnels for half a mile; then sitting astride a slide were shot with great velocity to a lower level where the miners were at work excavating in the huge rocks of salt. On reaching a lake in these subterranean regions where a weird reflection is cast upon wave and shore by myriad oil lamps, we entered a boat and crossed to the opposite side, where mounting a small hand-car, we threaded the narrow passages, and emerged once more into daylight. This mine which is of great depth, has been worked for 250 years, and is a monopoly of the king of Bavaria. Salt is not only extracted in crystallized form from the mine, but also by evaporation, in certain localities water being pumped in and left standing for a month, when it is found to have absorbed 28 per cent of saline matter.

The Königssee, a romantic lake six miles long and one wide, is hemmed in on all sides by mountainous rocks towering to a height of from 5,000 to 8,000 feet, rising up so perpendicularly that nature has left no space for man to build and mar its natural beauty. Taking a small boat, rowed by stalwart peasant girls in bright, national costume, we sailed its entire length, whence we crossed to Obersee, a smaller lake, separated from it by a narrow strip of land.

Innsbruck, the capital of the Tyrol, surrounded on all sides by mountains 10,000 feet high, has a population of 17,000 and derives its name from the "bruck" or bridge which crosses the river Inn. This is the scene of the exploits of the famous Tyrolean chief, Andreas Hofer. He was an inn-keeper noted for his honesty, eloquence, and piety; and such was the influence that he exerted over his countrymen, that under his leadership the French were repeatedly driven from the country. After many victories, he was elevated to the head of the government, but he still continued to wear his peasant's costume, and while occupying the palace cost the government only $5 per day for his personal expenses. He was finally betrayed by a Judas named Roff, and conveyed to Mantua, where he was shot by order of Napoleon in 1810.

In the Franciscan church is the tomb of Maximilian I., the principal object of attraction in Innsbruck. The marble sarcophagus, on which is the bronze effigy of the emperor, is ornamented with 24 bas-reliefs of Carrara marble, representing the most prominent events in his life, of such exquisite beauty and delicacy of workmanship, as to resemble fine cameos. Surrounding the monument are 28 figures of heroic size in bronze of distinguished personages of the house of Austria, and in the same church is a marble statue of Andreas Hofer, beneath which repose his remains.

In the Museum near by, are the clothes, gun, and decorations of this remarkable man, whose history is concentrated within the compass of a single year, but to whose memory every hill, vale, and pass of the Tyrol are enduring monuments.

Among these mountains dwells an old man whose very original occupation deserves mention. Having discovered a peculiar kind of spider whose web is remarkably even, strong, and pliable, he conceived the idea of cultivating it, and utilizing its web. After selecting the most uniform

of these productions, he stretches and prepares
them by a process known only to himself, and
after framing so that the webs retain their trans-
parency, they are consigned to artists, who with
extreme delicacy of touch, paint upon them,
usually scenes appropriate to the Tyrol; one of the
largest of these, portraying a hunting-scene in the
mountains, we were fortunate enough to secure.

Continuing through the Tyrolean Alps we went
to Brixlegg, a small village surrounded by high
mountain peaks in the vicinity of Oberamagau, to
witness the production of the Passion Play. The
performance of this sacred drama was sanctioned
by the Catholic clergy, and the services of the
church were held at an earlier hour to enable all
to attend. The large temporary theatre built for
the occasion, was filled with over 1,000 religious
and devout people, and a large number of the
clergy. The play given on Sunday began at 9.30
A. M. and continued, with a short intermission,
throughout the day. The performance was a
representation of the Life and Passion of Our
Saviour, rendered with a most thrilling and rever-
ential realism; its 18 acts alternated by tableaux
of scenes from the Old Testament.

CHAPTER XI.

MUNICH: CONSTANCE: SCHAFFHAUSEN: ZURICH: LU-
CERNE: LAKE LUCERNE: RIGI: SACHSELN: GIES-
BACH FALLS: INTERLACHEN: BERN: FRIBOURG:
LAKE OF GENEVA: GENEVA.

MUNICH, the capital of Bavaria, is on the river
Isar, with a population of 230,000. It is mostly
of modern architecture, and its principal thoroughfares are adorned with numerous statues. It is
celebrated for its extensive collection of fine paintings, its bronze foundry, its stained-glass factory,
and its excellent beer.

Most of the fine bronzes of the world come
from Munich, one of the largest is the figure of
Bavaria represented in the form of a colossal
woman. It is 100 feet high, and within it is a
spiral staircase which ascends to the interior of the
head where eight persons can be comfortably
seated at once. This statue was cast in the Royal
Bronze Foundry, in 1850, by Miller, and was
made of 78 tons of the metal of captured cannon.
Here we saw another colossal female figure of
Germania in course of construction, destined for
the banks of the Rhine.

The principal statues in the public places of
the city are those of Maximilian I. on his throne,
Ludwig I. on horseback, Maximilian II. surrounded by figures of Justice, Peace, Science, and
Power; and over the Gate of Victory, Bavaria is
represented in a chariot drawn by four lions.

In the Royal Palace, the main apartments are
the throne room in which stand twelve colossal
bronze-gilt figures of the princes of the house of
Bavaria, from Otho the Illustrious, 1253, to
Charles XII. of Sweden, and the bedroom of
Charles VII. containing the magnificent couch
of that monarch, the hangings of which, richly
embroidered in gold, employed the labor of 40
persons for 15 years, and are valued at $400,000.
Among the relics in the Royal Chapel, are a fragment from the flagellation column; one of the
stones cast at the Saviour; the skull of John the
Baptist, and the *prie-dieu* carried for Mary Stuart
to her execution.

The Palace Treasury contains several crowns
and many fine jewels, among the latter of which
is the largest blue diamond in existence, set
in the order of the Golden Fleece; and a miniature equestrian statue of St. George and the
Dragon, of gold and white enamel thickly set with
diamonds and rubies, is a most exquisite piece of
workmanship.

The Royal Library is next in extent to the
largest in the world. In it is a collection of

10,000 Greek and Roman coins, besides tablets of wax of the 15th century; the Gospels, written in gold, on purple vellum, of the 9th century; and an Egyptian document, dating 400 years B. C., which was found in a tomb, and said to have been bestowed by a priest upon the deceased, as a passport to heaven.

The National Museum, whose walls are ornamented with 143 frescoes, illustrating the history of Bavaria, has among its objects of interest tapestries from the earliest periods of manufacture to the present perfect productions of the Gobelins; arms used previous to the Christian era, and every variety of instrument of torture, including the stocks, rack, cat o' nine tails, screws, weights, cages, and spiked chairs and barrels.

In the Gallery of Sculpture are the statues of Alexander the Great, and the Barberini Faun, or Sleeping Satyr, said to have been thrown from the top of a wall by the Romans, when defending themselves against the Goths.

The Old Pinacotheca, or picture gallery, contains 1,400 paintings by old masters, among which are Rubens' celebrated Rape of the Sabines, and several gems by Murillo, of Italian beggar children.

The New Pinacotheca has a fine collection of paintings on porcelain, and pictures by modern artists, among which are the Destruction of Jerusalem, by Kaulbach; the Deluge, by Karl Schorn;

9

and Thursnelda, in the triumphal train of Germanicus, by Piloty.

In the Maximilianeum are thirty of the largest and finest modern paintings, the most notable being, Mohammed entering Mecca, by Müller; the Building of the Pyramids, by Richter; and the Destruction of Carthage, by Conrader.

In connection with the cemetery of Munich is the Lichtenhaus, or home of the dead, a building where all bodies, irrespective of rank or wealth, are kept for three days before burial, as a precaution against premature interment. As soon as the coffins of the deceased are brought here, the bodies are removed and laid on marble slabs, with a wire attached to the right forefinger, which communicates with an electric bell, numbered, in the watch-room adjoining, where an attendant keeps constant vigil.

Constance, an ancient city of the Duchy of Baden, situated on Lake Constance, is interesting from its association with John Huss. In the Grand Hall were held the sittings of the famous council of 1414-18, which was composed of 400 of the magnates of Europe, the Pope, cardinals, bishops and archbishops, and presided over by the Emperor Sigismund. They disposed of the schisms in the Church, elected Martin V., and condemned John Huss and Jerome of Prague to be burnt at the stake.

In the Münster Cathedral is shown the place

where Huss stood while receiving sentence from
Bishop Hallam, and a mile distant is a large, ivy-
covered stone, with an inscription to the effect
that John Huss was burnt here July 6th, 1415.

Schaffhausen, a small village in Switzerland,
two miles from Neuhausen, is charmingly located
on the Rhine, with a view of the snow-capped
Alpine range in the distance, and the Falls of the
Rhine below, which, though less grand than those
of Niagara, are more picturesque. In the midst
of the falls is a high rock, which has been tunnelled through by the force of the water. This
rock is approached by the venturesome, in a
small boat through the rapids, and climbed to its
summit for a finer view of the falls. On the east
side of the river is the old castle of Laufen overhanging the falls, and here a camera obscura
gives a miniature picture of the cataract and surrounding country.

Zurich, on a lake of the same name, is noted
as being the scene of the beginning of the Reformation in Switzerland, and the home of the
celebrated physiognomist, Lavater. In the cathedral here Zwingli, the reformer, denounced the
errors of the Church of Rome, and enforced the
doctrine of the Reformation.

The Museum, among other relics, contains the
helmet, sword and banner of Zwingli, and the
cross-bow of William Tell, with which he shot the
apple from the head of his son.

From Zurich to Lucerne, the rail passes through Zug, on the banks of the pretty little lake of Zug.

Lucerne, on the lake of the same name, is the capital of the Canton, and has a population of 15,000. It is still surrounded by its old walls, with numerous and picturesque watch-towers, and is noted for the exquisite beauty and grandeur of the surrounding scenery, the lake of Lucerne having, from time immemorial, been acknowledged the most beautiful of the Swiss lakes. The principal attraction of the town itself is the Lion of Lucerne, a monument dedicated to the officers and soldiers who died in Paris in 1792, defending Louis XVI. It is of colossal size, cut in the solid rock. Under the lion's paw is a fleur-de-lis, which he is endeavoring to protect with his latest breath, the life-blood oozing from a spear-wound in his side.

Taking the steamer, we traversed the lake revelling in its exquisite scenery, and landed at the small village of Altdorf, in the centre square of which is a fountain surmounted by the figure of Gessler, marking the spot where the Austrian governor caused his hat to be hung as an object of reverence to the people, and near by is the spot where Tell's son stood, while his father, in obedience to the mandate of the cruel tyrant, gave evidence of his wonderful marksmanship. Six miles distant, over a most beautiful and romantic carriage-road, skirting the lake, and in many places cut through the solid rock, is the chapel of William Tell, the Mecca of all Switzerland. It was here the hero sprang from the boat and made his escape, after having been unfettered, in order that he might be enabled to row Gessler through a storm which had suddenly arisen on the lake.

From Vitznau we ascended by means of an inclined railroad to the top of Mount Rigi, which is 6,000 feet high, and overlooks Lucerne. From its summit one looks down upon the grandest panorama conceivable, the snow-capped peaks of the Alpine range, outlined against the blue horizon, eleven lakes nestling amid the foliage at their base, with here and there tiny villages clustered on the banks. The sunset and sunrise, seen from the top of the Rigi, is a sight we will not be apt to forget. Just above the horizon the orb appeared like a great ball of rayless fire, tinting cloud and mountain peak with gorgeous coloring, creeping softly down to arouse the sleeping scene beneath, and gradually dispelling the mist midway, which rolled at our feet like the billows of a vast grey sea.

From Lucerne, we crossed the lake to Alpnach, and there took carriage over the beautiful and picturesque Brunig Pass, stopping en route at the village of Sachseln, on Lake Sarnen, in whose small church are the remains of St. Nicholas, the Santa Claus of universal childhood, who ac-

tually lived here, and is the patron saint of this
section.   A portrait represents him as tall,
slender and serious, and altogether the reverse of
his traditionary picture   According to the legend, the saint was the father of ten children, and
deserted them for a hermit's life in the mountains,
a portrayal of character differing as widely from
the original of our childhood's fancy as does his
pictured semblance.

Behind the high altar, and above it, concealed
by a movable metal screen raised by means of
machinery, is the skeleton of St. Nicholas kneeling
in prayer, his cloak about him, in death as in life;
in the sockets of his eyes are immense diamonds,
on his bony fingers are many rings, and on every
rib numbers of precious stones.

A few miles further on the road is the village
of Gyswyl, half swept away in 1629 by a fearful
torrent from the Larribach, which formed a lake
that lasted 120 years, until the inhabitants dug a
tunnel and drained off its waters.

Leaving our carriage at Brienz, we crossed the
lake to the Giesbach Falls, one of the loveliest in
Switzerland.   They consist of a succession of
seven cascades, embowered in foliage, leaping from
a height of 1,100 feet, and finally losing themselves in the waters of the lake.   The scene is
illuminated at night, during certain seasons, by
colored Bengal lights, which produces an effect of
fairy enchantment.

Interlachen, so called from its situation between two lakes, Brienz and Thun, is surrounded
by high mountain peaks, and is the great nucleus
from which excursions are made to neighboring
points of interest. The principal one of these is
to Grindelwald, 15 miles by carriage, at the base of
the Wetterhorn. Here we took horses to visit the
immense glacier which lies between Mounts Eiger
and Mittelberg. This huge mass of ice is sixty miles
in extent, and is tunnelled through a distance of
150 yards leading to an ice grotto; here, in the
weird, blue reflection of the crystal walls, we found
the strangely incongruous presence of two witch-
like crones, who, for a small coin, crooned their
monotonous ditties to the accompaniment of their
twanging lutes.

The Glacier, the accumulation of time untold,
has cut its way through the solid mountain of
rock, five hundred feet deep, by means of what is
called glacier mills; these are boulders moved and
hurled around by rapid currents with such velocity as in the course of time to cut immense basins
in the rock. These excavations, besides formation
of shell and fragments of rock showing impressions
of vegetable petrifaction, illustrate the successive
epochs of the globe, when the northern hemisphere was buried under a mass of ice, with only
an occasional oasis inhabited by animal life long
since extinct.

Another point radiating from Interlachen is

Lauterbrunnen, which means many fountains, and
derives its name from the number of streams—some
twenty in all — which fall from the high mountains into the depths of the valley below.   The
principal of these are the Falls of Staubach, drop-
ping a distance of 1,100 feet in an unbroken line.
The scene from below is surpassingly grand; perpendicular rocks resembling giant castles with
their glittering turrets and white-bannered walls;
towering above these the Jungfraü, the Mönch,
and the Eiger, some 13,000 feet high, losing their
hoary heads in the eternal clouds.

Bern, the capital of Switzerland, is on the
river Aar, with a population of 36,000.   The
town is old and quaint, with narrow streets, miniature and grotesque figures surmounting its
fountains, and sidewalks under the projections of
the second stories of the houses.   Bern takes its
name from *baren* the German for bear an animal
which the aboriginal tribes formerly worshipped.
The chief sight of this city is the bear pit, a government institution, where a number of these
animals are kept for the amusement of the public.

Fribourg is noted for its fine Suspension
bridge, and its Cathedral, over the entrance of
which is an alto-relievo, in stone, of the Last
Judgment; the devil is here represented weighing
down the balance on the side of the righteous, in
order that Justice may add a preponderance in
the opposite scale.   Within the sacred edifice is

an organ noted for the purity and strength of its compass.

Lake Geneva — or Leman — is the largest of the Swiss lakes, being 55 miles long and from 2 to 9 in width. Its waters are clear, and of a beautiful deep blue, its banks, bordered with the high mountain range of Savoy on one side, contrasting strongly with the vine-covered slopes of the opposite shore.

Midway up the lake is Lausanne, on an elevation which commands a fine view. Further on is Vevay embosomed in vineyards; and at the eastern extremity is Montreux, noted for its mild climate, and as the scene of Rousseau's "Nouvelle Héloise." Near by on a small island is the celebrated Castle of Chillon, which Byron's poem has immortalized. Here Bonnivard was confined for six years; the chain which bound him to the stone pillar of his donjon, being still in its place.

> " Lake Leman lies by Chillon's walls ;
>   A thousand feet in depth below
>   Its massy waters meet and flow ;
>
>   *   *   *   *
>
>   Below the surface of the lake
>   The dark vault lies. "

From Montreux we embarked by steamer for Geneva at the opposite extremity of this romantic lake.

Geneva sits enthroned a queen on the shore of this beautiful sheet of water. The city is divided by the river Rhone which is spanned by some of the finest bridges in Europe. On a small island in the river is a bronze monument to Jean-Jacques Rousseau, who was a native of Geneva; and there is also to be seen an elaborately designed monument to the Duke of Brunswick, who left his entire fortune to this city. Geneva is celebrated for its manufacture of watches, gold ornaments, and exquisite wood-carvings. Among the many places of interest one should not fail to visit are, the Cathedral in which Calvin preached for thirty years; the villa of Lord Byron; Ferney, the residence of Voltaire; and the château and grave of Madame de Staël. It was in this château she held her intellectual court where Shelley and Byron were wont to join the brilliant galaxy that surrounded her.

CHAPTER XII.

CHAMOUNI, a small village in Savoy, is at the
foot of Mont Blanc, three thousand feet above the
level of the sea. It was here, among her native
mountains, that the familiar strains of her village
airs lured poor Linda's wandering feet to peace
and rest.

In the village we found mules and guides, and
climbing the mountains over a narrow, precipitous
trail, reached Montanvert. Here we dismounted,
and securing the services of an additional guide,
proceeded on foot to cross the Mer-de-Glace — or
Sea of Ice.

We had not gone far when a blinding
snow-storm overtook us, which added to the
perils of our undertaking; underfoot a sea of ice,
its surface broken by innumerable crevices, 300
feet in depth, yawning to engulf us at every step;
around us an impenetrable shroud of mist and
snow; above, fathomless, illimitable space. For
over two hours we groped our uncertain way

across this trackless waste of frozen waters, and at last reached the opposite shore. Here we descended a series of steps called the Mauvais Pas, roughly hewn on the side of an almost perpendicular rock from whose eminence we could look down thousands of feet beneath us.

At the Chapeau, a mountain station, we found our mules awaiting to convey us to the valley below.

By private conveyance we passed through the romantic vale of Chamouni; over the Tête Noire, a wild and rugged mountain pass; and descending into the valley of the Rhone, arrived at the Gorge of Trient. This is a stupendous rent in the rock, six hundred feet in height, and extending a distance of several miles; at the base of the chasm flows a rapid torrent emanating from distant glaciers, which rushes madly on its way, boiling and seething, over boulders and jutting crags that intercept its course.

Leaving Brieg by diligence, we crossed the Alps by the Simplon Pass over the military road made by Bonaparte for the passage of his troops. Arriving at the Fifth Refuge, one of the stations instituted as places of shelter for the wayfarer, we exchanged our carriage for a sleigh, as recent snow-storms had rendered the roads otherwise impassable. For a distance of 20 miles we traversed vast plains of snow, and penetrated deep chasms cut through fallen avalanches, then resuming our former mode of conveyance, began the descent through the Gorge of Gondo — awful in its sublimity — and emerging from rocky tunnels, amid scenes of wild and rugged grandeur, we were suddenly transferred into the vine-clad slopes and balmy air of sunny Italy.

Stressa, on Lake Maggiore, is situated just opposite the Borromean Islands, the property of Count Borromeo. On Isola Bella, the most beautiful of these little islands, is his palace: the bare rock having been metamorphosed into a scene of enchantment. This fairy creation is a series of ten terraces adorned with statues, obelisks, and vases, and here in sight of Alpine snows, tropical flowers bloom, and tea, indigo, citron, and magnolia thrive luxuriantly.

Sailing through Lake Maggiore, and then taking a carriage, we drove over a delightful road to Lugano, a small village nestling on the banks of the lake under the beetling shadow of Mt. St. Salvador. After a short sojourn here, we sailed through Lugano, the smallest and one of the prettiest of the Italian lakes, and continued our journey to Bellagio on the banks of Lake Como.

Bellagio, on a small peninsula formed by the three arms of Lake Como, commands from its eminence views of unsurpassed beauty, but a more extended range is obtained from the villa Serbelloni, on the heights above. Embowered in a rich luxuriance of tropical growth, this pretty little villa is almost concealed from view, but from its secluded elevation are obtained glimpses of the panorama of mountain and lake so vividly portrayed by Claude Melnotte: "A deep vale shut in by Alpine hills from the rude world, near a clear lake margined by fruits of gold and whispering myrtles."

Lake Como, 30 miles long and 2½ wide, is set like a precious gem in the midst of ever-green hills; along its shores are picturesque villas, and romantic ruins, standing out from a dark background of foliage; here the Villa d'Este, the fair casket that once enshrined Tasso's beautiful Leonora, and later the peaceful refuge of the unhappy Caroline of Brunswick; there, the Villa Taglioni, the lovely home of the famous *danseuse*, and again the Villa Carlotta, filled with the masterpieces of Canova and Thorwaldsen.

Como, at the southern extremity of the lake, has a population of 25,000, and is defended by double walls and environed by hills. The city has four gates, one of which leads to Milan and is a grand specimen of architectural beauty. In front of the Cathedral are statues of the elder and younger Pliny, the latter having been born here A. D. 62.

Taking rail from Como to Basle the road passes through the finest of the Italian and Swiss scenery, skirts Lakes Como, Lugano, Lucerne, Zug, and Zurich, and enters the Alps through the

St. Gothard Tunnel.   This, the most wonderful
piece of engineering in the world, penetrates the
mountain like a cork-screw, making four complete
loops within a distance of twenty miles in order to
attain the requisite elevation, when it emerges
into daylight only to enter again the main tunnel
which is nine miles in length.   On the opposite
side the road winds around cliffs, through rocky
gorges, and crosses chasms of fearful depth, presenting a scene of surpassing grandeur.

CHAPTER XIII.

FREIBURG : STRASBURG : BADEN BADEN : HEIDELBERG :
FRANKFORT : MAYENCE : THE RHINE : COLOGNE : AIX-
LA-CHAPELLE : METZ : RHEIMS : DIJON : MÂCON :
LYONS.

FROM Basle to Freiburg where in the latter city
is a monument to Berthold Swartz, the monk
who, it is claimed, in 1320, invented gunpowder,
the rail follows the Rhine, and skirts the Black
Forest so intimately associated with the legends
of Germany.

Strasburg, the principal city of the German
provinces of Alsace and Loraine, has a population
of 105,000 and is noted chiefly for its wonderful
clock, and its manufacture of patés-de-foie-gras ;

this well-known delicacy is composed of geese-livers unnaturally enlarged by a process of excessive feeding. A singular sight is that of the great storks standing beside, or building their nests on the chimneys of many housetops. It was in Strasburg that Guttenberg first used type, and gave to the world one of the most useful of inventions.

The city, while in possession of the French, was bombarded by the Prussians, in August and September, 1871, from Kehl, the batteries being placed out of sight of the French, and under the direction of an officer stationed on a high steeple, who communicated by telegraph to the distant trenches.

The Cathedral which has a spire 470 feet in height, the highest in the world, contains the celebrated astronomical clock made by Schwilgué in 1838-1842 to replace a similar one of great antiquity. At the hour of 12 the cock crows, the twelve apostles appear, and other puppets are set in motion.

In the Church of St. Thomas is a fine monument to Marshal Saxe, and in glass cases are the bodies of the Duke of Nassau and his daughter, preserved for 400 years.

Baden-Baden, the famous German watering-place, is in a valley on the northern extremity of the Black Forest. Along the banks of the river Oos are shaded avenues for public resort, leading to the Trinkhalle whose waters are sought by invalids affected with gout and rheumatism, and to the Conversations Haus formerly the gambling hall, but now a place of rendezvous, where people meet to chat and drink beer, while listening to strains of music discoursed by a fine band outside.

A most delightful excursion from Baden-Baden is, by carriage, to the Merkur Tower, situated on the mountain top in the midst of the Black Forest, from which is obtained an extended view of the forest and adjacent mountains. En route one passes the New Castle founded 1,100 years ago, at present the summer residence of the Grand Duke, the picturesque ruins of an old Roman castle, and further on the fantastic Felsen, or rocks, in form somewhat resembling pulpits, where legend avers an angel once discoursed from one of them, the devil from the other; which of the two succeeded in obtaining the greater number of disciples, tradition revealeth not.

Heidelberg, so celebrated for its Castle and University, is situated on the Neckar, and has a population of 25,000. The Castle is on an elevation commanding a fine view of town and river; it is partly a ruin, half palace and half fortress, and is surrounded by charming grounds. In its cellar is shown the great Heidelberg Tun, with a capacity equivalent to the measure of 283,000 bottles of wine: in order to realize the size of this monster cask, one must climb to its top, by means of a

ladder, and standing upon its broad surface look
downward to the stone floor beneath. In the
same room is a wooden effigy of the court fool
Porkes, who never went to bed sober, his moderate allowance being 18 bottles *per diem*.

The Church of the Holy Ghost is an old and
quaint structure, and is divided by a partition
through the middle, which separates the Protestant from the Catholic services, held under the
same roof.

On the opposite side of the river from Heidelberg is a building where, once a week, the students repair to settle their quarrels by means of
duels fought with swords. These duels are as
much an institution of the University as is the
scholastic course, and " honorable scars " thus obtained are the object of the students' fondest ambition. In order that these wounds may be worn
in open view upon the face, the body is protected
by padding, while the eyes are shielded by iron
goggles; a surgeon is, of course, in attendance,
whose duty it is to prevent the combat from resulting seriously.

Frankfort-on-the-Maine, with a population of
138,000, was formerly a free city of Germany, but
was annexed to the Kingdom of Prussia, October
8th, 1866. It is a very ancient city, having in
794 been the residence of Charlemagne. At
present it is chiefly noted for its large banking
houses, and the great wealth of its citizens; it is

the native place of the original Rothschild, the house in Jew street still standing where the famous banker was born. The present Baron Rothschild is the king of bankers, and the banker of kings. The principal public monuments are those of Guttenberg, Schiller, and Goethe, the latter being born here August 28th, 1749. In a private villa is a statue of faultless marble, by Danneker, representing Ariadne seated on a tiger —one of the most perfect productions of modern art.

The Rhine ranks first among European rivers in variety and beauty of scenery, and in the historical associations and traditional reminiscences which haunt its shores. From Mayence to Cologne it winds with rapid current among high hills crowned with ruined castles, the river's sloping banks covered with luxuriant vineyards. On the right bank is the Castle of Johannisberg surrounded by the vines which produce the most celebrated of the Rhine wines distinguished for their delicate bouquet. Beyond, are the vineyards of Steinberg and Rudesheim, from the former of which is obtained wine noted for its body, warmth, and peculiar aroma, while from the latter, planted as far back as the reign of Charlemagne, is produced a wine which, although less expensive, is almost equal in quality to the Steinberg.

Bingen on the Rhine is best known from the

beautiful poem bearing that title: opposite is
the ruin of Bishop Hatto's Castle of Ehrenfels, and
on an island in the river is the Mouse Tower
where the wicked Bishop sought refuge when
pursued by the rats. Besides these points of interest are, the Castle of Rheinstein, where is
buried Prince Frederick of Prussia; Pfalz, where
Louis le Debonnaire retired, weary of the cares of
empire, to end his days on a barren rock in the
river; the Lorelei Rock where the syren sat and
sang, and combed her golden locks, luring the en-
tranced boatmen to destruction; the Castle and
Fortress of Reinfels, an imposing ruin; the Castle
of the Two Brothers whose unnatural love for
their beautiful sister culminated in a fatal combat;
the Castle Stolzenfels, the property of the King
of Prussia; the Fort of Ehrenbreitstein, opposite
Coblentz, so strongly fortified that it is styled the
Gibraltar of Germany; Bröhl, a small village,
celebrated for its tufa stone used by the Romans
for coffins on account of its property of absorption, and from which is derived the name of
sarcophagus — or flesh consumer; the Castle of
Rolandseck, built by Roland, a nephew of Charlemagne, that he might overlook the convent to
which his bride had retired from the world; and
Drachenfels, commandingly situated on the highest hill-top, once the fortress and watch-tower of
the robbers of the Rhine.

Cologne, the capital of the province, and the

third city of importance in the empire, has a population of 145,000. It is as celebrated for its filthy streets and bad odors, as for the superior article of cologne-water manufactured here by the Farina firm. In its public squares are bronze statues of Frederick William III., Frederick William IV., and the present Emperor William.

The Cathedral, a magnificent specimen of Gothic architecture, was commenced in 1248 and only completed in 1880. Behind the high altar is the Chapel of the Magi, or three kings, who came from the East to worship, and bring offerings to the Infant Christ; the remains of these three wise men — Caspar, Melchior, and Balthasar, are, here inclosed in a casket of solid gold, studded with precious stones, (valued at $2,000,-000), their skulls, which are exposed to view, bearing crowns of diamonds. In the church treasury are three links of the chain with which St. Peter was bound, and a bone of St. Matthew, and in the aisle is a plain slab covering the heart of Marie de Medici.

In St. Peter's church is the font where Rubens, a native of Cologne, was baptized; and here also is his celebrated painting of St. Peter's crucifixion, head downwards — considered by himself his *chef d'œuvre*.

The Church of St. Ursula enshrines the bones of that saint, with those of her 11,000 virgins, who were murdered on this spot by the Huns in

450 A. D. on account of their refusal to break
their vows of chastity; the walls of the church
are covered with their ghastly relics, arranged
in hideous display. Another of its treasures is
one of the six porphyry jars, which it is claimed,
was the means used by the Saviour in the performance of His first miracle of changing water
into wine, at the marriage feast of Cana.

Aix-la-Chapelle is celebrated as having formerly been the city where the earlier sovereigns
of France and Germany were crowned; it is noted
for its highly medicinal waters and received its
name from the chapel erected by Charlemagne
for his place of sepulture.

The present Cathedral which adjoins the
chapel, is one of the oldest in Europe, and is unsurpassed in the value of the relics it contains,
which were presented to Charlemagne by the
Grand Patriarch of Jerusalem. These consist of
the white gown of the Virgin; the swathing clothes
of the Infant Christ; a cloth on which lay the body
of John the Baptist; the leathern girdle of Jesus;
part of the rope with which He was bound; one
of the nails that fastened Him to the Cross; a
fragment of the reed with which they mocked
Him; bones of the twelve apostles; and the pulpit
from which St. Bernard preached the second crusade. Here, encased in a golden coffin, are the
remains of Charlemagne; and also the marble
coronation chair in which he was found, sitting

erect, with the crown, sceptre, and orb of his imperial state, when his tomb was opened by Otho
III., in 997. This same chair, crown, orb, and
sceptre, were used at the coronation of successive
emperors of Germany, for centuries afterward.

The Rath-haus stands on the site of the
palace where Charlemagne was born, 742; and
contains an ancient hall beautifully frescoed with
scenes from the emperor's life, and another,
called the Great Hall, used for the coronation
ceremonies of emperors, for the assemblage of the
Diets, and for other important celebrations. In
this hall is a magnificent stained-glass window
representing a life-size portrait of the present Emperor, William I.

From Aix-la-Chapelle to Metz the rail follows, part of the way, the Moselle river, whose
scenery much resembles that of the Rhine; and
from this district is produced the famous Moselle
wine.

Metz, on the Moselle river, with a population
of 54,000 is one of the most strongly fortified
towns in Europe. Four miles distant the battles
of Vionville and Gravelotte were fought August
16th and 18th, 1870. Metz has always borne the
name of the Virgin Fortress, and can easily be
defended against six times the number of its garrison; but on the 27th of October, 1870, the
whole French army under Marshal Bazaine, cap-
itulated; and 3 marshals, 66 generals, 6,000 of-

ficers, and 173,000 troops surrendered themselves prisoners of war to the Germans.

From Metz to Rheims we traversed the great Champagne district, stopping at Epernay, where are the extensive cellars of Moet and Chandon.

The ancient city of Rheims is noted not only for its world-renowned wines of Champagne, but for its having been the city where have been crowned nearly all the kings of France since Philip Augustus. It was here that the virgin hand of Joan of Arc caused the crown of reunited France to be placed on the head of Charles VII.

In Rheims are the celebrated champagne vaults of T. Roederer & Co. These excavations, which extend half a mile underground to the depth of 120 feet, are cut out of the solid rock; and were once stone quarries which yielded a white, chalk-like substance hardening on being exposed to the air.

Traversing the Burgundy district, we stopped at Dijon and Mâcon, the exporting centre of the Burgundy wines. The strength and flavor of these wines is partly owing to the soil on which the grape is grown — a reddish strata of earth overlaying a white chalky rock. The wine is both red and white in color, of a heavy body, and far superior to the ordinary claret wines; but very little of the finer qualities are exported, the French preferring to retain this their favorite beverage in their own country even at the high rates demanded for it.

Lyons at the confluence of the Rhone and Saône, has a population of 343,000. It is the second city in France in point of size and population, and is the centre of extensive manufactures. It is of great antiquity, having been the capital of Celtic Gaul, and in modern times had its share in the great revolution, and was the chief scene of the Jacobite excesses. It was here that Bulwer laid the first scenes of his popular play The Lady of Lyons.

Lyons is the great manufacturing mart for silks and velvets, and although it has 30,000 weavers of these fabrics, there are no large factories, the work being done by small establishments, in each of which, only from eight to twelve men are employed. Jacquard, the inventor of the loom, was born here.

A fine view of the city and suburban landscape is to be obtained from the tower of the Church of Notre Dame on the heights of Fourvières. On this height is the Hospice de l'Antiqueille built on the site of the palace in which the Roman emperors Claudius, Germanicus, and Caligula were born; and in the Museum is a bronze tablet on which is carved a speech which Claudius delivered before the Roman Senate, A. D. 48. Near here is the Church of St. Iranée, erected on the spot where Septimus Severus, in the year 202 caused the massacre of 20,000 Christians who had assembled for prayer.

In the Hotel de Ville, the Revolutionary tribunal consisting of Couthon, Fondée, and Collot d'Herbois sat in council, after the siege of Lyons. The latter of these who was their leader, had, when an actor, been hissed from the stage, and maddened at the insult swore to be revenged. When the opportunity presented itself, he wreaked a terrible vengeance for his fancied wrongs; the citizens were killed at the rate of 100 a day; the knife of the guillotine working too slowly for the satisfying of his cruel impatience, fifty human beings at a time, were tied together and shot as they stood, with grape and canister. After 2,000 had been butchered in this manner, the city was razed to the ground.

From Lyons we now turned our faces towards Paris; where after a brief sojourn we started forth again on our travels, with Spain as our point of destination.

CHAPTER XIV.

ORLEANS: BLOIS: TOURS: POITIERS: BORDEAUX: BAY-
ONNE: BIARRITZ: BURGOS: VALLADOLID: MADRID:
ESCURIAL: CORDOVA: SEVILLE: GRANADA: MAL-
AGA: GIBRALTAR.

ORLEANS one of the most ancient cities of
France, has a population of 52,000. In 1429 this
city was besieged by the English for six months;
but in the following year Joan of Arc, in full
armor, bearing a sacred banner, entered the city
at the head of a very small force, bringing supplies to the besieged. In opposition to the judgment of the French commanders, she crossed the
Loire in boats, accompanied only by a chosen
number of men, and attacked the Bastile des Tour-
nelles. Although pierced by an arrow, she waved
her banner, scaled the walls and carried the fort.
Hence her name of Maid of Orleans.

The city has a fine Cathedral, and an equestrian statue of Joan of Arc.

Blois on the river Loire, was the native city
of Louis XII., Peter the Divine, and Papin, inventor of the steam engine. The old castle overlooking the river, was once the palace of Francis
I., and of Charles IX. In it is a room where

Catherine de Medici consulted the stars and con-
cocted her most diabolical plots; foremost among
these was the cold-blooded murder of the Duke
of Guise; when, at her instigation, her son
Henry III. placed daggers in the hands of his attendants to stab him as he entered the chamber.

Napoleon I. dated his last imperial decree at
Blois to which place he had previously dispatched
the empress with the young king of Rome and
the remnant of his court.

Tours, the principal city of Touraine, has a
population of 48,000. It was near here, in 732,
that the battle took place between the Christians
under Charles Martel and the Mohammedans
under Abder Rahman, which resulted in the
death-blow to the Koran in the West.

Poitiers is chiefly noted as having given the
name to the famous battle fought near by, between King John and the Black Prince, which
resulted in the defeat and captivity of the former.

Bordeaux the second sea-port town of France,
is on the Garonne, 60 miles from its mouth, and
has a population of 216,000. It has a quay 3
miles long, surpassed by few in Europe. The
city is particularly celebrated for its extensive
trade in claret wine, of which it exports large
quantities to foreign ports. Among its most remarkable edifices are the ruins of an old Roman
palace; a fine theatre built by Louis XIV.; and
St. Michael's Church; in a cave of the tower, are

a large number of wonderfully life-like bodies standing upright against the walls; their preservation being attributed to the nature of the soil in which they had been buried 400 years before.

Bayonne is situated at the junction of the Nive and Adour rivers, on the high-road to Spain; and is one of the most strongly fortified towns of France. Its citadel is considered the best work of Vauban the engineer. From Bayonne the bayonet derives its name; it was invented in the 17th century, originating from the incident of a regiment short of ammunition, defending itself against the Spaniards by means of long knives which they stuck in the barrels of their muskets.

Biarritz on the Bay of Biscay, 8 miles from Bayonne, is a fashionable watering-place, and was a favorite resort of the Emperor Napoleon III.; its mild climate rendering a sojourn here attractive during the fall and winter months. The shore is rugged and wild, with cliffs from thirty to forty feet in height.

After crossing the Spanish frontier at Irun, where a most thorough search is made by the custom-house officials, the first city of importance reached is Burgos, the former capital of the kingdom of Castile. It is situated 3,000 feet above the level of the sea, and contains 30,000 inhabitants. The streets are narrow and dirty, and the houses high and inclosed in glass verandas. At intervals of 15 minutes throughout the night, the voice of the watchman may be heard in loud tones announcing the hour and the state of the weather. The ladies still adhere to the picturesque lace mantilla, and the graceful fan; while the men invariably envelope themselves in the voluminous folds of their mantles. Before being admitted into a house, the stranger is first jealously scanned through a grating in the outer door; a custom having its origin in a time of general insecurity. The small donkey, the only beast of burden seen on the streets, is often so heavily laden as to be scarcely observable under his bulky load.

Burgos is celebrated as the birthplace and tomb of the Cid, a Moorish name meaning unconquerable. This celebrated Spanish hero was a great warrior, whose deeds have been recorded in prose and verse by writers of all countries and periods for the last eight centuries. Even after his death he is said to have won a great victory; his followers having secured his corpse to his favorite horse, conducted him to the battle-field, where the foe, having heard of the death of the great leader, were appalled at sight of the ghastly apparition, and, conquered by their own superstitious terrors, fled ignominiously from the field.

Valladolid the ancient capital of Spain, is at the confluence of the Pisuerga and Esgueva rivers, and has a population of 52,000. It was here that Christopher Columbus, who gave a continent to the world died,— May 20th, 1506 — in a small

dimly-lighted room, in a narrow street of the
poorer quarter of the town. Valladolid was the
birthplace of Philip II. and in the Cathedral —
one of the finest in Spain — were married, in
1469, Ferdinand and Isabella.

Madrid, the capital of Spain, is in the centre
of the kingdom, in a barren, rocky plain 2,200
feet above the level of the sea. Owing to its
situation, the city is exposed to cold winds and
the climate is particularly unhealthy. Madrid
has 400,000 inhabitants and though of very ancient origin, has, owing to its handsome buildings
and wide streets, a modern appearance. The
most conspicuous public ornaments are, the
statues of Spain's gifted sons, Murillo the artist,
and Cervantes the author of Don Quixote; and
of Philip IV. on horseback surrounded by the
early kings; besides the fountains of Neptune and
Sibyl. The Park, of an afternoon is thronged
with the élite driving out in their elegant equipages, among them that of the Royal family, in
which is the little Infanta accompanied by her attendants.

The Royal Palace is an immense structure
built of granite, and covering, with its surroundings, 80 acres of ground. Favored with invita-
tions from the Palace we attended the Christening
of the Royal Infant of Spain. The ceremony
was performed in the Royal Chapel by a Cardinal, assisted by the highest dignitaries of the

Church; and was attended by members of the
Royal household and cabinet, generals of the
army, and foreign ambassadors in full uniform,
wearing their numerous decorations.

In the Royal Picture Gallery are several hundred paintings, among them those of Velasquez,
master of the Spanish school, whose best work is
the portrait of Æsop; here also are many of Murillo's original works — the Conception, and the
Infant St. John being among the finest. Of the
productions of modern Spanish artists are, the
Bell of Huesca, the Death of Lucrezia Borgia,
Defending the Pass, and the Death of Seneca.

In the Naval Museum are the compass of Columbus and the original chart with which he
demonstrated his discovery of a new continent.
The armory contains the swords and coats of mail
of Columbus, Ferdinand, and Cortez, besides those
of Boabdil and other Moorish kings.

The Amphitheatre where bull-fights take place
is built of stone and brick, with a capacity for seating 16,500 people; this barbarous entertainment
being held Sunday afternoons from the hours of
2 to 5. The bull-fight which we witnessed was an
especially grand affair given in celebration of the
birth of the Royal child. At the hour specified,
the streets were thronged, and the vast building
crowded to its utmost. The entertainment was
inaugurated by a grand procession entering the
arena, composed of all who were to take part,

dressed in gay and fantastic costumes, glittering
with gold and silver.   After saluting the king and
audience, two heralds advanced from among them
and received from the governor the large iron key
with which they proceeded to open the gates
separating the arena from the inclosure in which
the restive animals were confined.   One at a time
the bulls were admitted.   The animal entered the
circle, evidently bewildered at the novelty of his
situation, and evincing no sign of his natural belli-
cose propensity.   Then came the matadores who,
flourishing their blood-red mantles in his face, and
launching their bandarillos — or barbed arrows —
into his sides, soon succeeded into goading him
into mad fury.   With a low roar like the sound of
distant thunder, the bull rushed upon his assailants, who, to escape his attack, performed marvellous feats of agility, now dodging from beneath
his very horns, and again casting themselves on
the ground in his path, that unable to make so
sudden a halt in his mad career the animal should
pass him by ; and — more wonderful than all —
quickly planting a spear in the ground, by its aid
vaulting clear over the beast to the opposite side.
Next the Picadors, or mounted men, entered
upon the scene, bearing long spears, their sole
mode of defence against the furious onslaught of
the now thoroughly aroused and pain-maddened
bull.   Then the hideous interest of the spectacle
became intensified.   The wretched horses, with

one eye bandaged in order that they might not be
fully conscious of their peril, vainly essayed to
elude the repeated attacks of the bull, flying
wildly around the ring, their entrails protruding
from their bleeding wounds and trailing in the
dust as they ran. By this time the bull, having
overcome his assailants, and being thoroughly ex-
hausted from loss of blood, stood at bay with re-
laxing muscles but undaunted eye, as a matador
entered the arena for the final scene of the barbarous sport — the Blow of Mercy. He approached on foot, and armed only with a sharp
dagger, confronted the bull, and as the animal
lowered his head for a last attack, the daring matador plunged the blade into his neck adroitly and
instantaneously severing the main artery.

On this occasion, these fearful scenes were repeated until no less than six bulls and seven horses
had been killed and several men wounded.

The present king and queen, although much
averse to bull-fights, are compelled to sanction
and even yield to the requirements of custom and
prejudice, and attend these national exhibitions.

The Escurial, 40 miles from Madrid, is an immense granite building comprising palace, tomb,
and convent. It is one of the wonders of Spain,
and was built by Philip II. as a royal vault for
kings and mothers of kings. Over the entrance
are large statues of David, Solomon, Jehoshaphat, Hezekiah, Manasseh, and Josiah. The palace

apartments are hung with the finest of modern Spanish tapestry, the chapel contains pulpits of the most exquisite Mexican onyx, and over the altar is the largest round topaz in the world. The vault beneath, whose steps and walls are of porphyry and polished stones, is of a circular form, the granite coffins arranged on shelves in chronological order bearing the names of the occupants engraved in gilt letters, several vacant places awaiting the living. Outside this receptacle for dead royalty, but still within the church, lies all that remains of the young and lovely Mercedes, first wife of Alfonso, who having been denied the motherhood of a son, is debarred the honors of sepulture within the precincts of the royal circle.

Cordova, with a population of 50,000, was once the principal city, and capital of the Moors, and contained at one time 1,000,000 inhabitants, and 300 mosques. It was the birthplace of the two Senecas, and of Lucan the poet.

The Cathedral, formerly a mosque, still retains its Moorish style of architecture, and is exceedingly beautiful and picturesque. It has 850 pillars of jasper, porphyry, and every variety of marble; the arches and ceilings are of the most exquisite mosaic, and everywhere are fine carvings inscribed with quotations from the Koran. In the south end of the edifice is the Zancarron, or Moorish sanctuary of octagon shape, highly ornamented, and canopied with a scallop shell cut from a solid block of marble 15 feet in breadth.

In Cordova is manufactured a preserve made from the orange-blossom — some 200 blossoms being required to the pound,— which is delicate in flavor, and grateful to the taste. The great industry of the place is the pickling of olives; the process being to soak the fruit in a brine impregnated with anise-seed and bay leaves.

Seville, on the Guadalquivir, is claimed to have been founded by Hercules, captured by Cæsar, and subsequently in 711, by the Moors. It was at one time the centre of science and art, but declined rapidly after having been conquered by the Christians. Seville was the birthplace of the Emperors Trajan and Theodosius; also of Magellan the famous navigator, Las Casas the defender of the Indians, and Lope de Vega the father of Spanish comedy. It was here in 1480 the Inquisition was established; the Square still existing, where the grand tribunal met, passed judgment, and dispatched their victims. The streets are crooked, and some of them barely six feet in width; the Plazas are bordered with palm and date-trees, and the surrounding country is luxuriant with growth of olive and orange, cactus and aloe.

The Alcazar or Palace, of Moslem architecture, was the residence of the Moorish and Catholic kings of Spain. On one side of the court once

stood the throne . before which were yearly
brought one hundred of the most beautiful virgins
of Seville, from among whom the Moorish monarch
might select his wives. Opening from the opposite side is the Hall of Ambassadors, where Don
Pedro not only killed his own brother, but also
the former King of Granada, Abu Said, to whom he
had promised protection, and whom, after feasting
and flattering, he assassinated and robbed of his
jewels; among the latter was the heart-shaped
ruby which he afterwards presented to the Black
Prince, and is now conspicuous in the crown
of England. On the floor above is the private
chapel where Ferdinand and Isabella gave audience to Christopher Columbus. Adjoining the
beautiful gardens of the Palace are immense baths,
where Maria de Padilla and her attendants dis-
ported in the presence of the king.

In the Cathedral are many of Murillo's finest
works; and a slab on the floor marks the spot
where is buried Ferdinand son of Columbus, —
the body of the great discoverer having been removed to Havana. Adjoining the church is a
library containing the log-book of Columbus, with
charts indicating his route and the distance travelled each day; also a history of the world with
his marginal notes and corrections.

In the Bourse, or Exchange, are the archives
of Spanish South America, with the correspondence of Cortez and Pizarro.

Among other places are, the studio, and
house where Murillo died; that called the House
of Pontius Pilate,—a fac-simile of the one in Jerusalem; and the home of Figaro, the barber of Seville, the scene and subject of one of the prettiest
of modern operas.

At the Escuela de Bailes, or Dance-hall, we
witnessed the Spanish Fandango danced in all its
originality and boldness.

Granada is in a beautiful plain on the banks of
the Darro near the snow-capped range of the
Sierra Nevada. Its present population is 76,000,
not one-tenth of what it was when taken from the
Moors by Ferdinand and Isabella.

The Alhambra, or acropolis of Granada, is on
the top of a high hill overlooking the city. It
was built 600 years ago by the Moors; is surrounded by walls and towers, and was at one
time capable of accommodating 40,000 soldiers.
This palace was to them a terrestrial paradise, and
it was here they made their last stand for empire
in Spain. Though somewhat faded and damaged
by the ravages of time and war, it still retains
much of its former grandeur; and resembles
more an abode fitted for fabled queens of Love
and Beauty, than a human habitation. Its ceilings are of honey-combed stalactite, of blue, red,
and gold, and inlaid with mother-of-pearl; the
walls of stucco resemble fine lace-work of various
intricate designs inscribed with quotations from

the Koran; and the floors and columns are of alabaster and marble. The most beautiful and interesting apartments of the palace are, the Hall of
Ambassadors where Ferdinand and Isabella received Columbus, prior to his departure for the
great voyage of discovery; beneath it, the dungeon, and the balcony from which Boabdil when
a child was lowered in a basket, by his mother,
and sent beyond reach of his cruel father; the
Repose Room where the Sultan rested with his
Sultana after the bath, listening to strains of music
from the balconies above; the Toilet-room, in one
corner of which is a perforated marble slab in the
floor, over whose ascending perfumes the Sultana
stood while her attendants ministered to her toilet;
the Hall of Two Sisters, whence the royal couple issued their orders; the Hall of Justice where the
nobles received sentence; the Court of Lions, so
called from its fountain supported by twelve
huge lions, surrounded by 136 marble pillars;
and the Hall of Abencerrages where Boabdil
killed thirty-six of the tribe of that name; the
marble fountain flowing with their blood. This
massacre was caused by a report made by some
of the rival tribe Zegri, to Boabdil, that his beautiful queen was seen in the garden in the embrace
of the chief of the Abencerrages. The queen,
dreading the king's vengeful wrath appealed for
protection to four Christian knights, who came,
disguised as Moors, vanquished the Zegri in a

hand-to-hand fight, and compelled them to confess their villainous plot in the presence of the
king and assembled people.   In the Tower of
Comares is the room in which Washington Irving
wrote his fine description of the Alhambra.

The Generalife, on an adjacent hill was the
summer palace of the Moorish kings, and in it are
portraits of Moslem and Christian sovereigns.   In
the terraced gardens of this palace are sparkling
fountains, and perpetual bloom of oleander, pome-
granate, lime and orange.

From an elevated rock called the Seat of the
Moor, can be seen the bridge where Columbus
was overtaken by the king's messenger, while
he was on his way, disappointed and dejected, to
submit his disdained projects to the Court of
France.   Near by is the point called the Last
Sigh of the Moor, whence Boabdil looked back
and wept at the city he had lost, and was re-
proved by his mother's sarcasm: "you do well to
weep as a woman over what you could not defend
as a man."

The chief object of interest in the town itself
is the Cathedral whose highly ornamented interior
contains the magnificent marble tombs of Ferdinand and Isabella, and those of their daughter,
Jane the Demented, and her husband Philip I.

In the Treasury is the sword of Ferdinand,
and the flag he carried at the siege of Granada:
also Isabella's crown and sceptre, and the golden

casket which once contained the jewels she caused
to be sold to enable Columbus to sail on his voyage of discovery.

The Convent of Cartouja, two miles from
Granada was once the abode of an order of monks
who were allowed to speak only once a week;
and if by chance they met one another they
crossed themselves piously, with the adjuration:
"brother we must die!" This order has been
suppressed; but the edifice still exists in good
condition. The Chapel walls are of a variety of
exquisite marbles brought from the Snow mountains, the doors and cabinets are of ebony, ivory,
and tortoise shell; and set in the altar are two
immense agates three feet each, in circumference.

Malaga, a seaport town of Andalusia, founded
by the Carthagenians, and successively under the
rule of the Romans, Goths, and Moors, is situated
on a mountain-girded bay; and above the town
towers the ruin of an old Roman castle. Malaga
is celebrated for its grapes, figs, oranges, lemons,
raisins, wine, and olive oil, which are exported in
large quantities to the United States. The manufacture of olive oil is most primitive in its
process; the fruit is picked in December, when
very ripe, and crushed between two large stones
turned by a cow or mule; it is next placed in
straw baskets and the oil forced out by heavy
pressure, after which it is poured into large jars to
settle and refine.

Gibraltar, an English possession on a peninsula in the extreme south of Spain, contains a population of 25,000, of whom 6,000 belong to the army.

The Rock so celebrated as the strongest fortress in the world, rises above the town 1,400 feet and extends to the end of the peninsula, a distance of four miles. Heavily mounted with guns on solid fortifications, its strongest side is that facing Spain. Within the solid rock have been cut to a great height, roads and galleries; while nothing is visible from the exterior but the portholes through which the muzzles of the guns protrude.

On the top is the signal station from which is a fine view of sea and land. On the side of the hill, midway between the fort and the town, is St. Michael's stalactite cave; and near by, numerous monkeys infest the crevices of the rock, and leap, with chatter and grimace from cliff to cliff.

The Rock, which overlooks the bay, is a thorn in the side of Spain, and serves England as a coaling station for its India-bound steamers; it by no means commands the strait, however, as at this point it is 13 miles wide, and the guns could not carry half that distance.

Ten miles from Gibraltar, are the extensive Cork forests of Spain, where the bark is annually gathered and shipped in large quantities to all parts of the world.

From Gibraltar we crossed the strait and after
an exceedingly rough passage reached the northern shores of Africa.

CHAPTER XV.

TANGIERS: ORAN: BLIDAH: ALGIERS: MARSEILLES:
CHATEAU D'IF: TOULON: NICE: MONACO.

TANGIERS, a seaport town of Morocco, has a
population of 10,000.   It presents from the sea a
beautiful aspect, its white houses rising in terraces, one above another; but a closer proximity
shows the city in a disgustingly filthy condition;
its narrow streets swarming with beggars, ragged,
crippled and diseased.

The women are enveloped in a voluminous,
shapeless, white garment, their faces, with the exception of one eye, completely concealed from
view.   The men, who are very dark of complexion, wear loose white burnooses, between the
opening folds of which is occasionally seen the
gleam of their silver mounted daggers; their bare
legs terminating in yellow leather slippers, and
their heads incased in a red fez, over which is
wound the many folds of the conventional white
turban.

The bazaar shops are generally about ten feet square; here the Moor sits cross-legged, surrounded by his wares, and transacts business from the door; the chief article of commodity being that fine grade of leather which takes its name from the country.

The city contains three mosques, before entering any one of which the Moor must first wash his feet in a stone trough at the threshold. From the top of each minaret, at sunrise, noon, and sunset, a flag is raised, and the faithful called by voice to prayer.

The Prison is simply a dungeon with a dirt floor, light and communication being obtained only through an aperture in the door. The prisoners are not only chained and beaten unmercifully, but are left by the government to starve, unless food or money is furnished them by private charities.

The Market-place is an open space outside of the city walls which on market days is a scene of great activity and bustle; hundreds of camels and donkeys loaded with dates and other articles of merchandise from the interior, are grouped around; the camels kneeling while their owners relieve them of their burthens, and spread their wares on the ground before them. In the midst of this motley throng, wild, half-naked men from the Atlas mountains — religious fanatics — dance their uncouth measures, writhing, and foaming at the mouth, while they strike their closely-shaved heads with sharp instruments, cutting, bruising, and mangling them to a mass of bleeding, quivering flesh, apparently unconscious of the self-inflicted pain. Here the snake-charmers ply their singular avocation, displaying their perfect control over the movements of the huge reptiles to the sound of their peculiar instruments. A portion of the market-place is devoted to the sale of slaves; the auctioneer standing in the midst of the wretched creatures, cries in a loud voice for the highest bidder; after the auction, those remaining unsold are driven through the streets to be sold for whatever price they may bring.

A man who wields a wonderful degree of power in Morocco without being absolutely in official authority, is the Prince Hadj Abdes Salem, or the "Saint," as he is called, a direct descendant of Mohammed, who is not only worshipped by the people, but to whom even the Emperor of Morocco must kneel for permission before assuming office. In person he is a man of apparently 45 years of age, weighing some 250 lbs., and so dark of complexion as to be almost black; in dress he is plain, distinguished from other Moors only by the green fez which indicates a descendant of Mohammed. The Saint has a decided partiality for the English and Americans, perhaps induced by the influence of his American wife, who visiting the country as governess to an English

family, charmed the Moslem by her beauty and
grace, and consented to accept the dubious honor
of being his favorite wife. In the suburbs she
dwells in her own private residence, while in the
town is the prince's harem, consisting of several
hundred women, which is jealously guarded by
a large number from among his many thousand
slaves.

A cordial invitation was extended us by the
prince to attend a nine days' boar hunt, escorted
by his suite and attendants numbering some
2,000 men ; the slaves attending the hunt in the
capacity of beaters.

Only the ladies of our party were admitted
into the harems. One of these is worthy of description. The entrance was through a court-
yard whose gates were guarded by black eunuchs.
The reception-room was a fair example of the
oriental style ; the walls were hung in draperies
of silk and gold tissues ; the floor covered with
costly Persian rugs ; while scattered around were
cushions and divans of rare stuffs and inviting
shape, suggestive of ease and repose ; and over
all the reflection of the vast mirrors lent additional
brilliancy to the scene. Here reclining in various
graceful attitudes, were the beauties of the harem ;
fair Georgians, lovely Circassians and dark-eyed
Persians, gorgeously apparelled, and decked in
resplendent jewels. Refreshments—tea, sherbets,
and comfits — were served in delicate porcelain,

by kneeling slaves, incense burned and highly-aromatic perfumes proffered.

At Tangiers we took steamer coasting along the African shore; and after touching at various ports of minor importance in Morocco, we landed at Oran in Algeria.

Oran, the capital of the province of the same name, contains some 50,000 inhabitants, and is almost surrounded by high hills on the summits of which are strong fortifications whence magnificent views are obtained of the harbor and adjacent country.

The rail from Oran to Algiers, 260 miles, traverses a fertile and productive valley 20 miles in width, and one is surprised at the richness of the soil, and the luxuriant growth of vegetation; here, in the month of December, the climate resembles that of spring; and the large vineyards, recently planted, promise great future revenues to France.

Blidah lies at the foot of the Atlas mountains, its streets gradually sloping for miles into the Metidja plain. Although located in the fairest portion of Algeria, with a mild and balmy climate, and tropical growth of vegetation, snow covers the mountain peaks which overlook the city. In the Tivoli Gardens, where the band of African Chasseurs discourses fine music, throngs of the military and citizens resort in the cool of the evening to saunter among the groves of date, palm and banana.

The French purchase many of their horses for
cavalry service in Blidah; the stables containing
several hundred of the finest animals of pure
Arabian stock. They are constantly bought
from the Arabs who obtain as high as from $500
to $1,500 apiece, according to color, the sorrel
being most highly esteemed.

The Gorge of Chiffa, ten miles from Blidah by
carriage, is a rent in the Atlas mountains, through
which flows the river of the same name; it is
wild and rugged, and is considered the finest
mountain scenery of all Algeria.

In a narrow ravine leading from the Gorge is
the Monkey brook, where innumerable apes and
monkeys leap from rock to rock and from branch
to branch uttering their discordant accents. Although permitting a near proximity, these animals
are difficult to capture owing to their intuitive
suspicion of mankind; their less wary progeny
alone falling sometimes in the snares laid to entrap them.

Algiers, the capital of Algeria, has a population of 60,000. Its white, flat-roofed houses,
rising one above another on the sloping hill-side,
present a singularly oriental aspect. This city
was for many years the terror of the civilized
world; it was the headquarters of pirates whose
ravages extended over the Mediterranean; Christians of all nationalities being captured by them
and cast into slavery. The modern part of the

city is that nearest the sea, it has wide streets
with handsome buildings — the second stories
projecting over the sidewalks—and arcades roofed
with glass, offering shelter in inclement weather.

The Boulevard de la République is a magnificent avenue built sixty feet above the water
level, on arches of stone masonry, and extends
several miles along the bay. It is inclosed on one
side by the principal mosques, hotels and public
squares, and on the other by a balustrade with
occasional openings from which steps or roads
lead down to the water's edge.

The old or Arab part of the town is on the
rise of the hill, above the modern or French portion; the streets which are very narrow and
crooked, form an intricate net-work, their precipitous ascent broken by a series of stone stairs,
the Rue de la Kasba being simply a continuation
of 497 steps. The houses, which are very high,
project from the upper story, almost meeting
mid-air. Bordering these streets are the native
shops, mere niches in the walls, where business is
transacted; the barber shops and cafés presenting
the greatest interest to seekers of novelty. On the
street one is struck by the variety of costumes, the
Jew with fez, dark colored jacket, red sash, and blue
stockings; the Moor in white turban, embroidered jacket, full, short trousers, and white stockings; bare-legged Arabs wrapped in white burnooses; negroes, black as ebony, from Nubia; the

Greek, Spaniard and Maltese; with the French
and native soldiers in their gay uniforms, all jostle
one another in the busy thoroughfares.

The Place Bresson is a lovely square filled
with tropical plants; the Place du Gouvernement
has in its centre an equestrian statue of the Duke
of Orleans; and the Place d'Armes, the former
place of execution, is celebrated as being the spot
where St. Gerónimo was buried alive.

The Kasba — or citadel, once the palace of
the Deys, stands on the summit of the hill overlooking the city. It was here that, in 1827, the
Dey struck the French consul in the face with his
fan, an insult which cost him his empire and led
to the conquest of the city by the French.

Of the several mosques in Algiers, the Old
and the New Mosques are the finest in external
architecture. In accordance with the simplicity
of the Moslem form of worship, their interior
consists of bare white walls, divided into naves by
columns which are wrapped about with matting
to the height of some three feet; the floors are
covered with prayer-rugs; lamps are suspended
from the ceilings, and the Mihrat, a niche in the
wall, indicates the direction in which Mecca lies.
On Friday — which is the Mohammedan Sabbath
— the Moslem repairs to the Mosque, and after his
preliminary ablutions, enters with uncovered feet,
and prostrates himself upon the ground, touching
his forehead frequently to the floor, invariably

turning his face towards Mecca, and apparently
lost to the outward world.

Overlooking the Jardin Marengo is a mosque
and koubba combined, which enshrines the tomb
of the saint Aba-er-Rahman, surrounded by those
of pashas and deys; lights are kept continually
burning on this tomb, which is hung around with
flags, ostrich eggs and other offerings from the
faithful.

On a brow of the hill overlooking the sea is
the handsome church of Notre Dame d'Afrique;
the interior of whose walls are covered with
wooden crutches, and with waxen imitations of
hearts, heads, and limbs, as offerings to its tutelary saint for having effected miraculous cures of
disease in each respective portion of the human
body. Every Sunday afternoon the priest, followed by the devout, marches in procession to a
projecting point overhanging the sea, and per-
forms the service for the dead over that vast
grave.

Directly below the church, on the sands of the
beach, a weird religious ceremony takes place
once a week, at sunrise. A sect composed of
various nationalities — Jew, Arab, Moor, and Ne-
gro — assemble here with their priest to perform
their singular rites, which are supposed to effect
miraculous cures. The afflicted each bring with
them a chicken, which is offered to the priest, who
adroitly cuts its throat in a manner to preserve

the blood; with this he anoints the parts affected, muttering the while certain incantations or exorcisms; after which the subjects proceed to bathe in the cleansing waters of the sea whence they are supposed to issue purified.

The Aïssaoui is another sect of fanatics, somewhat similar to the Dervishes, composed of Arabs, Kabyles, and Negroes, and derives its name from its founder Sidi-Mahomet-Ben-Aïssa. Their religious rites, which are now rarely permitted by the French authorities on account of the barbarity exercised, take place under roof, accompanied by the primitive, monotonous sounds of drums beaten by the hand. Working themselves up to the required pitch of nervous excitement, the fanatics rush with an unearthly yell into the ring, and execute a frantic dance, their bodies swaying and writhing with the violence of their emotions, while they utter growls similar to those of beasts of prey. Among the ceremonies we witnessed were the ordeals of walking barefooted on red-hot irons, the burning flesh impregnating the air with its sickening odor; holding live coals in their mouths; beating their bare breasts with great stones; standing on the sharp edges of swords, running steel blades through their cheeks, tongues, and bodies; and eating live scorpions, and the leaves of the prickly pear.

Three miles from Algiers is the Jardin d'Essai — an extensive farm, with beautiful avenues

of bamboo, palm, date, banana, and magnolia,
where are raised large numbers of ostriches.
These birds which are of white, black, and grey
plumage, are caught on the desert with some difficulty; in order to capture one of them, the speed
of ten swift horses stationed at certain intervals, is
required to run it down. The ostrich averages
200 lbs., is valued at about $300, and lives to the
age of 40 years. Between this garden and the
city is the Arab cemetery where every Friday
afternoon the women assemble to pray upon the
graves of their dead. On the road we passed
caravans of camels, heavily laden with fruit and
various merchandise, on their way to and from
the city.

From Algiers we crossed the Mediterranean,
passing between the islands of Majorca and Min-
orca, and landed on the southern coast of France.

Marseilles is the great commercial seaport of
France on the Mediterranean, and has a population of 325,000. It was founded by the Phœni-
cians 600 years B. C., and in its vicinity is the
battlefield where Hannibal and his Carthagenians
on their march upon Rome encountered the Roman legions.

The quays of Marseilles are magnificent, and
its harbor the finest in France, accommodating
hundreds of vessels, and is so arranged as to allow of the entrance of but one at a time. The
streets are wide and clean, the principal of which

are bordered with trees and handsome buildings;
the Prado, a lovely shaded avenue, several miles
in length, being a favorite drive of an afternoon.
Its principal edifices are, the Church of Notre
Dame de la Garde, located on an eminence, the
Palais de Longchamps; the Cathedral, and the
Bourse.

The Château d'If on a rocky island in the bay,
five miles from Marseilles, was the scene of
Dumas' greatest work of fiction — the Count of
Monte Cristo. The water surrounding the island
is deep and rough but it is accessible by sail boat
in fair weather. On the wall of a prison cell
are still visible the mathematical calculations of
the abbé Ferrier. The size of his small donjon
cell barely measures the length of the narrow
bed that concealed the aperture in the wall,
which he made at cost of such peril and sleepless
vigils, thus enabling the wretched prisoner to com-
municate with Edmond Dantes. A point on the
battlement, reached by stone steps, is shown
where the living sewn up in a bag was thrown
into the sea in place of the dead man; and a rock
two miles distant is seen where Dantes first placed
foot after making his almost miraculous escape.

The Château d'If is also notable as the temporary place of confinement of the man of the
Iron Mask, whose identity is to this day enshrouded in mystery, and of other better known,
but perhaps less distinguished prisoners.

From Marseilles to Nice, the railroad passes through Toulon, the great naval arsenal of France on the Mediterranean, which is strongly fortified, and now considered impregnable. Toulon was taken by the English in August 1793; but as 5,000 troops were inadequate to garrison such extensive works, the important pass of Ollioules on the west was left unguarded, and was entered by 50,000 mad Republicans recking with the gore of the inhabitants of Marseilles and Lyons, who killed all whom they met whether friend or foe. Six thousand were massacred by order of the Committee of Public Safety, of which Robespierre was at the head, notwithstanding the protestations of the French general, Du Gommier, and those of his lieutenant Bonaparte.

It was at Toulon that Napoleon — for the first time in command, had an opportunity of displaying his military genius, and so planted his batteries on the heights as to command all the forts held by the enemy.

A few miles beyond Toulon, on the coast, is the village of St. Raphaël where Napoleon embarked for Elba in 1814, the beginning and closing of his wonderful career taking place in such near proximity.

Cannes, delightfully situated on a bay of the same name, is a winter resort noted for its mild climate. It has many lovely villas, and pleasant walks and drives in every direction.

Nice, on the Mediterranean, with a resident population of 54,000, is a favorite resort on account of its perfect climate. Some of its streets and buildings may compare favorably with those of Paris, while the Promenade des Anglais, which faces the sea, is thronged every afternoon with the élite and fashion of the place.

It was in Nice that Massina was born, 1758, and Garibaldi in 1807. A marble cross commemorates the visit, in 1538, of Pope Paul III., who came to effect a reconciliation between Francis I. of France and Charles V. of Germany, and a monument is also erected in honor of the visit of Pope Pius VII. in 1814.

A charming drive in the suburbs of the city leads to the Franciscan monastery, the road passing through an old Roman amphitheatre and near many lovely villas.

In Nice a specialty is made of bonbons made of the real petals of the violet, orange, and rose, coated with sugar in such manner as to retain their natural fragrance.

Monaco, the smallest sovereign principality in Europe, being only one mile in width, and having an army of only 72 men, projects into the Mediterranean from the south-eastern corner of France, and is protected from the winds of the north, by a spur of the Alps which rises behind it like a vast amphitheatre.

On one of the peninsulas is the town of

Monaco and the palace of Prince Grimaldi, while on the opposite point is Monte Carlo, the famous gambling place of Europe, which the prince rents to a French company for a fabulous sum.

On the top of the mountain stand romantic ruins of old Roman towers, further down, magnificent gardens, filled with palm and date trees, beautiful flowers, and a luxuriance of other tropical growth, while below, the blue curves of the bay, combine to render the scene a most charming one. The Casino is a magnificent harmony of frescoes, gildings, mirrors, and paintings. The Concert room seats 1,000 people, and is free to the habitués of the place, who congregate there daily to listen to the strains of the finest string band in Europe. The Gambling rooms, three in number, open one into the other, and contain seven tables for the game which begins at 12 M. and closes at 11:30 P. M. No one is permitted here under sixteen years of age, but in singular contrast is tottering old age and blooming youth, dazzling beauty and frivolous fashion, nobles, plebeians, actresses, and demi-mondaines, all intent upon the game ; money flowing lavishly, fortunes made and lost in a few hours.

The Cornice road, which extends from Nice to Spezia, runs parallel with the railway skirting the shores of the Mediterranean, passing near a number of small villages and places of resort, one of the most attractive of which is San Rémo.

CHAPTER XVI.

GENOA: TURIN: MILAN: VERONA: VENICE: BOLOGNA: FLORENCE: CARRARA: PISA.

GENOA, is a city of 162,000 inhabitants, built on and between hills overlooking the bay. Its streets are very narrow, especially in the old quarter, and its houses, many of which are of marble, rise to a great height, having as many as eight and ten stories. As a rule the exterior of the houses are stuccoed, painted red or yellow, and frescoed from top to bottom, while the roofs being flat and filled with plants and shrubs serve as a promenade for the owners.

Genoa is especially noted as having been the native city of Columbus, who was born here in 1436. His statue adorns a square in the city, and represents him leaning on an anchor, America kneeling at his feet, and surrounding him figures typical of Wisdom, Strength, Geography and Religion.

The city is celebrated for its delicate filagree work in gold and silver, and is a great manufacturing place for silks and velvets.

The Cathedral of San Lorenzo, a portion of which was a heathen temple of worship in olden times, is built of black and white marble in horizontal stripes, and is adorned with handsome columns, and grotesque figures representing animals. In the treasury of this church is the Sacro Catino, the dish from which it is said Christ ate the Last Supper. It is of dark green glass, ten inches across and four deep, and was kept in the Temple until Cæsarea was taken by the combined armies of Pisa and Genoa, when the latter took it as their share of the booty. So great was the veneration in which this dish was held, the Jews loaned 5,000,000 francs — $1,000,000 — on it, and when on exhibition once a year, it was attached by a strong chain which was held by a priest, and was guarded by twelve noblemen.

The Church of the Annunciation has the finest interior of any in Genoa, being finished in a great variety of marbles, its ceiling and dome frescoed to represent scenes from the Old and New Testaments.

The palaces of Genoa are of marble with an open court inclosed in pillars; the entrance doors or gates are frequently forty feet high, and surmounted by the coat-of-arms of the owner, and both exteriorly and interiorly, they are dingy, damp, cold, and prison-like. The principal of these are the Pallavicini, Doria, Brignoli, and Doria-Torsi palaces, in all of which are fine paintings, while the ducal palace, formerly the residence of the Doges, is now used for public offices.

The Campo Santo, or Cemetery, three miles from Genoa, is on the side of a hill, and is justly celebrated for its many magnificent monuments; these, the best works of Villa, Benetti, and Moreno, are cut from the purest white marble; their originality of design and delicacy of execution, being truly wonderful. The humble graves of the poor offer a striking contrast, being simply mounds of earth surmounted by lanterns.

Seven miles from Genoa is the villa of Count Pallavicini, in the grounds of which are a great variety of plants and trees, miniature mosques, pagodas, and temples, with numerous jets of water, leaping up here and there at most unexpected turns, and a stalactite grotto in which is a small lake, winding through to an opening on the opposite side, where a scene of unexpected beauty greets the eye.

Turin, on the river Po, with a population of 193,000, differing from other Italian towns, is well built, with streets running at right angles, and houses massive and substantial, its several squares containing many fine monuments. In the Piazza Castello stands the old castle of the dukes of Savoy, also the present palace, adjoining, which is the Royal Armory, noted for its fine display of arms. In the chapel of St. Sinode attached to the Cathedral, is preserved the winding sheet of the Saviour.

From Turin, there is a magnificent view of the

Alps, and from this point rail is taken to Iorea, thence stage and horse to the Hospice at the summit of the great St. Bernard.

Milan, the capital of Lombardy, with a population of 261,000 and noted for its manufacture of silk and velvet, is the finest and most modern-built city in Italy, full of activity and thrift, and free from those evidences of decline visible in other Italian cities. It is nearly circular in form, and seven miles around, with thirteen gates of massive proportions, the finest of these being the Porta della Pace, on the Simplon road; it is of marble ornamented with statues, and surmounted by the bronze figure of Peace in a chariot drawn by six horses.

Within the city are the well-preserved remains of an ancient Roman arena, sufficiently large to accommodate 30,000 spectators. Here Napoleon witnessed a regatta in 1807, water having been introduced into it by artificial means.

The Duomo, or Cathedral of Milan, the finest in Italy, is one of the most beautiful existing specimens of Gothic architecture. It is constructed of white marble, from the quarries of Gandolia, which was bequeathed to the Cathedral by Gian Galleazzo, and is in the form of the Latin cross, 477x183 feet, surmounted by hundreds of spires and 4,000 statues. The interior, with its double aisles, lofty arches, and clustered pillars — ninety feet high, and eight in diameter, is very imposing, and beneath the dome are the remains of St. Charles Borromeo, who was archbishop of Milan in the 16th century.

On the wall of the Refectory in the Dominican Church of Santa Maria delle Grazie, is Leonardo da Vinci's fresco of the Last Supper. This, one of his first works — 30 feet in length by 15 in height, occupied sixteen years of his life. Though greatly damaged by dampness, age, and violence — the monks having cut a door through the feet of the principal figure, and Napoleon having used the room for a stable — it is still considered the finest painting in the world.

In the Church of St. Ambrogio where the German emperors received the crown of Lombardy, they claim to have the Brazen Serpent made by Moses in the Wilderness.

The Biblioteca Ambrosiana comprises 175,000 volumes, and 20,000 MSS. among which are, a note-book of Leonardo da Vinci; a lost oration of Cicero; translations from Homer, Josephus, and Livy; and the correspondence of Cardinal Bembo and Lucrezia Borgia, with a lock of her hair.

In the centre of the Piazza della Scala — a public square, is a monument, in Carrara marble, of Leonardo da Vinci surrounded by his pupils. Facing this stands the famous Teatro della Scala, which contains six tiers of boxes seating 4,000 people, and whose acoustic properties are superior to those of any other theatre in the world.

In the Monumental Cemetery is the Cremation house, containing furnaces and all other necessary appliances for the incinerary rites. The body is placed on an iron slide and pushed into an oven which after being rendered air-tight, is brought to intense heat by means of brush twigs, but two hours being required to reduce the body to ashes.

Verona, on the river Adige, with a population of 67,000, was once the capital of the kingdom of Italy, and afterwards that of quite a large territory governed successively by the Scaligers and Vicontis. It was near here Marius fought his famous battle against the Cimbri; here Theodoric the Great won the victory over Odoacer; and in the 13th and 14th centuries transpired the contentions between the Capuletti and Montecchi, which Shakespeare has immortalized in his story of the loves of Romeo and Juliet.

Verona is celebrated as having given birth to Julius Cæsar Scaliger, Caius Secundus, Pliny the elder, whose tragic death occurred at Vesuvius, and Paul Cagliari, surnamed Veronese. The principal objects of interest in the city are, the old Roman amphitheatre, which seated 25,000 persons, and is in a perfect state of preservation: the Church of Zanzenone, in which are the statue of the black African bishop St. Zeno, and the tomb of Guiseppi della Scala to whom Dante refers. The Palazzo del Consiglio is adorned by statues of Catullus Fracastorio, poet and astronomer, Pliny and other sons of Verona.

In a public thoroughfare yet stand, as they have for 500 years, the tombs of the Scaligers, the old lords of Verona; while still to be seen are the houses of the Montagues and Capulets — the latter bearing the armorial crest of the Capulet bonnet: here Juliet's room and balcony are pointed out, and her grave is shown in a remote part of the city. The play of Romeo and Juliet was produced by Shakespeare in 1596, but the original author of the story, a fact not generally known, was Luigi da Porta, a gentleman of Vicenza, who died in 1529.

Venice, the queen of the Adriatic, was founded in 462, by the inhabitants of Aquilera, who fled to the shallow lagunes for safety, when Italy was invaded by Attila. It is built on 117 islands on a bay in the Gulf of Venice, intersected by 150 narrow canals which are spanned by 380 short bridges. As there are few or no sidewalks, the mode of conveyance used either for business or pleasure is the gondola — a long narrow boat rowed by two men who stand erect one at the bow and the other at the stern, propelling it with grace and skill. These boats, which hold from two to six persons, are painted black by legal ordinance which was established to prevent the growing rivalry of extravagance. They are comfortably and luxuriously appointed, but in bad weather a

wooden covering is thrown over that portion
occupied by passengers, which with its gloomy
trappings gives it the appearance of a hearse.

The city is chiefly noted for its glass manufactures and wood carvings, and contains many
fine churches and palaces built mostly after the
Byzantine-Moorish style, while many of its towers
and houses, on account of their sunken founda-
tions, lean almost as much as the Tower of Pisa.
The city by daylight is unattractive, as the houses
are mouldy and out of repair, but by moonlight
it is exceedingly beautiful, showing the light,
open style of architecture to advantage.   Gliding
over the glassy surface of the canals, with music
pulsing in the air, and the sheen of the moonlight
casting a glamour over the scene, is enchanting
and attractive for a time, but after a few weeks'
stay the novelty wears off, and the fact of being
dependent upon a gondola and gondolier gives
one a sense of infinite helplessness; for as some-
one has said: " Venice is a paradise for cripples,
as a man has little use for his legs."

The Grand Canal which is two and a half miles
in length, three hundred feet in width, and six in
depth, runs through the heart of the city in the
form of the letter S.   On it are situated most of
the fine buildings, and mid-way it is spanned by
the famous Ponte di Rialto — a marble bridge
bordered on either side by shops — which connects
the two large islands of Rialto and San Marco.

The Piazza di San Marco is the principal square in the city, where the band plays in the evening, and all Venice promenades from 7 to 9. At 2 P. M. when the clock strikes the hour hundreds of pigeons fly from all directions to its centre to be fed, an old lady having bequeathed her fortune for this purpose. Around this square are the principal cafés, shops, and public buildings, including St. Mark's Church, and the palaces of the Doge and the King. At the water-front are two granite columns from Syria, on one of which is the statue of St. Theodore, the protector of the Republic, standing on an alligator, and on the other the Lion of St. Mark, with one foot on the Bible and another on a ball; between these two columns public executions formerly took place.

St. Mark's Church standing at the head of the Square, was founded in 828 to receive the remains of St. Mark brought from Alexandria, Egypt, and is of the Gothic and Oriental styles. In front of the church are the three staffs which formerly bore the flags of Candia, Cyprus, and Morea, and above the main entrance are the four famous bronze horses of Chian origin. These horses were taken to Constantinople by Theodosius, from thence they were removed by the Venetians, in 1206, when they plundered the capital of the Eastern Empire; they were afterwards carried to Paris by Napoleon, and subsequently restored to Venice. The pulpits and walls of the church are of costly marble decorated with Biblical illustrations in glass mosaic, and of its 500 pillars of alabaster and stone, the four centre ones supporting the canopy over the relics of St. Mark, are said to have been brought from the Temple of Solomon. The altar of the baptistry is formed of a granite slab on which, it is said, Jesus stood when he preached to the inhabitants of Tyre, and near the central portal is a red marble block inserted in the floor marking the spot where Pope Alexander III. was reconciled to the Emperor Frederick Barbarossa, July 23d, 1177.

To the left and right of the church are the bell and clock towers, up the former of which Napoleon rode apparently in imitation of the feat performed by Peter the Great in Copenhagen; while the latter contains a large and complicated clock with two life-size bronze figures of men which strike the hour with sledge hammers.

The Doge's Palace, on the east side of St. Mark's Square, is built of red and white marble, in the Oriental style, and is supported on the Square and water-front sides by colonnades. It is entered by the Giant Staircase, which derives its name from the gigantic statues of Mars and Neptune; besides these are those of Adam and Eve, while ranged around the corridor are busts of celebrated Venetians; here the doge, Marino Faliero, was beheaded for plotting against the Republic.

At the head of the Giant Staircase is The Lion's Mouth — a small hole in the wall formerly covered with a lion's head, in the mouth of which informers were wont to place anonymous communications warning the authorities against suspected conspiracies; this means was not infrequently taken advantage of to gratify personal animosity, and many an innocent victim was arrested and sentenced to death.

Ascending the stairs one enters the Library, which contains the first book printed in Venice, in 1469, and the will of Marco Polo, dated 1324.

The Hall of the Great Council is a vast apartment, its walls and ceiling covered with frescoes, at one end of which is Tintoretto's painting on canvas of Paradise, 84x33½ feet in size, while bordering the walls are the portraits of the 72 doges, that of Marino Faliero being obliterated.

When the patricians governed Venice, plebeians had no vote or voice in state affairs: from the 1500 patricians, 300 senators were chosen; from the senators, a council of 10, who elected from their number a doge, and by secret ballot these 10 chose a council of 3, who judged all political criminals, and from whose sentence there was no appeal: these met at night in the Dark Room, masked, and unknown to each other or even to the Doge. In the vestibule leading into this apartment was another Lion's Mouth in which the patricians deposited their accusations signed with

their own names—unlike those of the plebeians.
The Chamber of the Council of Three is of dark
wood, imparting a gloomy aspect in keeping with
the mystery of their transactions : in closets in
this room were kept their masks and gowns, and
secret passages connected it with the prison.

Mystery and darkness likewise enshrouded all
dealings with the suspected. The accused was
arrested in the secrecy of night and conveyed in a
gondola to the water door of the prison, where he
was confined in a donjon cell, until taken across
the Bridge of Sighs to receive sentence in the
Chamber of the Council of Three, which sentence
invariably meant a horrible death.

> " I stood in Venice, on the Bridge of Sighs ;
> A palace and a prison on each hand."

The Ponte dei Sospiri, or Bridge of Sighs, is
a covered passage, divided by a lengthwise partition, one small window admitting light within,
and permitting to the condemned a last glimpse
of the outer world he was quitting forever.

At the entrance of the Arsenal are the four
marble lions brought from Piræus in 1687, and
within it, is a model of the Bucentaur — the
Doge's gilded barge used at the annual ceremonial of his marriage with the Adriatic when
the nuptial ring dropped into its waves consum-
mated the poetic rites.

In the private palace of Treves are the colossal marble statues of Hector and Ajax, the last works of the great Canova. Of the other objects of general interest in Venice are, the house of Shylock, the "Merchant of Venice," situated in the Jews' quarter near the Grand Canal; that of Cristoforo Moro, the original of Shakespeare's Othello; the house of Desdemona, now a part of the Grand Hotel; the house of Lucrezia Borgia, now a museum; and the palace occupied by Lord Byron while writing his beautiful description of Venice.

The Church of Santa Maria di Frari, magnificently adorned with a variety of marbles, contains the beautiful monuments to Titian and Canova, and a most peculiar one to the Doge Giovanni Pessaro, consisting of four gigantic Nubians in black marble, their drapery of a strongly contrasting white marble, bearing on their heads sacks of India coffee.

While in Venice we witnessed a grand illumination on land and water, given in honor of a visit from the English fleet. An immense barge gay with colored lights, and flags of all nations, and bearing a fine band of music, was drawn by smaller boats, and followed by hundreds of illuminated gondolas, through the canals. These latter were bordered by brilliantly-lighted buildings, while colored rockets sped like meteors through the air.

Taking rail from Venice in a southerly direction, we stopped at Bologna, celebrated for its
manufacture of sausages; crossed the Apennines
range, having a succession of beautiful views, and
passed through Pistoria, where pistols were originally manufactured, and whence they took their
name; and near here Cataline was defeated and
slain.

Florence, in the province of Tuscany, on both
banks of the Arno, has a population of 170,000.
It has been immortalized by Byron and Rogers,
and revered as the birthplace of Dante, Petrarch,
Boccaccio, Galileo, Michael Angelo, Leonardo da
Vinci, Benvenuto Cellini, and Andræa del Sarto.

In the Piazza della Signoria stands the Palazzo Vecchio, formerly the residence of the superior magistrate, near which is the Fountain of
Neptune on the site where the reformer, Savona-
rola, suffered martyrdom; and under the Loggia
di Lanzi are fine sculptures of the Rape of the
Sabines by Giovanni di Bologna; Perseus, by
Benvenuto Cellini; the Rape of Polixena; and
the Dying Ajax.

Florence is noted for her large collections of
the fine arts; and for the manufacture of mosaics,
which are composed of colored stones blended
with such artistic skill as to resemble the most
delicate painting.

The Uffizi Gallery, one of the largest and
most valuable collections existing, contains Titian's

Venus Reposing; the Mater Dolorosa by Sasso-
ferrato; and the marble statues of the Venus di
Medici, found in Hadrian's villa during the reign
of the Medici; the Wrestlers; the Young Ath-
lete; and the Dancing Faun; besides a vase cut
from a single block of Lapis Lazuli 14 inches in
diameter; and a mosaic table, which required the
labor of fifteen years, and is valued at $200,000.

The Pitti Palace the residence of the king
when in Florence, has a collection of 500 paintings by old masters; the most celebrated of these
are Raphaël's Madonna della Seggiola,—or Madonna of the chair; Titian's Magdalene; Murillo's
Madonna and Child; and a painting representing
Diogenes in the act of throwing away his cup on
seeing a boy drink from his hand; besides these
are Canova's sculptured Venus, and other fine
marbles.

In the Academy of Fine Arts are Michael Angelo's colossal statue of David; and a fair collection of paintings by modern artists; while in the
National Museum formerly the State prison are
Michael Angelo's Leda and the Swan; and Giovanni di Bologna's Mercury in bronze.

The Tribuna dedicated to the memory of
Galileo contains his statue in marble; also, in a
glass case, one of his fingers; and his telescope
and other astronomical instruments. On the walls
are three beautiful frescoes representing scenes in
the life of this great astronomer; one depicting

him in the Cathedral at Pisa swinging the lamp
from which he originated the theory of the pendulum; another, his demonstration of the power
of the telescope before the Doge and Council of
Ten; and the last representing him as blind with
one hand resting on the globe, the other pointing
heavenward as he demonstrates to his pupils the
motion of the heavenly bodies.

The house in which Dante was born is still
extant; and in that of Michael Angelo, the illustrious Italian painter, sculptor, and architect,—
born in 1474 and died in 1564 — are his manuscripts, swords, canes, designs, and his portrait by
himself.

The Cathedral of Santa Maria del Fiore, built
of black and white marbles, has the largest
dome in the World, and served as a model for that
of St. Peter; its campanile — or bell-tower —
designed by Giotto, rises to a height of 275 feet;
and near it are the statues of the two architects
Arnolfo and Brunelleschi, while not far off is the
Seat of Dante where the poet contemplated the
beauties of the Cathedral.

The Baptistry, built after the model of the
Pantheon at Rome, from material taken from the
temple of Mars, contains Ghilberti's celebrated
bronze doors representing scenes from the Old
and New Testaments, which Michael Angelo declared worthy of being the gates of Paradise.

The Church of Santa Croce is the favorite

burial-place; and contains the tombs of, and fine
monuments to Dante, Galileo and Michael Angelo
Buonarrotti.   Over the entrance are the letters
I. H. S.— anglicized Jesus Saviour of Men —
placed there by St. Bernadino of Sienna; who,
reproving one of his flock for the manufacture of
playing cards, suggested the substitution of these
letters for the usual characters.   The unique
novelty of the inscription pleased the popular fancy
and the sale of his cards realized him a fortune.

In the Church of Ognisanti is the tomb of the
discoverer Amerigo Vespucci marked only by a
simple slab; and in the Church of San Lorenzo
is the Medicean Chapel, originally intended for
the Holy Sepulchre, which the Tuscans intended
stealing from Jerusalem, but failed in the attempt.
The Chapel contains some magnificent mosaics
and frescoes; the walls are inlaid with valuable
marbles and precious stones, with armorial bearings the very perfection of mosaic art.   Here are
the tombs of Guiliano and Lorenzo di Medici, and
of other members of that wicked race.

The Cascine is the Hyde Park of Florence,
deriving its name from the dairy houses of the
Grand Duke; here the fashion of the city congregate of an afternoon, for the society of Florence
makes no further requirements than an attendance at the Opera, and an equipage in the
Cascine.

Carrara is celebrated for its perfect white

marble, which is used exclusively for statuary.
The quarries, of which there are several, are on
the side of a mountain overlooking the town, and
give employment to about 6,000 men. The
marble having been blasted, the huge blocks are
carried by rail down the mountain side and hauled
by ten or more oxen to the mills where they are
sawed into more portable size. In the town are
several fine studios of which Pietro Lazzerini's is
the best known.

Pisa, an ancient and much decayed city, is on
the Arno, five miles from its mouth, and contains
50,000 inhabitants. The Leaning Tower, 183
feet in height, is built of white marble, and consists of eight stories, with outside galleries, which
project seven feet, with an interior ascent of 294
stone steps. The topmost story overhangs the
base on one side 14 feet, and underneath this
point Galileo is said to have studied the principles
of gravity. This tower was erected by Bonanno of
Pisa, in 1174, and has probably taken its present
inclination from the sinking of the earth at its
foundation, although the Pisans claim it to have
been produced by a miracle of architectural skill.

The Cathedral which is composed of a variety
of marbles has several old paintings and fine
statues, while in the nave is suspended the large
bronze lamp, the swinging of which first suggested
to Galileo the theory of the pendulum.

The Baptistry situated opposite the Cathedral

is an immense circular building 160 feet in height surmounted by a cupola ; its interior is rich in marbles and mosaics, and contains a pulpit of exquisite workmanship.

The Campo Santo is the most ancient burial ground of any in Italy, and the earth in this inclosure was brought from Jerusalem in 50 galleys in the year 1228.

In the Piazza di Cavalieri is the Torre della Fame, or Tower of Fame, celebrated by Dante's description, and near this is the palace Lanfranchi where Lord Byron dwelt with the Countess Guicioli, and wrote his Werner and Don Juan.

A small insignificant-looking house in the via Forbesas bears a marble slab with the inscription : "Galileo Galilei was born here February 18th, 1564." This eminent astronomer and inventor of the telescope, undertook in Rome, to demonstrate the theory of the Solar System discovered by Copernicus, but his theories being in advance of the unenlightened age in which he lived, aroused the ire of the priest-ridden people, and he was thrown into prison and compelled to deny his principles ; on his release, however, he exclaimed : "*eppúr si muove*,"—"but it does move after all."

The rail from Pisa to Rome passes through Leghorn, celebrated for its manufacture of straw hats, and in sight of the small island where Garibaldi is buried, and of that of Elba, the scene of Napoleon's first exile.

CHAPTER XVII.

ROME, — ITS ENVIRONS.

ROME is the most celebrated of European cities, famous in both ancient and modern history. It was once the capital of the most powerful nation of antiquity, and later the ecclesiastical capital of Christendom, and the place of residence of the Pope; since 1871 it has become the capital of United Italy and the city where the king holds his court.

Rome is situated on both banks of the Tiber, 16 miles from its mouth, and has a population of 250,000. It once boasted 4,000,000 inhabitants, and its area encompassed seven hills, several of which are now marked but by ruins and decay.

The origin of the city is involved in mystery, but the generally conceived idea is that it was founded 753 years B. C. by Romulus and Remus who, as the legend runs, were found on the banks of the river by a she-wolf, which had come to drink of the stream, carried them into her den hard by and suckled them.

The Palatine Hill was first settled by a Greek colony under Evander 2,000 years B. C. and was afterwards the site of the city founded by Romu-

lus, who inclosed it with a square wall, which
gave it the name of Roma quadrata.   Just outside
of this wall was the sacred boundary over which
Remus leaped in token of his contempt, and
thereby incurring his brother's resentment was
slain by him.

At the beginning of the Empire Augustus
built the first palace on the Palatine, to which were
subsequently added those of Tiberius, Caligula,
Domitian, and Septimus Severus, and consolidated
into one is called the Palace of the Cæsars.
Among the ruins of this palace is the temple of
Jupiter Stator where the Lares and Penates, or
household gods, were enshrined; where Nero
condemned St. Paul to death, and where Cicero
delivered his first scathing denunciation against
Catiline; and in the palace of Domitian is an
amphitheatre where foot-races and other sports
took place.   Near by is the Circus Maximus,
the scene of the rape of the Sabines by the
Romans.

The Capitoline Hill was the citadel of ancient
Rome.   It was betrayed by Tarpeia, the daughter of the warden of the gates, to the Sabines, who
entered the city, and after a time reigned jointly
with the Romans.   It was in this citadel that were
kept the sacred geese whose cackling, on the approach of the Gauls, aroused the garrison and
thus saved Rome; and it was from the Tarpeian
Rock that the Roman commander Marcus Man-

lius on this occasion, hurled the enemy headlong down the precipice.

The Temple of Jupiter Capitolinus adjoins the Senate-chamber upon the steps of which Rienzi — the last of the Tribunes — fell beneath the daggers of the populace while attempting his escape.

The Capitoline Museum, in front of which there is a fine equestrian statue of Marcus Aurelius, and also of the twin heroes of the mythological era, Castor and Pollux, contains the following celebrated statuary: The Dying Gladiator, the Faun of Praxiteles, the Venus of the Capitol, Romulus and Remus nursed by the wolf, heroic figures of Julius and Augustus Cæsar, busts of other Roman Emperors, besides a beautiful ancient mosaic of Pliny's Doves.

The Roman Forum, which occupies the low land between the Palatine and Capitoline hills, was formerly the market-place and general place of assembly; here was the scene of important social, religious, and political events, and here were grouped the finest buildings of ancient Rome. The Forum is crossed by the Via Sacra, or Sacred Way, over which the household gods were carried from the Palatine to the Temple of Jupiter on the Capitoline, and where returning victors marched in triumphal procession. Its ruins comprise the temples of the Sun, of Saturn, Concord, Janus, Castor and Pollux, Faustina, and Vespasian; the Colonnade of the Twelve Gods, the column of Phocus, the Basilicas Julia and Constantine, the house of Julius Cæsar, the Tabularium — or House of Records, — and the arches of Septimus Severus, Constantine, and Titus.

The Arch of Titus has on one side a bas-relief of this Emperor returning in triumphal procession from Jerusalem, while on the other is a representation of the seven-branched candlestick, and through this arch it is said Josephus marched, a prisoner, with other captives.

The Forum was the scene of the death of Virginia, and the ruins of the shop where Virginius snatched the knife to save his daughter's honor, is still extant. Here is the rostrum where Mark Antony made his oration over the dead body of Julius Cæsar, the spot where it was burnt and the ashes buried; also the rostrum from which Cicero discoursed, and where, after his death, his head and hands were exposed to public gaze.

In the centre of the Forum once stood a column on which was enscribed the distance from Rome, of every important city in the world; hence the expression used : " that all roads lead to Rome."

In close proximity to the Forum is the Mamertine Prison — an underground donjon where Saint Peter and Saint Paul were confined, and in it is a spring of water which is said, gushed forth to enable Saint Peter to baptize his converted jailers.

The Colosseum, a vast amphitheatre was

commenced by Vespasian and finished by Titus,
A. D. 80. It is 157 feet high, 1,900 in circumference, and was built by 60,000 captive Jews,
who were engaged ten years in its construction.
It once seated 87,000 spectators, the seats rising
in tiers one above another; the Emperor's box
occupied a prominent position, and on either side
of it sat the Senators and the Vestal Virgins.
Beneath are subterranean passages and chambers
where both men and beasts were confined, and
whence they were brought into the arena by
means of elevators. After the close of the
gladiatorial sports, water was let in by means of
aqueducts, and galleys introduced for the purpose of representations of naval engagements.
At the inauguration of the Colosseum, the festivities of which lasted 100 days, 5,000 wild beasts
and 10,000 captives were slain and many Christian martyrs perished.

The Golden House of Nero, so called from its
magnificence and splendor, and which was inlaid
with gold and mother-of-pearl, still shows on its
walls the remains of exquisite frescoes, a design
from which was adopted by Napoleon for the
standard of his army. In the portico stood a
colossal bronze statue of Nero 120 feet in height,
the mutilated remains of which are now to be
seen in the capitol. It is said to have been for
the purpose of enlarging the grounds around his
palace that Nero caused a portion of Rome to be

burned: his name was so obnoxious to the people
on account of his many crimes, that after his
death his palace was partly buried under ground,
and on top of it Titus built his magnificent and
extensive baths.

The Castle of St. Angelo, formerly the mausoleum of Hadrian, and the tomb of subsequent
emperors to the time of Septimus Severus, was
during the middle ages converted into a fortress
and prison. In its donjon cells were confined
and tortured Galileo and Beatrice Cenci, and the
square opposite was the scene of the execution of
that unfortunate girl. The Castle is now connected with the Vatican by a covered passage,
and here the popes take refuge in times of trouble.

The Baths of Caracalla, a superb ruin, were
built by that emperor in 212, and covered 140,-
000 square yards. They consisted of swimming,
hot, and steam baths, with an accommodation for
1,600 bathers, and were surrounded by pleasure
grounds and stadium—or course for foot-races.
Among these ruins were found the marble group
of the Farnese Bull.

The Vatican, the residence of the Pope, is the
largest palace in the world, having 5,000 apartments and 20 courts. The Sistine chapel contains the Last Judgment, by Michael Angelo — a
painting 60 feet in height by 30 in length. The
Library has 120,000 volumes and manuscripts,
besides many fine vases, and the largest block of

malachite known. The Gallery of Sculpture and Painting is considered one of the most complete and valuable in existence, and comprises among its statuary the Apollo Belvidere, the Laocöon, Ariadne, and Cleopatra; among the paintings are Raphäel's Transfiguration, the Communion of St. Jerome, by Domenichino; the Baptism of Constantine, and the Crucifixion of St. Peter, by Guido Reni. In the Museum are, a Roman chariot, an iron grating used for cremation, the porphyry sarcophagus of the daughter and wife of Constantine, and the Pope's state carriage, containing his arm-chair, and a seat for his Prime Minister.

Of the other palaces of Rome are, the Royal — the residence of the King; the Barberini, in which are the portraits of Guido's Beatrice Cenci, and Raphäel's Fornarina; the Spada where is the marble statue of Pompey — formerly in the Senate-chamber — at the base of which "great Cæsar fell;" the Borghese, with a valuable collection of old and rare paintings; the Rospigliosi, which contains Guido's fresco of Aurora strewing flowers before Apollo in his chariot of the Sun; the Farnese, once the residence of Pope Paul III.; and the Borghese villa, in which are the statues of Pauline Borghese, by Canova, David with his sling, and Daphne being transformed into a laurel tree.

St. Peter's, the great marvel of ecclesiastical architecture, is built on the site of the Basilica erected by Constantine upon that of the Circus of Nero, and on the very spot consecrated by the blood of the martyrs slaughtered by order of that tyrant. The present edifice was begun during the reign of Pope Julius in 1506, and completed at a cost of $60,000,000, the architects being Bramante and Michael Angelo. It is built of white traverstine stone, in the form of a Latin cross, is 607 feet in length, 448 in height, and covers 8 acres of ground. At its entrance are the equestrian statues of Constantine and Charlemagne, and its dome is surmounted by a ball capable of holding sixteen people. In the interior are 46 altars and 400 statues of saints and popes, while the dome and walls are covered with beautiful marbles and glass mosaic pictures. In the centre of the church is a bronze baldachino over the remains of St. Peter and St. Paul; at the extreme end is the gilded tribune containing the chair of St. Peter, while his statue in bronze is an object of great veneration to the devout, whose kisses, through successive generations, have considerably reduced the proportions of the toe. In the Sacristy are the robes of the pope — 14 in number — and the crown and mitre of St. Peter, with which, on rare occasions, his statue is adorned.

St. Paul's, next to St. Peter's, is the most magnificent church in Rome. It is rich in variegated marbles, malachite altars, oriental alabaster pillars, besides 80 granite columns, and 261 mo-

saic medallions of the popes, from St. Peter to
Leo XIII.

Of the remaining 365 churches in Rome, may
be mentioned that of St. John Lateran, where
the coronation of the popes take place, and in
whose Baptistry Charlemagne was crowned.   It
was in its font that Constantine was baptized, and
Rienzi bathed, for which sacrilegious act he was
excommunicated by the Church.

In a building opposite is the Scala Santa — or
Holy Staircase, supposed to be those of Pilate's
house which Christ was compelled to ascend to
receive sentence.   On the steps are spots of His
blood which are reverently kissed by those who
following His footsteps, ascend on their knees.
Down this stairway, contrary to usage, Luther
walked, in defiance of the superstitious reverence
of the Catholics.

The Pantheon — as its name signifies — was
formerly a Pagan temple, in niches of which once
stood statues of gods and goddesses, now a mausoleum for the late King Victor Emanuel II., and
for Raphäel the artist ; once the scene of the dei-
fication of heroes, and again that of the canoniza-
tion of martyrs.

The Church of Santa Maria dei Angeli, built on
the site of the Baths of Diocletian, contains several
fine paintings, and an ancient sun meridian on the
pavement.

The Church of St. Peter-in-chains has Michael

Angelo's statue of Moses, and contains the chains which once bound St. Peter.

In the Church of St. Maria della Concezione is Guido Reni's famous painting of St. Michael, and in its vaults are the remains of 4,000 departed Capuchin monks whose skeletons are ranged in hideous and ghastly attitudes.

The Church of St. Sebastiana is over the Catacombs where St. Sebastian is buried, and contains one of the arrows with which he was pierced, and a stone bearing a footprint of Christ.

Among other points of interest in Rome are the Temple of Vesta where the Vestal Virgins guarded the sacred fire, the Mausoleum of Augustus now a circus, the Theatre of Marcellus now the palace of the Orsini, the Temples of Juno and Minerva, the Portico of Octavia, the Baths of Agrippa and of Diocletian, the Temple of Fortune, the Theatre and Senate-hall of Pompey — the place where Cæsar fell, the Villa of Sallust, the Aqueduct of Nero, the Column of Marcus Aurelius, the Obelisk of Augustus Cæsar, the houses of Rienzi, Beatrice Cenci, and Tasso, in the latter of which the poet died, the Fountain of Treve, the Forums of Augustus, Nerva, Domitian, and Trajan, — the latter containing the column from which Napoleon modelled the Column Vendome, and the remains of the Sublician Bridge which was defended by Horatio alone.

While in Rome we were especially favored by

an audience with his holiness Pope Leo XIII.
The stipulated written requirements of toilet were,
for gentlemen, full dress, for ladies, black, with lace
mantillas of the same sombre hue covering the
head.

Arriving at the Vatican we passed the Swiss
Guard, in their gay striped uniforms, and were
ushered by attendants in red satin and knee-
breeches through several apartments until we
reached the one in which we were left to await the
entrance of the Pope.   As he entered, surrounded
by his cardinals, all present knelt, comformably to
etiquette, while he passed around the circle laying
his hand in blessing upon the bowed head of each
of his visitors.   The more devout kissing his foot
and the hem of his garment.   Pope Leo XIII. is
a man of 70, tall, slender, and very frail, so weak
as to be unable to walk without assistance.

We also witnessed the Carnival in Rome
which begins several days before the commence-
ment of Lent.   The balconies on the Corso were
decorated with bright-colored bunting, and
thronged with grotesquely-costumed masquerad-
ers.   Certain days are allotted for the throwing of
flowers and confetti, but horse-racing down the
Corso being now abandoned, this festival has lost
much of its zest, and though mask balls take
place every night, and other amusements are
indulged in, the Carnival is altogether inferior to
that of many other cities.

The Appian way, which extends from Rome to Brindisi, was first made in 312 B. C., by Appius Claudius. It was bordered with temples, villas, and tombs, for it was the custom of the Romans to bury their dead on either side of the principal roads leading from the city. The monuments yet remaining are the Columbraria, or Pagan Sepulchre, which is an underground chamber with niches in the walls where were placed the cinerary urns; the tomb of the Scipios, and that of Caecelia Metella, daughter of Crassus. On the Via Appia are also the Circus Maximus, where the chariot races occurred, and the aqueducts of Claudius and Marcia.

Tivoli is a Sabine town nestling at the foot of the mountains. Near it are the romantic villages of Santangelo and Monticelli, and en route from Rome are passed the camping ground of Hannibal; Palatio, where Lucretia killed herself, unable to survive her dishonor, and Gabbi, which was taken by the Romans under Tarquin through the artifices of his son Sextus.

Hadrian's Villa, on the slopes of Tivoli, once covered an area of several square miles. Its magnificent grounds unequalled in the Roman Empire, were designed by Hadrian to combine models of all that had most pleased him during his travels; accordingly they comprised palaces, temples, theatres, circuses, and many of the finest specimens of statuary. This mundane paradise was destroyed by the Goths in the 6th century, and many of the finest of the antique statues were uncovered from beneath these ruins.

CHAPTER XVIII.

NAPLES: VESUVIUS: HERCULANEUM: POMPEII: CAS-
TELLAMARE: SORRENTO: CAPRI: CASERTA: BRIN-
DISI.

NAPLES, which was founded by a Greek colony 1,000 years B. C., has 450,000 inhabitants, and though prettily situated on the curves of the bay which bears the same name, is not so fascinating that one would wish to "see Naples and die." Approaching from the sea, the city at a distance, stretching lazily down to the blue waters, with the old fortress of St. Elmo towering in the background and mighty Vesuvius standing sentinel, as it has stood since the beginning of time, is extremely picturesque, but on closer view the pleasing illusion is dispelled. The streets, with few exceptions, are narrow and filthy; the houses are of several stories and swarming with occupants— many families huddled under one roof — poor, ragged, and uncleanly.

The Neapolitans as a class are apparently devoid of feeling, as is evidenced by their cruelty to their beasts of burden; a characteristic feature being their country wagons loaded with from twenty to thirty people and drawn by one poor, staggering animal.

A strange sight witnessed on the streets of Naples is a funeral procession. The coffin — the corpse often exposed to view — is borne on an open bier by monks of the order of Misericorde concealed underneath the velvet pall, while preceding and following it are others bearing lighted candles, and completely enveloped in white garments in which are small openings for the eyes.

This city is celebrated for its manufacture of corals, shell, and maccaroni; the latter is a favorite article of diet with the lazzaroni who may be seen swallowing it by the yard, as they lounge about the streets.

The fashionable drive extends for several miles along the bay, and is bordered on one side by the National Park; here large crowds congregate in the cool of the evening to admire the views and enjoy the refreshing breeze from the sea.

In Naples are the fine marble statue of Dante, and the equestrian figures, in bronze, of Charles III. and of Ferdinand I.

The Royal Palace is of no special interest, but adjoining it is the Theatre of San Carlo, at the entrance of which are the bronze horses presented by the Emperor Nicholas of Russia.

The Castle of St. Elmo is built on a high hill overlooking the city. It was erected by Robert the Wise in 1343, and its numerous historic reminiscences of love and daring render it an object of interest to the romantically inclined.

The Cathedral is supposed to occupy the site of the Temple of Apollo, and contains the tombs of Charles I. of Anjou, and of Charles Martel and his wife Clementina of Hapsburg.

The Grotto of Posilippo is an old Roman tunnel 750 yards long and 60 feet high, on the road between Naples and Puteoli. Over the entrance of this tunnel is the tomb of Virgil — a chamber containing 10 niches for cinerary urns, that of Virgil having once, it is said, occupied the centre of the sepulchre.

The National Museum of Naples is interesting and extensive, comprising large collections of paintings, mosaics, statues, frescoes, and inscriptions, many of which were found in the excavations made in Herculaneum and Pompeii. Here are the Farnese Bull, considered one of the finest groups of ancient art; the Psyche of Capua— which inspired Bulwer's conception of Ione ;—the Dancing Faun ; a mosaic pavement bearing the figure of a dog, from the house of Glaucus; shopsigns from Pompeii ; and the marble pillar which stood in its forum, upon which is a bronze plate that once served as a bulletin board ; also the remains of fruit, milk, loaves of bread, a variety of

household utensils, and a Roman calendar on a
square block of marble, each side embracing the
period of three months.

Taking a conveyance with three horses, from
Naples we drove a distance of 6 miles to Herculaneum. This town, which with Pompeii was
overwhelmed by an eruption of Vesuvius, unlike
the latter was buried under lava, to the depth of
80 feet, which in cooling acquired the consistency
of stone, rendering excavations virtually imprac-
ticable; so far the principal building unearthed is
the theatre which once seated 10,000 people.

From Herculaneum we commenced the ascent
of Vesuvius, the road winding for five miles up
the mountain in the midst of a vast stretch of lava
in its various stages of induration. At the foot of
the cone a chain-railway ascends almost perpendicularly a distance of one mile; from here we
were borne in chairs on the shoulders of excited
Neapolitans to the crater. At this point the
ground was a mass of steaming, yellow sulphur;
sulphurous clouds, with their asphyxiating fumes,
hovered around, wavering and dispersing here and
there before the violence of the ascending flame.
Up from the seething cauldron of the crater, red-
hot stones and liquid lava were thrown with
incredible force high in air; and far below, from
the very bowels of the earth, issued low, rumbling,
ominous sounds, all uniting in one vivid conception of hell.

Pompeii, which contained 40,000 inhabitants, was overwhelmed A. D. 79, by an eruption of Vesuvius, and remained buried under the ashes for 1,700 years. Walking through this dead city, its silent streets, which are well paved, though worn in deep ruts by the wheels of chariots, its sidewalks bordered with straight lines of houses and shops in a surprising state of preservation, one almost expects to meet the inhabitants at every turn. Here are public buildings — the Forum with its temples and basilicas; theatres for tragedy and comedy; shops, with their fixtures and utensils; baths, fountains, the Temple of Isis, houses of pleasure with the frescoes still visible upon their walls; private residences from the cottage of the poor to the mansion of the patrician, including those of Arbaces the Egyptian, Glaucus the tragic poet, Ione, and Sallust, and the Villa of Diomedes the wealthy, an edifice twelve stories in height, in whose cellars 17 human bodies were found in various attitudes showing their efforts to escape.

Leading from the Herculaneum Gate is the Street of Tombs lined on either side by sepulchral monuments.

Castellamare occupies the site of Stabia, which was destroyed by an earthquake A. D. 79: from here we witnessed the strange and fearful sight of a river of red-hot lava rolling slowly down the sides of Vesuvius.

The drive from here to Sorrento is a delightful one, skirting the blue shores of the bay, winding along the base of the mountains, crossing ravines and passing picturesque villages.

Sorrento, with a fine view of Vesuvius and the Bay of Naples, is celebrated as the birthplace of Tasso — 1544. Here the Tarantella is danced in all its original grace and vivacity by the peasants in their picturesque costumes.

The Island of Capri, ten miles from Sorrento, is 1980 feet above the level of the sea, and is chiefly noted for its Blue Grotto. This is an interior space 160x80 feet in extent, and 40 feet in height above the water, which is 8 fathoms deep. It is entered by an aperture only three feet high — ingress being impossible during high tide — and the visitor is compelled to recline in the boat as it passes under the low portal. The Grotto is lighted only from the opening, and the reflection from the deep-blue water gives a weird and indescribable effect to the scene.

Brindisi, once the great seaport town of the Romans on the Adriatic, is the terminus of the Via Appia, and is noted as the place where Cæsar beseiged Pompey, and where Virgil died 19 B. C.

Taking steamer of the Peninsular and Oriental Line, at Brindisi, we skirted the shores of Albania and Greece, passing the islands of Corfu, Kephalonia, and Crete, arriving, after a three days' sail, on the coast of Africa.

CHAPTER XIX.

ALEXANDRIA : CAIRO : HELIOPOLIS : PYRAMIDS OF GIZEH :
THE NILE : TEL-EL-KEBIR : PORT SAID.

ALEXANDRIA, situated on a peninsula between
Lake Mareotis and the sea, was founded by Alexander the Great, 332 B. C. It was once celebrated
for its library of 700,000 volumes, which was
established by Ptolemy Philadelphus, 284 B. C.,
and partly destroyed by Julius Cæsar ; also for
its lighthouse Pharos, the seventh wonder of the
world.

It was in Alexandria the Christian religion
first took root, and here St. Mark preached the
Gospel.

One of the few relics of antiquity yet remaining is Pompey's Pillar — a red granite column 100
feet high, on which is a Greek inscription showing
that it was erected by Publius, prefect of Egypt,
in honor of Diocletian who besieged and took
Alexandria, 296 A. D.

Its population numbered at one time 500,000,
but the present census shows only 212,000 inhabitants. The city has many fine streets and buildings, but the heart of it is in ruins, having been
burned by Arabi's soldiers on evacuating, and the

fortifications surrounding the city were dismantled
by the English in the late bombardment.

The rail from Alexandria to Cairo—a distance
of 131 miles — runs parallel with the canal and
wagon road, and affords scenes of varied interest:
here groups of natives scantily clothed; there
caravans laden with merchandise; and frequently
an immense camel, a buffalo, and a tiny donkey
yoked together to a primitive wooden plough, or
employed turning a *sakieh*—a wheel upon
which are fastened earthen jugs to dip up water for
irrigating purposes. Again at short distances is
seen the *shadoof*,—a long pole balanced on an upright one, at one end of which is a weight, and on
the other a vessel which is lowered into the water
and raised filled; and a still more primitive
mode of irrigation is that of men dipping up the
water in mat baskets and pouring it over the
earth, while others direct its course with their
bare feet, as described in the Bible.

Cairo, founded by the Arabs, is situated near
the right bank of the Nile, and has a population
of 350,000. It is the largest city in Africa, and
the residence of the Khedive, and next to Constantinople the most important city of the Mohammedan world.

Cairo is built on low ground, partly surrounded
by low, rugged, and barren hills. Many of its
streets are wide, well paved, and bordered with
tropical trees, and its hundreds of mosques and

minarets viewed from an eminence, combine to
make a picture of Oriental beauty: but the pas-
sage-ways of the older, native portion of the city
are narrow, dirty, and crowded, and it is both difficult and disagreeable to thread one's way through
its swarms of debased humanity.

On the streets of Cairo one sees Oriental life in
its native aspect; the various sects and ranks
arrayed in their distinctive garbs, the ladies of the
harems—attended by the inevitable black eunuchs
— richly dressed and be-jewelled, with thin gauze
covering their faces below the eyes, and their
finger-nails stained with the red henna; the fat
Turk astride a small donkey whose deafening bray
protests, to the extent of its no small ability,
against the thickly falling blows of the urchin who
follows on behind for that purpose; hundreds of
camels moaning under their heavy loads; the
water-carriers selling water from their dirty goat-
skins; the oil dealers with their primitive jars,
recalling so vividly the story of the Forty
Thieves; and the grand official in his equipage
before which run two bare-legged Arabs in gold-
embroidered jackets, loose white trousers, and red
fez, with long sticks in their hands, shouting, in
loud tones, a command to clear the way for the
high and mighty Somebody; all of which gives
a suggestion of out-door life at Cairo, and recalls
at every turn vivid scenes from the Arabian
Nights.

The people as a class, are filthy, ignorant, and
mendicant, and owing to the combined influences
of indolence and cowardice, the men mutilate
themselves in order to avoid being drafted into
the army. The turban is held in high favor by
the Egyptian, especially by the *fellahs:* it consists of a light, white material wound around the
fez, and is always of sufficient length to be converted into a shroud. The women are partial to
jewelry, often wearing rings in their noses. They
carry their infants astride their left shoulder or
hip, and the children, not being allowed to brush
the flies from their faces owing to some religious
prejudice, are consequently generally blind or sore-
eyed.

The bazaars occupy several squares of the narrowest streets which are roofed over with straw
mats and palm-leaves effectually excluding the
glare and heat of the sun. The shops are two feet
above the level of the street, and are from five to
ten feet square, each one having its own specialty,
and the aggregate presenting an array of almost
every commodity desired.

The Citadel stands on a high hill, and commands a fine view of the city. It is surrounded
by a wall, and in its inclosure is the palace of the
pasha, and the magnificent mosque of Mohammed
Ali, built of Oriental alabaster, and the finest in
Egypt. Within the citadel is Joseph's Well — a
square shaft 15 feet across and 280 deep — cut in

the solid rock, at the bottom of which donkeys are kept at work forcing the water to the top. This well is supposed to be the work of the ancient Egyptians and was discovered by the Sultan Saladin while erecting the citadel, who called it Yusef — or Joseph — after himself. It was from the outer wall of this citadel that occurred the memorable leap of the mameluke Emin Bey, who being entrapped, with 300 of his comrades, by Mohammed Ali, and seeing them all perish before his eyes, urged his horse over the precipice to the frightful depths below, and thus effected his escape.

The Mosque of Sultan Hassan is considered the finest existing specimen of Arabian architecture, and its high dome and lofty minarets present a majestic appearance. It is said the Sultan was so much pleased with its construction that he caused the hands of the architect to be cut off to prevent him from designing another like it.

The Mosque of Tayloon, the most ancient in Cairo, is partly in ruins and according to one legend occupies the spot where Abraham sacrificed the goat in place of his son Isaac, and is called Kal-at-el-Rebsh — or Castle of the Goat. Another legend points out this spot as being the place where Noah's ark ran aground on the 10th of Moharrem which is the first month of the Arabian year, and observed as a great festival in this country.

The Palace of Shoobra, in whose court there is a small lake around which are ranged divans where the Sultan and his suite were wont to lounge, sipping their coffee and smoking their *nargileh*, was the summer residence of Mohammed Ali. It is four miles beyond the city precincts, and is reached by a beautiful avenue shaded on either side by the flowering acacia. This is the favorite drive of the people of Cairo, and on a Sunday afternoon the Khedive may be seen there in royal state, escorted by a mounted guard.

The tombs of the Mamelukes and Caliphs at the foot of the citadel resemble miniature mosques, and are not only picturesque in appearance but are interesting from their historic associations.

Old Cairo, which is a short distance from the new city, and now almost a mass of ruins, is built on the site of new Babylon, which was founded by the Babylonians in the year 525 B. C.

The Jewish Synagogue is claimed by the Jews to have been the place where Elijah once appeared, and where Moses prayed for the cessation of the seventh plague of lightning and hail. In a niche, within this edifice, guarded with jealous care is a scroll of the Thorah said to be written by the hand of Ezra.

The old Coptic Church contains some very ancient pictures, and carvings in wood and ivory, and is built over a subterranean cave in which

Joseph and Mary with the Infant Jesus dwelt for a time on reaching Egypt after the Flight.

The Boolak Museum has the finest collection of Egyptian antiquities in the world, comprising sarcophagi, mummies, hieroglyphics, statues, sphinxes, ornaments and other relics found in the tombs and temples of the ancient Egyptians. Among the objects most noted are the mummy of Rameses II.— supposed to be the Pharaoh of the Exodus,— and the Village Sheik — a wooden statue said to be thousands of years old. In a granite sarcophagus lie the remains of Mariette Bey, who devoted his life to unearthing these relics.

The island of Rhodda is in the Nile, directly opposite ancient Cairo, and contains the Nilometer — a graduated stone pillar 40 feet high, covered with measures indicating the rise and fall of the river, and is placed in a well some 20 feet square, and 50 deep. The minimum tide of the river is 32 feet; 40 feet is considered the desirable medium; and the maximum of 42 entails incalculable destruction. In August when the Nile is sufficiently high for irrigating purposes, the embankment of the river is cut, and the ceremony attended with great rejoicing and festivities. On the upper end of the island of Rhodda is located the spot where Moses was found in the bulrushes by Pharaoh's daughter.

The Howling Dervishes comprise a religious sect who meet in their temple every Friday—the

Mohammedan Sabbath — for the celebration of
their religious rites. Forming a circle around
the priest, they frantically sway their bodies back
and forth to the frightful accompaniment of their
howls and wails, and the beating of tabors, a
species of drum. Many of these are old men,
half-clad, with long white hair waving with the
motion of their swaying bodies.

The Kieswah is a Holy Carpet which Cairo
sends to the Kaaba at Mecca, once a year. This
is conveyed on the back of a camel, and escorted
by thousands of pilgrims; who, on their return,
deeming themselves prepared to die, prostrate
themselves on the ground, to be trampled under
foot by a horse ridden by the *Sheik ;* and blessed
is the man whose injuries are the most severe.

The ancient city of Heliopolis — an hour's
drive from Cairo, is marked only by a single
obelisk of red granite, 70 feet in height, supposed
to be the oldest extant.

Near this are the Tree and Well of the Virgin,
where the Holy Family first rested after their
Flight into Egypt. In this neighborhood grew
the celebrated Balsam shrub, the balm of which
is said to have been presented to Solomon by
the Queen of Sheba.

The Pyramids of Gizeh, a drive of an hour
and a half from Cairo, are nine in number, and
surrounded by ruins of temples and tombs partly
buried beneath the sands of centuries. These

monuments, which are supposed to be the tombs
of early Egyptian kings, are built of enormous
stone blocks, and were originally covered with
white marble casings. Of this number three
are of immense proportions, the largest being
classed among the seven wonders of the world.

Cheops, the largest of these pyramids is 820
feet across its base on each of its four sides; and
470 feet in height, not including 15 feet already
lost from the apex, which leaves a flat surface of
120 square yards. The interior is entered by a
small opening 48 feet from the ground; first
through a long descending inclined passage of
polished granite at an angle of 26 degrees which
afterwards ascends as abruptly, and leads to the
King's Chamber. This room is the largest in the
pyramid, being 19 feet high, 17 wide, and 34
long; and is of polished granite. In it is a stone
sarcophagus which is supposed to have contained
the mummy of a king, or ancient records. On
each side of this room are air-tubes for purposes
of ventilation; and above it are five small chambers difficult of access. At the end of the Great
Hall which is 155 feet long and 28 high, is a passage leading to the Queen's Chamber; and a shaft
150 feet deep, known as the well, which descends
to the lower passage, and connects with a subterranean chamber. The difficult ascent of this
pyramid we accomplished with the aid of four
Bedouin Arabs, each; one at each hand, above,

to pull, and two others below, to push. The
descent was scarcely less perilous: with a strong
rope about our waists, held by one of our Bedouins while the others lent support, we jumped
from block to block, scarcely daring to look below, lest a misstep should hurl us into Eternity.

An exploration of the interior of the pyramid
though attended by less danger, is accompanied
by a far greater degree of discomfort, owing to
the foul air, heat, and darkness.

While many scientists believe these to have
been constructed as mausolea for the Pharaohs,
others contend they were built before the flood,
for astronomical purposes, or as receptacles for
historical archives. These gigantic structures
will yet, in all probability yield up to the world
the secrets of past ages, for in exploring Cheops
soundings in its interior developed the fact of the
existence of chambers yet unrevealed.

The Sphinx, the oldest and most famous
monument in the world, supposed to have existed
2,000 years before the pyramids, is the recumbent
form of a lion with the head of a man hewn from
the natural lime stone rock. It measures 128 feet
in length; 66 feet from the paws to the crown of
the head; the ears are 4½ feet long; the nose 5
feet 7 inches; the mouth 7 feet 7 inches in width;
and the extreme breadth of face 13 feet 8 inches.
Investigation developed the existence of two
wells within the body partially filled in with sand,

and from the top of the head a shaft descending
a depth of six feet in which the priests probably
concealed themselves in order to work upon the
superstitious fears of the credulous with mysterious and oracular enunciations.

The Sphinx was the deity of the ancient
Egyptians; and offerings were made before an
altar between its paws; the smoke of their sacrificial fires issuing from its nostrils. This silent
figure, defying time, immovable as the fixed stars;
enthroned amid these desert wastes for thousands
of years, has witnessed the rise and fall of nations; mighty cities springing from nothingness,
wielding their powerful sceptres, and descending
into the abyss of oblivion; has gazed undaunted
into the face of Osiris, the Sun-king, and looked
down upon the countless myriads of grovelling
humanity who have passed away forever.

The Temple of the Sphinx and a mausoleum
recently discovered by Campbell the explorer, lie
near by, buried to the depth of 100 feet in the
sand; and surrounding them on all sides are
partially exhumed tombs and temples.

Leaving Cairo by boat for a three weeks' trip
up the Nile, we made our first landing at Badra-
chin, and mounting donkeys set out to visit the
ruins of the far-famed ancient city of Memphis,
once the capital of Lower Egypt and one of the
greatest cities of antiquity. These ruins retain
but few vestiges of past grandeur; the most con-

spicuous object of interest being the Serapeum—
the tomb of the sacred Bulls Apis which contains
24 gigantic sarcophagi, of granite and black
marble, each 11 feet high and 18 feet long,
highly polished and inscribed with hieroglyphics. Above this tomb once stood the
temple in which the sacred bulls were worshipped.
The Egyptians believed that the soul of Osiris,
after his death, became incarnated in the body of
a bull,— born of a virgin cow,— which they called
Apis; this animal was distinguished by certain
marks required also in his successors; these consisted of a triangular white spot on the forehead,
the figure of an eagle on the back, a white cres-
cent on the right side, and a sacred scarabæus—
or beetle — under the tongue. To the god Apis
were assigned a temple, two chapels, and a court
for exercise, and his food was served in vessels of
gold. On attaining the age of 25 years he was
drowned by the priests in the sacred cistern; and
his body carefully embalmed and placed in one of
the sarcophagi in the Serapeum, when the whole
country was thrown into mourning until a successor had been announced. Among the other
ruins of Memphis are immense prostrate stone
figures of Rameses II. and those of his wife and
daughter, the pyramids of Sakkara, and the
tombs of Onas and Ti.

Returning to the Nile we sailed past the
False Pyramid, the villages of Wasta and Fesh-

neh, and the mountain Gebel-el-Dayr, on the summit of which stands a Coptic convent, and landed at Minieh which contains a fine palace, and the extensive sugar factory belonging to the Khedive.

Further up the river are the tombs of Beni-Hassan, chambers cut in the solid rock far up the hill, and supposed to be the oldest tombs of the kind in Egypt. These are ornamented with figures of animals, fish, and birds, and designs representing the life and customs of ancient times, in all of which the imperishable red and blue are almost as distinct as when painted thousands of years ago. One tomb is dedicated to Pasht the Egyptian Diana ; in another is the Grecian Doric column — unique in Egypt; and beneath all are pits where numerous mummies were found.

A few miles beyond are the ruins of Antino-öpolis — a city built by the Emperor Hadrian to commemorate the death of his beautiful favorite Antinous who drowned himself in the Nile ; and along the river for twelve miles are the celebrated Crocodile mummy-pits, cut in the rock of Mount Gebel-abou-faydah.

Assioot, the metropolis of Upper Egypt stands on the site of ancient Lycopolis or city of wolves, a place noted for the worship of these animals. It is the terminus of the railway from Cairo ; is the residence of a pasha, has a fine palace, mosque and bazaar, and was once the principal slave

market in Egypt. From the mountain in the
rear of the town is a fine view of the valley of the
Nile, and numberless tombs extend under the
hill below.

The ruins of Abydos are situated six miles
back of Girgeh at the base of the Libyan
mountains. They at one time ranked next to
those of Thebes, and owed their importance to
the fact that the god Osiris was buried here ; and
wealthy Egyptians from all parts of the country
desired to have their bodies lie in the sacred dust
which their god had hallowed. The principal ruins yet remaining are the Temple of Setee
I., the Temple of Rameses II., and the Necropolis.

Here, in the Temple of Osiris, the Tablet of
Abydos—or list of Pharaohs was found, which
is now one of the most valuable objects in the
British Museum.

Keneh is a place of considerable importance ;
chiefly noted for its porous jugs, and dates.
From here we made an excursion across the river
to the Temple of Denderah, one of the finest and
best preserved on the Nile, dedicated to the goddess Hathor—the Egyptian Venus ; the ceiling which is carved with the signs of the
zodiac, is supported by 24 massive pillars with
beautiful capitals ; the outer wall has the cartouch
and figure of Cleopatra with that of her son the
young Cæsarion by Julius Cæsar ; while on the
portico, erected by the Emperor Tiberius, is the

name of that monarch with those of Claudius,
Nero, Caligula, Cæsar and Ptolemy.

Luxor, a place of debarkation, is a small Arab
village on the site, and in the midst of one of the
finest ruins of Thebes.   It was here at the Consul's
house we witnessed the Egyptian Nautch or muscle
dance, rendered by the native women to perfection.

Thebes extended for seven miles on both
sides of the river.   It was the most celebrated
and the most magnificent of all the ancient capitals of Egypt, and was the capital of the kingdom of the Pharaohs when in the zenith of their
power.   Looking upon these ruins of a long past
grandeur — these palaces, temples, and tombs of
extinct races, one gathers a faint conception of
the customs and habits of its people.

The Temple of Luxor 800 feet long by 200
broad, has yet many magnificent columns standing, and at the main entrance are three colossal
statues of kings.   In front of these once stood
two granite obelisks ; one of which was presented
to Louis Philippe, and now stands in the Place de
la Concorde, Paris ; while the one remaining,
bears less evidence of the ravages of time than
any other in the world.

The ruins of Karnak — a portion of Thebes —
comprise a vast collection of palaces, temples,
obelisks, and columns from 80 to 100 feet high,
and avenues of sphinxes surpassing in grandeur
and extent all other ruins on the Nile.

On the opposite side of the river, extending back eight miles, and strewing the plain where once stood the western portion of Thebes, yet remain the ruins of the temples of Medeenet Haboo, Koorneh, and the palace-temple Memnonium or Rameseum. Near the latter is the prostrate colossal figure of Rameses II., weighing 1,000 tons and measuring 63 feet around the shoulders, the largest statue ever hewn from a solid block of granite. This king, supposed to be the Pharaoh of the Exodus, after having conquered the then known world, in order to perpetuate his memory, built the Rameseum as a lasting memorial of his greatness and glory.

The Colossi are two sitting figures in stone, 60 feet high, well preserved, and in all probability, statues of Amenophis II. or III., and once guarded here the entrance of the Temple-palace of this Pharaoh, " who knew not Joseph." One of these known as the vocal Memnon was celebrated for the musical sounds said to issue from the statue when touched by the first rays of the morning sun; and the religious and poetic version is that it represents Memnon, a king of Egypt, who was killed by Achilles at the siege of Troy, and the dew-drops which appear in the morning are the tears which Aurora sheds for her son.

In a desolate valley in the heart of the Libyan Mountains are situated the Tombs of the Kings excavated in the solid rock, some of which are 470 feet deep, and extend for half a mile into the mountain, the walls and ceilings being decorated with carvings and paintings representing every phase of Egyptian life. The finest of these are the tomb of Setee I., father of Rameses II., in which was found a beautiful alabaster sarcophagus; the tomb of Rameses III. in which are the paintings of the famous harpists; those of Rameses IV., Rameses VI., and Rameses IX., and that of the rich priest Assef: while others contained the mummified bodies of animals of various kinds.

Returning to Luxor, where our steamer was awaiting us, after an exploring tour which occupied three days, we continued up the river to Esna.

Here is a palace of Mohammed Ali, and in the centre of the town the portico of the Temple of Keneph with its 24 columns 19 feet in circumference and 65 feet in height, whose capitals represent the doum palm, the vine, and the papyrus. Of the temple which is entirely covered up, this portion alone has been excavated, and is one of the most beautiful and well preserved on the Nile.

Edfoo is the next place of importance reached, and its temple one of the grandest monuments of Egypt. Its entire length is 440x200 feet; it was built by Ptolomaeus Philometer, 180 B. C. and was dedicated to the god Horhat, and to Athor, his mother, the Egyptian Venus. In one cham-

ber, beautifully ornamented with carvings, is a
grey granite monolith in which was kept the
sacred hawk.

At Gebel Silsileh are the quarries from which
the ancient kings of Egypt procured the stones for
erecting the mammoth structures at Luxor, Karnak, and Medeenet Haboo; and here where the
river is very narrow, a chain was thrown across
by an ancient king to arrest navigation.

The Temple of Kom Omboo, 18 miles further
up, is fast going to decay and falling into the
river. It comprises two temples, one dedicated to
Light and the other to Darkness, the latter consecrated to the crocodile god Sebek; the tank is
still to be seen where the sacred crocodile bathed,
and the brick terrace where he sunned himself.
Besides this animal, cats, wolves, and birds were
worshipped by the ancient Egyptians, as is proved
by the numbers found mummified in the surrounding caves.

Asswan is the border town between Egypt
and Nubia, and the terminus of navigation for the
large Nile steamers. In its bazaars are to be purchased the skins of serpents and wild beasts, elephants' tusks, ostrich eggs and plumes, and
various other articles peculiar to the country.
Here the Nubian, black as night, first makes his
appearance, his naked body shining with oil, and
hair grotesquely arranged. The wardrobe of
many of the women consists of but a leathern

girdle fringed out and ornamented with shells,
while their kinky hair is worn plaited in multitu-
dinous small braids.   The childrens' attire is of
an even more primitive description — a ring in
the right nostril, and three or four in each ear, to
complete which elaborate costume a cord is sometimes worn around the waist.   The Nubians, as a
race, are less corrupt than the Egyptians, and
decidedly more dignified, frank and cheerful.

In the river opposite Asswan is the island of
Elephantine, where there are ruins of temples and
statues, and also of a Nilometer.

In the mountains beyond are the famous
granite quarries from which were wrought the
colossal statue of Rameses, and the obelisks now
at Heliopolis, Alexandria, Constantinople, Paris,
London, and New York. A monolith 100 feet
long and twelve feet square at the base is still
here, never having been removed from the quarry,
and like its mates is of a light red color sprinkled
with green, very hard and susceptible of the highest polish.

The great problem to the inquiring mind is
the means used by the ancients in cutting into
this adamantine material; from a thorough examination and from the numbers of partly-hewn
blocks abandoned on account of the rock having
split in a contrary direction, it is reasonable to
suppose that holes were cut in line, plugged with
wood and soaked with water which, expanding

these wedges, divided the rock and accomplished with long and tedious labor the work which modern machinery achieves with so much ease.

The first Nile cataract, seven miles above Asswan, is a series of rapids down which the Nubian boys float or shoot on logs, to amuse spectators, after which they vociferously demand *backsheesh* — a gift of money.

The Island of Philæ in Nubia, above the first cataract, is by far the most picturesque spot on the Nile. It is surrounded by wild and rocky scenery, while the island itself is covered with rich verdure, and groves of palm and acacia, intermingle with beautiful ruins. These consist of the Temple of Isis, Pharaoh's Bed,— formerly the Temple of Osiris, and the Temple of Athor. Philæ was the last stronghold of the Egyptian faith, and here Osiris, Isis, and Horus were worshipped 60 years after the Egyptian religion was abolished by Theodosius.

This was the terminus of our trip up the Nile, and from here we turned our faces towards Cairo and lazily floated down the river.

The rail from Cairo to Port Säid, a distance of 150 miles, follows the Sweetwater canal which supplies the stations, and towns on the Suez canal with drinking-water, and runs through that Land of Goshen so fertile in olden times, but now a barren and sandy desert. The principal places of importance passed are Belbeis and Bordein, near the latter of which are the remains of the ancient city of Bubastis — in the Coptic language Pi-Beseth — the city of which Ezekiel prophesied that it should go into captivity, and its young men fall by the sword.

Tel-el-Kebir passed en route, is a dirty Arab village of no importance, but rendered notable as the scene of the decisive battle of the recent Egyptian war fought on September 13th, 1882, when Arabi was vanquished by the English, and his army of 30,000 men destroyed and taken prisoners.

In taking steamer from Port Säid to cross the Mediterranean for a sixteen hours' sail to Jaffa, we left with regret this ancient and interesting country strewn with colossal ruins which speak so plainly of a past and powerful nation; for, to see the palaces and monuments of Egypt is to see the Egyptians as they lived and moved before the eyes of Abraham and Moses, to see the temples and tombs of Egypt is to see the Egyptians in the most solemn moments of their lives.

CHAPTER XX.

PALESTINE is a long strip of land bordering the Mediterranean, and is bounded on the east by the river Jordan. It is nowhere over 50 miles in breadth, and from Dan to Beersheba 180 miles in length. The country is hilly and mountainous, and with the exception of a few green valleys is rocky and barren. Only from Jaffa to Jerusalem, and Baalbec to Beyrout, are wheels available, and what here are called roads are simply rocky paths which only a sure-footed horse and experienced rider can travel.

This is the ancient Canaan or Palestine, so called by the Israelites who were expelled thence, three tribes of which, Reuben, Gad, and Mannasseh having territory assigned to them east of the Jordan. In the time of Moses they numbered over 2,000,000, but the present population is probably only 700,000, who are mostly Arabs, Turks, Mohammedans, Druses, Jews, Armenians, Greeks, Syrians, and Latins.

Jaffa, the ancient Joppa, has a population of

8,000, and tradition says was first founded by Japhet, son of Noah. It is the principal seaport town of Palestine, and has the worst harbor in the world; the rugged and projecting rocks rendering a landing dangerous at all times and impossible in stormy weather.

Here Andromeda was chained to the rock until rescued by Perseus from the devouring monster; here Noah built his ark, and Jonah embarked for Tarshish — instead of going by Divine command to Nineveh, and on which voyage he was swallowed by the whale : here Solomon received the cedars of Lebanon from Hiram, king of Tyre for building his temple, and here Peter recalled Tabitha to life (Acts, IX.— 36–41). Here also is the house of "one Simon the tanner," where Peter on the house-top saw the vision of animals let down in a sheet from heaven (Acts, X.—5–16).

Jaffa was taken by Napoleon in 1799 after an obstinate and bloody siege, and it is said that previous to his retreat across the desert he caused 1,200 Turkish prisoners to be cruelly put to death.

At Jaffa we made a contract for a tour of 30 days or more through Palestine and Syria, and selected three tents, a dragoman (Antonio Maclouf), a cook, waiter, and six muleteers, besides 3 good riding-horses and seven mules for transportation.

From Jaffa to Jerusalem we passed en route Lydda, in the plain of Sharon where St. George killed the Dragon; Ramleh with its ancient tower, where were buried 40 Christian martyrs, and where we first met victims of that scourge of the East — leprosy, in the various stages of the loathsome disease: the locality where Samson caught his 300 foxes and tied brands to their tails to burn his enemies' grain fields, and stopped for the night at Latroon in the valley of Ajalon, where Joshua commanded the sun and moon to stand still (Joshua, X.—12).

Next day we visited the village near by, where the penitent thief was born, and the cave where the two thieves lived while committing their robberies, and entered into the land of the tribe of Benjamin, passed Kirjathjearim, Job's Well, the site of the house of Abinadab, where the Ark of the Covenant was kept (I. Samuel, VII.—1·2), the town of Ain-Karim, where St. John the Baptist was born, and where the Virgin visited her cousin Elizabeth (Luke, I.—39-60); the site of Emmaus, where Christ appeared to Cleopas (Luke, XXIV.—13-31); looked upon the two hills where the army of Saul and that of the Philistines confronted each other; and picked up a pebble from the stream which flows between, at the identical place where tradition says David selected the stone with which he killed the giant Goliath.

After passing the site of ancient Gezer, which
one of the Pharaohs of Egypt took from the
Canaanites and gave to his daughter the wife of
Solomon (I. Kings, IX.—16), we saw the mountains of Moab in the distance, and those "round
about Jerusalem;" and riding through the Valley
of Gihon, in which Solomon was anointed king
over Israel, we entered the Holy City through the
Jaffa Gate.

Jerusalem which is called, even by the Mohammedans, the Blessed City, is situated on a
sloping hill surrounded by a stone wall 3 miles in
circumference, which is 40 feet high and some 3
feet in thickness. It has 34 towers, and is entered
by 7 gates—that of Damascus on the north, of
St. Stephen on the east, Jaffa on the west, and
Zion and Dung on the south; the latter being low
and crooked, was anciently called the Needle's
Eye, hence the saying: "It is harder for the rich
man to enter the kingdom of Heaven, than for a
camel to pass through the eye of a needle," while
Herod's and the Golden Gate, have long since
been walled up. Jerusalem has a population of
36,000 inhabitants, one-third of which is Mohammedan, one-third Jew, and the remainder Copt,
Assyrian, Persian, Syrian, Greek, and Latin.

The streets, some of which are arched over,
are narrow and filthy, and the houses and shops
shabby and neglected. This is Jerusalem the
Golden, the city that men call the perfection of

beauty, which apart from its historical association appears not worth possessing, even without the trouble of conquest.

On the high ground to the north overlooking Jerusalem is the point from which Titus made his attack; here is the grotto where Jeremiah wrote his lamentations; and the tombs of the kings and judges: these are many in number, cut in the solid rock, their entrances being closed by means of large round stones which fitted into grooves and required great strength to remove. On the west is the Valley of Hinnon, with the upper and lower pools of Gihon. On the south in the valley is the Fountain of the Virgin, and the Pool of Siloam; beyond, is the Hill of Scandal where King Solomon had his immense harem, and the Potter's Field or Field of Blood, where Judas after betraying Jesus went and hanged himself: and in a cave close by, the apostles concealed themselves during Christ's imprisonment and crucifixion.

On the east rises the Mount of Olives from the summit of which Christ ascended to Heaven, and close by is the cave in which He taught His disciples the Lord's Prayer. At the base of this mountain is the Tomb of the Virgin, with her husband Joseph, and those of her father and mother,— Joachim and Anna.

Near the spot where St. Stephen was stoned to death, is the Garden of Gethsemane, where

Judas betrayed Christ with a kiss, and close by the Grotto of the Agony, where the Saviour endured his agony and bloody sweat.

Between Jerusalem and the Mount of Olives lies the Valley of Jehoshaphat, through which flows the brook Kedron; and here among thousands of Jewish tombs are those of St. James, Jehoshaphat, Zachariah, and Absalom, cut in the rock, the latter being ornamented with Doric columns, and partially buried beneath small stones thrown by the Jews in token of contempt for his conduct.

Mount Zion on which a portion of Jerusalem is built is a large hill, and on it, just outside of the Zion Gate, is the tomb of David over which the Mohammedans have erected a small mosque: here in the house of the High-Priest Caiaphas is the room said to have been the scene of the Last Supper; on this mount is also the spot where Christ appeared to his Apostles after the resurrection, and where the Holy Ghost descended upon them on the day of Pentecost.

In an Armenian church just within the Gate of Zion, is kept the stone on which the cock crew when Peter denied his Lord; and its altar is formed of a large circular stone 6 inches thick, and 15 feet in circumference, which the angel rolled away from the door of the Sepulchre.

The Mosque of Omar, the Mohammedan Holy of Holies, is of octagon form, and is situated on

Mount Moriah.   It is on the foundation walls of
the Temple of Solomon, and with its grounds
covers an area 1,500 feet long by 1,000 broad.
This has been considered by the Jews the most
sacred ground in Jerusalem since the time of
David; it was then used as threshing floors, for
which he paid 50 shekels of silver.   The Mosque,
which is rich in gilding and glass mosaic windows,
has beneath its dome the Holy Rock, 57 feet long
by 43 wide, rising 6½ feet above the ground,
on which consistent with Biblical authority, Abraham was on the point of sacrificing Isaac.

On this Rock is the impression of Mohammed's
foot, which he left when taking his flight from
earth, also that of the angel Gabriel's hand as
he restrained it from accompanying the prophet in
his ascension.   In a cavern beneath the Rock are
preserved two hairs of Mohammed's beard, and
here are shown shrines indicating the places where
once prayed Abraham, Elijah, David, Jesus, and
Mohammed.

In the grounds inclosing the mosque is a
small temple where David and Saul sat in judgment; and another shows where once stood Solomon's throne.   In a subterranean passage are
some of the original walls and arches of the
Temple, and in another, containing 3,000 pillars,
were the stables of this wise son of David.

Outside the walls, where still remain some of
the original stones of the Temple, is the Jews'

Wailing Place, where every Friday men, women, and children of that dejected and outcast race assemble to read their testament, to bring their written prayers, which they insert in the crevices of the wall, and with hands outstretched upon the stones worn smooth by their kisses, to weep and wail in piteous accents over the destruction of their Temple.

The Church of the Holy Sepulchre was built by St. Helena, mother of the Emperor Constantine, about the year 325 A. D, and not only covers the supposed site of Calvary but those of every incident connected with the Passion and sepulture of the Saviour.

The exterior of the church is shabby and fast going to decay, while the interior, owing to the jealousy and unwillingness of either of the Christian sects to allow the other to keep the edifice in repair, presents a dingy appearance, lamps, ostrich eggs, cheap pictures and other gewgaws being the sole ornaments of its walls and altars.

In consequence of the antagonism existing among the various Christian sects, a Turkish guard of 100 soldiers is constantly on duty to keep the peace, and they are frequently bribed by one sect to persecute another. Owing to this state of affairs, each sect, except the Protestants, has a separate chapel or altar near the Holy Sepulchre, and one is not allowed to trespass upon the premises of the other. Occasionally may be seen the Greeks and Latins with their backs turned on each other holding their different forms of worship at the same time.

On entering the edifice the first thing notice-able is a marble slab which covers the Stone of Unction where the body of Jesus was laid and anointed for the grave, and near it is a circular railing inclosing the spot where Mary and Martha stood during the ceremony. In the centre of the church is the rotunda directly beneath which is the Holy Sepulchre inclosed in a square temple of yellow marble, 15 feet high and 12 feet square; this is divided into two chambers; the first one containing the stone where the angel sat guarding the entrance to the tomb, and the other the Sep-ulchre. Surrounding this are large wax-candles, each sect providing one, and besides these are 40 gold and silver hanging-lamps presented by dif-ferent sovereigns, which are kept continually burning.

On either side of this small temple are holes through which, during the Easter celebrations of the Greeks and Latins, which occur one month apart, flames are seen to issue; attributing to this manifestation a miraculous origin, the devotees in their eagerness to secure a portion of the Holy Fire, as they consider it, rush forward frantically, trampling one another underfoot and converting this holy place into a veritable pandemonium.

Opening from the rotunda is a cavern in the
natural rock, claimed to be the tombs of Nicode-
mus and of Joseph of Arimathea, where they laid
the body of Jesus immediately after the crucifixion. Various shrines in the church indicate the
spots where Christ was imprisoned, put in the
stocks, and crowned with thorns, also the site and
a remnant of the flagellation column, and the
place where the soldiers cast lots for His vestments.
A colored marble slab on the floor marks the
spot where the Saviour stood when He appeared
to Mary Magdelene, and a star inserted a few
yards further off is where Mary received this
manifestation ; besides a place shown where Jesus
also appeared to His mother after His resurrection.

Ascending a flight of steps to the upper part
of the church is Calvary, or Golgotha — the place
of a skull, where are two shrines ; that of the
Latins showing where Christ was nailed to the
Cross, and that of the Greeks, a hole in the rock
where the Cross was raised, as well as the rent
made by the earthquake.

A few steps below the church level is the
Chapel of St. Helena, where in 350 A. D. she
explored and found the True Cross.

In a Greek chapel is a globe inserted in the
floor, marking the centre of the earth ; close to
which is the tomb of Adam, whose resting-place
at the foot of Calvary is said to have been revealed
by an angel.

In the Sacristy are the spurs, sword and neck-
lace of Godfrey de Bouillon, and near it is his
tomb and that of his brother Baldwin.

On Holy Thursday we witnessed in the
church of the Holy Sepulchre, the ceremony of
the Washing of Feet by the Latin High-priest;
in remembrance of our Saviour's washing of the
feet of His twelve apostles.

On Good Friday, to commemorate the last
scenes of the Passion, the Latins have a life-size
wax-figure of Christ which is borne through the
Via Dolorosa — or Way of Sorrow — the procession pausing at each station held sacred in His
passage to the scene of the crucifixion. The Via
Dolorosa commences at the Tower of Antonio
where Christ first took up the cross; then passes
under the Ecce Homo arch, from which Pilate
said " Behold the Man;" past the site of the
house of St. Veronica, who, witnessing the
Saviour's suffering, offered Him a handkerchief
upon which was left the impression of His face in
blood; and other shrines indicating, by impressions left upon the stone wall, the places where
Christ in falling under the weight of the cross,
struck His face or arm. Further on is the house
of the Wandering Jew, where stopping to rest,
Jesus was told by him to " move on," in reply to
which, according to tradition, the Saviour said:
" Move thou on likewise;" and ever since, the
Jew has been moving on, permitted neither to

rest nor die; which legend suggested to Eugene Sue the motive for his celebrated novel.

Arriving at the Church of the Holy Sepulchre, the procession proceeds to offer prayers at the various shrines; after which they perform the ceremony of the crucifixion. The effigy is nailed to the cross, and lifted into position in the so-called identical hole where once stood the original cross; when appropriate ceremonies and prayers ensue, after which the cross is lowered, the body placed on the stone of unction and anointed, and finally laid in the Sepulchre.

These religious ceremonies we witnessed under the protection of our Consul, attended by his guard together with our own; for so great is the fanatical excitement of the Christians, that one's very life is endangered by their demonstrations.

From Jerusalem to Hebron, southward, a distance of 20 miles over the most rocky road imaginable, we first passed the Magician's Well where the Star of Bethlehem was reflected in the water to direct the Wise Men; then Rachel's tomb near the village called after Benjamin (Gen. XXXV.—19), and Abraham's oak, under which his tent was pitched when he was commanded by God to sacrifice Isaac.

Hebron which, next to Damascus, is the oldest city in the world, contains about 5,000 inhabitants; here Abraham bought from Ephron

the Hittite, the cave and field of Machpelah; and
under a large Mohammedan mosque which neither
Christian nor Jew is allowed to enter, lie buried
Abraham and Sarah his wife; Isaac, Rebecca
and Leah; and the Mohammedans claim Joseph
also.

From here, proceeding northeast, we passed
the immense Pools and Gardens of Solomon,
where he once had a summer palace (Ecc. II.—
5-6), and went through the village of Etam where
Samson was bound with cords, and after breaking them killed 1,000 Philistines with the jaw-
bone of an ass (Judges, XV).

Bethlehem, the City of David, situated on the
knob of a mountain, surrounded by valleys and
picturesque views, is one of the prettiest and most
interesting spots in Palestine.

The Church of the Nativity covers the grotto
stable where Christ was born; the spot being
marked by a silver star inserted in the floor.
The first one placed there having been stolen, the
Greeks and Latins contended for the honor of
providing a substitute; which contention afforded
a pretext for the inauguration of the Crimean
war.

Another grotto is where the angel appeared
to Joseph in a dream bidding him take the young
child and its mother, and flee into Egypt; in the
Milk grotto the Holy Family took refuge; in another St. Jerome lived and died; and in still an-

other, 20,000 of the Innocents were thrown after the massacre ordered by Herod.

This church, built by St. Helena, is said to be the oldest in the world, and was of great magnificence when Baldwin was crowned here, King of Jerusalem; the ceiling is composed of beams of cedar from the forest of Lebanon, and its walls still show traces of the golden mosaic which once adorned it.

Leaving Bethlehem we passed David's Well, the water of which he so thirsted after (II. Samuel, XXIII.—15-16); crossed the field of Boaz where Ruth gathered the sheaves (Ruth, II), and where the shepherds watched their flocks by night (Luke, II); stopped for lunch at the grotto where the angel appeared to the shepherds, announcing the birth of the Saviour; and camped for the night at Mar-Saba.

This locality is noted for its convent cut in the solid rock, which is occupied by dirty Greek monks who are never allowed to look upon the face of a woman, and who pass their days guarding the tomb of their Saint Saba.

Leaving camp early in the morning we rode four hours through the wilderness of Judea; passing the ruined castle where John the Baptist was beheaded, and the valley in which were the warm baths where Herod bathed for his illness, and reached the Dead Sea.

This sheet of water which is 46 miles in length

17

and 11 in breadth, is of a dark-green color and so
bitter and briny that no living creature can exist
in it, though birds, contrary to the general belief
are frequently seen flying over it. It is situated
1,300 feet below the level of the ocean, and its
specific gravity is so great that in bathing one
finds it impossible to sink. The Dead Sea is
inclosed by mountains not less than 2,000 feet
high, and at its head is Mount Neba, while on its
shores, now desolate and devoid of all life and
vegetation, once stood the cities of Sodom and
Gomorrah.

It may not be inappropriate, although somewhat anticipating events, to recount here an incident of a second visit to the Dead Sea which I
made alone.

Mounting my thoroughbred Arab horse I was
conducted by an Arab attendant to a Bedouin
village — an assemblage of tents — where the
sheik resided. Each tribe, inhabiting a certain district, is governed by a sheik, and in order to
obtain permission to pass through their territory,
tribute money is exacted, when they furnish an
escort to the neighboring tribe, who in turn enact
similar proceedings.

After some deliberation and delay, the sheik
furnished me a guard armed with a gun, a brace
of pistols, and a sword, and mounted on a thoroughbred mare as swift as the wind, which he
rode without bridle and with such perfect control

as to be able to turn her in an instant, to gallop
her up and down almost perpendicular ascents,
while he shouted at the top of his voice, waving
on high his gun and sword, and often crossing
blades with other Arabs whom he met.   Finally
reaching the shores of the sea, the question arose
in my mind how I was to obtain a bath without
leaving all my effects at the mercy of the Bedouin,
whose manifestations — such as reloading his gun,
examining his ammunition, and whetting his
sword — were anything but reassuring. Such was
my situation in the desert, alone, and twelve miles
from any human being of my own race.   Finally
I bethought me of a ruse.   As well as I could
make myself understood by means of signs, I in-
timated to my companion my misgivings as to the
safety of the contemplated plunge : and finally
after some difficulty, succeeded in persuading him
to precede me into the water.   Once in, I kept a
position between him and the shore, in order to be
master of the situation, and seizing the opportunity when he had swam out some distance, I stepped out, and as quickly as possible resumed my
clothing and arms.

On my return trip, the Bedouin's appearance
and demonstrations being anything but agreeable,
I kept him in advance of me until we reached
the precincts of the next tribe when I will-
ingly exchanged him for another guard, con-
gratulating myself for the narrow escape from

the danger into which a spirit of adventure had led me.

From the Dead Sea we followed the course of the river Jordan for an hour, lunching and bathing at the traditional spot where Christ was baptized by John the Baptist (Matt. III). Here the river is about 50 yards wide, quite deep and muddy, with a current running at the velocity of 8 miles an hour: the banks are low, marshy, and treacherous; a fact which we well recall from the circumstance of the partial loss of our lunch, and the narrow escape of our sumpter horse, who, poor beast, suffering from heat and thirst, ventured to the edge of the stream, and losing his foothold came near being carried away by the swift current.

This is supposed to be the place where the Israelites crossed; where Elijah divided the waters, and passing over ascended in a chariot of fire to Heaven, and where Elisha on whom the mantle of Elijah had fallen, smote the waters and again divided them.

During Easter Monday after Passion Week Christian Pilgrims from all parts of the world come, mounted on horses, donkeys, and camels, to bathe in the Jordan at this spot. This motley throng composed of every sect and nationality, men, women, and children in every variety of costume, shouting and wrangling in every known language under the sun, present a most novel and animated scene of the cosmopolitan life of the East.

Crossing the plain of the Jordan where the heat is intense, we camped at the site of ancient Jericho at the foot of the high mountain where Christ, after his forty days fast, was tempted by the devil (Matt. IV.—8-12); and above the Fountain of Elisha whose waters he healed and converted from bitter to sweet (II. Kings, II—21-23).

Jericho was built by Herod, and it was here he died: and near it was the tree climbed by Zaccheus to enable him to view Jesus as he passed through the vast concourse of people (Luke, XIX. 1-5). Here also grew the famous Balsam shrubs which possessed the virtue of healing wounds, presented by Mark Antony to Cleopatra, and which she caused to be removed to Heliopolis when she sold the ground to Herod.

From Jericho we crossed the brook Cherith, passed the cave where Elisha was fed by the ravens, the place where the she-bears lurked to tear the "forty and two wicked children" (II. Kings, II.—24), and lunched among the ruins of the Samaritan inn: afterwards passing the spot where a certain man fell among thieves (Luke, X. —30-36) we reached Bethany, where we descended into the tomb of Lazarus, and visited the ruins of the house of Mary and Martha (John, XI.).

From Bethany we followed the road by which Christ made his triumphal entry into Jerusalem,

passing the site of the fig-tree which he cursed
(Mark, XI.); the field which henceforth produced but stones; and camped on the Mount of
Olives from which point is obtained a magnificent
view of the Holy City.

CHAPTER XXI.

SINJEL: NABLOUS: SAMARIA: JEZREEL: NAZARETH:
THE SEA OF GALILEE: TIBERIAS: CAPERNAUM:
DAN: CÆSAREA PHILIPPI: DAMASCUS: BAALBEC:
BEYROUT.

LEAVING Jerusalem for the north we crossed the
hill of Neby Samwil — the Biblical Mizpah where
Saul was elected the first king of Israel; descended to the village and pool of Gibeon where
Solomon asked of God wisdom to govern his
people; passed Ramah where Samuel was born
and Beira where Joseph and Mary missed Jesus,
after a day's journey. We stopped for rest and
refreshment at Bethel where Jacob with his head
on a stone dreamed of a ladder that reached to
heaven, and saw angels ascending and descending
thereon; and camped for the night at Sinjel near
the Robbers' Fountain.

From here we passed through Shiloh where
the Ark of the Covenant rested for 300 years;

and where Eli fell down and broke his neck ; further on the well of Haran where Jacob first met
Rachel (Gen. XXIX.) ; Joseph's tomb where he
was buried after being brought up out of Egypt
(Josh. XXIV.—32); and the well which Jacob dug
after buying the land of the sons of Hamor for
100 pieces of silver, and where Jesus sat talking
to the woman of Samaria (John, IV.—5-31).

Nablous — or Shechem — one of the cities of
refuge whose history dates back 4,000 years, is
situated in a beautiful valley at the foot of Mount
Ebal and Mount Gerizim, between which Moses
commanded Joshua to read the laws before the
congregation of Israel.   Here Abraham first
pitched his tent in Canaan ; here Simeon and
Levi murdered the male population to revenge
the dishonor of their sister Dinah ; and here Re-
hoboam was proclaimed king over Israel.

The inhabitants, who are Samaritans numbering about 1,000, believe only in the Pentateuch
or first five books of Moses ; they claim to be the
true Jews ; and in their synagogue show the
celebrated Samaritan Codex said to be 4,000
years old.

On the top of Mount Gerizim where the
twelve stones of the tribes of Israel were set
up, traditions say that Abraham met Mel-
chisedec ; and that here also he prepared to sacrifice his son.   On this mountain during the
months of April and May the Samaritans en-

camp, and on the traditional spot offer up a burnt sacrifice of a ram.

After leaving Nablous we rode through a fertile and well-cultivated valley to Samaria, and camped on the ruins of Ahab's Ivory Palace which stands on the top of a lone hill 300 feet above the level of the plain, with expansive views in every direction. Here are the remains of Herod's noble colonnade of which about 100 of the granite columns yet stand ; and it was on this site that once stood the great temple of Baal. The city was besieged during the reign of Ahab,— who married the notorious Jezebel,— by the king of Damascus ; and the suffering of the inhabitants during the three years' siege, was one of the most frightful on record ; it is recounted among other horrors that mothers actually boiled their dismembered infants for food. The siege was finally raised, as predicted by Elisha the prophet (II Kings, VI.—24-33 ; VII.—1-20).

From Samaria we visited the site of Dothan where Elisha dwelt ; and near by the pit into which Joseph was cast by his brethren ; thence to Jenin and through the plain of Esdraelon which is environed by the hills of Samaria, those of Galilee and of Gilboa, and Mount Carmel. This plain which is 20 miles long by 12 wide was the scene of the great battles of Palestine. It was here, near the river Kishon that the battle was fought between the armies of Baruk and

Jabin; when Sisera, general of the army of the latter fled on foot to the tent of Jael, who after inviting him in to rest and giving him drink, drove a nail into his temple; here also Joshua, Benhadad, Saul, Gideon, Tamerlane, Tancred, Cœur de Lion, Saladin, and Napoleon have fought bloody battles and added pages of history to this already celebrated spot.

At night we camped at Jezreel the capital of Ahab and the wicked Jezebel, the scene first of their crimes, and later of their retribution (I Kings, XXI.), and from here we passed the Fountain of Gideon, where he encamped his army previous to the attack on Shunem (Judges, VII).

It was in Shunem that Elijah restored the child of the Shunamite to life; from this town we rode around the mountain of Little Hermon to Nain, where Jesus resuscitated the widow's son (Luke, VII.—11-16), and beyond, to Endor where we visited the cave in which lived the witch whom Saul consulted before going into battle (I Samuel XXVIII. — 7-15).

After thus diverging, we returned, and continued through the plain of Esdraelon, stopping at Debiereh the home of the prophetess Deborah; and ascended Mount Tabor, the scene of the Transfiguration, which rises like a cone in the midst of the plain, whence is obtained a magnificent view of the adjacent country.

Nazareth, the scene of the Annunciation and

the home of the Saviour during his boyhood's years, contains a population of 6,000 inhabitants. It is situated on the side of a hill overlooking a lovely valley; but its streets, like those of all Eastern cities are narrow, crooked and filthy. At the entrance of the town is the Fountain of the Virgin where Mary was in the habit of drawing water, and which the Greeks claim was the scene of the Annunciation; while to-day as then, it is the favorite resort of the Nazarene maidens, who assemble here to fill their jugs which they carry away gracefully poised on their heads.

The Church of the Annunciation where the Latins claim the angel appeared to the Virgin, is built over the house of the Holy Family which is divided into three small underground apartments; a broken column indicating the spot where the angel appeared, and a cross where the Virgin stood while receiving his message.

A church also covers the site of the carpenter shop where Jesus and Joseph worked at their trade: another incloses an immense rock on which Christ and his disciples ate; and the synagogue is shown from which Jesus was driven while preaching.

In Nazareth as elsewhere throughout the country, the sites of holy places are covered by churches of the Latins or Greeks, each sect often claiming a different locality for the identical association, and building thereon a commemorative church.

From Nazareth to Tiberius, we passed Gath
Hepher ; and Cana of Galilee where Christ performed his first miracle—excepting those recorded
in the rejected books; and here we visited an old
church in which are two huge earthen pots
which are claimed to be the identical ones used at
the marriage feast (John, II.—1-12). ·

Passing Lubieh and Beth-arbel, we stopped
for our mid-day repast on the summit of Horn-
Hattin — or Mount of Beatitudes — where Christ
preached His famous sermon on the Mount (Matt.
V. VI. VII). Here the last great battle of the
Crusade of 1187 was fought, the Sultan Saladin
completely exterminating the army of the Christians.

The Sea of Galilee, or Lake of Tiberius, is 14
miles in length and 6 in breadth, and of the many
cities that once clustered along its shores only a
few scattering villages now remain. While Josephus describes its surface covered with vessels,
and naval conflicts taking place upon its waters, it
is now as quiet as the grave, with only a few rude
fishing boats with their drowsy occupants, breaking the monotony of the scene.

After the expulsion of Jesus from Nazareth
He dwelt upon the banks of the Sea of Galilee,
and consequently nearly every foot of its shore is
consecrated ground. Here He passed three of
the most eventful years of His life : here He chose
His apostles, while the multitudes followed Him,

and here He performed his most noted miracles.

The town of Tiberias on the borders of the sea, was built by Herod Antipas and named after the Roman emperor. It once extended for two miles along the shore from the site of the present town to the natural hot baths, which are still extant; but it is now confined to a very small area. Its walls are in many places in a ruinous condition, and the place looks quaint and old. On the water's edge is a small convent built on the site of Peter's house and near which it is said the miraculous draught of fishes took place (John, XXI. 1-15 and Luke V.—1-12).

The inhabitants of Tiberias are mostly Jews who believe the Messiah will yet come and establish his throne at Safed.

Taking one of the small fishing-boats on the Sea of Galilee which ply at the rate of two miles an hour, giving rise to the irreverent but very suggestive remark of an impatient American "it was no wonder Christ got out and walked," we passed Magdala, the village where Mary Magdalene was born; the place where the miracle of the Loaves and Fishes was performed (John, VI.—1-22); Bethsaida, where are yet to be seen large columns and stone ruins lying in every direction; and camped for the night on the site of ancient Capernaum, at the upper end of this beautiful sheet of water so teeming with his-

torical interest. Capernaum commands the finest
situation on the Sea of Galilee, and its extensive
ruins show it to have been a place of great
importance.

For the first time since our sojourn in the Holy
Land we were impressed with the solemnity of
our surroundings : here the desecrating hand of
man has not marred the effect of association by
the rearing of shrines and churches, but Nature
alone chants the solemn requiem : here no Eblis
of contention and rivalry exists, but the spirit of
peace and holiness broods like the dove over
the quiet scene.

Continuing north we passed in view of Safed
on the summit of the mountain, which is identified
as " the city set on a hill that cannot be hid,"
crossed the rocky highlands of Napthalie, where
we met large caravans, one of them alone numbering 500 camels, and continuing up the valley of
the Jordan, camped for the night at the waters of
Merom, surrounded by about 100,000 Bedouin
Arabs, with their large herds of buffaloes. This
is the strongest tribe in Syria ; in time of war
mounting 10,000 men on blooded mares, and
90,000 on camels. Riding around the Great
Marsh, and passing by Beth-Rehob, we crossed
an old Roman bridge and halted for lunch at Dan
just above a large spring of clear water, one of the
sources of the Jordan. Dan is the ancient Laish
which the children of Dan took, and named after

their father, and is situated on the northern border of Palestine as Beersheba is on the southern ;
hence the saying : " from Dan to Beersheba."

From here we rode to Cæsarea Philippi,
where we camped for the night near another
source of the Jordan whose waters rise in a cavern
formerly dedicated to the god Pan. It was in
Cæsarea Philippi, that Jesus delegated to Peter the
keys of Heaven, saying : " Thou art Peter, and
upon this rock I will build my church " (Matt.
XVI.—18-19).

On the roofs of the village houses are structures, resembling birds' nests, formed of branches
and leaves, and supported by poles at either
corner, in which the inhabitants sleep in summer
to avoid the heat and insects.

From Cæsarea Philippi we ascended the rough
slopes of Hermon, and visited the ruined castle
of Banias standing on a height of 5,000 feet
above the level of the sea, supposed to have been
built in the time of the Herods; and commanded by Josephus.

Further on we passed the village of Medjee
Eshshems whose inhabitants are Druses; Beit-
Jenn on the banks of a tributary of the Parphar
and at the foot of high and rugged rocks in which
are cut numbers of tombs, and camped for the
night at Kafr-Hauwar, where is the reputed
tomb of Nimrod, the mighty hunter.

Damascus, the oldest and most Oriental city

in the world, was founded by Uz, the grandson
of Noah; dates back over 4,000 years; and now
contains 175,000 inhabitants.   It is situated in a
fertile and well-watered valley between the rivers
Pharpar and Abana; this oasis of the desert
being claimed by some to be the site of the Garden of Eden.

From the heights of Salihneh, before entering
the city, there is a magnificent view of Damascus
with its many domes and towering minarets.   It
was from this point that Mohammed, when a
camel driver, first viewed the city, and refused to
enter, saying: "Man can have but one Paradise,
and my Paradise is fixed above."

In Damascus one sees the Arab and Turk in
their original state, free from the taint of European civilization; and business transacted as it
was thousands of years ago.   The interior of
many of the houses are richly furnished, and have
large courts filled with flowers and sparkling
fountains.   In the narrow and tortuous streets
may be heard to this day, men relating the story
of Joseph and his brethren, and the adventures
of Haroun Al Raschid; as centuries ago the blind
Bard of the seven cities went from place to place
reciting his undying epics.

The bazaars far surpass those of Cairo and
Constantinople in cleanliness, variety and beauty
of display.   The merchants are richly dressed
in gay-colored attire, and sit cross-legged on

Turkish rugs among their wares; here are displayed all the various products of the Orient—
spices and perfumes from Arabia; dates from
Nubia; ivory and ostrich plumes from Egypt;
tobacco from Latakia; satins from Aleppo;
rich fabrics from India; silks from China;
pearls from Ceylon, and steel blades and brazen
ornaments, manufactures of Damascus

The city is divided into sections, separating
Mohammedans, Jews and Christians, by iron
gates which are closed at nightfall and in times of
disturbance. The Mohammedans bear a great
antipathy towards the followers of Christ; and in
1860 massacred all the Christians in the city excepting those who effected their escape to their
stronghold.

Damascus is noted for its cafés, and for its
manufactories of silks and jewels; and is a great
centre for the fitting out of caravans for the
Bedouin districts; whence they return laden with
rugs, skins and other articles of traffic.

The Great Mosque, one of the finest of all the
Mohammedan places of worship, is built on the site
of an ancient temple, many of the columns of which
are still standing. It has two courts and three
minarets and in its centre stands a gilt iron cage,
in which they claim is the head of John the Baptist.

In the cemetery are the tombs of Mohammed's
numerous family; and that of St. George, the tutelary saint of England.

In the city are: "the street called Straight;"
the house of Judas where Saul was taken; the
house of Ananias and Sapphira whom the Lord
destroyed for their perjury: the Leper's hospital
on the site where once stood Naaman's house;
and the wall from which Saul was lowered
in a basket. A short distance beyond the city
gates is the spot where Saul on his way from
Jerusalem to Damascus, to persecute the Christians, saw the Divine light and was converted
(Acts, IX.).

From Damascus we followed the Abana river
to the Fountain of Fijeh, where tradition says
Balaam watered his ass; passed the town of
Columns, and camped at the village of Suk, located at the base of a steep mountain, on top of
which we visited the ruins of an old marble
temple said to have been built on the spot where
Cain killed his brother, and beyond, about 30
yards, covered by a shrine, is the reputed tomb
of Abel.

Making an early start the following morning,
we passed over a road and along an aqueduct cut
in the solid rock by the Romans 164 years B.
C. Further on we reached the town of Abi-
lene, where there are tombs cut high up in the
rocks; then Bludan the summer residence of the
consuls of Damascus; and passing Yafufeh, and
the tomb of Seth, we arrived at Baalbec after
having been ten hours in the saddle.

The ruins of Baalbec are among the finest on earth; their magnificence and magnitude of columns and blocks of stone having been for centuries the wonder and admiration of the world. These ruins are 900 feet long by 500 wide, built on an artificial platform raised thirty feet above the plain, and have immense vaults underneath, the foundation blocks being bevelled and fitted together similarly to those in the Temple at Jerusalem. Owing to the discovery of Jewish architecture amid the Doric, Tuscan, and Corinthian ruins, it is considered by many archæologists to have been the House of the Forest of Lebanon which Solomon built for his Egyptian wife, and which is not improbable from the fact that his successors were idolaters; and this his dwelling place was consecrated to the worship of Baal, or the sun; Baalbec of the Syrians having the same meaning as Heliopolis of the Greeks — City of the Sun.

On the immense foundation where rise these ruins, several stone blocks of which measure 63 feet long, 15 wide, and 13 deep, stood two or more temples of immense magnitude: the Temple of the Sun was surrounded by Corinthian columns 80 feet high, and 22 in circumference, only six of which remain standing: the Temple of Jupiter is yet comparatively intact, and is about 230 feet long by 125 feet broad: many of its columns are crowned by magnificently-carved capitals, of such extent as would compare with the size of a cottage.

A mile distant, in the quarries, there yet remains a huge block of stone partially hewn, measuring 70 feet long, 17 wide, and 14 thick, and of sufficient area to allow of two wagons being driven on it abreast. Viewing these relics of long past eras the question is naturally suggested as to the means employed to elevate these huge masses to their designated positions at a period when the science of engineering was still in its incipiency.

From Baalbec we rode through the valley between Anti-Lebanon and Lebanon proper, and traversed the country to which the spies were sent by the Children of Israel to explore, and who returning, brought with them immense bunches of grapes as evidence of the richness of the land.

On the road to Estura, where we proposed camping for the night, we visited the tomb of Noah, which is 70 yards long, and inclosed in a Mohammedan shrine.

On the following day, we crossed the mountains of Lebanon, stopping for rest and refreshment under its famous cedars, after which we resumed our route reaching, in the evening, Beyrout, a town of 100,000 inhabitants, on the sea-coast; its hotels, banks, and shops recalling us once more to the essentials of civilization.

CHAPTER XXII.

LEAVING Beyrout by an Austrian Lloyd steamer, we had a most delightful trip through the Mediterranean, and the Grecian Archipelago, sailing amid the beautiful islands so celebrated in historic and classic lore, and landed on the island of Cyprus, one of the first places where Christianity was established, and where Paul and Barnabas preached.

We went ashore at Larnica, a small town inhabited by Greeks, and spent the day rambling about the place. Here we visited the Greek church which contains the tomb of Lazarus, who having moved here after his resurrection from the dead, became the first Christian bishop of Cyprus. This was also the birthplace of Zeno, who founded the sect of Stoics and taught at Athens the doctrine that men should be free from all passion or emotion.

Rhodes on an island of the same name and so called from its abundance of roses, is a most favored spot. It is situated on a hill which slopes down to a miniature bay, and has a delightful climate.   Rhodes is chiefly renowned for the Colossus which once spanned the bay at its entrance.   This was the figure of a man in brass 105 feet in height, his extended legs forming an archway through which the small crafts of the period could readily pass, and was classed as the 6th wonder of the world.   It was built 290 B. C. and was destroyed by an earthquake, the fragments being sold by the 6th caliph to a Jew who loaded 900 camels with 800 lbs. each.

Rhodes was also distinguished in ancient times for its liberty, learning, and valor, and in modern times for its defences conducted by the knights of St. John; the Rue des Chevaliers—or street of the knights — yet containing many old houses on which are sculptured in stone the armorial bearings of the knights.

From here we entered the Archipelago passing the site of Halicarnassus where stood the Mausoleum of Mausolus, king of Caria, erected by Artemisia, his wife and sister, 350 B. C. and reckoned the 5th wonder of the world; Symi, noted for its corals and sponges and the expertness of its male and female divers; Patmos, where St. John wrote the Revelations, having been banished there by the Emperor Domitian for preaching the Gospel of Christ; Samos, celebrated in classic literature as the birthpiace of Juno and Pythagoras, and for a long time the home of Herodotus, who here compiled the greater portion

of his history; and Scio, which we saw partly in
ruins, having been recently visited by a fearful
earthquake, and under whose fallen walls yet lay
buried the remains of hundreds of human
beings.

Smyrna, which stands foremost among the
cities of Asia Minor, has a population of 160,000,
and is supposed to have been founded by Alexander the Great. It is the only city of the Seven
Churches addressed by the apostle St. John,
which has retained its importance down to the
present time, and is also one of the seven cities
that lay claim to having given birth to Homer:

" Seven Grecian cities strove for Homer dead,
   Through which the living Homer begged his bread "

Its inhabitants have erected a temple near the
grotto where it is said he conceived his immortal
epic, the Iliad.

On Mount Pagus, a hill overlooking Smyrna
are the ruins of an old castle, near which is the
spot where Polycarp the first bishop of the city
was burnt at the stake, and near by is his tomb.
The principal export of this city is figs, and caravans daily import the indigenous products of Asia
Minor.

A two hours' trip from Smyrna, by rail,
brought us to the ruins of Ephesus once one of
the most remarkable cities of the world, whose

origin was attributed to the Amazons; and especially noted for the Temple of Diana, the 3d
wonder of the world. This temple which was
425 feet in length, and 225 in breadth, the whole
supported by 127 superb columns, each the gift
of a king, was built 552 years B. C. Its erection
required an incredible number of workmen; the
most skilful painters and sculptors being employed
in the decorations of the edifice. The statue of
Diana was of ebony; and legend avers was a gift
direct from Jupiter to the Ephesians. This
temple was burned by Herostratus, who sought
thus to acquire a meritricious fame; the event oc-
curring on the very day of the birth of Alexander
the Great, 356 B. C.

At Ephesus are also the ruins of the great
theatre which seated 60,000 people, and into
which Demetrius with his fellow craftsmen drew
Gaius and Aristarchus — Paul's companions —
shouting: "Great is Diana of the Ephesians!"
(Acts XIX — 21-41.) Here also are the ruins of
the school of Tyrannous; the Agora, or market-
place; the Odeum, and the Stadium which seated
75,000 people; the Gymnasium; the old Aqueduct,
40 columns of which still remain, and on the top
of several we saw storks standing guard over their
curious nests; the cemetery with numbers of stone
sarcophagi; the prison of St. Paul, on an elevation; the tombs of St. Luke and St. John, and the
baptismal font of the latter. In the side of the

hill of Prion, is the cave of the Seven Sleepers, where the seven young men slept for over 200 years. Near Ephesus, flows the river Meander from whose tortuous course is derived the word meander.

It was in this city that Apollo and his sister Diana were born; here Syrinx was changed into a reed, and here also the god Pan dwelt in the caves of the hill of Coressus; here roamed the Amazons, and here their contests with Bacchus and Hercules; and here also, is claimed the nativity of Homer.

Ephesus was visited by successive celebrities of the different eras — Alcibiades, Lysander, Agesilaus, Alexander the Great, Hannibal, Antiochus, Scipio, Lucullus, Sulla, Pompey, Brutus, Cassius, Cicero and Augustus.

Here Antony administered justice; and leaving his seat in court followed Cleopatra as she passed the door. Later he sailed with her from this port, in a galley ornamented with gold and silken sails rowed by black slaves and filled with beautiful dancing girls, and winged Cupids; while they made love in the midst of perfumed breezes, to the sound of voluptuous strains of music and the dipping of silver oars.

Returning to Smyrna we crossed the Archipelago to Piræus, once the great sea-port of Greece and seven miles from Athens.

Athens, the capital of Greece, with a popula-

tion of 64,000 owes its celebrity to its record of
past grandeur, its numerous ruins of architectural
and sculptural art, and its historical landmarks of
many ages.

Of the modern city, the Palace, the Academy
of Science, and the Museum are its finest buildings; the latter contains a fine collection of old
Grecian statues, among which is that of Minerva,
modelled after the lost masterpiece, the Palladium,
which the Greeks had stolen from Troy and
placed in the Parthenon; besides quantities of
arms, gold plate, ornaments, and coin found in the
tomb of Agamemnon.

The public gardens and open air theatres of
Athens are numerous and well patronized, and
often combine arenic and dramatic performances.

The Acropolis or Citadel crowns the summit
of a rocky hill which rises abruptly to a height of
150 feet from the plain in the midst of the city,
and has been a fortress from the earliest ages. The
Acropolis which was the pride of Greece, the perfection of art, and the envy of the world had four
distinctive features — the Fortress of the city; the
Sacred Shrine for sacrificial offerings; the Treasury; and the Museum of Art. It was entered
by the Propylæa — a massive marble gate-way
of the Doric order, and was approached on either
side by steps between which the chariots drove
up on the natural rock. To the right of the entrance stands the Temple of Victory without

Wings; and on the left is the Pinacotheca which
now serves as a museum for the statues, inscriptions, and other antiquities found in the Acropolis.

The Parthenon — a temple dedicated to Minerva, was built during the time of Pericles 436
years B. C. at a cost of $3,000,000. It was of
white marble, 230 feet long by 100 wide; the
walls were surrounded by 48 marble columns of
the Doric order — 34 feet high — most of which
are yet standing; while on the façade still remains
a portion of the celebrated frieze supposed to have
been the work of Phidias representing the faces of
the gods, the ceremonies of the temple, and
chariot and horse races. In the centre of the
temple stood the colossal statue of Minerva, 60
feet high, and covered with gold and ivory; and
in its vaults was kept the public treasure.

To the west stands the temple of the Erec-
thium dedicated to the joint worship of Minerva
and Neptune who disputed for the guardianship
of Athens; the preference being adjudged to that
deity who should confer the most useful gift to
man. Neptune struck the ground with his tri-
dent and forthwith a horse sprang to life; but
Minerva caused an olive-tree to grow out of the
earth — the emblem of peace and plenty; and to
her was given the coveted prize; when she called
the city Athena, after her own name in Greek.
The portico of the temple is supported by six

beautiful marble figures or Caryatides, women of Caria, who were condemned to support the temple on their heads, for joining Xerxes against their own countrymen, the Athenians. Its Ionic columns are the finest type of that style of architecture existing; and in its inclosure were entombed the remains of Cecrops.

Below the Acropolis were the temple and the theatre of Dionysus, or Bacchus; the latter built 500 years B. C. and in a wonderful state of preservation. The stage, orchestra and seats are of marble; the front row of arm-chairs being reserved for the priests of the temples, each having the name of the owner inscribed upon it.

The Temple of Theseus surrounded by a colonnade was erected to receive the remains of that hero, who, in order to abolish the ceremony of the sacrifice of seven Athenian maidens and as many youths, sent annually as tribute to Minos, king of Crete, to satisfy the rapacity of Minotaur a monster confined in the Labyrinth, went himself as one of the allotted victims, to Crete. Here having been cast into the Labyrinth, he sought the monster, and slew him, and finding his way out by means of a ball of thread given him for the purpose by Ariadne, the king's daughter, fled with her from the island.

In the temple are preserved the code of laws of Solon written on tablets of stone; and the marble bas-relief of the soldier of Marathon who bringing back the glad tidings of success expired with the word " Victory " upon his lips.

Other objects of interest in Athens are, the Stadium, an immense amphitheatre built in the side of the hill where the games and chariot races were celebrated annually; the Odeum of Herodes Atticus, a well-preserved Roman theatre; the Temple of Jupiter of which there remain only 16 Corinthian columns, 60 feet in height, one of which lies prostrate, broken into singularly symmetrical sections from the effects of an earthquake; the arch of Hadrian which divides old Athens,—the city of Theseus, from new Athens,—the city of Hadrian; the Lantern of Diogenes, also known as the monument of Lysicrates, a circular building of white marble, and the only one remaining of a series that ornamented the street of Tripods; the Tower of the Winds, an octagonal-shaped water-clock, each of its sides facing the points of the Athenian compass, and the Bema, or stone pulpit from which Themistocles, Pericles, Alcibiades, and Demosthenes addressed the people.

On Mars hill that god was tried for the murder of the son of Neptune by the Areopagus which was the highest judicial court of Athens: and here Socrates was tried for theism, found guilty, and sentenced to death: close by is his dungeon-prison, cut in the solid rock, where he drank the hemlock, and where it is said he was buried 398 B. C.

It was from Mars hill that St. Paul preached to the Athenians, saying: — "for as I passed by and beheld your devotions, I found an altar with this inscription ' *to the unknown god.'* Whom therefore ye ignorantly worship, Him declare I unto you."

On Mount Lycabettus is a small Greek chapel dedicated to St. George, and on the Hill of the Muses is a marble monument to Philopappus; both points affording fine views of the city, and of the Plain of Marathon.

The most interesting excursion from Athens is by carriage to Megara, a drive of four hours or more.

En route the first point of interest is the Temple of Apollo in the Daphne pass. Here Daphne who had bestowed her love upon the Ocean, was walking, when seen and pursued by the enamored Apollo, and unable to reach her lover was transformed by Jupiter into a laurel-tree at the moment the god was about to embrace her, whereupon he plucked a branch therefrom and entwined it about his head; hence the origin of the laurel wreath.

From here we continued along the Sacred Way to Eleusis, where are the ruins of the temples of Ceres and Proserpine, in which the celebrated Mysteries were held. It was in Eleusis that Euclid, the great mathematician, was born, and from here, on a distant hill is visible the point

called the Seat of Xerxes from which he witnessed
the destruction of his fleet in the battle of Sala-
mis.

At Megara we found crowds of Greeks assembled to celebrate the festival of Easter Tuesday. On
the village green, with the sunny skies overhead, and
frequent glimpses of the blue waters of the bay
seen through the intervening foliage, the peasants
dressed in their fanciful and beautiful costumes,—
the rich ornaments of which are frequently inherited through successive generations—held this
their high festival with national games, dances,
and music.

After enjoying this gay and picturesque scene
for several hours, we retraced our way to Athens,
thence to Piræus whence we embarked for Constantinople.

CHAPTER XXIII.

THE DARDANELLES: SEA OF MARMORA: CONSTANTINO-
PLE: THE GOLDEN HORN: THE BOSPHORUS: THE
BLACK SEA: BUDA-PESTH: THE DANUBE.

SAILING through the Archipelago, we passed the
island of Mitylene, the ancient Lesbos, which once
rivalled Athens in learning and art, and where the
" burning Sappho loved and sang ;" and the island
of Tenedos where the Greeks concealed them-

selves when they pretended to abandon the siege of Troy.

From here entering the Dardanelles, or Hellespont, we passed the site of ancient Troy; the tombs of Ajax, Hector, and Achilles; the harbor in which the fleet of Agamemnon lay at anchor; and Abydos, at the narrowest part of the channel where Xerxes, with an army of 5,000,000 men, consumed seven days and nights in crossing, and which Leander nightly swam to visit his beloved Hero: a feat which Lord Byron successfully imitated.

After entering the Sea of Marmora we passed Mount Olympus in Asia Minor, at the foot of which is Brusa, the ancient capital of Turkey; and further on was Nicæa where the first Ecumenical Council was held. This was presided over by Constantine, and was convened for the purpose of compiling the New Testament; when certain books were retained and others rejected by ballot; A. D. 325.

Constantinople, as known in a general way embraces four cities, namely: Stamboul, or Constantinople proper, Galata, Pera, and Scutari; these are located on three approximating peninsulas, and are separated by the Sea of Marmora, the Golden Horn, and the Bosphorus. Their aggregate population numbers 1,000,000 inhabitants comprising almost every nationality. The nobles and public officials are covetous and corrupt,

often selling offices to the highest bidder; and
the lower classes are ignorant and fanatical; peaceful enough habitually, but dangerous when their
passions are aroused by their priests.

The city occupies one of the finest natural
situations in the world; and as approached from
the sea is very beautiful, exhibiting to view a
multitude of domes, minarets and palaces, with a
background of the foliage of the cypress-trees
which shade the extensive cemeteries beyond the
walls.   Its interior is a perfect labyrinth of winding, steep, and dirty streets; many of them un-
named, and all swarming with dogs — often as
many as from 50 to 100 in a single block — who
lie basking on the pavement all day to the great
discomfort of pedestrians who must either walk
around or step over the lazy canines.   These for-
lorn-looking brutes are owned by no one; dividing
themselves into gangs, they inhabit certain self-
apportioned districts, going every morning from
house to house in search of food, thus monopo-
lizing the office of public scavengers.   This sys-
tematic division of territory by these canines is
something curious to the observer of animal char-
acteristics; peaceably inclined towards their fellows as long as they confine themselves to their
own districts, woe to him who oversteps the
boundary of his neighbor's province, for from that
moment he is a doomed dog.

That portion of the city known as Stamboul —

the ancient Byzantium, is on a tongue of land between the Sea of Marmora and the Golden Horn.
It was founded in 656 B. C. by Byzas, a Greek
from Megara, who consulting the Oracle of
Apollo at Delphi was commanded to build his
city on this favorable site opposite Scutari.

It was taken and rebuilt by Constantine A. D.
328, who made it the capital of the Roman Empire, from which time it has borne his name; and
since then, through numerous sieges has been
captured only twice; first in 1204 by the Crusaders and lastly by the Turks in 1453 under
Mohammed II., who slaughtered the Christians
that had taken refuge in the Church of St. Sophia, and left the mark of his sword, and blood-
stained hand on one of its pillars.

The city is surrounded by a wall which though
15 centuries old, is fairly well preserved; that
portion on the west, or land side, being very
strong and protected by the Seven Towers, a
fortress and prison on whose walls are carved the
names of many a doomed captive.   It was at this
point the Russian army made its attack in the
late war, and outside of the gates the treaty of
peace was signed.

The Acropolis, in which is the Seraglio, is
situated on the extreme point of the peninsula
and was for many centuries the imperial and min-
isterial residence; it is shut in by lofty walls with
gates and towers nearly 3 miles in circumference,

and is entered by the Sublime Porte — a gate once guarded by 50 sentinels — from which the government of the Ottoman Empire takes its name. Within the enclosure is the throne of the sultan, who, unseen, gave audience to his ministers; and here also is the harem prison through whose mysterious underground passages many a disgraced favorite was hurried to her doom beneath the silent waters of the Bosphorus.

Outside of the Gate to the right, is the stone block where State offenders were decapitated; on crosses over the Gate, their heads were publicly exposed; and on another stone to the left, their skulls were broken previous to burial.

The Mosque of St. Sophia which was built by the Emperor Justinian in 538 for a Christian church, is the finest Mohammedan mosque in existence, and compares favorably in size and grandeur with St. Peter's at Rome. This mosque which, it is said, employed the labor of 10,000 workmen for 7 years, is in the form of a Latin cross surmounted by an immense dome surrounded by eight smaller ones and four minarets; and is 270 feet long, 243 wide, and 200 high. Of its 170 columns of marble, granite and porphyry taken from various heathen temples, are those from the Temple of the Sun at Baalbec, those from the Temple of Diana at Ephesus, and others from the temples of Heliopolis and of Athens. On the walls are yet faintly discerned the figure of

Christ, and Christian symbols, painted over with the names of the Mohammedan prophets in Arabic characters 30 feet in length.

The Mosque of Soliman the Magnificent, was built in 1560 by that sultan, to imitate and rival that of St. Sophia; and in his tomb which adjoins it, is a model of the Kaaba at Mecca. Near this mosque was the Slave Market; the grated pens, yet to be seen, where the unfortunate slaves were displayed for sale.

The Mosque of Sultan Achmed ranks next in magnificence and is the only one that boasts of six minarets, which is the greatest number allowed; the Kaaba at Mecca having seven, consequently all others are restricted to a less number.

Of the remaining mosques — each vieing with the other in magnificence — are those of Mohammed II. and of Benjazid; the latter giving shelter to thousands of pigeons which being held sacred are fed at public expense.

The finest of the mausolea of the sultans is that of Mahmoud; the tomb within it, which is of great size, is covered with black velvet richly embroidered in silver with Arabic characters and other Oriental designs, and inclosed by a silver railing; at its head are costly camel's-hair shawls and the sultan's fez, in which is a magnificent diamond ornament.

The Hippodrome Square, formerly a Greek

circus, contains the Obelisk of Theodosius brought
from Heliopolis; the Pillar of Constantine and
the Serpentine Column; the latter consisting of
three twisted bronze serpents brought from Delphi where it supported the tripod which the victorious Greeks dedicated to Apollo after the great
Persian war when the army of Xerxes was
defeated. It was in this Square that Justinian's
great general, Belisarius, was eulogized for his success and conquest, and after having become old and
blind, was suffered to be led by a child, and beg his
daily bread at the foot of the very monuments
his valor had preserved. Near this are the Burnt
Column once surmounted by the bronze statue of
Apollo, and the Thousand and One Columns—an
underground cistern built by Constantine, whose
grave lies neglected in the most wretched and
filthy part of the city.

Galata and Pera on the northern peninsula
between the Golden Horn and the Bosphorus are
those sections of Constantinople inhabited chiefly
by the Franks, or Europeans, and here are the
headquarters of all the foreign ambassadors.

On the shore of the Bosphorus is the immense
white Palace and harem of the present sultan who
rejoices in the possession of 150 wives. Every
Friday at noon the sultan can be seen on his way
to the mosque, escorted by his ministers, 20 generals, a large staff of officers in dazzling uniforms,
and 5,000 troops; with a suite of attendants, state

carriages and led saddle-horses.   All this display
for one man to pass 20 minutes in prayer!

The Dervishes, a religious sect of the Mohammedans, are   divided   into   two   orders — the
Dancing, and the Howling.   The former, wearing
tall, pointed hats and full skirts, with outstretched
arms, maintain an incessant spinning motion, often
revolving at the rate of fifty times a minute until
the mind becomes so disassociated from the body,
that they enter into a state of trance. The Howling Dervishes observe the same ceremonies here,
as those already described in Cairo, with the addition of walking over the prostrate bodies of
persons of all ranks and ages, who believe in this
means of effecting cures of the diseases that afflict
mankind.

Scutari, on the Asiatic side of the Bosphorus,
contains a fine summer palace of the sultan, with
beautiful grounds, kiosks, and large cages containing fine specimens of tigers, lions and other
wild animals.   Near by is the hospital where Florence Nightingale nursed the sick and wounded
soldiers of the Crimea : and the English cemetery
containing the graves of 25,000 victims of this
war.

In the Turkish cemetery beyond, is a monument to the horse which was ridden by the messenger who was sent to announce the taking of
Constantinople to Mohammed II. in 1453, and
which fell dead immediately after. The government

employs a Dervish priest to place a sack of oats
on the grave each night, and as by morning it has
disappeared, the superstitious regard the fact as
evidence of the horse's acceptance of the tribute.

On the north of the city is the Golden Horn,
an arm of the sea, so-called from the abundance
of fish found in its waters by the first settlers,
which yielded them an immense revenue. One of
the favorite excursions from the city is to sail up
the Golden Horn, passing the ruined palace of
Belisarius, to the Sweet Waters the popular resort
of the Turkish ladies ; for this purpose the caique
is most in vogue,—a long, narrow, pointed boat,
somewhat resembling a canoe, in the bottom of
which its occupant is required to sit upright, and
perfectly motionless, with the alternative of an
impromptu plunge into the water.

Leaving Constantinople we sailed through the
Bosphorus passing numbers of palaces and
mosques which border its shores; the Castle of
Asia, and the Castle of Europe, the latter built by
Mohammed II., and from which he shot marble
cannon balls when besieging Constantinople.

Therapia is a pretty summer resort of the
ambassadors and wealthy citizens; and the spot
where Medea landed with Jason on his return
from Colchis after the Argonautic expedition.

Crossing the Black Sea we took a direct course
to Buda-Pesth the capital of Hungary, situated on
both banks of the Danube, with a population of

308,000. Buda on the right bank contains the
Royal palace in the midst of beautiful terraced
gardens, with a stern-looking old castle guarding
the heights above; and Pesth, on the left bank
connected with Buda by several bridges, is a
modern-built city, with wide streets containing
several statues, and is celebrated for its Tokay
wines and immense flour mills.

From here we took steamer on the Danube—
a twelve hours' sail to Vienna, passing en route
Presburg, Komorn, Gran, and other points of interest, but being wide and muddy, with low banks,
the river does not compare here in point of
scenery with that already described.

CHAPTER XXIV.

CARLSBAD : HOMBURG : WIESBADEN : EMS : BOULOGNE :
AGINCOURT AND CRESSY : ST. OMER : AMIENS : DIEPPE.

HAVING by this time traversed the length and
breadth of Europe, with the most interesting portions of Morocco, Algeria, Egypt, Syria, and
Turkey, and deeming it inadvisable during the
summer months to continue our travels through
the Red Sea and under the Equator, we concluded
to while away the intermediate time visiting the

most noted and frequented watering-places of
Europe.

Carlsbad—or Charles bath—has a permanent
population of 8,000, and is located in a ravine in
the mountains of Bohemia.

During the season,—from April to October,
there are often as many as 40,000 visitors from all
parts of the world, who come, not as votaries to
the altars of Fashion, but as worshippers at the
shrine of Hygeia.

The mountains and hills environing Carlsbad
are intersected by beautiful and romantic walks,
where invalids seek in healthful exercise an efficient adjunct to the medicinal effects of the
waters. Owing to the oppressive atmosphere of
the valley, visitors, as a rule, seek the cool shelter
of the many pretty villas which dot the hill slopes
surrounding it. The Springs, 9 in number, located along a stream in the bottom of the ravine, take their name from the Emperor Charles
IV. who discovered them while hunting, his dog
chancing to fall into one, and emerging scalded
by the natural heat of the water: the Emperor,
afterwards returning here, was benefited by the
baths which he took for wounds received in
battle.

The principal of these Springs are the Mühl-
brun, and the Sprudel, whose waters are 165 degrees Fahrenheit, and contain sulphate, carbonate
of soda, lime and potash, considered highly bene-

ficial for rheumatism, liver, and kidney diseases.
Every morning from six to eight, while the band
plays, crowds of visitors may be seen strolling
towards the springs carrying their small glasses,
and taking their places in line, to await their turn
to be served from the medicinal waters.

Homburg, one of the most famous watering
places of Germany, is 15 miles from Frankfort,
and is situated on a commanding elevation.

The Kursäal is decidedly the handsomest
building of its kind in the Empire; its theatre,
concert, and ball-rooms, together with the extensive grounds and promenades surrounding it,
combine to render it a delightful place of resort.
The springs, four in number, are beneficial for
rheumatism and skin diseases; while the large
park in which they are situated, laid out in flower-
bordered walks, and the conservatories filled with
orange-trees and other tropical plants, add much
to the attractions of the place.

Wiesbaden, with a population of 50,000 is the
capital of the Grand Duchy of Nassau in Prussia,
and the residence of the Grand Duke; it is
beautifully situated in the midst of gardens, orchards, and handsome villas.

The springs, numbering 30, which are alkaline,
and of a high temperature, were known to the
Romans; and are frequented during the season,
by at least 30,000 people. Its Kursäal which is
devoted to reading-rooms, restaurant, and formerly

to gambling-halls, is in the midst of a park containing a beautiful little lake on the margin of which are tables and chairs where visitors retire after dinner to sip their coffee, while listening to a fine band of music.

Ems, another fashionable place of resort much frequented by Germans and Russians, is situated on both banks of the river Lahn, in a long narrow valley shut in on both sides by steep wooded hills, and has a population of 6,000. It has a fine Kursäal and a covered colonnade for promenading in inclement weather besides many shaded walks. It was here the Emperor — then King William — gave Benedetti his final answer — July, 1870 — which led to the Franco-Prussian war.

Boulogne derives its importance from its proximity to the shores of England, and is a fashionable watering-place much frequented by English visitors for its surf bathing. On one side of the harbor is the circular basin excavated by Napoleon to contain the flat-bottomed boats intended to convey his army of invasion to England.

Not far from Boulogne are the celebrated battle-fields of Agincourt and Cressy; in connection with the latter of which is noted the incident of the brave blind king of Bohemia anxious to participate in the battle, insisting upon being led by two knights into the thickest of the fight, where he fell covered with wounds. His standard was presented to the Black Prince after the English victory, who adopted for his own, the crest it bore,—three ostrich plumes with the motto *Ich Dien*,— I serve,— which has been borne ever since by the successive Princes of Wales.

The town of St. Omer, one of the oldest in France, is situated in this vicinity. It contains the ruins of a monastery, whose founder, Omer, assuming the cowl at the death of his wife, devoted his large possessions to this purpose; for which deed he was afterwards canonized. His descendant Geoffrey de St. Omer was one of the founders of the order of Knights Templar in the time of the Crusades.

Amiens, on the Somme, has in its Cathedral a head which the inhabitants claim as that of John the Baptist.

Dieppe is another popular bathing resort particularly frequented by the French people, and is situated on the coast of Normandy in northern France.

CHAPTER XXV.

PARIS: BRINDISI: PORT SÄID: SUEZ CANAL: RED SEA:
ADEN: INDIAN OCEAN: COLOMBO: KANDY.

AFTER equipping ourselves in Paris with medicines, clothing, and other requirements necessary for travel through hot, unhealthy, and dangerous countries, we took rail direct for Brindisi, and from there, steamer for Port Säid at the head of the Suez Canal.

The Suez Canal from Port Säid to Suez, a distance of 100 miles, is a water highway extending through a number of lakes and ancient canals,— and connects the waters of the Mediterranean with those of the Red Sea. The project of constructing this canal was entertained by both Napoleon I. and Mohammed Ali; but it was reserved for Vicomte Ferdinand de Lesseps of France to bring it to a successful issue. He first conceived the idea while in quarantine at Alexandria, in 1831; in 1859 a company was formed of 21,000 Frenchmen, inaugurated by Prince Jerome, who took shares when the entire capital of 200,000,000 francs, $40,000,000, was subscribed; and in 1869, the work being completed, the canal was opened with great festivities under the auspices of the Empress Eugénie, the Emperor of Austria, the Crown Prince of Prussia, and other guests of the Khedive.

The Canal is 26 feet deep, and 72 feet wide, and while being navigable for the largest steamers and iron-clads, sidings are necessary to enable them to pass one another. This route has shortened the trip from London to Bombay by 5,000 miles, or 24 days, and proves such a benefit to the English especially,— as two-thirds of the vessels passing through it carry the English flag —

that in 1875 she secured, out of the 400,000 shares, 176,602 shares of the stock. The canal alternately passes through miles of sandy desert, and large, bitter, and salt lakes; while the great, ungainly dredging machines are kept constantly at work clearing the channel, on which the immense naval vessels of the English government are frequently seen going to or from India. The rate of speed allowed steamers on this canal, is six miles an hour, and even this washes away the banks considerably, and fills up the channel.

The principal towns passed are Daphne the Tahpannes of the Bible, and Kantara, formerly called Meses. This town, one of the most ancient in the world, is the spot where the Asian tribes entered to settle Egypt, and was the birthplace of Horus—the oldest of the Egyptian deities — like the Greek Apollo, typical of the Sun. Further on is Ismailia, on the shore of Lake Timsah, now a healthy and thriving town of 3,000 inhabitants, on a spot where a few years ago no living thing could exist.

Suez, with a population of 13,000, is on the gulf of the same name near the Red Sea. It owes its importance to its being a station on the route of pilgrimages to Mecca; and also for vessels plying between European ports and India. Four miles below the town on the African shore are the mountains Gebel Attakah, or Mountains of Deliverance — at which point tradition locates the spot where Moses crossed the Red Sea with the Children of Israel. Our guide at this place who spoke with the assurance of a contemporary informed us it was not Pharaoh, but a horde of Bedouin Arabs — who then, as to-day, lived by attacking travellers on the desert — that followed the Israelites for the purpose of plunder: Moses being acquainted with the rapid rise and fall of the water, selected a favorable time to effect a crossing, while the Bedouins, ignorant of such matters, were in their wake when the returning tide overtook them and they were drowned. As a proof of his assertion the guide contended that had the pursuing party been Pharaoh's host, his chariots would undoubtedly have been found afterwards. However much our guide's account may differ from Biblical records, the fact is incontestable that Napoleon once narrowly escaped sharing the same fate as that of the pursuers of the Israelites.

On the Asiatic coast further south, on the Red Sea we saw the Wells of Moses, dug by the Children of Israel after reaching the shore in safety; and further on at the extreme end of the peninsula, is Mount Sinai where it is said Moses received from God the Ten Commandments. The intense heat of the Red Sea, swept by the hot desert winds of either shore, now began to make itself felt, and our steamer keeping in view the coast of Hedjaz Jemen in Arabia, we passed Jeddah, the sea-port for Mecca and Medina. This latter city,

only second in the veneration of the Mohammedans, contains the remains of the Prophet in a
silver coffin beneath a marble slab, over which a
fine mosque is erected. It was hither the Prophet
fled from Mecca, a distance of 240 miles, when
the skeptical, deaf to his teachings, rose up against
him, and from this flight, or Hegira, dates the
Mohammedan era. Mecca, the birthplace of Mohammed, and the Rome of Islam, is 65 miles from
Jeddah. Its natural position hemmed in by hills, its
passes guarded by Arab sentinels, and the fanati-
cism of its inhabitants, render it almost impossible of access to Christians.

Mr. Keane, an Englishman, led by a spirit
of adventure, accomplished the perilous feat of effecting an entrance, disguised as a Mussulman, into
this city: but being detected, he was stoned in
the streets and escaped by almost a miracle.

The following account may prove interesting
to those who, like ourselves, have been debarred
the privilege of entering the sacred precincts.

"Mecca," says Mr. Keane, "is a walled city,
situated in a narrow, sandy valley, inclosed by
rocky eminences from 200 to 500 feet high. The
valley is scarcely 600 yards broad, narrowing
southward to about 300 where it is almost blocked
by the Beit-Ullah — God's House — the great
mosque enshrining the famous Kaaba. The entire
building forms a rectangle 250 yards long by 200
broad, the north side of which is formed by four

rows of pillars, the other three, of three rows each, arched over, and so disposed, that each group of four supports a small cupola, making in all 152 of these structures along its four sides. The oldest pillars are hewn out of the neighboring rocks; the others consisting of marble, granite, and porphyry, are mostly offerings of the faithful, and include some from the most ancient temples of Syria and Egypt. Within the mosque is the Kaaba, a small, massive building about 40 feet in height. Tradition associates this unpretending and curious little structure with a multitude of marvels and legends. On the north side is a door-way leading over steps inlaid with gold and silver, to the inner sanctuary, in one corner of which lies the famous Black Stone which they claim was a gift from God to Abraham, but which is evidently a meteoric formation descended, if not from heaven, at least from the interplanetary space. To the west of the Kaaba is the Golden Channel carrying off from the flat roof the rain-water which is reputed to be endowed with miraculous properties."

Continuing through the Red Sea we passed Mocha noted for its finely-flavored coffee, and Aden, located on a rocky, volcanic soil, serving England as a coaling station, and as a guard to the Red Sea. In our sail through the Arabian Sea and Indian Ocean, the Southern Cross, seen only in these latitudes, shone brightly in the heavens above us by night, and nearing India we passed the Maldive Islands, which are coral reefs — formed by the labor of millions of insects — with small lakes in their midst, fringed by rows of palm-trees.

On approaching the island of Ceylon, our attention was first attracted to the peculiar boat used by the natives. It is about 20 feet long, 20 inches wide, and 3 feet deep, with a balance log the same length of the boat, 10 to 20 feet off one side, and attached to it by bamboo poles; this out-rigger, as it is called, is always kept to windward, and when a breeze springs up, one, two, or three men, will sit on it in order to balance the boat, and in speaking of a storm they call it a one, two, or three man breeze according to the number of men on the outrigger; these boats sail at the rate of 10 miles an hour, and venture 20 miles out to sea in the severest storm.

Ceylon is a pear-shaped island at the extreme south of India and has a population of 2,500,000. Its government is entirely separate from that of India, and the governor is appointed by the British Crown. It is almost connected with India by a rocky reef called Adam's Bridge, so named from the Mohammedan legend that on his expulsion from the Garden of Eden Adam passed over this singular causeway into Ceylon. By the Brahmans the Island is called the Resplendent; by the Buddhists, a Pearl upon the brow of India; by the Chinese, the Island of Jewels, and by the

Greeks, the Land of the Hyacinth and the Ruby. It was to Ceylon the ships of Solomon came for gold, silver, ivory, apes, and peacocks; and Fable has also contributed to its fame by locating it as the place where Sindbad of the Arabian Nights was wrecked.

Near a marine mountain of lodestone his ship fell asunder, and the nails and every iron thing about it flew to the lodestone: even to this day, native boats are constructed without the use of iron.

The island is filled with the richest and rankest of tropical growth; wild elephants and other large animals abound, and the spices, ivory, and precious stones — such as cat's-eye, sapphires, pearls, and rubies found here are world-renowned.

Ceylon, though the stronghold of Buddhism, contains many followers of the Christian, Mohammedan, and Hindu faiths, while Polyandry, which allows of a plurality of husbands, is largely practised here.

Colombo, which was named by the Portuguese after Columbus, has a population of 98,000. It extends about 4 miles along the coast and is divided into the European quarter, and the black, or native, town. Here one sees the Singhalese chiefly as servants — the men wearing skirts, and their long hair in a knot at the back of the head held by a high comb, giving them a resemblance to women; the Parsees as merchants; the Tamils as laborers, and the Moors as retail dealers; while upon the Coolies, or lower classes, devolves the menial duties : these latter wear only a cloth about their loins, and oil their bodies until they shine like polished ebony.

The natives as a rule are clean in their personal habits, but their mouths are invariably discolored from betel chewing. This consists of a compound of the leaves of the betel, some lime, and the sliced nuts of the Arèca palm, which quenches thirst without being intoxicating in its effects, while it possesses strong tonic properties. This mixture, on being chewed, imparts a blood-like hue to the mouth, and has been used by the natives, both here and in India from time immemorial.

There are palms in great variety around Colombo, but the cocoanut is the most plentiful, and yields many of the necessities of life : its fruit furnishes food ; its shell drinking-vessels ; its milk palm wine and sugar ; its stems material for building, and its leaves, roofs, matting, baskets, and paper.

We drove through the European quarter, and along the beach, seeing nothing particularly noticeable beyond the cinnamon gardens, which are cultivated for the bark of this shrub.

In the native quarter we visited a Buddhist temple in which is a gilded, recumbent figure of Buddha, measuring 80 feet in length, with angels with drawn swords, keeping watch over him. A poetic feature of the Buddhist religion is the floral sacrifice, and in this temple we first saw, among a great variety of lovely flowers offered at the shrine of Buddha, the sacred lotus.

Driving 3 miles out of town, through the rankest of tropical vegetation, we called on Arabi Pasha, who was exiled here after the battle of Tel-el-Kebir in Egypt, and is now a State prisoner of the English. Arabi is a man of large frame and mild countenance, speaking some French, and but a little English. He received us with native grace and hospitality, offering us refreshments and tobacco, and rendering our visit an altogether pleasant one.

From Colombo we took the rail 75 miles to Kandy — the ancient capital of Ceylon — situated in the interior of the island. The entire route afforded a varied and grand panorama, winding through vales and among hills, combining Alpine grandeur with tropical luxuriance.

Kandy though only a small village is beautifully situated on the shores of a miniature artificial lake. It has lovely walks and drives, and handsome villas dot the hill-sides which environ the lake: on the margin of which is the palace of the late king of Ceylon and a fine Buddhist temple enshrining a tooth of Buddha, an object of great veneration, and exposed to the view of worshippers only on rare occasions.

Near Kandy we visited large plantations of tea and coffee, and saw growing the clove-tree from whose flower-bud the spice is named; the nutmeg, the outer covering of which is the mace: also the vanilla, cocoa, rubber, and banyan trees, and clumps of gigantic bamboos. Here we saw almost every variety of the palm; the Travellers' — one stem of which, when cut, yields a quart of the purest drinking water; the Palmyra, from the sap of which a wine is produced, and the Taliput, whose single leaf measures 10x14 feet, and will shelter 15 men. It blooms but once in 100 years, and has a flower, which we were fortunate enough to see, measuring twelve feet in circumference, and of a yellowish color.

Returning to Colombo, we took steamer to the extreme southern point of India, landing at Tuticorin.

CHAPTER XXVI.

INDIA: ITS HISTORY: ITS RELIGIONS: BRAHMANISM: BUDDHISM: HINDUISM: MOHAMMEDANISM: THE JAINS: THE PARSEES: CASTE.

INDIA, the vast Asiatic possession of Great Britain, stretching 2,000 miles from north to south, and nearly as many from east to west, has

an area of 1,490,000 square miles; and embraces
almost every variety of climate; with high mountains, low marshes, densely-populated and unin-
habited regions, immense rivers, and jungles infested by the most formidable of wild beasts.   Its
chief official is the Viceroy, who resides at its capital,
Calcutta, and under him are native independent
princes, lieutenant-governors, and agents who pre-
side over states and districts.

The population of India at the present time
numbers 250,000,000 of people of different religious sects, and speaking many languages and
dialects.   As this country is the mother of the
oldest religions known, it will not be amiss to
give here some details of its history and religious
creeds, as derived from other authors, and from
our own observation.

The early non-Aryan races of India, divided
into three great groups, are the Thibeto-Birmans,
the Kolarians, and the Dravidians.

The Thibeto-Birmans occupy the Himalayas,
and include many mountain tribes, akin in feature
and in tongue to the Chinese.

The Kolarians, supposed to have come in
through the mountain passes, are now scattered
in every direction, their chief tribes being the
Sontals and Khands.

The Dravidians who also came through the
mountain passes, forced their way on in a com-
pact phalanx, and found a secure resting-place in

the south. They attained a high state of cultivation long before the Aryan invasion; their chief languages, polished and cultivated, are the Telugu — melodious as Italian: the Tamil — rich in its literature; the Canarese and the Malayan.

The Aryans — or nobles — is the wide-spread Indo-European race whose western branch extends over Greece, Italy, Germany, and England. They, in turn, entered India by the northwest passes, speaking the stately Sanscrit, driving the inferior hordes before them, and finding a permanent home in the great river plains. They soon asserted their supremacy over the earlier people, as Brahmans and Rajputs; they established Caste and gave to the East the two giant religious systems of Brahmanism and Buddhism; their languages were the Sanscrit and Pali with their branches Panjabi, Sindhi, Hindi, Bengali, Marhatti and Singali.

The Greeks invaded India 327 B. C. under Alexander the Great; but left no permanent settlement, though the Greek type of sculpture long survived in Indian art. Scythian influences and a Scythian era also marked the annals of India from 57 B. C. downwards; and some of the Rajput tribes are traced back to them.

The next wave of conquest was that of the Mohammedans, who entered India in the 11th century, and made successive conquests. They brought with them their native Arabic; and

Arabic inscriptions adorn the magnificent mosques, halls, palaces and tombs, which they erected chiefly in the 17th century.

Brahmanism, the religion of the Aryans which found its earliest exposition in the hymns of the Vedas, and its development in the institutions of Manu, was originally monotheistic.

The Rig-Veda, usually placed 1400 B. C. consists of a series of hymns addressed to the bright friendly gods Divas — literally the shining ones, the great powers of Nature, the father-heaven, the mother-earth, the encompassing sky. Brahma, the creator, has no separate existence in these hymns; Vishnu, the preserver, is but slightly known; and Siva, the destroyer, appears as Rudra the god of tempest. The potent prayer was called Brahma, and he who offered it was called Brahman. Already, in the Vedas, sacrifices are enjoined; the man-sacrifice, and the great horse-sacrifice of 600 animals that was substituted for it. Thus, by degrees, sprang up the four great Castes; the Brahmans, or priests, sprung from the mouth of Brahma, and distinguished by a sacred cord about their bodies; the Kshatriyas, or warriors, now called Rajputs, taken from his arms; the Vaisyas, or husbandmen from his thighs and beneath these, the Sudras, or servile class, the slaves of black descent issued from his feet.

After a long struggle between the priestly and warrior castes, the former prevailed and es-

tablished their supremacy as the makers of Sanscrit literature; and the priests and teachers of
the people. The Brahman's life was one of dis-
cipline; study occupied his early years; then
marriage and family life; next seclusion and devotion; and lastly mendicancy, asceticism and
absorption.

Throughout life he practised strict abstinence,
recognizing the transitory vanity of human life.
"What is the world?" says a Brahman sage: "It
is even as the bough of a tree on which a bird
rests for a night, and in the morning flies away."
Self-culture, self-restraint, was the ideal life.
Hence amidst all the changes of history the Brahman in India, refined in feature, tall and slender,
has calmly ruled. Brahmanism in its growth and
spread is strikingly illustrated by the teachings of
Christianity regarding the lapse of man from a
pure and simple faith — from the knowledge of
God into idolatry and superstition: "knowing
God they glorified him not as God, but became
vain in their imaginations." Brahma, the Creator, became a mere abstract name; Vishnu, the
Preserver received 10 avatars — or incarnations —
Rama and Krishna being the chief; and Siva, the
Destroyer and Reproducer, became the embodi-
ment of wrath and lust. The most prominent
doctrine of philosophical Brahmanism became the
transmigration of souls; ending with absorption
in the Supreme Being.

Buddhism, now the religion in a degraded form of one-third of the human race, had its origin in India, whence it has long been exiled. Its founder was Gautama son of a prince of the Sakyan clan, born 623 B. C. a hundred miles north of Benares. After his student and married life he retired when 30 years old to a cave near Gaya in the Patna district, and this epoch in his life is called his Great Renunciation. But instead of finding peace in his fasting and seclusion, he reached a crisis of despair, passed through a conflict with the powers of darkness, and emerged with new light and knowledge, to be henceforth known as Buddha the Enlightened, and this era that of the Enlightenment.

Now he began to live and preach a new life of love and kindness among men, condemning Caste, proclaiming the equality of men, and setting before them Nirvâna, that is, cessation, not of existence, but of sin and sorrow as their final goal. He began his public teaching at the age of 36, and for 40 years he labored. His last words were: "Work out your own salvation with diligence, keep your minds upon my teaching, all things change, but this changes not. I desire to depart, I desire Nirvâna, the eternal rest." The date of his death is 543 B. C.

Buddhism was a missionary religion and it spread as a gospel throughout India. Its apostle was Asoka, grandson of Chandra Gupta, and king of Maghada, whose edict in Pali inscriptions indicate the humanity and kindness of the teachings which the system promulgated.

The son of Asoka became a Buddhist missionary to Ceylon, and the systems spread as the Topes and Caves of early Buddhism indicate. But it borrowed much from Brahmanism: namely, the doctrine of transmigration, the practice of asceticism, and the recognition of a priestly order. Relics of Buddha were cherished and adored and shrines built over them; images of the Saint himself were multiplied, and became objects of worship.

But in process of time Brahmanism triumphed over its rival. Buddhism lacked a personal god, it was a form of atheism; it failed to recognize the doctrine of the expiation of human sin by sacrifice; and here the Brahmans had the advantage, and in time regained their influence and their supremacy. By the 10th century of the Christian era, Buddhism was in India an exiled religion, finding its home in Thibet and Ceylon, in China, and in Burmah. It has since degenerated into an elaborate ritualism akin to Romanism, with the image of Buddha in place of the crucifix; the goddess of Mercy for the Virgin; a shaven, robed and celibate priesthood; altar and lights; rosary and penance; monks and nuns; purgatory and hell, and in Thibet a pope.

Hinduism is the modern development in India,

of the religion of the Brahmans, modified by
Buddhist teachings; and here again we find only
degeneracy from the primitive standards. The
Brahmans or priests themselves have in many
places degenerated, and are self-indulgent, gross,
immoral, worldly-minded men. Caste with all its
tyranny prevails. Women are immured in ignorance, and doomed to slavery : married in childhood — as early as the age of ten — if the child-
husband dies she is a widow for life, doomed to
drudgery and neglect. The temples are adorned
with revolting and obscene sculptures and frescoes,
the images of idolatry are hideous, and the objects
of adoration countless.

Vishnuism, or the worship of Vishnu and his
many incarnations, and Sivaism — or the worship
of Siva, form in the present day, the very heart
and soul of Hinduism. The old idolatry of serpents, trees, and stones, borrowed perhaps from
the non-Aryan tribes has been adopted into the
system, and the Linga bedaubed with oil and red
ochre is the popular idol.

The Puranas are the writings that form the
basis of modern Hinduism, and they disclose
Phallic worship in all its loathsomeness.

The chief daily ceremony in all temples, after
washing and decorating the idol, and burning
lights and incense before it, consists in offering it
food — rice, sweetmeats, flowers, and grain. The
smallest village has its own peculiar symbols of

worship, which are often merely rough blocks of stone.

Mohammedanism first appeared in India about the 11th century, and gained a permanent footing by the conquest of the Moslems. In the 17th century its sway was universal in north India. It proclaimed the doctrine: "there is but one God and Mohammed is His Prophet;" and it built its giant mosques in the great cities, and made many converts. The Mohammedan population to-day numbers 45,000,000.

The Jains, a small, but very ancient sect, are akin to the Buddhists, but have an independent origin. They are a very wealthy community distinguished by the beauty and costliness of their temples, and the multiplicity of their hospitals, especially those for diseased and decrepit animals. They lay great stress upon the doctrine of the transmigration of souls, and actually strain the water which they would drink, brush the seat upon which they would sit, or the path upon which they would walk lest they should unwittingly crush an insect. Their distinctive feature is saint worship, and their most important holy place of pilgrimage is Mount Abu.

The Parsees are of Persian origin and are settled chiefly in Bombay where they have become wealthy and prosperous. They hold the tenets of Zoroaster, and worship the four elements, fire, air, earth and water. The Supreme Being called Ormuzd is, with them, not self-existing but derived. Their scriptures are the Zend-Avesta, which contains the doctrines of Zoroaster.

The religious and social system of India, is everywhere based on the institution of Caste which was originally introduced, as before mentioned, to uphold the political supremacy of the fair Aryan intruders over the dark aborigines; but before its introduction a considerable intermixture had already taken place except perhaps among the very highest classes of the Aryan conquerors. The indigenous elements being by far the most numerous, the Aryans were thus threatened with ultimate absorption; and in fact had become in many places largely assimilated with the native. They could be saved from extinction only by checking further alliances; marriage with the dark races was accordingly forbidden, and a definite grade assigned to each shade of color which had already been developed. Hence Caste, originally meant color, and had therefore an ethnical value. But once established, the institution gradually acquired an indefinite development, and the four original castes, already mentioned, have in the course of ages expanded into minute subdivisions almost innumerable.

The last census returns give 2,500 main divisions; and in Madras alone, nearly 4,000 minor distinctions. The consequence is, that every child is born in a caste, and must follow the oc-

cupation of its father, neither rising above nor falling below it, hence in the domestic provinces, it requires a dozen men to accomplish the work of one
ordinary servant; the punker-boy can do nothing
else but pull the punker — or swinging fan,
which is an invariable feature of Indian life; the
man who makes the fire cannot remove the ashes,
or the one who makes the bed, sweep the room;
while the Brahman feels himself defiled if he
comes in contact with the Sudra, and immediately
seeks through prayer to rid himself of the pollu-
tion.

CHAPTER XXVII.

TUTICORIN : MADURA : TRICHINOPOLY : SERINGHAM :
TANJORE : CHILLAMBARAM : MADRAS.

TRAVEL in India is for the most part attended by
discomforts; the government bungalow — or
rest-house — is often only a place of shelter, and
the hotels are little better, even in the largest
cities, and one is compelled to provide himself
not only with a servant, but with bedding, and
often with provisions. The railroad officials are
mostly natives; and one may travel for days on
some of the lines without seeing a white face.
The first-class cars are but few, and in them are
separate compartments for men and women.

To resume the course of our travels: after landing at Tuticorin — a wretched, dirty town in the extreme south of India — celebrated only for its pearl-fisheries, we took rail to traverse the country in its entire length and breadth.

At Madura we first saw the masterpieces of Dravidian architecture for which the Madras presidency is famous; and which, in their number, their extent, and the elaborateness of their workmanship astonish and almost bewilder the beholder. The Dravidians offered their labor to their gods, and reared immense temples to their worship.

These temples, though differing in size and magnificence, are similar in their component parts. The most conspicuous feature from the exterior are the Gopuras or pyramidal gate-ways, towering from 150 to 300 feet high; elaborately carved with grotesque figures in stone of their gods, which are from 6 to 10 feet each in height, painted in every color imaginable, and in various attitudes; some having as many as 20 heads and arms. These figures are symbolical of the gods they represent; rising one above the other in diminishing tiers, some ten to fifteen, over the arched gateway; the summit crowned by an immense head with open mouth, great teeth and eyes, grinning down upon the inferior gods with Satanic mien.

The Vimana, or adytum, is a square, sur-

mounted by a pyramidal roof overlaid with gold;
here in a dark cubical cell, the idol with its altar
is immured, and a lamp is kept dimly burning
night and day.   Around the Vimana, and leading
up to it, usually from the four points of the compass, are the Mantapas, or huge stone porches,
richly carved: besides these, are · the Hall of a
Thousand Pillars, all of which are of elaborately
carved stone from 10 to 40 feet high, supporting
a flat roof; and the Sacred Tank surrounded with
corridors, and with flights of steps leading down
into the water.   All these gates, halls, courts, and
shrine, centred around, and leading to the adytum, form the monster temples of South India
covering from 30 to 40 acres, and called Pagodas.

The pagoda — or temple of Siva in Madura,
to which the above general description applies,
covers 20 acres, and though not the largest, is one
of the most interesting and best preserved in India.   It dates from the 3d century B. C. and is
dedicated jointly to Menakshi, the fish-eyed goddess and to Siva.

Entering the Temple we passed through a
succession of 9 gopuras, and along corridors
used for bazaars, where the principal articles sold
were paints and oil, essentials of their religious
rites, and entered the hall of a Thousand Pillars,
one of which is subdivided into 24 smaller ones,
and all are elaborately carved in stone; one of

these pillars represents the Devil holding a woman
by the hand in the act of leading her into temptation; and boys are taught, as a religious duty to
spit in his face. In one of the courts was the
sacred tank filled with dirty water in which the
worshippers were busily engaged cleansing themselves from their sins; and continuing on we passed
through halls and apartments where the columns
represented men on horseback hewn out of the
solid blocks of granite. In this temple there are
three different statues of the Bull sacred to Siva,
besides many other idols, and all are covered with
oil and besmeared with red ochre which impreg-
nates the atmosphere with a disagreeable odor.
In the centre of the main hall of worship was an
immense live elephant painted in many colors and
used in their religious processions in transporting
the idol.

It chanced to be a fête day when we visited
the temple, and we found it crowded with the
natives. The men, nude except for the loin cloth,
bore on their foreheads in painted characters token
of their caste, and of the special idols of their
worship: while the women profusely decked with
ornaments — ear, nose, finger, and toe-rings,
bracelets and anklets, necklaces and diadems of
glass and tinsel — had their faces and bodies entirely besmeared with yellow paint.

A prominent building in Madura, now partly
in ruins, is the palace of Tirumala, one of the

greatest rulers of the province, built by him in
1623.   The Throne-room or Hall of Audience is
of a peculiar style of architecture, the ceiling consisting of several domes supported by massive
pillars.

A lovely drive of three miles beyond the city,
shaded with banyan trees meeting overhead, leads
to the Teppu-Kulam — a large, sacred tank containing in its centre a small island upon which is
a temple; once a year it is illuminated, and the
idol placed in a boat and rowed on the waters
with the pomp and circumstance of their religious
rites.

Continuing by rail to Trichinopoly Junction
where we passed the night, we drove next morning a distance of 3 miles to Trichinopoly Fort, the
main feature of which town is the rock fortress
from which it takes its name.   It rises abruptly
500 feet above the level of the sea, and towers
250 feet over the town; while half-way up the
rock, and built against it, is a temple dedicated to
Siva.

A three mile drive northward from Trichinopoly brought us to the famous Dravidian temples
of Seringham, the largest in all India, built on an
island formed by the branches of the Cavery river.
The greatest of these pagodas is seven miles in
circumference; and includes many bazaars and
streets of Brahmans' houses, more resembling a
walled town than a temple.   In its centre shrine

we saw the Golden Idol one of whose glittering
eyes, abstracted in the last century by a French
deserter, proved to be a diamond of almost match-
less purity: it was subsequently purchased by
Count Orloff and presented by him to his royal
mistress Catherine. This gem known as the
Orloff diamond, now figures as the most conspicuous ornament in the imperial sceptre of Russia.

While this temple differs but little from the
general description already given of the Indian
pagodas, the wonderful carvings in its Column
Hall are worthy of special notice. Its pillars,
formed from a single block of granite, are sculptured into grotesque, gigantic figures of men in
the act of spearing tigers, others mounted on
rearing horses, and some of these animals hold in
the mouth a loose stone ball: all indicating a
wonderful degree of skill.

Here we happened to witness a religious procession entering the temple; this comprised first,
a band of music consisting of various kinds of
queer native instruments; next the elephants, immense beasts, their foreheads, ears, and trunks
painted red, white, and yellow, and their bodies
covered with rich trappings and large ringing
bells; these followed by white horses and an en-
thusiastic crowd of worshippers. We enquired
with interest the object of this ceremonial, and
were informed it was the occasion of the elephant's
bath.

Tanjore is 3 hours by rail from Trichinopoly, and has a population of 52,000. Here we visited the palace of the Rajah, two forts, and a church, built by the Protestant missionary Schwartz, in which his remains lie buried.

In the great Pagoda is the colossal bull Mundi, sacred to Siva: it is in a recumbent posture, formed of stone which is saturated with oil, and is 15 feet in length and 12 in height. Within the court is the temple of Soubramanya, an exquisite piece of architecture; while the corridor surrounding it is filled with hundreds of Linga shrines.

On the way to Chillambaram — a town of 40,000 inhabitants, and the very hot-bed of idolatry, we travelled with vast numbers of the natives, on their way to worship at the temples. On reaching our destination we experienced an adventure full of thrilling interest. Disappointed in not seeing at the station the customary bungalow, we found ourselves isolated amid a curious crowd of non-English-speaking natives, and evening closing in upon us. After some moments of anxiety we were fortunate enough to discover a converted heathen who by means of signs and the few English words he knew, conveyed to us the welcome information of the residence of an English missionary a few miles beyond the town. Procuring for us a rough grain-cart drawn by two bullocks,--the only mode of conveyance to be found, he accompanied us as a guide, and we set forth for the house of the missionary to beg hospitality for the night.

On our way through the town we saw the two temples combined in one, of Siva and Parvati, enclosed by a high wall: and notwithstanding the protestations of our guide determined to enter. He, for reasons best known to himself, refused to accompany us, but promising to meet us with the cart at another gateway, sent a native — who could not speak a word of English — as his substitute.

In the former temple we saw the sacred image of the Dancing Siva, besides some fine carvings, and a chain cut from the solid stone connecting two pillars. We were in the very heart of the temple, examining these interesting objects when a crowd of natives surrounded us, gathering by hundreds as we moved, and pressing us on all sides, with threatening accents and menacing gestures. In the midst of our bewilderment we perceived that our guide had deserted us. Leading us on from shrine to shrine, and finally forcing us into a dark chamber, the priests compelled us to comprehend by means of the words "gold" and "three thousand," their demand for a large sum of money.

Notwithstanding the exigencies of the situation, acquiescence in their requirements was a virtual impossibility as we were totally unprepared for such excessive extortion.

Followed by the excited mob closing in upon us and blocking our way at every step we attempted to make our escape, while the gathering darkness, and an utter ignorance of the modes of egress filled us with terrible forebodings. In this emergency, an "angel in disguise" in the form of a small native boy to whom we had previously shown some small act of charity, crept through the crowd, and gave us an almost imperceptible signal which our sharpened wits readily interpreted into an invitation to follow him, which we managed to accomplish with much difficulty through devious and tortuous ways, until we reached our conveyance and awaiting guide; and set forth with all the speed of which our bullocks were capable, to our haven of safety and rest, where the missionary and his good wife gave us most hospitable welcome.

Madras, the capital of the Presidency of the same name, is a city of 400,000 inhabitants, and extends a distance of 2 miles along the coast of the Bay of Bengal. It is the third city of importance in India, but its harbor is a dangerous one owing to the high surf; and its climate is wretched on account of the cyclones and typhoons which prevail from October to January.

The main thoroughfares are Mount Road leading to Fort St. George, and Mowbray Road which is a fine avenue of banyan trees. The principal statues of the city are the equestrian one of Sir

Thomas Munro, a marble one of Lord Cornwallis, and one of General Neil; and near the city is the suburb of St. Thomé — the traditional site of the martyrdom of the apostle St. Thomas.

From Madras to Bombay, by rail, the trip consumes 36 hours, and along the route we were continually passing pagodas and small villages, in the latter of which were immense elephants and horses made of stone, and painted in a variety of colors, standing in rows before some shrine, awaiting the convenience of the gods.

The route passes through the independent State of Hyderabad, governed by the great Nizam, whose capital is Hyderabad near the old capital of Golconda. In the southern part of this territory, we traversed the Kistnah Valley, where are the famous Partial and Kollur diamond fields, where the Great Mogul, the Orloff, the Koh-i-noor, the Pitt or Regent, and many other historical and magnificent gems were found. The rough stones yielded by these mines were formerly cut and polished in the town of Golconda, about 100 miles further north, and from this circumstance the diamonds were popularly supposed to be produced at or near Golconda which is not a diamond-bearing district.

Beyond the State of Hyderabad is Poonah, prettily situated, and a great resort for the Government officials and residents of Bombay; and further on we arrived at the Bor Ghat—mean-

ing steps,—which are immense wash-outs of land
2,000 feet deep. Here the mountains are precipi-
tately scarped, and the railway wends its way
around precipices and in zig-zags from the summit
to the ravine below.

At Lanowlee station, ponies are taken six miles
to the celebrated Karli caves — or Buddhist temples which date about 78 B. C. and whose interior
walls are formed of huge statues of elephants and
other figures cut in the solid rock. In its centre
is the Dagoba, a dome on a circular drum surmounted by a Chattar, or umbrella, light being
thrown upon it by a horseshoe-shaped window in
the side of the cave.

CHAPTER XXVIII.

BOMBAY: SURAT: BARODA: AHMEDABAD: JEYPOOR: AM-
BER: DELHI: AGRA: CAWNPORE: LUCKNOW.

BOMBAY — fair haven, as the name signifies — is
the capital of the Bombay Presidency. It is
built upon a chain of islands branching out southward from the mainland; and incloses a splendid
harbor of 40 square miles, one of the largest in
the world. The fort was ceded by the Portuguese in 1661, to Charles II., who relinquished
it to the East India Company in 1668 for an an-

nual rent of £10. in gold. Owing to the increased
growth of Indian cotton, and to the opening of
the Suez Canal, it has rapidly advanced, and has
a greater future before it than any other city in
India, if not Asia.

The population of Bombay is 750,000. Of
these 400,000 are Hindus, 150,000 Mohammedans, 50,000 Parsees, and the remainder Jains,
Eurasians, and Europeans.

The variety of nationality and costume, is
perhaps more striking here than elsewhere in
India; crowds of coolies, or laborers, with
their dark, shiny skins, turbaned heads and the
strip of cloth around their loins; native women,
graceful in figure and feature, arrayed in many
colors — crimson, yellow, orange, green, and blue
— and decked in jewelry; Parsees in white garments, and dark, towering, mitre-shaped hats;
and Mohammedans, proud and stately; all bust-
ling along through the native streets beneath the
tropical sun.

The native town, which stretches northward
several miles, is mostly the business quarter; and
here are also the bazaars, temples, mosques, and
shrines; while the houses are painted in every
imaginable color, and often exquisitely carved and
ornamented.

Between the Apollo Bunder, a quay, and
the old fort, are the finest European buildings in
the city, consisting of the High Court, Tower, Li-

brary, University, Sailors' Home, Post Office, and Watson's Hotel, all built of stone, brick, and iron, and creditable to any European city. Here also are erected, the white marble statue of Queen Victoria, and the bronze equestrian one of the Prince of Wales.

On the Green of an evening, from 5 to 6 P. M. the band plays; and for five miles along the beach, Europeans, and the rich native Baboos, or gentlemen, drive their fine teams with a great display of liveried servants.

Malabar Hill the favorite suburban residence of the wealthy, is a lofty ridge, 500 feet high, stretching, as a separate promontory for two miles out to sea, in a southwesterly direction, and from it are obtained glorious views of the city and ocean.

On the summit of this hill are the Towers of Silence — five mysterious stone receptacles for the Parsee dead, which are located in a garden of flowers. These towers, which are painted white, are about 100 feet high, and 150 in circumference; and all around their upper edge and covering the trees in the neighborhood, sit thousands of large vultures, waiting to devour the dead deposited there.

As the Parsees,—although claiming to be monotheists, worship the four elements, they will not contaminate earth by burial, or fire by cremation, consequently they give their dead as prey to the vultures. When a funeral takes place the mourners stop in the garden of flowers; the corpse is then silently conveyed by the bearers to the tower, and laid uncovered at the top of one of these stone receptacles; and scarcely have they departed leaving their funeral garments behind, when the vultures swoop down upon the inanimate remains, and in half an hour's time not a vestige is left but the bones, which drop through the grating into a well at the bottom of the tower, upon which is a layer of charcoal which prevents them from defiling the earth.

Another curious sight in Bombay is the Panjrapul, a hospital for diseased and decrepid animals. This has been founded, and is mainly supported by the Jains, with whom tenderness for animal life is a distinguishing tenet, induced by their belief that life — whether it be in man, animal, or vegetable product, is identical.

In the Panjrapul all sick, maimed or helpless animals are treated free of charge — from the mammoth elephant to the tiniest insect; and we saw numbers of buffaloes, cows, monkeys, birds and other animals there for treatment.

The Caves of Elephanta are on an island 6 miles from Bombay, which we reached by a steam launch. A stone pathway and many steps led us to the famous caves which are Brahman temples hewn out of the solid rock. Three massive columns divide the entrance and support a huge overhanging cliff, mantled with verdure, on which grow trees with hanging bird's nests. The cave is 130 feet deep and equally wide, hollowed out of trap-rock with huge pillars left to support the roof. Just within the entrance is a colossal figure of the Hindu trinity: Brahma, the creator, in the centre; Vishnu, the preserver, on the left, and Siva, the destroyer, on the right; besides various other images cut in the walls.

From Bombay we took the rail directly north, passing through Surat, one of the first English settlements in India. Here there are many cotton factories, and the immense tombs of the governors of the English and Dutch mills.

At Baroda, a curiously built native city with streets crossing one above the other, we visited the Gaikwar's palace, and were shown his gold and silver cannons — their carriages covered with the same material. We also inspected his collection of wild animals, and visited the square stone arena, where are given the tiger and elephant fights with which he entertains his European guests with the most extraordinary magnificence.

In Ahmedabad we went to see the Jain temple — a splendid structure with many spires and elaborate carving. The interior walls and the floors are of a variety of polished marbles, while the images in niches around the temple and in the centre are of the purest alabaster covered with gold and quantities of precious stones and having large pearls and diamonds for eyes.

As we drove through the town there were numbers of wild apes on the housetops, gates and fences; and in the streets, going from house to house, begging for food which they are seldom refused, and all along the line of rail, for two days, we saw hundreds of these animals, many of them as large as a lad of 12, sitting by the roadside looking at the passing train. At noon we reached Mount Abu, the Mecca of the Jains; on the summit of which are some of their finest temples in India.

Jeypoor, the capital of Rajpootana, is a walled city containing 150,000 inhabitants. It being the province of a native prince, no European or white man is allowed within the limits of the city without a pass from the Maharajah. Presenting a letter of introduction from Sir Richard Temple, late governor of Bombay, to the English political agent, we received a permit from His Highness to visit the city, palace, and old capital Amber; and were given a special escort with staff of office.

The streets of Jeypoor are 40 yards wide, and run at right angles; at the main crossings of which, are the market-places, with fountains, and temples having two stone elephants at each entrance. The houses are stuccoed, painted pink, and ornamented with barbaric frescoing. The palace of the Maharajah is in the centre of the city, painted yellow, and occupies with its grounds two square miles. It is five stories high, and has

many fine apartments, some being of marble;
while the garden comprising 70 acres, is filled
with fountains, and at its extremity is a lake
where there are immense turtles and crocodiles 14
feet in length.

We were also shown the Maharajah's extensive
collection of birds and wild animals among which
were white pea-fowls, and the finest specimens of
tigers in India; several having just been caught
in the jungle two miles distant from the palace,
from the roof of which these animals are plainly
visible in all their native freedom and ferocity.

Amber, the ancient capital, is six miles from
Jeypoor, and hither the Maharajah sent us, with
an escort of several attendants, on one of his State
elephants, the largest we had ever seen; decked
with showy trappings and richly caparisoned howdah, its tusks ornamented with burnished bands.
The *mahout*, a native who guided his course, sat
on his neck; and so perfect was his control of the
huge beast that at a word of command he would
kneel, in order to facilitate our mounting and dis-
mounting; notwithstanding which a ladder was
necessary to enable us to ascend or descend his
sides.   In this novel manner we wended our way
along the edge of the jungle where large apes
sporting among the overhanging branches of the
trees grinned down upon us, in such close proximity that we instinctively grasped our hats in the
not unfounded fear of having them snatched away.

After passing many ancient temples and shrines we arrived at Amber which retains of its former magnificence only the ruins of its fine palace, which is situated on a high hill overlooking the native town, and a beautiful little lake.

Delhi whose ancient wealth and grandeur has been described by Moore, in the departure of Lalla Rookh from her father's capital to Cashmere where she went to meet her betrothed, the king of Bucharia, is situated on the Jumna river, and dates from 1400 B. C. It has been destroyed seven times, but its extent and magnificence can somewhat be imagined when one beholds its temples, columns, and tombs strewn thickly over an area of 45 square miles. It was governed in turn by Hindus, Mohammedans, Tartars, Afghans, and Moguls; and its treasures rifled by each successive conqueror; but many of its finest buildings yet stand, in a remarkable state of preservation, as monuments of its past grandeur.

The city of to-day, whose population numbers 155,000 was built by Shah Jehan in 1637, who inherited the great wealth and genius of his grandfather Akbar the Great. The city wall, which is of red sandstone, is five miles in circumference, and has eight gates; the citadel is inclosed within another wall one mile and a half in circumference, entered by the Delhi and Lahore gates, and comprises the fort, palace and other fine buildings. Entering the fort by the Lahore gate—called the

king's umbrella from its splendid Gothic arch,—we
first visited the Diwan-i-Am — or hall of public
audience — a large apartment open at three sides,
and supported by rows of red sandstone pillars
formerly adorned with gilding and stucco work.
Behind the throne is a doorway by which the
Emperor entered from his private apartments;
and the wall is covered with mosaic pictures in
precious stones, of some of the most beautiful
fruits, birds, flowers, and animals of Hindostan.
These were executed, as was also the work in the
palace by Austin de Bordeaux, who after defraud-
ing several of the princes of Europe by means of
false gems which he fabricated with great skill,
sought refuge at the court of Shah Jehan, where
he was in great favor with the Emperor, and made
a large fortune.

Next we saw the Motee Musjeed — or Pearl
Mosque built of marble and so called from its
pearl-like whiteness and beauty.

The palace of Shah Jehan is a beautiful structure of the purest marble raised on a terrace four
feet high, with floors, walls, and supports of the
same material inlaid with gold, silver, and precious
stones. The top of the building is surmounted
by four marble pavilions with gilt cupolas, and
the ceiling was originally completely covered
with silver filigree; but in 1759 the Mahrattas,
under Sedasheo Bhad, after the capture of the
city, possessed themselves of it and caused it to

22

be melted into coin — the value of the same being
estimated at $850,000. At one end of the build-
ing are the baths of the Shah, and those of the
ladies of the harem, decorated in extravagant style;
and these are connected, by a stream of water, running through the building in a shallow trough
cut in the marble floor, with their repose and
sleeping apartments. These latter surpass even
the baths in richness, and have open-work marble
screens through which the ladies of the harem
could look upon the outer world. Adjoining
them is a small apartment on whose walls are
golden representations of the sun and moon, and
of a pair of balances before which the Emperor
paused for prayer before entering court, and
asked that he might deal justice in his judgments.

The Diwan-i-Khas—or Hall of private Audience—particularly set apart for the reception of the
nobles, is by far the finest and most interesting
apartment in the building. It is a quadrangle of
moderate dimensions and constructed entirely of
the purest of white marble, with massive pillars of
the same material, the whole of which are richly
ornamented with flowers of inlaid mosaic work of
different colored stones, and with gildings; and on
the side looking out upon the river, there is
a marble balustrade chastely carved in intricate
designs of perforated work. In the centre
of this hall once stood the famous Peacock
throne, so called from its four peacocks, two

above and one on each side, with expanded tails,
which with their bodies were so inlaid with sapphires, rubies, emeralds, pearls, and other precious
stones of appropriate color, as to impart a wonderful resemblance to the real bird. The throne
itself was an oblong platform 6x4 feet; it stood
on six massive feet which like the body were of
solid gold inlaid with emeralds, rubies, and diamonds. It was surmounted by a canopy of gold,
supported by twelve pillars all richly emblazoned
with costly gems, and a fringe of pearls ornamented its outer edge. Between the two topmost
peacocks stood the life-size figure of a parrot,
said to have been carved from a single emerald.
On each side of this throne was a chattar, or
umbrella, one of the Oriental emblems of royalty:
they were formed of crimson velvet richly embroidered and fringed, like the canopy, with
pearls: the handles were eight feet in length, of
solid gold, and studded with diamonds. The cost
of this superb work of art has been estimated at
$30,000,000.

The Peacock throne with nearly all the treasure in the imperial city, was carried off by Nâdir
Shah the Persian conqueror, who in 1739 having
defeated at Karnaul the reigning emperor, Mohammed Shah — grandson of Shah Jehan —
marched with that sovereign, a captive in his
train, to Delhi. The inhabitants enraged on
beholding this, rashly attacked the Persian guard;

whereupon Nàdir Shah ordered a general massacre, and caused the eyes of the dethroned monarch to be put out. The city has never recovered from the work of destruction to which it was then doomed.

In one end of this famous Audience Hall, is yet distinctly visible in golden Persian characters, these words: "if there is a paradise upon earth, it is this — it is this!"

The principal mosque of Delhi is the Jumma Musjeed, or Friday mosque, built on a rocky eminence considerably elevated above the ground, 200×120 feet, and surmounted by 3 cupolas of white marble with gilt spires; while the main building with lofty minarets and extensive court, is built of red sandstone. Here on the 12th of November, we witnessed the Mohurrum a great festival of the Mohammedan Shiah Sect, when they paraded gilt representations of the tomb of Hussien, — grand-son of Mohammed, through the streets, after which they buried them with great ceremony.

The Kutab Minar, a fluted column 240 feet high, 110 feet in circumference at the base, and gradually diminishing in a series of 5 stories like the joints of a telescope, to 30 feet in circumference at the summit, is built of stuccoed stone, and handsomely carved with the 99 names of the Almighty, in Arabic letters. It is supposed to have been built by the Hindus, and subsequently con-

verted into a minaret by the Mohammedans. It
is said to have been the highest column standing
alone in the world, before the erection of the
Washington monument, and is one of the gigantic reminders of old Delhi.

Near by, and almost adjoining the Kutab
Minar, is Aladdin's Gate — a majestic arch, beautifully carved and built for the entrance of a palace; while connected with it are the remains of a
mosque built of red sandstone from the ruins of
eleven Hindu temples whose site was once on this
spot. In the midst of this ruin stands the enig-
matical iron pillar, weighing about 17 tons, and 60
feet in length but now only 22 feet above the
ground. It is supposed to be of Brahmanical
origin, and legend gives it the symbolical significance of the strength and subsequent downfall of
the city.

From here we stopped at a tank filled with
water, to witness a performance of the natives; who jump into it, from the roofs of the
neighboring houses, feet foremost, to a depth of
some fifty feet, falling with the dull thud of an inanimate body; after which, in a state of exhaus-
tion, they come to beg an *anna* — two and a half
cents — from the bystander.

We then drove to the Lat of Fyroz Shah — a
monolith of red sandstone upon which is an inscription in Pali indicating that it was erected by
Asoka; then to the tomb of Humayun, Akbar's

father, a tyrant of great cruelty and patron of
thuggism, which is of colossal size, built of red
sandstone, and required 16 years in its construction; and further on to the tomb of a certain king of Delhi who was so partial to cherry
brandy that he consumed it at the rate of a glass
an hour, until it was the cause of his untimely
death.

But more affecting than all these grand tombs
built of stone, with towering domes and hand
somely-carved marble screens and porticos, is the
grave of the lovely daughter of Shah Jehan,
who remained faithful to him when his son had
caused his imprisonment. It is simply a sodded
mound, bearing on the headstone the following
inscription in Arabic: "Let no rich canopy cover
my grave: this grass is the most appropriate covering for the poor in spirit."

From here we returned to the city of Delhi
and drove through its chauk — or main street,
where are the bazaars and principal shops. It was
here, in the late mutiny of 1857, that Captain
Hodson, an English officer exposed to public view
the bodies of the two sons of Behadar Shah —
the last, and aged king of Delhi — whom, after
their surrender, he had caused without trial, to be
shot.

Agra, formerly the seat of government of the
northwest provinces, is a scattering city situated
on the river Jumna. The fort, which is one of

the finest in India, is of red sandstone, with walls
40 feet high, and comprises many fine buildings.
It was built by Akbar the Great, who had three
wives, a Christian, a Hindu and a Mohammedan.
He built a church for the first, a temple for the
second, and a mosque for the third, declaring his
determination to be on the safe side. Within the
fort, we visited the palace of Akbar; the public
and private Judgment Halls; the throne of Jehanjeer where this sovereign sat to witness the
elephant and tiger fights in the arena below; the
palace of Shah Jehan where he was imprisoned
by his son, and the very room in which he died;
also the Sultana's bath-room with walls and ceilings formed of thousands of pieces of convex
mirrors casting innumerable reflections; the Pil-
lared Hall where the sultan and sultanas played
hide and seek; and the dungeons beneath it
where the ladies of the harem, falling into dis-
favor, were hung, and their bodies washed into
the river through an underground passage.

We drove across the Jumna over a bridge of
boats, to see the tomb of It-mâd-ud-Daulâh —
the prime minister to Jehanjeer. He came from
Persia a poor man, his sole possession the ox
upon which he rode; and subsequently became a
great favorite with his sovereign, who married his
daughter, and loaded him with benefits, and
placed this magnificent tomb over his remains.

The Taj-Mahal, erected by Shah Jehan, as a

mausoleum for his favorite wife, whose title
was Begum Muntaz Mahal, is by far the
most beautiful structure in Agra, if not in the
world, and might well be reckoned as one of the
Wonders. It was commenced in 1630 and is said
to have occupied 20,000 workmen for 17 years,
at a cost of about $60,000,000. It is in a beauti-
ful garden 2 miles from Agra, on the bank of the
Jumna, rising from a double platform; the first
of red sandstone some 20 feet high and 1,000
broad; the second of marble 15 feet high and 300
square, at the corners of which stand 4 marble
minarets, 180 feet high each. In the centre of
this platform reared high in air, stands the Taj
with giant arches and clustering domes. Its base
is a square of 186 feet, its height is 200 feet, and
it is built of the purest white marble with Arabic
inscriptions traced over the entrances. On either
side of it are mosques, the one facing Mecca designed for worship, the other serving only to
complete the unity of appearance. Within the
mausoleum are the remains of Shah Jehan and
his favorite wife Taj,—the pet name of the
Begum Muntaz — in whose honor it was named.

One characteristic of the Tartars was their
tomb-building propensity; and each Mogul in
turn built a tomb for himself.

The symmetry of outline, the imposing and
dazzling effect of the materials used, as well as
the delicate inlaid work, and the intricate marble

carvings, render the Taj an object that must be seen by both daylight and moonlight in order fully to realize its perfect beauty and finish. All parts of the Orient have contributed their treasures to the embellishment of this marvellous mausoleum: Jeypoor its white marble; the Narbudda its rock-spar and yellow marble; Charkoh its black marble; China its crystal; the Punjab its jasper; Bagdad its carnelian; Thibet its turquoise; Yemen its agate; Ceylon its sapphires; Arabia its coral; the Bundelkund its garnets; Punnah its diamonds; Gwalior its lodestone; Villate its chalcedony; and Persia its onyx and amethyst. Many of the most valuable of these precious stones have been rifled from their settings by the Jats and Europeans; and consequently a guard is now kept constantly on watch day and night. What is huge and massive is usually associated in the mind with what is rough and ponderous; but here is the majesty of a giant building combined with the lightness and delicacy of a costly jewel-casket.

The tomb of Akbar the Great, is 8 miles from Agra, near Secundra, in a court a quarter of a mile square, with a heavy fortress-like wall surrounding it. It is 30 feet square and 100 high; rising in terraces of pyramidal form with cloisters, galleries and domes, to the height of 5 stories. The body of Akbar is interred in the vault beneath; but on the extreme top, in the centre of the building, is his white marble tomb, with the 99 names of the Almighty beautifully inscribed upon it in Arabic characters; and at its head stands a marble urn upon which once was— placed there by his grandson Shah Jehan — the great gem known as the Koh-i-noor diamond, now the centre ornament in the crown of England.

Cawnpore, situated on the Ganges, is a busy, populous town, with cotton factories, flour mills and leather works; but its principal interest centres in the monuments and commemorative spots which testify to the hardships and cruelty that prevailed during the mutiny of 1857. Of these is a well, which is now covered over and surmounted by the marble statue of an angel, with drooping wings, leaning against a cross; her arms folded over her breast, and in her hands two palm-leaves emblematical of martyrdom and victory. On the pedestal is the following inscription:

"Sacred to the perpetual memory of a great company of Christian people, chiefly women and children, who, near this spot were cruelly massacred by the followers of the rebel Nana Dhoondopunt of Bithoor; and cast, the dying with the dead, into the well below on the 15th day of July, 1857."

A memorial church, a short distance away, stands in the midst of what was Wheeler's intrenchment; where that general, gathering to-

gether the 330 women and children, surrounded
and guarded them with 250 soldiers and 300 citizens, the balance of his army having mutinied;
and when at length this worn-out band, reduced
by sickness and death, yielding to the treacherous
promises of the Nana Sahib of safe conduct down
the river, surrendered, they were cruelly massacred at the Suttee Chaore — a temple now
marking the spot — on the banks of the Ganges.

Lucknow the capital of Oude, is a city of
262,000 inhabitants, situated on the banks of the
river Goomti, a tributary of the Ganges. Like
Cawnpore it was the scene of much suffering and
bloodshed during the great mutiny. It was in
the Residency here that in 1857, 2,200 souls
consisting of 1,000 European residents with their
families sought refuge; and that 1,000 soldiers
under the English general, Sir Henry Lawrence,
kept a large army of Sepoys at bay for six
months.

The building is a large three-story house,
with towers and thick walls, standing on an elevation in the midst of extensive grounds. We
descended into the vast cellars where the women
and children had found refuge; shot and shell
having left their traces on every side. The
tombs of Lawrence and other brave men are
within the grounds, bearing touching epitaphs
commemorative of the events attending their
deaths. The house is a ruin and a melancholy

spectacle; but Nature has mantled the spot with verdure, and the gardens are blooming with flowers.

Lucknow has some very grand and imposing buildings, especially those in the fort; among which are, the Imaun Barra — an old palace — and several mosques and gates crowned with domes, of a very pleasing style of architecture.

Among the most important buildings which we visited are the Kaisar Bagh with its large grounds and Turkish pavilion; the Chattar Manzie, surmounted by a gilt umbrella, — the emblem of ancient royalty; the Hooseinbad — or Palace of Light; and the Dilkusha palace where Henry Havelock died.

The Martinière College is an immense building styled a second Versailles. It was built by a Frenchman named Martin who came out to India a private soldier, and after having become a general, with a large fortune, built this edifice for his private residence.

At the Elephant Stables, 3 miles from Lucknow, the English government keeps 100 of the largest of these animals, which are used on state occasions, or in time of war for transporting cannon. The obedience of these huge brutes who *salaam*, or salute, and lie prostrate at the word of command, is proof of their remarkable intelligence and docility.

CHAPTER XXIX.

BENARES: THE GANGES: SERAMPORE: DARJEELING: CALCUTTA — ITS ENVIRONS.

BENARES, the sacred city of the Hindus, located on the west bank of the mighty Ganges, has a population of 208,000. It dates from 1200 B. C. and was frequently alluded to in early Sanscrit literature. What Jerusalem is to the Jew; what Rome is to the Latin; what Mecca is to the Mohammedan, Benares is to the Hindu.

It contains 1,400 temples, over 3,000 shrines, 300 mosques, and 25,000 Brahmans, or priests. Its chief source of revenue is obtained from the offerings of the horde of pilgrims who resort there daily to worship at the shrines.

In Benares one sees what Hinduism practically is, idolatry of the basest description; the worship of Vishnu, the preserver, and of Siva, the destroyer, being represented by numberless idols and symbols of the most revolting character. Here Brahmanism and Caste hold sway, and Hinduism has acquired a stony compactness and solidity almost impenetrable. The sanctity of Benares — its temples, reservoirs, wells and

streams — has been famed for thousands of
years; and it is the aim of every good Hindu to
visit it once annually; and if possible, when sick,
to be conveyed there either to seek life or to find
death within the sacred precincts.

In the holy Kasi, or Benares, each native
Hindu prince owns his private palace which he
occupies during his sojourn. The Brahmans, or
priests, are among the richest of her citizens,
their wealth being derived from the offerings of
the pilgrims; and although some of them are
intelligent, they are usually worldly and immoral.

Idolatry seems to have a charm for the
masses, the persuasive teachings of their priests
having for them a singular fascination; and their
zeal and earnest observance of their rites might
well teach a lesson to those who claim the light of
a Revealed religion.

We traversed on foot the narrow dirty streets
and bazaars of Benares, inspecting the brass
wares, toys, and embroideries for which this city
is celebrated; and at every few steps were
brought to a sudden halt by some sacred bull —
these animals being permitted to wander at ran-
dom whithersoever they please, even into houses
and shops, demolishing stands of eatables with
perfect impunity. But filthier by far than the
streets, are many of the temples and shrines filled
with live sacred animals, such as bulls, dogs,
monkeys, serpents, doves and pigeons; and idols

besmeared with oil and ochre, which with the
food offered to the latter, as well as to the more
appreciative live stock, combine to create an almost unbearable stench. Each temple, shrine,
well, and idol of Benares, has its distinctive legend,
which is invariably extravagant.

The Golden Temple is dedicated to Siva, the
presiding deity of Benares, and is considered the
holiest of all the places in the city; while the
symbol of the god is a plain Linga of uncarved
stone.

In the Temple of Ampura, all beggars are fed
daily The goddess Ampura is their divinity of
love and beauty; and her charms are enhanced
by ornaments of gold and silver. In one shrine
of this temple is an idol representing the sun
seated in a chariot drawn by seven horses; in
another is Gauri Shanker; in another Hanoo-
man — the monkey-god; and in yet another Ganesh, with his elephant trunk.

The Temple of Bhaironath enshrines a god
who is the protector of Benares. The idol is
of stone with a face of silver, and head encircled
with garlands; he has four hands, and is armed
with a stone bludgeon. Behind him is the
image of a dog, on which the deity is supposed to ride. Before the temple sits a priest
with a *chowry* or switch of peacock feathers in-
flicting gentle punishment upon the worshippers
who offer themselves for chastisement. In this

temple there congregate numbers of dogs which are fed daily by men appointed for the purpose.

Near by is the Temple of Sukreswar — a creative god; that of Sitla, the goddess presiding over small-pox; and the Temple of Naugrah dedicated to the planets in which every Hindu must inaugurate each important religious ceremony.

In the Temple of Ganesh is its god painted red, with three eyes, a silver head, and an elephant's trunk; while at his feet is the figure of a rat on which the god is supposed to ride.

The Trilochan Temple which is devoted to Siva has at its entrance a marble bull; while the paintings on the wall represent hell with the river of death in the foreground, and figures in it endeavoring to make their way to the opposite shore.

The Temple of Kameshwar is dedicated to the god of wishes, whose prerogative it is to grant the desires of his worshippers; and as the wants of mankind are legion, it is not surprising that Kameshwar has a host of devotees.

The Nepaulese Temple occupies one of the most conspicuous places in the city, and from a distance presents a handsome appearance; but on a closer examination, it is found to be defiled with carvings of an obscene character.

At the extreme end of the city, and near the river's bank, is the Durga Kund — or monkey temple, so called from the hundreds of brown monkeys, sacred to Durga, who inhabit the temple, bathe in the tank, and rear their young in a hollow tamarind tree near by. Here every Tuesday morning sacrifices of goats and buffaloes take place; and the ground around is saturated with the blood of these animals.

The Wells of Fate, Knowledge, Salvation, of the Moon, and of Hindu mythology, are as full of curious legends as they are of putrid water from which emanate the most noisome smells. Opposite the Nepaulese Temple is a Well whose waters are so pestilent that the effluvium pollutes the air around; but notwithstanding this fact the sick and aged, believing in its miraculous properties of imparting health and longevity, bathe in this well and even drink its waters. Lepers, the very sight of whom is sickening, and those suffering from other contagious diseases, bathe in common, an act which is calculated to shorten life rather than to prolong it.

One of the oldest and most interesting houses in Benares is the Manmandil, the whole top of which is covered with huge astronomical instruments built of stone, which excite the wonder of all scientific men. Here are instruments used for taking the sun's altitude and zenith; for ascertaining its greatest declination; its distance at noon; its ascensions; the latitudes, and for finding the degrees of azimuth of a planet or star; and here also is an equinoctial stone.

23

The great sight of Benares is its river front in the early morning, when the rays of sunrise flood the city with brightness, and its inhabitants bathe in their sacred river, the Ganges. Seated on the deck of a *dinghy* with four men to row, we floated slowly along with the lazy tide, watching the panorama of humanity at its devotions. Men, women, and children of all ages were crowding the ghâts, or steps, leading down into the water, performing their ablutions in the yellow tide as a daily act of refreshment, of purification, and of religion; worshipping the river, basking in the sun, filling vessels with the sacred water for purifying purposes at home; and finally repairing to the Brahmans seated on the banks of the river under large palm-leaf umbrellas, in order to have the distinctive marks of their castes painted upon their shiny foreheads; for which service they deposited a coin in the grasping hands of the officiating priests.

Bordering one side of the river, the temples and palaces rose, one above another on the steep bank, and several of the largest of these, having been undermined by the water, had partially sunk into the river.

The Dasaaswameah Ghât — or steps, is one of the five chief points of pilgrimage in the city. It derives its name from dasa, ten,—aswa, a horse, and meah—a sacrifice; for here, according to Hindu tradition, Brahma offered a sacrifice of ten horses.

On this spot have been erected ten commemorative shrines, each containing an idol. Here we
saw several of the religious devotees called *Fakirs*,
who live upon charity, and obtain a reputation for
sanctity by abstinence, by severe penances, by
anointing their greasy bodies and faces with
ashes—allowing their hair to grow until the long
shaggy locks touch the ground—and by assuming
an upstretched position of the right arm, which is
retained until the limb becomes immovably fixed
in that attitude.

At the Burning Ghât, are several slabs set up
on end called Suttee, which mark the spots where
widows have been burnt alive on the funeral pyre
of their husbands ; but this custom was prohibited
by the English government in 1829. The word
Suttee means " chaste " or faithful woman ; and
these memorials are held as objects of great veneration.

At this place most of the cremating ceremonies take place, and we saw seven bodies
consumed in one day. When a Hindu is about
to die, he is laid upon the ground to breathe his
last ; and a few hours later, the body is placed on
a bamboo litter with simply a covering of thin
cloth, and borne through the streets on the shoulders of four men, chanting, to the river side.
Arrived at the banks of the Ganges, the corpse is
laid on a pyre of wood, and more wood piled
over it. The nearest relative of the deceased,

after having his face and head shaved, and a bath
in the river, receives from a *dôm* — one of the
lowest Caste — a lighted torch which, after walking around the pile five times, he applies to the
wood, and within an hour or so the body is reduced to ashes, and cast into the river.

Unlike almost every other people under the
sun, the Hindus evince no respect for their fellow-
beings after the spirit has departed from its frail
tenement; but go through the last rites with a
seeming indifference strange to behold.

Leaving these repulsive scenes, the depression
to which they had given rise was changed for a
sense of the poetic and beautiful, as we saw floating past us the tiny boat with flower-encircled
lights, freighted with the fate of the Indian maiden,
who by the continuance of the flame tests the fidelity of her lover.

Further on we reached the Mosque of Aurung-
Zeb, the bigot and persecutor, who imprisoned
his father Shah Jehan, murdered his brothers, and
imposed a tax upon all who were not of the Mohammedan faith. Its minarets tower over the
city, and from the top of one of these, we obtained a magnificent view.

Benares is not only the centre of Hinduism,
but also the cradle of Buddhism. After six years of
asceticism and solitude at Gaya, a town 50 miles
south of Benares, Buddha having experienced his
temptation and his enlightenment under the Bo-

tree, made his way to this city, affirming: "I am going to give light to those enshrouded in darkness; and to open the gates of immortality to men." The place where he taught, once called the Deer-park, now Sarnath, lies four miles north of Benares, and is marked by a large tope —a pile of brick and stone resembling an immense bee-hive, about 120 feet high, and 90 feet in diameter at the base. It is handsomely carved, and has eight niches around it intended as receptacles for life-size statues of Buddha, and is supposed to contain a relic of this great Reformer.

Continuing from here by rail, we stopped at Serampore, which we visited to see the temple and great idol Juggernaut — a hideous figure with an immense head and big eyes. Outside of the temple is the car of Juggernaut, one of the largest in India, being 60 feet high, covered with images and paintings and mounted on 16 broad wheels. On top of this the idol Juggernaut is placed and drawn through the streets in their religious processions; on which occasions the fanatics throw themselves on the ground before it, to be crushed beneath the wheels, notwithstanding the efforts of the English government to suppress this barbarous custom.

From here we took a boat to the opposite side of the Ganges, and visited Barrackpoor, a pretty suburban village, and a great resort for Europeans. In the centre of a large garden here, stands the summer residence of the Viceroy of India, and in this section is cultivated the poppy, the opium from which having been extracted is shipped from Calcutta to China.

Darjeeling, appropriately called "the city above the clouds," is prettily located in the Himalaya Mountains 8,000 feet above the level of the sea. It is surrounded by the highest peaks of the range, 12 of them within line of vision from this point, each being over 20,000 feet high. Mt. Everest, the highest in the world, 29,002 feet; Kinchinjinga, 28,156; and Chamalari, 27,200 feet, all located in Nepaul and Thibet, stand out like sentinels with their snowy caps, and present a scene of grandeur unequalled on the globe. Here is seen the thickest crust of the earth's surface—5½ miles; casting the eyes from the snowy peaks above the clouds to the great ravines below clad in rankest tropical vegetation, one is filled with awe at beholding these sublime contrasts of nature.

Here are seen a variety of people — the Nepaulese, with intelligent and pleasing countenances, active and brave to a degree, but whose country Europeans can only view from a distance; the Bootiers with almond-shaped eyes, high cheek-bones, and wearing the queue, who make use of a praying machine — a toy resembling a child's large-sized rattle in which, on yards of paper, their prayers are inscribed; this they revolve while repeating the formula, which may be translated "Oh, the Jewel on the Lotus!" — referring to Buddha; and again other sects who rarely wash themselves, but coat their faces with tar to preserve their sight, and as a protection from the cold.

The modes of conveyance used here are palanquins — a kind of box open at either side and of sufficient length to allow one to recline, borne by four coolies; and dandies — a sort of recumbent chair on two poles carried on the shoulders of the natives.

From Darjeeling to Calcutta the distance is 250 miles, and going thither we first took a miniature narrow-guage railroad down the mountain, whose grade was a fall of one in every eighteen inches, and having many loops and reverse stations.   The train rounded the spurs of the high knobs, crossing bridges over deep ravines and roaring torrents, passing through luxuriant tropical vegetation, tree ferns, rhododendrons, flowering creepers and plantations of tea and chinchona, all rendering it one of the most beautiful railroad trips of our experience.

At the foot of the mountain, we passed through ten miles of the densest jungle in India, infested with great numbers of wild elephants and tigers, and stopped at a small station where the government employs men to entrap the former for military purposes. These animals are first driven into

corrals by means of decoy elephants, after which
the latter with heavy chains held in their trunks,
advance upon the strangers and beat them into
submission.

Calcutta, the capital of India, is situated on
the Hoogly mouth of the Ganges, 100 miles from
the Bay of Bengal, and with its suburbs, has a
population of 795,000. Its mid-day sun is hot
and treacherous, and the evenings and nights are
foggy and cool, producing so unhealthy a climate
that its deleterious effects have won for it the title
of "the city of pale faces."

Old Court-house street, and Chowringhee
Road are the principal thoroughfares, on which
are situated the finest residences and shops;
while between the latter and the river, is the
Maidan — a large common, with several fine
statues, among which is the handsome equestrian
one of Sir James Outram. Here between the
hours of 5 and 6 P. M. may be seen hundreds of
Europeans and natives driving out with from two
to six attendants each, attired in garments more
gaudy than cleanly; and congregating around the
stand in the lovely Eden garden where the band
discourses sweet strains.

Government House, the residence of the Viceroy, is an imposing building in the centre of the
city, painted a bright yellow, and surrounded by
extensive grounds. In it is the Council-room,
with the portraits of Hastings and other English

notables on its walls, and where the fate of thousands of lives have hung in the balance.

The High Court, Great Eastern Hotel, and Post Office, are among the finest buildings in the city; and near the latter was the famous Black Hole, when on the 19th of June, 1756, 146 Europeans were imprisoned by the Nawab and Mahratta cavalry, in a room 18 feet square, and 123 of the number smothered to death.

In Calcutta we witnessed the opening of the great Exposition, under the auspices of the Viceroy, Lord Ripon, and the Duke and Duchess of Connaught, and attended by the native princes of India, who had come from all parts of the Empire. The display was on an extensive scale, the chief point of interest centring in the Oriental departments; here were to be seen the thrones, jewels, howdahs and trappings used in state ceremonials, besides other valuables loaned by the native princes for this occasion; the section devoted to Burmese exhibits being particularly interesting.

Caligat which gave the name to Calcutta, is a native village four miles south of the city, on a former bed of the Ganges, amid tanks of stagnant water and tropical vegetation. The legend runs that when the corpse of the goddess Kali, wife of Siva, was cut in pieces by order of the gods, one of her fingers fell here, and a temple was raised on the spot.

The streets near which the temple stands, are full of shops for the sale of charms, pictures, and images of idols; and on arriving at the place of worship, we found sacrifices already taking place, and the ground saturated with blood. This ceremony occurs every Tuesday and Saturday mornings, when great numbers of goats and buffaloes are killed; these animals are held by the hind legs, their heads fastened in a vise and severed from the body, the blood being caught in a vessel and poured over the tongue of the idol.

The Zoological Garden contains some fine specimens of animals, and is well worthy a visit. The Botanical Gardens, 3 miles from the city, cover 300 acres and combine the natural and the artificial in perfect harmony.

Besides many rare specimens of trees and plants, the avenues are bordered with various species of palms; while in the centre of the grounds is a Banyan tree, the largest known, whose hundreds of descending branches have taken root and cover a circumference of 900 feet, capable of affording shelter for 3,000 men.

Opposite the Gardens, on the east bank of the river, is the palace of the ex-king of Oude who is confined here, a state prisoner, having been deposed for attempting to poison the British agent. He maintains a harem of 600 women, and has a fine Snakery and Zoological collection. Here, as in many other parts of India, we saw the manœuvring of pigeons which is a great delight and pastime of the natives. These birds, flying in open air by the thousands, were made to separate into sections, deploy, form circles, and manœuvre like an army of soldiers, obeying strictly the commands of a native who, standing on an eminence, waves a flag and shouts at the top of his voice.

Leaving Calcutta by steamer for Rangoon, we sailed down the difficult Hoogly mouth of the Ganges; while "west stretched the great delta with its thousand mouths, its intricate net-work of countless channels and backwaters, and its almost impenetrable coast-region, covered with dense jungles, and still the prey of wild beasts, terrific cyclones and deadly exhalations. Here land and water still struggle for the mastery, while unbridled nature laughs at the feeble efforts of man to tame the jarring elements."

CHAPTER XXX.

RANGOON: MOULMEIN: MERGUIN ARCHIPELAGO: PE-
NANG: MALACCA: SINGAPORE.

RANGOON in British Burmah, located on the Ir-rawaddy river, 28 miles from its mouth, is surrounded by low paddy fields from which is produced large quantities of rice, shipped to all parts

of the world. This town has a population of
60,000, composed of Europeans, Chinese, and
Burmese, the latter being of light yellow complexion, slight in size, quiet in manner, dressing
neatly, and given to wearing flowers in their hair.

In the centre of the town rises a terraced hill
from 250 to 300 feet high, surrounded by a moat
that can be crossed only by drawbridges, and
beyond this is a lake. On top of this hill is the
Golden Pagoda, rising to a height of 300 feet,
which is the tallest and one of the most remarkable in the Buddhist world, and is visible 7 miles
off before reaching Rangoon; its gilded spire
which towers up far above the dark foliage shining in the bright sunlight like a fiery meteor. It
is shaped like a bell, and surmounted by a gilded
hitee or umbrella, from the edge of which hang
hundreds of small bells which are rung by the
breeze. At the base of the Pagoda are numbers
of small temples and shrines, beautifully carved
and gilded and adorned with colored glass, containing colossal figures in brass and marble of
Buddha, in both sitting and reclining postures;
while the entrances are guarded by stone images
of elephants, dogs, and other animals, some of
which are 60 feet in height.

Above Rangoon 200 miles, on the Irrawaddy,
is Mandalay, the capital of Burmah, where is kept
a sacred white elephant which ranks next to
royalty. This animal has a palace of its own, a

personal chamberlain and 30 courtiers; besides 4 golden umbrellas,— emblem of royalty,— and large real and landed estates.

Moulmein which is near the mouth of the Salwin river, and on the Gulf of Martaban, is surrounded by hilly islands; the town itself amounts to little, but from the base of its principal pagoda,—similar to the one described in Rangoon, standing on a hill 300 feet high, is one of the most beautiful and expansive views of numbers of islands and knobs, the summits of which are crowned with Buddhist shrines.

A most interesting sight to us in Moulmein was that of from 60 to 70 immense elephants at work in the lumber yards and saw-mills carrying huge logs from the river, adjusting them properly under the saw to be cut; afterwards carrying the long timbers well balanced with their tusks and trunks, and piling them together at a distance beyond, using both head and feet to arrange them in exact uniformity; every action betokening their wonderful brute intelligence.

From here, sailing along the coast of British Burmah, we passed through the Merguin archipelago, many of whose islands not only abound in rich tin mines, but have rock caves in which are found the bird-nests that furnish the delicate and expensive soup so much prized by the Chinese.

At Penang a town of 50,000 inhabitants situated on an island of the same name, off the coast of Lower Siam, we went ashore and spent the day visiting its bazaars, and driving two miles beyond the town to a lovely cascade nestled among the hills.

Two days later, we anchored at Malacca, a small town of no special importance, except as a stopping place for steamers on the Malacca coast; and the following day we steamed into Singapore harbor at the extreme south of the Malay Peninsula.

Singapore on an island at the south of Malacca, and only one degree from the Equator, is the capital of the English Strait Settlements. It has a population of 56,000, and abounds in beautiful gardens of tropical flowers and plants; and notwithstanding its proximity to the Equator, its seabreeze renders it more desirable for a residence than other places further north. Here we remained several days to pass a warm New Year's, and to witness the out-door sports participated in by both the native and European population. From its fort, crowning the summit of a high hill, is obtained a magnificent view of the beautiful miniature harbor and adjacent islands.

On this peninsula, but more particularly in Siam, is found the white elephant which is more of a dirty pink color than white, a phenomenon supposed to be caused by disease — a species of leprosy; besides these, the rhinoceros, hippopota-

mus and other wild animals abound; here also
are seen birds of brilliant plumage and butterflies
of gorgeous hues and unusual size, while in the
forests are teak, eaglewood, gum-trees, gutta-
percha, bamboo, dye-woods, cardamom, vanilla,
and all the spices of a tropical region.

CHAPTER XXXI.

SAIGON: CHINA SEA: CANTON: HONG-KONG: STRAITS
OF FORMOSA: YELLOW SEA.

TAKING the French steamer from Singapore, a
four days' sail brought us to Saigon, the French
settlement in Cochin China, where our vessel remained two days unloading arms and provisions
for the army in preparation for the threatened
war in Tonquin between France and China.

Saigon located 40 miles from the mouth of
the Saigon river, is a place of 90,000 inhabitants.
It is in the midst of low rice-fields, where both
heat and mosquitoes are almost intolerable, and is
surrounded by several native villages of considerable size.

Tonquin, though a part of Anam, is under the
protection of China; and its occupation by the
French will not only give them possession of its

mines, but will enable them to penetrate into the interior of China.

Five days continuous travel over the dangerous China Sea, and along the coast of Anam, brought us to Hong-Kong, or Victoria, where we immediately took advantage of the night boat going up the Pearl River to Canton. The steamer, a small one, was manned by English officers, and the cabin was provided with fire-arms to be used in case of an uprising or attack from the Chinese. This occurrence is not an unusual thing, owing to the hatred of the natives to foreigners occasioned by difficulties with the English, which incited them to burn the European quarter, destroy mission churches, and threaten the lives of strangers who enter the city walls; a sentiment which is greatly aggravated by the present war in Tonquin.

Arriving at Canton early in the morning, we immediately sent for Ah Cum, a Chinese guide, to conduct us through the city: and procuring chairs, borne each on the shoulders of Chinamen,— the usual mode of conveyance, we set forth single file through the narrow streets on a tour of inspection.

Canton is the pride of China from its being the largest, best preserved, and most flourishing city of the Empire. It is situated on the Pearl river, 90 miles from Hong-Kong, and has a population of 1,300,000 — 60,000 of whom live in

boats on the river. The city is surrounded by
walls 20 feet thick and 40 feet high, entered by
18 gates, while a large portion of it extends even
beyond the walls. The interior of the city is divided into districts which are separated by gates
that can be closed at an instant's warning in case
of trouble.

We first visited that portion of Canton built on
the island of Sha-Mien, where reside the consuls
and foreign population; then crossed to the native
city and passed through its crowded, narrow
streets, which are from 4 to 8 feet in width, and
often covered over above; these present a
strange but rather picturesque appearance, from
the array of board signs, ten feet in length,
painted in characters — in gold, black, and red —
indicative of the name and occupation of the in-
mate or proprietor; they are hung perpendicularly and fastened only by a hook at the top,
which in windy weather must render pedestrianism
somewhat dangerous. While threading our way
through these winding streets, we were followed
by large crowds of excited Chinese who, by
their threatening gestures and language, showed
that we were not at all welcome in their midst,
and decided us to make our tour of inspection a
hasty one, as at each halt we made on quitting
our chairs they pressed upon us more closely
and in larger numbers than we found agreeable.
The shops, bordering either side of the way, are

small and entirely open at the front, often displaying handsome goods and a variety of manufactures. Here we saw the workers in Jade stone, tortoise-shell, mother-of-pearl, wood, glass, silver and ivory. We also saw the feathers of the kingfisher set into jewelry in imitation of enamel; paintings on rice paper, embroideries in silk; opium dens, restaurants in which dog's, rat's and cat's meat is sold, and the establishments peculiar to that edible, in which we procured the gelatine from which 'the bird's nest soup is made. This delicacy, in its natural state, is suggestively repulsive; but after undergoing certain processes of cleansing and clarifying, assumes more inviting appearance, and is sold at the rate of $10 per lb.

We next visited the Temple of Longevity; the Flowery Pagoda, 9 stories high; the Temple of 500 Buddhas, filled with as many gilt images of Buddha and his followers; the Temple of the Five Genii, where in front of each image was a stone, said to be the remains of a ram on which the spirit rode to the city; and the Temple of Confucius, which the Emperor of China visits once annually.

In the older portion of Canton is the palace of the Tartar General, around which were native sentinels bearing primitive-looking shields made of painted straw: here also, is the Examination Hall with its thousands of stalls or small rooms for students; and the Prison, where we saw num-

bers of men with *cassques*—a large square wooden
yoke fastened around their necks, permitting of
no possibility of rest to the wearer; some loaded
down with heavy chains, by means of which the
body was held in unnatural positions; and others
undergoing various torturing punishments.

In the Execution ground, where on an average
365 criminals are despatched yearly, we saw
several barrels full of human heads lately severed
from the body, and 3 crosses used in crucifying.

Taking a boat we crossed the river to the
island of Ho-Nan, another portion of the city, to
see its temple, where are kept sacred pigs;
to visit the tea-firing and ginger-preserving establishments; and the Flowery boats, whose in-
teriors are finished in marble, and are used exclusively for pleasure parties.

On the delta of the Pearl or Canton river
250,000 people are said to pass their entire lives
on the water. The *Sampan*, a small boat which
serves as their floating home, is fitted up with
shrines and a few household articles, and it is a
common occurrence to see women, with infants
strapped to their backs, rowing them. As soon as
a male child is born, a life preserver, in the form
of a gourd, is fastened around its neck, as a precaution in case of its falling into the water; but
with a girl no such measure is taken, as the life
of female infants is held of little or no value. As
soon as a child can walk it is put to the helm or

oar, while the mother manages the sails, which are
made of matting. The Chinese fishermen are
probably the most venturesome in the world, and
are often seen in small boats 300 miles out at sea,
wearing in bad weather strange-looking cloaks
made of rice-straw and cocoanut-fibre, with straw
hats the size of umbrellas. Their boats, both
large and small, invariably have two big eyes
painted on the prow, and upon being interrogated
upon the significance of this, they make answer :
" No got eye, how can see ?"

The Chinese as a nation, though dirty and
superstitious, are industrious and apt; having for
thousands of years known many devices which
foreigners penetrating the country have appropriated and introduced at home as original inventions. The upper classes are reserved and observ-
ing ; the height of a Chinaman's ambition being
to possess a tiny-footed wife. While the women
are rarely permitted on the streets, we had the
opportunity of seeing several whose feet measured
about 4 inches in length ; but the standard of
perfection we were told is 2½ inches.

The density of the Chinese population renders them conservative, and opposed to improve-
ments of any kind that might be substituted for
manual labor ; and their history shows one
straight unbroken line of a nation unparalleled in
many respects by any other. Wheresoever a
Chinaman may die his bones are in course of time

taken to China for final interment; and their
opposition to having a limb amputated, even in
the worst state of fracture, is that a cripple is unable to make a living, and paupers are not
tolerated among them.

The Chinese religion partakes largely of
idolatry; the Dragon and the Tiger figuring ex-
tensively in their mythological legends. Though
Buddhism constitutes a large part of their religion,
ancestral worship is probably more general; one
of the rites of which consists in sending paper
clothes, money, and written prayers to their forefathers through the medium of fire and ascending
smoke. This latter religion, the most ancient in
China, was revised and elevated by Confucius 525
B. C., whose teachings of duty and morality, in
public as in private life, from the Emperor to the
serf, have endeared him to the people, and whose
laws, among which is the Golden Rule: "Do
unto others as you would they should do unto
you," have come down to us as the essence of
honor and of happiness, and have been incorporated into the Christian religion.

Hong-Kong, the most eastern of the British
possessions, with a mixed population of 250,000,
composed of Europeans, Americans, Chinese,
Hindus, Burmese, Malays, and Polynesians, is
situated on an island at the mouth of the Pearl
river. The city is built at the base of a high hill
on which are many beautiful residences with

shady and winding walks, affording fine views of
the large harbor.   Hong-Kong unfortunately lies
within the limits of the cyclones, during one of
which, in 1874, 1,000 houses were demolished,
hundreds of vessels wrecked, and vast numbers
of lives lost.   Here we passed several days, visiting its public gardens, witnessing the drill of the
English military, and, by means of chairs, borne
by four coolies each, ascended the Peak to the
Flag-staff point to obtain a view of the surrounding landscape.

On leaving Hong-Kong we were accompanied
by our Consul, Col. Mosby, in his private boat
flying the U. S. flag, as far as our steamer, the
"Takachio," of the Mitsu Bishi line, and after a five
days' sail along the coast of China, through the
Strait of Formosa and the Yellow Sea we reached
Japan, and anchored in the beautiful harbor of
Nagasaki.

CHAPTER XXXII.

NAGASAKI: INLAND SEA: KOBÉ: HIOGO: OTSU: LAKE
    BIWAKO: KIOTO: OSAKA: YEDDO: KAMAKURA:
    YOKOHAMA.

NAGASAKI, the extreme southwestern Treaty-
port of Japan, is a place of 30,000 inhabitants: it
occupies a commanding position at the head of a

romantic inlet which forms a magnificent land-locked harbor; and the houses built on the side of a hill, rising like an amphitheatre, combine to render it one of the most beautiful places of the Empire.

At the entrance of the harbor is the rocky island of Papenberg, from whose summit thousands of Christian martyrs were hurled into the sea at the close of the 16th century. A portion of the city is built on the artificial island of De-shima, where the Dutch resided, and monopolized the trade of Japan for 200 years.

Leaving Nagasaki our steamer passed through the narrow strait of Shimonoseki, and into the Inland Sea of Japan. This sea whose 3,000 islands of every conceivable size and form, many of which are crowned with a shrine, dot the surface of the waters, presents a scene of rare beauty, and has justly won the reputation of affording the most delightful sea-voyage in the world.

At Kobé which is the foreign port of the adjacent city of Hiogo, we passed the day riding in *Jinrikishas*—a small two-wheeled conveyance drawn by a native—seeing both towns and visiting the bazaars. Here our consul procured for us special passports to visit Osaka, Kioto, Otsu, and other places in the interior, beyond the Treaty limits.

Starting early in the morning we went the entire length of the railroad to Otsu, which is

situated on Lake Biwako. This lake is the largest
in Japan, being 50 miles in length, and 20 in
breadth, inclosed by hills on every side.

In this section is raised the finest tea in the
Empire; almost exclusively used by the Mikado,
who sends a detachment of soldiers yearly to
guard it en route to his capital.

While camphor and sulphur form some of the
exports of the country, tea is its principal source
of revenue. The shrub from which it is derived
grows about 3 feet high, having a small smooth
leaf, and is cultivated in small patches, by the
natives.

The Japanese manufacture of porcelain ware,
and their work in wood, ivory, mother of pearl
and bronze, are of great delicacy and finish, and
probably excel those of every other country.

Kioto, called the City of Temples, was the
ancient religious capital of Japan, and contains
over 100 Shinto, and 900 Buddhist temples, besides numbers of shrines, tombs and palaces.
The city, which has a population of 300,000,
covers a large area of ground, and while the temples and tea-houses or restaurants are generally
built on the hill-side, the city is on the low
ground, and extends along the banks of the river
Yodo.

The houses are, as a rule, from one to one and
a half stories high, and are built of light wood or
bamboo, with thin paper walls which keep out

neither cold nor heat, and are generally of such transparent texture, that by candle-light the movements of the occupants are distinctly visible from the outside. The walls and partitions are nothing more than sliding screens of paper, which afford but slight shelter from the wind; and strict privacy is out of the question as an intruder may enter from any quarter.

At night the streets present a singular appearance, each house being lighted by a square paper lantern bearing the number of the house, and the names of the occupants. Every individual, after dark, is compelled to carry a paper lantern in his hand or attached to his *Jinrikisha*, and these often igniting, with the frail combustible materials of the buildings, cause frequent conflagrations. The winters in Japan are severe, and the natives have a cold and pinched appearance, braziers being the only means by which they warm themselves.

We visited the Temple of Gion, with its red-painted gates, on each side of which were sentinel figures with terrifying expression; and the Chionin Temple, probably the most imposing, with tier upon tier of stone steps leading up to it. At the uppermost shrine stands the old Kioto bell, and surrounding it are the tombs of the Shoguns, or former military rulers of the country. The Temple of Kurodani, with its terraced cemetery of curious tombs of bronze and stone, was a sight well worth a visit. The Temple of Sanjus-

angendo — or 33,333 idols, — now contains, however, about 1,500 life-size wooden-gilt images,
and in a shrine to the left is the wooden figure of
Dai-Butsu, or Great Buddha, 60 feet in height,
and seated on the lotus flower; a former one of
bronze having been melted down and coined into
money.   The Temple of Noshi Honganji belongs
to the Monto sect, and is considered the largest
in Japan ; it is adorned with gilded panels, paintings, and carved wood.   At the Kitano Temple
we saw numbers of people, young and old, racing
madly around the building ; a hundred rounds
being their allotted penance imposed by the
priest, who presented them at each circuit with a
bamboo stick as evidence of the accomplishment
of their duty.   The Minizuka is a monument of
stone built over the ears and noses of the enemy
killed by the Japanese in the Corean war.   The
Golden Temple, in the garden of which is a large
cedar tree trained to resemble a full-rigged ship,
and the Imperial Palace, are other objects of
interest in Kioto.

At dusk we visited several tea-houses to test
the native beverage and to witness the singing
and dancing of the Japanese girls; and at night
went to the Bazaar quarter, where the shops were
brilliantly illuminated, and various kinds of amusements in progress.

In one theatre we witnessed the cleverest of
acrobatic performances.   In a concert hall a girl-

performer was seated on a circular, revolving platform, and as her song ended, a sudden rotation
of the section she occupied removed her from
view, and substituted another in her place.
Occasionally as the performance progressed the
appreciation of one or other among the audience
was manifested by the throwing of a handkerchief
or scarf to the favorite singer, who responded by
descending into the auditorium and spending a
few moments in conversation with her admirer.

At the Drama theatre the stage not only
occupied one end of the building, but extended
along the sides of the walls. Here we also witnessed some curious native customs. In lieu of
our modern calcium lights, a supernumerary held
a long pole at the end of which was a
candle serving to light up the hideous facial expression of the actor; in place of our elegantly
appointed stage, the performer was followed about
by a man carrying a low stool ready for use; instead of the shifting of scenes, a change was
indicated by the striking together of two wooden
blocks; and when in tragedy, the hero of a piece
died, a black cloth was held before him while he
rose and left the stage, his nether extremities
being plainly visible below it. The orchestra was
composed of men playing on native instruments,
while others chanted with great emphasis the
argument of the play. The audience occupied
cushions on the floor, which was divided off by

low partitions, with small braziers before them.
The Japanese play begins in the morning and
lasts until the midnight following; the price of
admission being only from 5 to 10 cents.

Osaka, which has a population of 280,000,
and next to Yeddo, the largest city of the Empire, is called the Queen City, or Venice of the
East, from its 3,500 bridges, and the manner in
which it is intersected by canals.

On the Ajikawa river, which flows through
the centre of the city, is located its strong Castle
surrounded by walls and moats, and erected in
1538 by the famous Shogun Tai-Ko-Sama.

Returning from here by the same route to
Kobe we resumed the steamer for a trip of 36
hours' duration to Yokohama, and from thence
by rail to Yeddo.

Tokio, or Yeddo, the present capital of Japan
and the residence of the Mikado or Emperor, is
situated on the Todagawa or Ogava River, and
covers an area of 36 square miles, with a population of 600,000 inhabitants. Its general appearance is that of other Japanese cities, with the exception of one or two streets on which are
modern-built houses and horse-cars, showing the
inroad of European civilization, which has been introduced since this city has become a Treaty-port.

The Castle occupies a commanding position on
a hill, and has 3 massive walls, one beyond the
other, with a moat filled with water outside of

each. Within the inclosure is the Fukiage, or Imperial garden, which covers several acres; and here stood the Imperial palace, destroyed in 1855 by a conflagration, which burnt 5,000 houses in Yeddo. From this point we had the best view of the city, stretching with its suburban towns and numerous temples far and wide.

We next visited a palace of one of the Daimios, which the present Mikado occupies until the rebuilding of the Imperial residence; and the ancient temple of Imanuon one of the most venerated and frequented in Japan. On either side of its entrance were two large idols, before which were hung numbers of sandals, the offerings of those whose diseased feet had been miraculously cured; while clinging to their faces and bodies were numberless spit-balls which were nothing less than written prayers thrown at the idol; the superstitious belief being that if they adhered, their prayers were accepted, but if otherwise, that they were rejected. Within the temple is a wooden idol whose features are worn smooth by the manipulations of the devotees, who believing in its curative powers, touch first the seat of their own affliction and then the corresponding portion of the idol. Surrounding the temple are various shows, which give it more the appearance of a place of amusement than of worship, and a garden filled with plants trained in the form of men and animals, a peculiarity of Japanese horticulture.

At Yueno, a suburban town of Yeddo, is a park overlooking the lake, containing a bronze statue of Buddha; and here are buried the five wives of the Shoguns, in tombs richly ornamented in lacquer and wood carvings, and surrounded by stone lanterns.

In the Zoological Gardens and Museums near by are specimens of animals and of Japanese art; and birds of fine plumage, among the most wonderful of which are cocks, of the game species, with tail feathers measuring 30 feet in length.

Surrounding the Senga Kuyi, or Hill Spring temple, is the celebrated cemetery where are buried the 47 Ronins whose devotion and patriotism form a prominent part of Japanese history.

The temples and tombs of Shiba, with probably the exception of those at Nikko, are considered the finest in Japan; and though small in size, are remarkable for their richness and fine carving. These temples which are entirely of wood, have highly polished black lacquered floors, with walls and shrines of the same material in gold and red; the ceilings are in arabesques of remarkable beauty; and the wood carvings of birds and animals are truly wonderful. Outside of, and surrounding each temple, are numbers of stone and bronze lanterns 5 feet in height, which are conspicuous adjuncts of the Japanese form of worship.

Returning to Yokohama, we took *Jinrikishas*

drawn by two natives each, in tandem style, and travelled 15 miles into the country, going at the rate of 5 miles an hour, passing through small villages and rice-fields, with Mount Fujiyama, the sacred landmark of Japan towering before us, to the town of Kamakura, which was the capital of Japan in the 12th century. Near this village, among the trees, is the colossal bronze statue of Dia-Butsu, or Great Buddha; this figure is over 100 feet in height, represented, as usual, seated upon a lotus flower, and within it is a shrine. Tourists ascend it from the outside by means of a ladder; the thumb alone being of sufficient size to offer a convenient seat. This statue was cast over 600 years ago, and yet stands as a monument of the past.

Returning by the same route and conveyance to Yokohama we passed several days in the latter city making purchases of old Satsuma china, and wooden panels with figures of mother-of-pearl and ivory; and at night visited the tea-houses which are its principal attractions.

Much has been said of the beauty of Japan, of the elegance of its temples and of the politeness of the people Although they have but little to learn of agricultural science, the land showing evidences of a high degree of cultivation, and while here and there one sees pretty bits of scenery, Japan does not compare on the whole with many other countries in point of landscape.

The religion which was almost entirely Buddhist is rapidly merging into Shinto — the religion of the court, and the temples although rich in wood-carving and polished lacquer are small in dimensions, and not as grand and imposing as those of India and British Burmah. The rich and picturesque native costume is rapidly changing into that of the European; which the Japanese adopt, together with an imitation of foreign manners, and often with ludicrous effect; while the carrying of two swords — a long one for defense, and a short one for *hari-kari*, or self-disembowelment — has become almost obsolete.

In the time of the Daimios, or feudal lords, a title which now no longer exists, the Japanese were exceedingly polite and obsequious, the lower grades prostrating themselves when addressing a superior, and serving them on bended knee; but the innovations introduced with the advent of the foreign element have to some extent modified the distinctions of rank; and the lower classes have, in the reaction, become indifferent and self-assertive.

Leaving Yokohama by the Steamship Oceanic, of the Occidental and Oriental line, we were 17 days crossing the Pacific Ocean, a distance of 4,600 miles to San Francisco.

The most notable occurrence of the voyage was the crossing of the line, or 180° parallel of longitude from Greenwich, from which our steamer reckoned; but as we had been travelling from west to east, we had gained about 24 hours, and in order to have the day of the week and month correspond to that of San Francisco, were compelled to insert an extra day; thus giving us two Sundays in succession, both dating February 10th, 1884.

CHAPTER XXXIII.

SAN FRANCISCO: NAPA VALLEY: PETRIFIED FOREST: GEYSERS: SANTA CRUZ: MONTEREY: SANTA BARBARA: LOS ANGELES: MARIPOSA BIG TREES: YOSEMITE VALLEY: CALAVERAS BIG TREES: SACRAMENTO: VIRGINIA CITY: LAKE TAHOE: PUGET SOUND: PORTLAND: COLUMBIA RIVER: YELLOWSTONE PARK: SALT LAKE CITY: MT. OF THE HOLY CROSS: PIKE'S PEAK: DENVER: GREENBRIAR WHITE SULPHUR SPRINGS: LEXINGTON: NATURAL BRIDGE: LURAY: CHARLESTOWN: HARPERS FERRY.

SAN FRANCISCO, the extreme western city of the United States of America, and the most important place on the Pacific coast, has a population of 250,000 inhabitants. It is situated on the end of a narrow peninsula six miles wide, one side of which is washed by the Pacific Ocean, and the other by the Bay of San Francisco, one of the finest harbors in the world, where the combined fleets of the globe might ride at anchor in safety and with abundance of room.

The Golden Gate, which is the only entrance for vessels to pass into this harbor, is a narrow strait of deep water one mile in width, and the forts on either side so completely command it that the entrance of a ship could readily be prevented. The narrowness of this passage, cut through high hills, and the great depth of water, give it an artificial appearance, and it is supposed by many to have been caused by earthquakes, which are of frequent occurrence in this section.

The city is built on a number of sand hills, many of its streets being so steep that it is impossible to drive up the ascent with horses; but its system of surface railroads, propelled by cable or wire ropes laid underground, is not only very general but complete in every detail, ascending and descending the steepest grades with rapidity and safety.

San Francisco is said to be one of the wealthiest cities in the world in proportion to its population and age, having been incorporated in 1850. Those who have been successful on this coast, whether in gold or silver mines, railroads or real estate, have as a general thing, located here, and built palatial residences, many of which have cost millions of dollars; while its public buildings, theatres, and hotels compare favorably with those of any on the globe.

The main artery and business thoroughfare of the city is Market street, along which are located the principal stores and public buildings, including the Palace Hotel, the largest caravansary in the world, accommodating over 2,000 guests; the Baldwin Hotel, comprising the prettiest theatre in the city; and the Odd Fellows' and City Halls, besides many other imposing structures.

Driving through this broad and busy thoroughfare, we stopped at Woodward's Gardens, the finest public resort of the kind on this coast, comprising within its beautiful grounds statuary, miniature lakes, and tropical plants; while its art gallery, conservatories, museums, aquarium, sealery, aviary, and zoological collections are as complete in detail as any on this continent.

Continuing from here to the Golden Gate Park with its magnificent conservatory, we drove through its broad avenues, thronged with stylish equipages, to the beach, where from the Cliff House verandah we were entertained watching the sea-lions upon the adjacent rocks, some lying full length sunning their huge proportions, others gambolling in the water and uttering sounds resembling the barking of dogs.

In the centre of the city is the Chinese quarter, where crowded into four squares are some 40,000 Celestials; and in visiting its Joss-houses, theatres, and opium-dens, one gets a good idea of the habits and customs of this race of people.

The city is healthy, owing to the strong southerly winds; and although the summer fogs are objectionable, the climate is so equable that a light over-coat is comfortable the year round.

The suburban towns of Oakland, Alameda, Saucelito, and San Rafael are on the opposite side of the bay, connected with San Francisco by ferry, and contain many handsome residences.

Taking boat and rail a distance of 100 miles north, and passing through the beautiful and productive Napa Valley, where are located the Soda, and White Sulphur Springs, we stopped at Calistoga, and drove 5 miles to the Petrified Forest, in which are some 100 prostrate petrified trees; then staging for several hours over mountains and through romantic ravines, we arrived at the Devil's Cañon, where are located the Geyser Springs. These wonders of nature in the midst of a ravine, consist of a series of boiling and cold springs of black, yellow, white, and red water; some of which bubble up and send forth steam, hot water and gravel high in the air.

The favorite and most accessible sea-side resorts are Santa Cruz and Monterey; the former having magnificent surf-bathing, while the latter has an extensive and delightful hotel called the Del Monte, situated in the midst of a large park, containing a thick growth of cedars and tropical plants and flowers, with artificial lakes and fountains. Here are to be found entertainments of every conceivable variety — lawn-tennis, croquet, bowling, boating, and driving — the most popular road being a twelve-mile drive that intersects the forest and skirts the coast, affording magnificent views of the ocean. One of the principal attractions of Del Monte is the four immense swimming-tanks inclosed under a glass roof, and filled with salt water heated at different temperatures to accommodate all ages and both sexes.

Leaving Monterey by steamer we followed the coast a distance of 275 miles south to Santa Barbara, a town of 6,000 inhabitants, lying in a sheltered nook, shut in by high mountain ranges, and enjoying a dry and mild climate. Its population is largely composed of people from the Eastern States seeking health and a warm climate, and the place has a select and refined society.

Continuing our journey by steamer 75 miles further south we arrived at Los Angeles, or "city of Angels," a prosperous and flourishing town, and whose suburban places of resort such as Santa Monica, Pasadena, and Sierra Madre Villa located among the vineyards, orange, lemon and olive groves, which thrive luxuriantly in this section, render a winter sojourn delightful, and are frequented by large numbers of Eastern visitors.

Returning north from Los Angeles by rail we stopped at Madeira, where we took stage, and after a long day's ride over the mountains arrived at Clark's station.

Near this are the Mariposa Big Trees, a species of red cedar, probably the largest in the world. The greatest of these monsters of the forest which is now fallen is said to have measured 90 feet in circumference, and 400 feet in height, with bark about four feet in thickness; the Monarch, one of the tallest standing, is nearly 300 feet high; and the Wyoming is of such size as to allow of a six-horse stage passing through an archway formed by a hole cut in the trunk of the tree.

Resuming our journey by stage, the following day at noon we reached the great Yosemite Valley, and halted at Inspiration Point to view the grand and wonderful scene before us. This valley is 6 miles long by ½ wide, with rocks towering up on every side almost perpendicularly from 3,000 to 6,000 feet in height; with torrents and river cascades falling from their summits, and almost lost in spray before reaching the valley below.

After locating ourselves at Hutching's Hotel, we procured both mules and guide, and spent three days riding up the precipitous trails to the various points for views; the finest of which are obtained from Glacier Point, Clouds' Rest, Sentinel Dome, The Three Brothers and El Capitan; while the Yosemite, Bridal Veil, Nevada, and Vernal Falls, are the grandest and most beautiful features of the Yosemite.

Mirror Lake at the end of the Valley whose placid waters reflect the precipitous foliage-crowned mountains which border it, well repaid an early visit, when to its usual beauty was added that of the sun rising in slow majesty above the mountain tops and mirroring itself in the calm waters at their base.

Leaving the Yosemite by stage over another route we visited the Calaveras Grove of Big Trees, similar to those just mentioned, the principal feature, however, being one which it took five men with pump-augers 25 days to cut down, and the surface of whose stump has been converted into a ball-room where 32 couples have danced at one time.

Resuming the rail again at Stockton passing on the way Sacramento, the capital of California, numerous placer gold-mines where whole mountains were being washed away by means of hydraulic power, the beautiful Blue Cañon with its numerous points of interest, and after rounding Cape Horn, from whose dizzy heights one gazes down awe struck into the depths below, we reached Reno.

Here changing trains, we passed through Carson, the capital of Nevada, and ascended the mountain to the great silver quartz mining district of Virginia City.

By special invitation from one of the " Bonanza kings " we visited the Consolidated Virginia

and California mines. Ladies as well as gentlemen donning the ordinary flannel outfit worn by
miners, and each carrying a lantern, we stepped
upon the cage — or elevator, and sped with the
rapidity of lightning down to the 1,600 foot level.
Here we saw some of the richest silver quartz deposits ever discovered; and miners stripped to
the waist, the perspiration streaming from every
pore, working in relays; the heat being so intense
that it is impossible for them to continue their
labor unremittingly for any length of time. The
tunnels in these subterranean regions extend in
every direction, and are lighted with thousands of
candles, which with the railroads, drills and other
machinery at work, present the animated appearance of an underground city.

From here we visited Lake Tahoe, a lovely
body of deep clear water, 25 miles in length, and
10 in width, located among the snow-capped
peaks in the Sierra Nevada mountains 6,000
feet above the sea level, where we spent the time
delightfully, hunting, rowing, and fishing.

Returning to San Francisco we took rail and
stage to Portland, Oregon, stopping en route at
Sissons, at the foot of Mt. Shasta, and thence
through the romantic Puget Sound, sailing among
its many islands. We then continued through the
Columbia River, which teems with salmon and
other fine fish, and on either side of which are
rocky cliffs and beautiful cascades to the Dalles;

where we joined the Northern Pacific R. R. and journeyed east as far as Livingston, where a branch railway and stage a distance of 60 miles south, brought us to the National Yellowstone Park, in the northwest corner of Wyoming Territory.

This Park which comprises 3,575 square miles, and is more than 6,000 feet above the level of the sea, embraces not only the grandest of scenery but the most marvellous freaks of nature; here are probably 50 geysers that throw a column of water to a height of from 50 to 250 feet each, and 5,000 springs depositing lime and silica, around their borders in elaborate ornamentation and in a variety of colors. The Yellowstone Lake with an altitude of 7,800 feet, sends forth the river of the same name, which after making a number of beautiful falls, cuts its way for 20 miles through the almost solid rock called the Grand Cañon, which is 1,500 feet deep, and only 500 yards wide; and remarkable for the variety of tints in its formation.

The mountain range which hems in this valley on every side rises to a height of 12,000 feet, and its numerous mud volcanoes show that this entire region was at a comparatively recent period the scene of remarkable volcanic activity.

Continuing our journey southward we stopped at Salt Lake City, or Zion, prettily situated near a lake of the same name, and on a gradual slope bordering the River Jordan. This is the residence and headquarters of the President and Saints who govern the Mormon world, uphold polygamy, and exact the payment of tithes as in olden times. While the Mormons as a class are very ignorant, the city is rapidly growing, owing to its charming situation, good climate, and adjacent rich mines.

Its great Tabernacle seating 15,000 people, with dome-shaped roof, and containing an immense organ, together with the Temple and Assembly Hall stand out as prominent landmarks of the place.

Proceeding from here along the Denver and Rio Grande R. R. we saw in the distance the Mountain of the Holy Cross, so called from a ravine about 40 feet deep at its summit, forming a perfect cross, which is filled with snow the year round, and is so prominent as to be visible 80 miles distant.

We passed through the Grand Cañon of the Arkansas, a narrow defile with perpendicular walls of rock on each side, rising to a height of 3,000 feet; while the railroad bed and bridges are suspended from the rock above, so as to enable the trains to pass over and along the rushing torrents that flow through it. Further on we passed Pike's Peak, 14,300 feet high, the mountain which created such great excitement several years ago, on account of its gold deposits; and at the foot of which are the Garden of the Gods, a curious upheaval and washing of rocks; and Manitou Springs, where are to be found both soda and iron waters; and which is so much frequented as to be called the "Saratoga of the Far West."

At Denver, the capital of Colorado, which is a well-built city with 50,000 inhabitants, we stopped over a day, and then continued our journey, changing cars at Council Bluffs after crossing the Missouri River, and at Davenport viewed the Mississippi, called from its great length the "Father of Rivers."

Chicago, situated on Lake Michigan in Illinois, with a population of 600,000 and the most important city of the West, is noted for its magnificent business houses, and fine residences, which are not surpassed anywhere in the world. The enterprise of its people is proverbial; as was evidenced by the quickness and solidity with which the city was rebuilt, when destroyed by the great fire of 1871, which consumed 17,450 buildings, covering an area of 3¼ square miles. Chicago is centrally located in the United States, has numerous fine hotels, and is a great railroad centre; these advantages have caused it to be selected of late years as a place of assembly for national delegations. Its parks and boulevards, especially those bordering on the lake, are particularly fine; and here the driving can be seen of an afternoon while enjoying the refreshing breeze from the water.

From Chicago we journeyed east, passing through Indianapolis, the capital of Indiana; crossed the Ohio River at Louisville, and passed through the Blue grass regions of Kentucky, to the Greenbriar White Sulphur Springs of West Virginia. This fashionable resort is located in a basin surrounded by mountains; the Springs and large Hotel being situated in the centre of the grounds and completely encircled by cottages, while morning, noon, and night, there is a round of gaiety, and dancing to the strains of a delightful band of music.

At Lexington we stopped to visit the two great colleges of the South; the Virginia Military Institute, and the Washington-Lee University; and to see the graves of Virginia's two noblest sons and greatest generals, Robert E. Lee and T. J. (Stonewall) Jackson. In a memorial chapel, in the grounds of the Washington-Lee University, is a life-size recumbent figure of Gen. Lee dressed in full uniform, with his sword beside him, cut from the purest of white marble; a magnificent piece of work, and a life-like portrait.

The Natural Bridge of Virginia is a sight well worth travelling thousands of miles to see. It is a solid arch of rock 200 feet high and 90 feet wide affording a safe roadway over a deep chasm which cannot be crossed for miles above or below; while beneath the bridge flows a rippling stream of water; and this with the surrounding beauties of nature are illuminated at night with calcium lights and colored lanterns, producing a most beautiful effect.

Near here is Appomattox, the scene of the surrender of Gen. R. E. Lee, with his Confederate army, to Gen. U. S. Grant, commanding the United States forces April 9th, 1865, which virtually terminated the civil war that had lasted for over four years.

At Luray where we found a magnificent hotel most charmingly situated amid mountain scenery, we visited the famous Luray Cavern, which extends several miles under ground, and is divided into sections or compartments, called the Hall of Giants, the Theatre, the Ball-room, Pluto's Chasm, and Skeleton Gulch, while the electric lights shining through the transparent lime formations of stalagmite and stalactite present a fairy-like scene, and are named, and perfect representations of, the Ghost, the Fish-market, the Saracens Tent, the Organ, the Bird's-nest, the Tower of Babel and Cinderella leaving the ball.

Charlestown, the county seat of Jefferson, West Virginia, is noted as the place where John Brown and his six surviving associates were tried, condemned for treason and insurrection, and hung December 2nd, 1859.

Eight miles beyond is Harper's Ferry, located at the junction of the Potomac and Shenandoah rivers, with high mountains on every side, which with the canal boats, and trains of cars continually passing, combine to form a scene of picturesque grandeur. It was here that John Brown and his comrades at dead of night seized the U. S. Arsenal and other buildings with their contents; and after taking from their beds the most prominent citizens of the neighborhood, held them as hostages, expecting the black slaves to uprise and flock to their standard, in the attempt to gain their freedom. This bold and daring plot proved a complete failure, caused much excitement, and cost many lives; but was undoubtedly the prelude to the late Civil War of 1861–1865, which occasioned so much bloodshed, and was the means of abolishing slavery in the United States.

CHAPTER XXXIV.

WASHINGTON: BALTIMORE: ANNAPOLIS: PHILADELPHIA: NEW YORK: LONG BRANCH: CONEY ISLAND: BROOKLYN: HUDSON RIVER: WEST POINT: CATSKILL MTS.: ALBANY: SARATOGA: LAKE GEORGE: NIAGARA FALLS: ST. LAWRENCE RIVER: MONTREAL: QUEBEC: WHITE MTS.: BOSTON: PROVIDENCE: NEWPORT.

WASHINGTON CITY, the capital of the United States of America, with a population of 150,000, is situated in an undulating plain on the banks of

the Potomac river. It is to-day one of the finest
cities in the world, and with its broad streets
paved with asphaltum, and bordered with grass
plots, and at every short distance a heroic statue
in bronze or marble of some statesman or general,
bids fair at no distant day to be unsurpassed by
any city on the globe.

The monuments in Washington are so numerous that it would fill a volume alone to describe
them; the principal ones, however, are the
Washington Monument, a four-sided shaft of
white marble, 465 feet high,—the highest in the
world, costing over one million dollars; the
Naval Monument, erected to the memory of sea-
men who fell in the war of 1861-5, a magnificent
marble group; while those of Generals Jackson,
Scott, Thomas, and McPherson, mounted on
horseback, with those of Presidents Washington
and Lincoln, and Admiral Farragut, standing on
high pedestals, are a few of the finest, located at
the intersection of the streets.

The Capitol building, whose corner-stone was
laid by Gen. Washington in 1793, stands on a
terraced hill 90 feet high, environed by beautiful
grounds, and is the most imposing structure of its
kind in the world. It is built of white marble
and freestone, measures 750 feet in length, and
covers an area of 3½ acres; its magnificent dome
surmounted by the Statue of Liberty, the grandest feature of this vast structure, being visible for

many miles away. At the main and central entrance of the building, where the Presidents take
the oath of office, is the colossal marble statue of
Washington ; on either side are figures symbolical
of Peace and War, and the bronze doors designed
by Rodgers and cast by Muller, of Munich,
weigh 20,000 pounds, and are a marvel of workmanship and beauty.

In the rotunda are eight large paintings with
figures, heroic size, illustrating scenes in American
history, viz.: Columbus discovering America, the
Baptism of Pocahontas, De Soto discovering the
Mississippi, the Surrender of Cornwallis, Signing
the Declaration of Independence, and the Resig-
nation of Washington ; above and extending all
around the dome is the celebrated fresco, which
stands out like an alto-relievo of marble figures,
and on the ceiling is a group of 63 portraits
covering a space of 6,000 feet.

The National Statuary Hall, semi-circular in
form, is surrounded by 24 columns of variegated
green breccia or pudding-stone taken from the
quarries near the city ; and here are statues of
statesmen and warriors, each State being allowed
to send figures of two of its most prominent men :
among whom are Washington, Jefferson, Hamilton, Allen, Green, Livingston, and Lincoln. In
other parts of the building are portraits of presidents and statesmen, besides paintings of the
settlement of California, and Perry's victory on

Lake Champlain; while the Marble Room, extravagant in its decoration, the Supreme Court, and the Library of Congress are all well worth an inspection. In one wing of the Capitol is the Senate Chamber, and at the other end the House of Representatives, where the Congress of the United States meets in session from December to March to make its laws; the gayest and most fashionable season of the Capitol is during the session.

Other important buildings at Washington are the Executive Mansion, usually called the White House,—the residence of the President of the United States,—the Treasury, State, War, Navy, and Pension buildings, Post Office and Agricultural Departments, all magnificent structures built of granite, which well repaid an interior investigation; and the Botanical Gardens, Smithsonian Institute, Naval Observatory, and Navy Yard we visited in turn, deriving from each both pleasure and information.

The Corcoran Gallery, a large brick and brown stone building, contains a varied and valuable collection, comprising among its statuary the Greek Slave, by Powers, and the Dying Napoleon, by Vela; and among the 200 paintings, many of which are gems, is the Procession of the Holy Bull Apis, in an Egyptian Temple, by a modern artist.

The Soldiers' Home for disabled veterans, located in a park of 500 acres, is reached through a beautiful drive, the principal resort of an afternoon.

Georgetown and Alexandria are pretty suburban towns in close proximity to Washington; in the former is Oak Hill Cemetery, where are the monuments of many eminent men, and the aqueduct which carries the water of the Chesapeake and Ohio Canal across the Potomac river; while in the latter is Christ Church, containing the pews number 59 and 46, which were once occupied by Washington and Lee.

Across the Potomac, on the Virginia side, is Arlington, the magnificent residence of General Lee before the war of 1861, and 15 miles further down the river is Mt. Vernon, where Washington lived and now lies buried.

At Baltimore, called the Monumental City from the number of its fine monuments, we drove through its natural and beautiful Druid Hill Park, and viewed its fine Washington and Battle Monuments; then taking boat down the Patapsco river, made a brief visit to Annapolis, which contains the U. S. Naval Academy with its well laid out grounds.

Philadelphia, a city of 900,000 inhabitants, located on the Schuylkill river, was founded by William Penn, who came over from England in 1682 with a colony of Quakers, and purchased this site from the Indians for $2,500. Here the first Continental Congress assembled in 1774, and the Declaration of Independence was issued July 4th, 1776; here the Convention which

framed the Constitution of the Republic assembled in 1787; and here was the seat of government of the United States until 1800, when it
was removed to Washington.

The city, which is 22 miles long by 8 wide,
covers an area of 130 square miles, and has more
buildings than any other city in America.
Its manufacturing interests are very large, and
while the streets as a general thing are narrow,
it boasts of one of the finest parks in the world;
among its principal buildings are Independence Hall, where July 4th, 1776, the Declaration
of Independence was read and adopted; the new
City Hall, the Masonic Temple, and the Penn-
sylvania Railroad depot.

New York city, the commercial metropolis of
the United States, and the most important city
of the Western Hemisphere, occupies the entire
surface of Manhattan Island, and a considerable
district of the mainland. It is bounded on the
west by the Hudson river, on the east by the
East river, and on the south by New York Bay,
which opens into the Atlantic Ocean.

Its location for a city is an admirable one,
surrounded on all sides by water of sufficient
depth for vessels of the largest draught, and its
population, which is rapidly increasing, numbers
now over 1,250,000 inhabitants.

The site of New York was discovered by Ver-
razzani, a Florentine, in 1524, but was visited

later by Sir Henry Hudson, an Englishman, in the
employ of the Dutch East India Co., who landed
here Sept. 3rd, 1609, and claimed this as well as
the surrounding country for Holland, by right of
discovery.   In 1614, a Dutch colony settled the
extreme end of the Island, or lower part of the
city, now known as Bowling Green, and called it
New Amsterdam, but in 1664 it was captured by
the British under the Duke of York, since which
time it has borne the name of New York City.

Broadway and Fifth Avenue are its principal
shopping and residence streets, running almost
the entire length of the Island in the centre of the
city.   Starting from the extreme southern end of
the Island called the Battery where is located Castle
Garden, a large building where all emigrants are
landed, we found ourselves in the commercial
and financial part of the city surrounded on every
side by colossal and imposing buildings, several
rising to a height of fifteen stories, with domes
and spires even towering above this, and some of
them marking the sites where once stood houses
occupied by Cornwallis, Howe, Clinton, Arnold
and Washington, when the colonies were strug-
gling for independence.

One of the finest buildings in the city is the
Produce Exchange, built of brick and iron, occupying an entire square on Whitehall Street, and
covering the site of the house where died Robert
Fulton, the inventor of the first steamboat " The

Clermont," which plied on the Hudson river in 1807.

At the intersection of Broad and Wall streets, the great banking centre, is the U. S. Sub-treasury, built of white marble, in front of which is a bronze statue of Washington, marking the spot where the old Federal Hall once stood, and the first President delivered his inaugural address.

On Broadway at the head of Wall street, stands Trinity Church, an old and rich corporation, dating back to 1696, built of brown stone, in the Gothic style, with a spire 284 feet high, from the top of which is obtained a magnificent view, and in its graveyard lie buried Hamilton, Fulton, Lawrence, and other distinguished men. Continuing up Broadway, crowded with hundreds of vehicles and a surging tide of humanity, we passed some of the finest structures of the city, and paused at old St. Paul's church, in front of which rest the remains of General Montgomery, killed in 1775 in the assault upon Quebec.

The City Hall, situated in the centre of a park, around and near which are located the leading newspaper buildings and lawyers' offices, may be termed the legal and literary centre; and in the Governor's room, on the second story of the City Hall, are the chair in which Washington sat when inaugurated President of the United States, and the desk on which he wrote his first message to Congress. In close vicinity are the Post Office,

built of granite, at a cost of $12,000,000, and the
Times and Tribune newspaper buildings, magnificent structures towering up to a formidable height.

The great East River Bridge, connecting New
York and Brooklyn,— the New York entrance
being at the City Hall Park — is the largest suspension bridge in existence, and a gigantic and
remarkable piece of engineering, deserving to be
styled one of the seven wonders of the modern
world.

The length of this bridge measures 5,989 feet;
the central span, which crosses the river from
tower to tower, is 1,595 feet; while the approach
and span from the New York side measures 2,493,
and that from the Brooklyn side 1,901 feet.

The towers on either side, built of granite, rise
to a height of 278 feet above high water, and
support the four cables of steel, each of which
measures 16 inches in diameter and contains 5,282
galvanized wires, to which the bridge is swung.

The floor of the span is 135 feet above high-
water mark, thus enabling the tallest ships to pass
under it; and it is 85 feet in width, allowing a
wide promenade for foot-passengers, two railroad
tracks, and two roadways for vehicles.

This stupendous triumph of engineering was
planned by Col. John A. Roebling, and commenced under his directions in January, 1870, and
completed by his son, Washington Roebling, and
opened to traffic May 23, 1883; having been

about 13 years in process of building, at a cost of $15,000,000.

Continuing up the city we passed through the Five Points, the London Petticoat Lane, viewing its depravity and wretchedness, and near which is the Tombs or city prison, covering an entire block, built of dark granite in the Egyptian style, where many notorious criminals have been confined.

Union Square, which contains bronze monuments of Washington, Lafayette, and Lincoln, is surrounded by fine buildings, and is in the centre of the great shopping district which extends up and down Broadway for many blocks. Madison Square, where Broadway, Fifth Avenue, and Twenty-third street intersect one another, is the hotel and theatre centre, and in the very heart of New York city.

Proceeding up Broadway we passed the principal theatres, including Wallack's, Daly's, the Casino, and Metropolitan Opera House; and hotels and apartment houses many stories high.

On Fifth Avenue, the principal street for driving to the Park, are located the Union League and other fine clubs, the Catholic Cathedral, St. Thomas' Episcopal, and Dr. Hall's Presbyterian, churches, and the palatial residences of Stewart, Gould, Astor, and Vanderbilt, the millionaire princes of New York.

Central Park, probably the finest in the world, extends from 59th to 110th Streets, and embraces

843 acres. It contains numbers of small lakes, magnificent fountains, lovely drives, romantic rambles, rock caverns, and rustic arbors. Here stands the Obelisk presented to New York by the Khedive of Egypt, the hieroglyphics on one side showing it to have been hewn during the reign of Thothmes III., while on the other are inscribed the victories of Rameses II.

Here also are bronze statues of Shakespeare, Scott, Burns, Webster, Goethe, Morse, and Halleck; and various groups add to the embellishment of this enchanting spot.

In one part of the grounds are the Zoological Gardens, with an interesting collection of animals, birds, and reptiles; and in another the Metropolitan Museum of Art, comprising a fine collection of statuary and paintings.

Within the Park of an afternoon is a constant throng of fine and stylish equipages, and on Harlem Lane may be seen some of the fastest trotters on record.

Among a few of the other points of interest in the city may be mentioned, High Bridge, by which the Croton River water is carried over Harlem River to be distributed in the city mains; Madison Avenue with its superb residences and lofty churches; the Lenox and Astor Libraries; the Academy of Design; and on Blackwells Island in the East River the massive structures of the Penitentiary, Asylums, and Hospitals.

Convenient to New York are many summer resorts which can be reached in an hour or more either by water or rail.

The principal of these is Long Branch, where there is fine surf bathing and a fashionable drive which extends for several miles along the beach. The hotels are large and numerous, and the cottages, many of which are built in the Queen Anne style of architecture, are environed by beautiful gardens, and well-kept lawns.

Coney Island being the most accessible seaside resort to New York, is the most popular with the masses, and here on a summer's day may be seen from 50,000 to 100,000 persons sporting in the waves, or enjoying the various amusements and attractions of the place.

The Hotels are on a very large scale, a truly unique one being built in the form of an elephant, 175 feet high, containing 30 rooms, and a hall 92 by 38 feet. Entering a door at a toe on the left hind leg, one ascends numbers of stairs, and traverses various sections of the beast's anatomy, and finally emerges in the gilded howdah on its back, from which there is a fine view of water and landscape.

Jersey City and Newark are suburban towns, with a population of about 140,000 each, and Brooklyn, the third largest city in the United States, with a population of 600,000, is directly opposite New York and connected with the latter

city by the East River bridge. We drove over
this obtaining a fine view of the harbor, and
reaching Brooklyn continued through its avenues
of brown stone houses to Prospect Park, containing 550 acres, and thence to Greenwood cemetery,
where are many rich and handsome tombs and
monuments.

Taking boat from New York we sailed up the
beautiful and romantic Hudson River, the Rhine
of America, whose banks teem with legends and
historic interest.

We first passed the spot where Burr killed
Hamilton in a duel; then Forts Lee and Washington of Revolutionary fame; Mt. St. Vincent, once
the home of Forrest the actor; Yonkers, where
lived Mary Phillips, Washington's first love;
Tappan, where Major André was imprisoned and
executed; Irvington, which contains "Sunny-
side" the late residence of Washington Irving;
Tarrytown, where André was arrested, where
Irving lies buried, and the scene of the author's
happiest fancies, including "Sleepy Hollow;"
Sing Sing, with its gloomy state prison; Croton
Point, above which the water of the Croton river
is conveyed to New York by the great Croton
Aqueduct 40 miles long, with 16 tunnels, and 24
bridges; and Caldwell's Landing, where it is said
the famous pirate, Capt. Kidd, buried his treasure.
Here we reached the Highlands, and passed
rapidly by Thunder Mountain, with its beautiful

cascade; Anthony's Nose, a rocky promontory; the picturesque Iona Island, a favorite picnic resort; Sugar-loaf Mountain at the foot of which is Beverly House, where Arnold was breakfasting when he heard of the capture of André; and Cranston's Hotel, one of the favorite summer resorts, commanding a fine view of the river and mountain.

We landed at West Point, by far the most charming spot on the Hudson, where is located the U. S. Military Academy, including an extensive parade ground where the cadets are instructed in infantry, artillery, and cavalry drill.

On one side are the residences of the commanding general, officers and professors, together with the barracks, mess-hall, chapel and observatory; and on the other side are the forts containing the heavy artillery, which command the river, and from which point are obtained glorious views in all directions.

Continuing our interesting trip up the Hudson we landed at Catskill, and there took rail and stage up the Catskill Mountains. About midway up the mountain in a secluded dell is pointed out the spot where Rip Van Winkle took his famous sleep; and near the summit are two magnificent hotels, the Kaaterskill, and Mountain House, from both of which one looks down upon a far-spreading panorama with the Hudson River running through it like a silver thread.

Albany, the capital of New York State is, next to Jamestown in Virginia, the oldest settlement in the country, having been a Dutch trading point in 1614. It is built on a hill sloping towards the river, on the summit of which is Capitol Square, and the finest public buildings of the city.

Saratoga, a place of 10,000 inhabitants, is celebrated for its famous mineral springs, which attract annually some 50,000 people from all parts of the globe. It has altogether some 25 springs, containing iron, sulphur and magnesia; the Congress and Hathorn, with large proportions of carbonic-acid gas, being, however, the most popular.

Besides a few fine residences, here are some of the grandest hotels in the country which are crowded to their utmost during July and August, the racing season, and on whose wide verandahs, during the hours that the bands play, the ladies may be seen arrayed in elegant costumes and wearing costly jewels.

From here we visited that lovely sheet of water, Lake George, stopping at Fort William Henry, and Rodgers Rock; thence by boat, and stage to the historic spot of Ticonderoga, and after doing the Adirondack Mountains, and skirting numerous beautiful lakes we arrived at Niagara.

The Niagara Falls, are formed by the Niagara River which drains Lake Erie, and falls perpendicularly 168 feet over a rock formation, of horse-

shoe shape 4,750 feet wide. In the centre of the
river, and on the brink of the precipice, is Goat
Island, which is reached by a bridge; from this
point the venturesome, enveloped in water-proofs
and accompanied by a guide, go under the Falls,
and through the Cave of the Winds, where on a
sunshiny day one stands in the centre of a perfect
rainbow circle. At night when the colored calcium lights are thrown upon the cataracts, the effect is most wonderful, the red light resembling a
sea of blood. It is estimated that no less than
100,000,000 gallons of water per hour pass over
the falls, which with the whirlpool rapids, and the
beautiful suspension bridge below, combine to
make a scene of unsurpassed grandeur, which
grows upon one the more it is seen.

We passed from here by rail through Lock-
port, so called from its numerous canal locks,
and afterwards taking steamer on the St. Lawrence
River, sailed among the Thousand Islands,
shooting the rapids, and landing at Montreal in
Canada. This is the largest city and commercial
emporium of British America, and contains in its
public square a marble statue of Queen Victoria.

Quebec, the oldest and most interesting city
in Canada, is on the north bank of the St. Lawrence 300 miles from its mouth. The old town is
surrounded by walls three miles in extent, and the
Citadel covering 40 acres, and crowning the summit of a rock hill, is styled the Gibraltar of America.

Along the edge of the cliff and 200 feet above the river is Dufferin Terrace, ¼ of a mile long, overlooking the St. Lawrence and the city; while in the vicinity are appropriate monuments erected to the memory of the gallant Wolf and Montcalm.

Continuing our journey we skirted the shores of Lake Champlain, and stopped at the Profile, Crawford, and Glen Houses, in the White Mountains, to see their various features of interest, and enjoy the fine mountain views; and ascended Mt. Washington 6,293 feet high, by a railway similar to the one up the Rigi.

Boston with a population of 400,000 is situated principally on a peninsular extending into Massachusetts Bay. It was here that on March 5, 1770, the Boston Massacre occurred when the soldiers fired upon the citizens, killing and wounding many people, and here on Dec. 16, 1773, the tea was thrown overboard into the harbor, which was one of the opening scenes of the Revolutionary War.

The business streets of the city, unlike most in America are crooked and narrow, but in the residence and newer portion they are wide and straight, and contain some fine churches and public buildings.

The Common, a park of 50 acres in the heart of the city, is not only historic, but the principal pleasure-ground, and near its celebrated Frog pond, is erected the Soldiers Monument, 90 feet high, with four statues of heroic size at its base; while in the Public Gardens adjoining are the statues of Washington, Everett, and Sumner.

The Bunker Hill Monument, on the site of the old fort at Breed Hill, is a square obelisk of Quincy granite, 220 feet high, and commemorates the battle fought on that spot June 17, 1775.

The buildings of greatest interest in Boston are Faneuil Hall of Revolutionary fame; the State House, with its collection of statuary, paintings and historic relics; Memorial Hall, and Music Hall, the latter one of the finest in America, containing the second largest organ in the world.

At Cambridge, a suburb of Boston, is located the Harvard University, founded by the Rev. John Harvard in 1638, and one of the oldest and richest institutions of learning in America.

After leaving Boston we stopped at Providence, the capital of Rhode Island, founded in 1636 by Roger Williams, who had been banished from Massachusetts on account of his religious beliefs. Here are Brown University, an old institution of learning, and the City Hall, one of the finest buildings of the kind in New England, which was erected at a cost of $1,000,000.

Newport, the queen sea-side resort of the East, is on Narragansett Bay, 5 miles from the ocean. It has limited hotel accommodations, and its beach is not as fine as that at Long Branch. It is principally the resort of wealthy New Yorkers, who have built magnificent and substantial houses which they call cottages. The season here continues later than at other resorts, for in September when business men have returned to the cities, a round of gaieties is inaugurated which renders this month probably the most enjoyable of the season.

Here taking one of the magnificent Sound steamers, we sailed through Long Island Sound and down the East River under the great Suspension Bridge, passing near Bedloe's Island, where Bartholdi's bronze Statue of Liberty, a gift from the people of France to the people of the United States is about to be erected. This is the colossal figure of a woman bearing a torch in her up-lifted hand, which with its pedestal when completed will stand 300 feet high, the tallest statue in the world, and with its electric light throwing countless rays many miles out to sea, will serve as a beacon of welcome to the stranger from foreign shores.

Viewing from the harbor the marvels of engineering skill, and the gigantic structures completed during our absence, we noted with pride the advancement and enterprise of our own people compared with those of many other countries, and hailed with joy our return to New York after a two years' tour, in which we had made the entire circuit of the globe.

INDEX.

27

ADVERTISEMENTS

MATILDA, Princess of England, by Mme Sophie Cottin, from the French by Jennie W. Raum, in two vols., paper, $1.00. Cloth, $1.75 per set.

"A good old-fashioned novel with a good old-fashioned hero and heroine, possessed of superhuman strength and virtues, is rare enough in the present day to be refreshing. 'Matilda, Princess of England,' would have been thoroughly satisfactory to our forefathers. It is crowded with incidents, has an exciting plot, is not sparing in sentimental love scenes, and describes the romantic times of the crusaders. The heroine is a sister of Richard Cœur de Lion, a novice in a convent, who desires to go with her brother on his pilgrimage to the Holy Land. The hero is Malek Adhel, a Mussulman and brother of the famous Saladin. The passionate love of the Eastern prince for the Christian maiden, and the chivalrous devotion which eventually won Matilda's heart, are but a part of the romance. After love on both sides is felt and acknowledged comes the long and terrible struggle of the lovers to be true to their different faiths. The agonizing efforts made by the Christian maiden to convert the Saracen, his loyal fidelity to his country and his people, and the subsequent tragedy, make the novel exceedingly powerful and interesting. The descriptions of scenery in the East are very fine; the situations are dramatic, and the language is highly colored and Oriental, perhaps too much so to be always agreeable. One may wish that Mme. Sophie Cottin had condensed her work and given us only one volume of 'Matilda;' but the novel as it is will be a valuable addition to the historical pictures of the days of the crusades. The boys and girls who have followed Richard Cœur de Lion's fortunes so gladly in 'The Talisman' and 'Ivanhoe' will rejoice to find him again foremost in battles and generous alike to friend and foe; while those who remember the venerable William, archbishop of Tyre, will find his life and character portrayed with wonderful truth and beauty. The first few chapters of any historical novel require a certain effort of the will to accomplish, but after the reader has left these behind he will find 'Matilda' as stirring and absorbing as a tale of modern times."--*Evening Transcript, Boston, July* 16, 1885.

EKKEHARD, a Tale of the Tenth Century, by **Joseph Victor von Scheffel,** translated from the German. Two volumes. Paper, 80 cts. Cloth, $1.50 per set.

"It is more than thirty years since the appearance of Herr von Scheffel's famous novel, 'Ekkehard,' which produced a profound sensation in Germany, and from that time to this has been recognized as a classic. The present translation of this brilliant work is excellent and unidiomatic, the original beauties of style being to a great extent preserved. The preface — an essay upon the office of the historical novel — is graceful and profound; it exhibits the author in the rôle of a critic who, rebelling slightly against the dry-as dust methods, prefers the poetical presentation of truth under a garb which is attractive as well as accurate. Not that the author would ignore the stern and unbending requirements of the historical conscience, but he would clothe the creature of the historian's toil and labor in garments which add to its beauty and attractiveness. No more brilliant and truthful picture of the age has ever been written : the waning yet still distinct influences of heathen rites and customs and heathen gods, the feudal spirit, the castle and the cloister, the prelate and the priest of that century which preceded the Carthusian reform, — the life, in a word, of the tenth century is portrayed with a pen directed by a scholar and an enthusiast.

Having studied the records of St. Gall and inspired by his own poetic and chivalrous nature, drawing deep breaths of inspiration from the mountains and valleys of Switzerland, Herr von Scheffel, with Ranke's love for truth and with Schlegel's sentiment, wrote with a burning pen the history of Ekkehard, the Monk of St. Gall, the preceptor of the beautiful Hadwig, Duchess of Suabia. Those were times when the muscle and brawn of the knight put the calm seclusion of the monastery to shame, when the Huns, looking back to Atilla as the demigod of their race, overran the south of Germany and harried the Rhine country — burning, devastating, destroying, foes to State and Church alike, and eager only for booty. All of this magnificent chaos of life is portrayed with a fire and enthusiasm which rouses the reader, and must have put the author into a state of exaltation. The characters are drawn vith vividness. The Greek girl Praxedis is a gem from Byzantium ; the Abbot, the boy-goatherd, the Hun and his German wife, and the chief personages, Hadwig and Ekkehard, have an actuality which makes them living and breathing personalities. And when one reads the song of Walthari, that most ancient of the ancient songs of German mediæval times, how pale and colorless seems the romance of 'The Fairie Queen' in comparison with the superb strength and daring of the contestants. Few historical novels are so charming, few deserve so careful study."—*The Critic*, N. Y., August 9, 1890.

A CHILD'S ROMANCE, by **Pierre Loti,** from the French by Clara Bell. One volume 16mo., paper 50 cents. 12mo. cloth $1.00.

"Childhood, like love and death, would seem to be much the same thing the wide world over. The story, here told with exquisite simplicity and vivid clearness, ot a childhood spent in a quiet old town of provincial France, will wake many a responsive sigh and smile of reminiscence in the hearts of readers whose childhood—whose wonder years—were passed under far other skies, and whose manhood knows far other ambitions, ideals and occupations than those of Pierre Loti, dreamer of dreams. All that makes childhood the strange and beautiful thing which under any normal conditions it is remembered as being, seems to belong to childhood, wherever lived; all the queer reticences, more unconquerable than any of after-life, all the formless sorrows, the unconfessed terrors, the lonely imaginings that turn, to a child's apprehension, the work-a-day world into a land of mystery and faerie, are the common property of childhood, under whatever skies; and however the spoken languages of children may differ, the unspoken language of childhood is one."—*Boston Transcript.*

"This delicious souvenir of the childhood of M. Pierre Loti is the idealist brother of Mr. W. D. Howells' realistic *Boy's Town.* Both books are inspired by the same tenacious and affectionate memory, the same same clear evocation of the past in its impressions as in its acts, the same wonderful naturalness in which every reader finds the image of his own childhood mirrored repeatedly. But M. Loti had an extremely sensitive infantile temperament, much more concerned with its imaginations than with the outer world, and very little social. He says that he might have given to his book the dangerous title, 'Journal of my unexplained sorrows, and of the tricks by which occasionally I sought to forget them.' Mr. Howells, on the contrary, might have named his book, "Journal of my natural good times, and the tricks by which occasianally I relieved them by conscientious gloom." M. Loti's book is a charming revelation of the intimate life of a little French boy, destined to be a literary artist. While we read, there vibrate again and again memories and impressions long silent, almost extinct."—*The Literary World.*

"The charming sentiment which characterizes the author's other works that have been given to American readers marks every page of this pleasing prose idyl."—*Philadelphia Inquirer.*

FROM LANDS OF EXILE.—By Pierre Loti, from

the French by Clara Bell, in one vol.   Paper, 50 cts.   Cloth, 90 cts.

―――――――

" THE FRENCH have a knack for dedications. The other day
we had occasion to notice Balzac's ' Modeste Mignon,' to which
was prefixed one of the most beautiful dedications we had ever
read : short, pregnant, eloquent, compressing in a single paragraph — but a paragraph of which Balzac alone is master — the
concentrated adoration of a life-time.   Pierre Loti, in this volume
of charming translations, shows himself hardly less skilful in his
introductory note, as he presents to us a brief memoir of the
inspirer and inspiration of some of his best work — Mrs. Edward
Lee Childe, ' whose never-to-be-forgotten image rises before me,
strangely vivid, whenever I have time to think.'   Between Loti
and this delicate, gifted Parisienne there existed sympathies of
which we have prescience and foreshadowing in these marvellous
sketches, — an Andromeda chained to a sofa in the Champs
Elysées while Perseus ran the Eastern seas, revelled in their gorgeous coloring, and brought back from them — ' seas of exile '—
impressions of the most exquisite vividness.   There is true Ori-
entalism in this book.   Fragmentary as its reminiscences are,
they are yellow with China, green with Singapore, glowing with
Aden, penetrated with the languor and intoxication of Annam and
Far India, tremulous with palms, grotesque with uprisen memories of pagoda and Buddha-worship.   An officer on a French
man-of-war in the Franco-Chinese war, Loti availed himself of his
opportunities, and drank in that golden, stagnant, inverted sort
of Chinese life which was afforded by Cochin China and its fantastic existence.   His note-book is a net with which he captured
butterflies, harvested impressions, wove the East into his cocoon-
hammock, and then hatched it out for us in this argentiferous
form.   A writer who writes mother-of-pearl, who thinks opal,
who ' tools ' his thought into all sorts of precious forms, and who
calls his strange spoil, ' From Lands of Exile;'   such is this
French officer, who is at the same time a great word-artist.   He
is certainly endowed with the ' fruitful river of the eye,' with a
retina of rare sensitiveness, with a sense of vision that dilates
your own almost to pain; what he sees you see twice over : for
yourself and through him.   China has passed through many
rarely gifted psychological organizations ; but it has never before
emerged so itself, so prismatic, so alive as a chameleon is alive,
with its great yellow goblinlike picturesqueness."— *The Critic.*

RARAHU; or the Marriage of Loti.— By **Pierre Loti,** from the French by Mrs. Clara Bell. *Authorized edition.* One volume. 16mo. paper, 50 cts. 12mo. cloth, $1.00.

Not long ago we had occasion to speak of Julien Viaud's "Pécheur d'Island" — that wonderful romance of the wild and frozen North in which marvellous descriptions of sea-faring life in Icelandic waters were intermingled with equally marvellous pages depicting the progress of a love affair between a wild young mariner and a beautiful daughter of Brittany. In the "Mariage de Loti," now translated by Clara Bell under the title of *Rarahu,* we are taken to the antipodes and the author lavishes all his power as a writer in painting in the most exquisite and idyllic colors the experiences of a young naval officer during a six months' stay at Tahiti. Tahitian customs are not based on Puritanic ideals, and this marriage of Loti would be regarded as something far different under less benignant conditions; but morals, like religion, are, as we all know, largely a matter of geographical location, and of this affair between the foreigner and the pearl of Papeete it may at least be said that it reflected the utmost devotion while it endured. The book is chiefly remarkable for its exotic flavor; it breathes the true atmosphere of the tropics. Tahiti, as Julien Viaud reveals that far-distant island, is a paradise of the senses, a veritable abode of syrens for those who go down to the sea in ships, and all its remote and unfamiliar charm, — the brooding silences of nature, the vast forests haunted neither by singing bird or venomous insect, the towering peaks, the ever-flowing cataracts leaping from the heights, the cool pools of refreshing water, the tremendous surf rolling in forever on the resistant shore, the gorgeous semi-civilization of Pomaré's court, the existence of a simple-minded, imaginative people who find their wants amply provided for by nature and who pass their hours with no thought or care for the morrow—all this gets a place in Julien Viaud's book. As for Rarahu she is a tropical flower born to dazzle for a time with her beauty and to intoxicate the soul with her adorable fancies, only to fade at last into something worse than death. This is Tahiti seen with the eyes of the poet, pictured by one who chooses his colors deftly and who has no call to portray the dreary or the commonplace. The book as it stands is a masterpiece of art, a symphony in words, expressing with graceful and often poignant modulation the emotions that stir the heart at twenty and make existence a vista of perpetual pleasure or a bourn of limitless despair. Viaud is one who at least in fancy has sounded all the heights and depths of passion, and yet there is in his method a reserve which piques interest. Being a genuine artist he knows with unerring felicity when and at what point to stay his hand. — *The Beacon,* Boston, *July* 26, 1890.

AN ICELAND FISHERMAN, *(Pecheur d'Islande)*

A Story of Love on Land and Sea, by **Pierre Loti,** from the French by Clara Cardiot. One Volume.

16mo, Paper, 25 cents.   12mo. Cloth, 75 cents.

———

" ' An Iceland Fisherman ' is a sad but wonderfully sweet story that established on a firm foundation the reputation of its talented author almost immediately upon its publication. Breton life is painted with a masterly hand, and the fine descriptions, tenderness and pathos of the story give it an interest for all classes of cultivated readers that can never wane."— *Boston Commonwealth.*

———

THE COURT OF CHARLES IV. a Romance, by B. Perez Galdós, from the Spanish by Clara Bell, in one vol.   Price, paper, 50 cts.   Cloth, 90 cts.

———

"To this house the American reading public owes many new and delightful sensations. It has brought into popularity here a number of authors of undoubted genius whose remarkable works have been strangely overlooked by other publishers. One of this brilliant company is B. Perez Galdós, the Spanish romancer, whose ' Gloria ' has recently made a profound impression in its English version at the hands of the accomplished linguist, Clara Bell. From the same author and the same translator we now receive a novel of love and war as powerful of its kind as Tolstoï's books which cover a similar range of human interest. The action takes place in the early part of this century, when Napoleon was the disturbing element of the universe. The characters who move through the thrilling pages are princes, princesses, grandees of all grades, generals and statesmen. They are mostly historical. Spanish scenery, climate, customs and manners are described with scrupulous fidelity. To read the book is like living in Spain during the eventful era to which the story is confined. As the Spanish peninsula is but little visited by American tourists, and as the ' Court of Charles IV.,' with its ambitions and intrigues, is a subject quite fresh to novelists, it follows that the present work will be eagerly bought and greatly enjoyed by all who love to explore new fields."— *The Journal of Commerce.*

THE MARTYR OF GOLGOTHA, by Enrique Perez Escrich, from the Spanish by Adèle Josephine Godoy, in two volumes. Price, paper covers, $1.00. Cloth binding, $1.75.

"There must always be some difference of opinion concerning the right of the romancer to treat of sacred events and to introduce sacred personages into his story. Some hold that any attempt to embody an idea of our Saviour's character, experiences, sayings and teachings in the form of fiction must have the effect of lowering our imaginative ideal, and rendering trivial and common-place that which in the real Gospel is spontaneous, inspired and sublime. But to others an historical novel like the 'Martyr of Golgotha' comes like a revelation, opening fresh vistas of thought, filling out blanks and making clear what had hitherto been vague and unsatisfactory, quickening insight and sympathy, and actually heightening the conception of divine traits. The author gives also a wide survey of the general history of the epoch and shows the various shaping causes which were influencing the rise and development of the new religion in Palestine. There is, indeed, an astonishing vitality and movement throughout the work, and, elaborate though the plot is, with all varieties and all contrasts of people and conditions, with constant shiftings of the scene, the story yet moves, and moves the interest of the reader too, along the rapid current of events towards the powerful culmination. The writer uses the Catholic traditions, and in many points interprets the story in a way which differs altogether from that familiar to Protestants : for example, making Mary Magdalen the same Mary who was the sister of Lazarus and Martha, and who sat listening at the Saviour's feet. But in general, although there is a free use made of Catholic legends and traditions, their effort is natural and pleasing. The romance shows a degree of a southern fervor which is foreign to English habit, but the flowery, poetic style — although it at first repels the reader — is so individual, so much a part of the author, that it is soon accepted as the naive expression of a mind kindled and carried away by its subject. Spanish literature has of late given us a variety of novels and romances, all of which are in their way so good that we must believe that there is a new generation of writers in Spain who are discarding the worn-out forms and traditions, and are putting fresh life and energy into works which will give pleasure to the whole world of readers." — *Philadelphia American*, March 5, 1887.

ASPASIA. — A Romance, by **Robert Hamerling,** from the German by Mary J. Safford, in two vols.   Paper, $1.00. Cloth, $1.75.

"We have read his work conscientiously, and, we confess, with profit.   Never have we had so clear an insight into the manners, thoughts, and feelings of the ancient Greeks.   No study has made us so familiar with the age of Pericles.   We recognize throughout that the author is master of the period of which he treats.   Moreover, looking back upon the work from the end to the beginning, we clearly perceive in it a complete unity of purpose not at all evident during the reading."

"Hamerling's Aspasia, herself the most beautiful woman in all Hellas, is the apostle of beauty and of joyousness, the implacable enemy of all that is stern and harsh in life.   Unfortunately, morality is stern, and had no place among Aspasia's doctrines. This ugly fact, Landor has thrust as far into the background as possible.   Hamerling obtrudes it.   He does not moralize, he neither condemns nor praises ; but like a fate, silent, passionless, and resistless, he carries the story along, allows the sunshine for a time to silver the turbid stream, the butterflies and gnats to flutter above it in rainbow tints, and then remorselessly draws over the landscape gray twilight.   He but follows the course of history; yet the absolute pitilessness with which he does it is almost terrible." — *Extracts from Review in Yale Literary Magazine.*

"No more beautiful chapter can be found in any book of this age than that in which Pericles and Aspasia are described as visiting the poet Sophocles in the garden on the bank of the Cephissus." — *Utica Morning Herald.*

"It is one of the great excellencies of this romance, this lofty song of the genius of the Greeks, that it is composed with perfect artistic symmetry in the treatment of the different parts, and from the first word to the last is thoroughly harmonious in tone and coloring.   Therefore, in 'Aspasia,' we are given a book, which could only proceed from the union of an artistic nature and a thoughtful mind — a book that does not depict fiery passions in dramatic conflict, but with dignified composure, leads the conflict therein described to the final catastrophe." — *Allgemeine Zeitung.* (Augsburg).

WAR AND PEACE. A Historical Novel, by Count Léon Tolstoï, translated into French by a Russian Lady and from the French by Clara Bell. *Authorized Edition.* Complete, Three Parts in Box. Paper, $3.00. Cloth, $5.25. Half calf, $12.00.

Part I. Before Tilsit, 1805 — 1807, in two volumes. Paper, $1.00. Cloth, $1.75 per set.

" II. The Invasion, 1807—1812 in two volumes. Paper, $1.00. Cloth, $1.75 per set.

" III. Borodino, The French at Moscow — Epilogue, 1812—1820 in two volumes. Paper, $1.00. Cloth, $1.75 per set.

OPINIONS OF THE PRESS.

"A story of Russia in the time of Napoleon's wars. It is a story of the family rather than of the field, and is charming in its delineations of quaint Russian customs. It is a novel of absorbing interest, full of action and with a well managed plot; a book well worth reading."—*Philadelphia Enquirer.*

"The story of 'War and Peace' ranks as the greatest of Slavic historical novels. It is intensely dramatic in places and the battle scenes are marvels of picturesque description. At other points the vein is quiet and philosophical, and the reader is held by the soothing charm that is in complete contrast with the action and energy of battle."—*Observer, Utica, N. Y.*

"War and Peace is a historical novel and is extremely interesting, not only in its description of the times of the great invasion eighty years ago, but in its vivid pictures of life and character in Russia."—*Journal of Commerce, New York.*

"On general principles the historical novel is neither valuable as fact nor entertaining as fiction. But 'War and Peace' is a striking exception to this rule. It deals with the most impressive and dramatic period of European history. It reproduces a living panorama of scene, and actors, and circumstance idealized into the intense and artistic life of imaginative composition, and written with a brilliancy of style and epigrammatic play of thought, a depth of significance, that render the story one of the most fascinating and absorbing."— *Boston Evening Traveller.*

POEMS, by **Rose Terry Cooke,** in one volume 12mo.,
Cloth, $1.50.

" IN writing of her, we recall the appreciative words
of Mrs. Harriet Prescott Spofford, who wrote of Mrs.
Cooke:

'It is genius that informs every line Rose Terry has ever written,—a pure and lofty genius that burned with a white flame in
such subtle metaphysical reveries as " My Tenants," and " Did
I ?" and showed its many-colored light in brief bits of poetic
romance, and in a succession of stories of New England life.
One marvels how such a genius became the ultimate expression
of generations of hard Puritan ancestry, as one marvels to see
after silent flowerless years some dry and prickly cactus stem
burst out into its sudden flaming flower.'

" The poetic temperament, sensitive to all influences,
mirroring impressions, swift to translate feeling into expression, is pre-eminently that of Rose Terry Cooke.
A singularly intense and passionate love of beauty ; an
insight into spiritual moods, fine and unerring; deep
sympathy with all human experience, characterize her
poems.   She has beside these an added gift of graphic
description that is a purely pictorial art.   With this
power of profoundly realizing and sympathizing with
all human experiences; with her wonderful color and
grouping that produces the perfect picture, and her
lyric gift — true singer that she is — we find in Rose
Terry Cooke the poet born and to some extent,—made."
Boston Evening Traveller.